the BOOKS of MAGIC

Reckonings

John Ney Rieber
writer

Peter Snejbjerg
Peter Gross
John Ridgway
artists

Sherilyn van Valkenburgh
colorist

Richard Starkings and Comicraft
lettering

Greg Spalenka
(pages 36, 62, 88)

August Hall
(pages 114, 140, 166)

Charles Vess
(page 10)
original covers

Neil Gaiman
...ultant

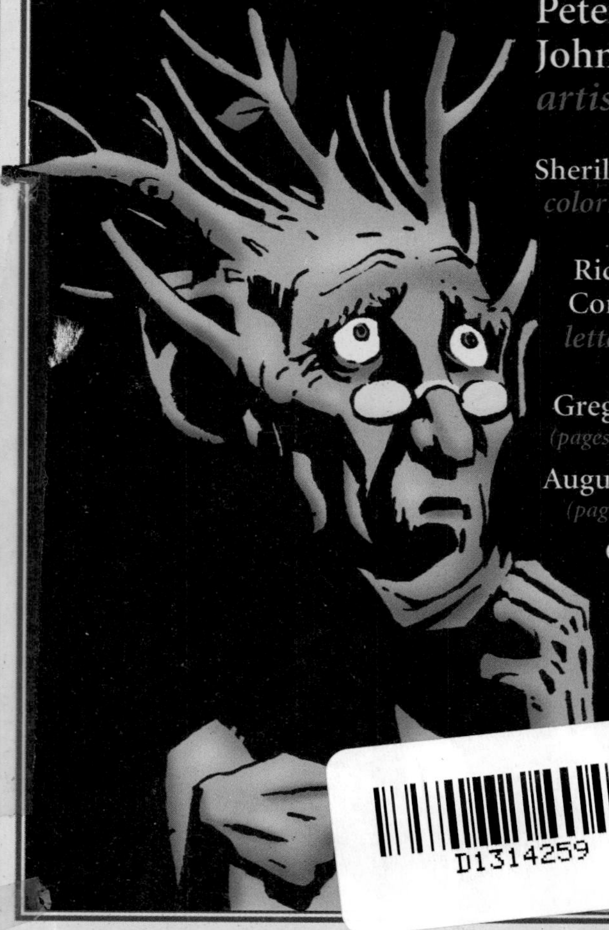

...ny Hunter and *The Books of Magic*
...d.by Neil Gaiman & John Bolton

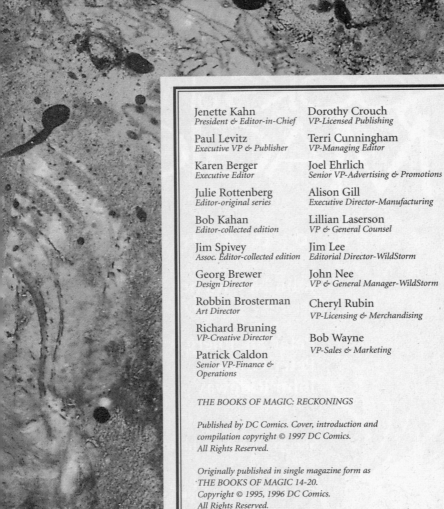

Jenette Kahn
President & Editor-in-Chief

Paul Levitz
Executive VP & Publisher

Karen Berger
Executive Editor

Julie Rottenberg
Editor-original series

Bob Kahan
Editor-collected edition

Jim Spivey
Assoc. Editor-collected edition

Georg Brewer
Design Director

Robbin Brosterman
Art Director

Richard Bruning
VP-Creative Director

Patrick Caldon
Senior VP-Finance &
Operations

Dorothy Crouch
VP-Licensed Publishing

Terri Cunningham
VP-Managing Editor

Joel Ehrlich
Senior VP-Advertising & Promotions

Alison Gill
Executive Director-Manufacturing

Lillian Laserson
VP & General Counsel

Jim Lee
Editorial Director-WildStorm

John Nee
VP & General Manager-WildStorm

Cheryl Rubin
VP-Licensing & Merchandising

Bob Wayne
VP-Sales & Marketing

THE BOOKS OF MAGIC: RECKONINGS

DC Comics, 1700 Broadway, New York, NY 10019
A division of Warner Bros. - An AOL Time Warner Company

Printed in Canada. Second Printing. ISBN: 1-56389-321-5

Cover by Michael Wm. Kaluta

Table of Contents

4
Introduction by Terri Windling

*All stories written by John Ney Rieber,
colored by Sherilyn van Valkenburgh and
lettered by Richard Starkings and Comicraft*

10
What Fire Leaves Us
(originally published in THE BOOKS OF MAGIC #14)
Artist-Peter Gross

Playgrounds

36
part one
Hell and Back
(originally published in THE BOOKS OF MAGIC #15)
Artist-Peter Snejbjerg

62
part two
Tag...You're It.
(originally published in THE BOOKS OF MAGIC #16)
Artist-Peter Snejbjerg

88
part three
Deformative Years
(originally published in THE BOOKS OF MAGIC #17)
Artist-Peter Snejbjerg

114
part four
Boys Will Be Boys
(originally published in THE BOOKS OF MAGIC #18)
Artist-Peter Gross

140
part five
Really-Pretend
(originally published in THE BOOKS OF MAGIC #19)
Artist-Peter Gross

166
epilogue
The Knight, The Dragon, & The Maiden
(originally published in THE BOOKS OF MAGIC #20)
Artist-John Ridgway

Introduction
by Terri Windling

To tell you the truth, I was surprised when Neil Gaiman and DC Comics asked me to write this introduction. *Why me?*

I thought as I put down the phone, since my name is not exactly universally known among readers of comics (working as I do in the alternate universe of Book Publishing); and I've never met Neil's talented collaborator, John Ney Rieber. Is it because I've published Neil's fiction in the past (in *Snow White, Blood Red, The Year's Best Fantasy & Horror,* and other anthologies co-edited with Ellen Datlow)? Or because the first BOOKS OF MAGIC collection was partially dedicated to me? Or perhaps Neil had asked for Terry Pratchett...or Terry Goodkind...or Terry Bisson...or Terry Jones...and ended up with me? The question nagged in the back of my mind, until an answer occurred to me. Neil knows me well. He knows I spend a great deal of time in the forests of Faerie, living as I do in the myth-haunted landscape of England's West Country (with painters Brian Froud and

4

Alan Lee for neighbors and native Faerie guides.) As an editor of fantasy books and a writer with incorrigible wanderlust, I've spent many years exploring the "windy road that lies across the fernie brae," the road that led Tam Lin and Thomas the Rhymer to Faerie before me. And so I suspect that what Neil wants from me is simply *corroboration*. He wants me to verify that he and Mr. Rieber (and co-creator John Bolton; and cover artists Charles Vess and Greg Spalenka; and interior artists Peter Snejbjerg, Peter Gross and John Ridgway) have all gotten their Faerie landmarks right, that this is the genuine article.

And indeed, it is. Right down to the river of blood, and old Baba Yaga's hut, and the Faerie Queen's seductive guile. Yo-yo the owl, Wobbly's appetite, Tanger with his hair of twigs — they all have the look, the feel, the sound, the scent of genuine Magic. True Magic, with its roots sunk deep in the soil of epics, sagas, myths, old fairy tales and riddling games and stories told by the fireside. Gaiman and Rieber's Faerie is a place that Katherine Briggs, Thomas Keightley, W.Y. Evan Wentz and the other great Celtic folklore scholars of the last century would recognize — yet it doesn't reside somewhere off in the Celtic Twilight of a romanticized past. Instead, their "road across the fernie brae" starts at young Tim Hunter's door, coexisting with asphalt and concrete, stretching from past to present and well within

5

reach of any of us. From this lively mix of the old and the new, Magic arises — potent and enchanting.

In creating the modern yet mythical version of London where Tim Hunter lives, the writers and artists of THE BOOKS OF MAGIC have joined the top ranks of what over here in the Book Publishing field we call the "Urban Fantasy" movement, pioneered by such novels as Charles de Lint's *Memory and Dream*, Emma Bull's *War for the Oaks*, Will Shetterly's *Elsewhere* and the Auberon section of John Crowley's classic *Little, Big*. Since the publication of the first BOOKS OF MAGIC collection, Rieber has taken up the tale and added his own spice to the rich stew originally cooked up by Gaiman and Bolton. Rieber 's additions include a delightfully fresh and quirky sense of invention, as well as good strong character studies, and a true under-standing of a basic Faerie rule: that for every outer transformation accomplished by an act of Magic, an inner transformation will also occur...for good or for ill.

Tim Hunter's story is a true fairy tale, in the most historical sense of the term — for it was not until Victorian times that fairy tales became the saccharine children's stories we're familiar with today (full of passively beautiful Cinderellas and shallow square-jawed Prince Charmings). In ages past, fairy tales were bold, dark, complex, and sensual; they were stories that were often never meant for children's ears at all. (Sleeping Beauty, for instance, was not wakened by a chaste kiss in older versions of the tale, but by the birth of twins after the prince had come and gone.) Molly would approve of the feisty heroines of the old, unbowdlerized tales — before Victorian publishers, and then Hollywood, turned them to pap. (Look for the fairy tale collections edited by the late Angela Carter for examples of traditional tales that would surely make Molly cheer.) Old fairy tales often take the form of a quest: the hero must leave the familiar world of home and/or childhood behind, setting out on a dark, unfamiliar road beset with dangers. A trial will be endured, a riddle solved, a monster overcome and a future claimed before he or she can reach for that

hard-won prize of a happy ending. Tim is a classic fairy-tale hero. So is the gutsy, headstrong Molly. So are many of the memorable secondary characters in Tim Hunter's tale — all of them flawed and believably human, whether they're human or angel or fey.

Like all the best fantasy, Tim's story works on two levels at once. On the one hand, it's simply an entertaining and suspenseful adventure tale. On the other, it speaks metaphorically about the quests we make in real life — both physical and psychological quests, each with their monsters to face. At an early

point in the story, Tim must make the choice to believe in magic — just as all of us who write, illustrate or simply love to read fantasy tales have made the choice to believe in magic long past the years of childhood. Rieber and the illustrators herein have drawn upon myths, memories, and desire to find the road to the Faerielands — just as Tim Hunter is learning to do. It is a road that is both dark and bright, shadowed by our deepest fears, illuminated by friendship and hope. Tim and Molly walk that road, side by side and hand in hand. I often meet Charlie Vess walking there, sketchbook in one hand, single malt in the other. I see Neil there less frequently these days, but still Faerie remains his true home. True Thomas is there, and the spirit of Katherine Briggs, and certain of my West Country neighbors....

I expect now that I've read all of THE BOOKS OF MAGIC published to date I'll also glimpse John Ney Reiber on that road, as well as Snejbjerg, Gross, Spalenka, Hall, Ridgway, and Bolton. Perhaps I'll meet you out on the winding road too, Yo-yo leading the way.

Terri·Windling
author of The Wood Wife, *editor of the* Borderland *Urban Fantasy series and other anthologies*

What Fire Leaves Us

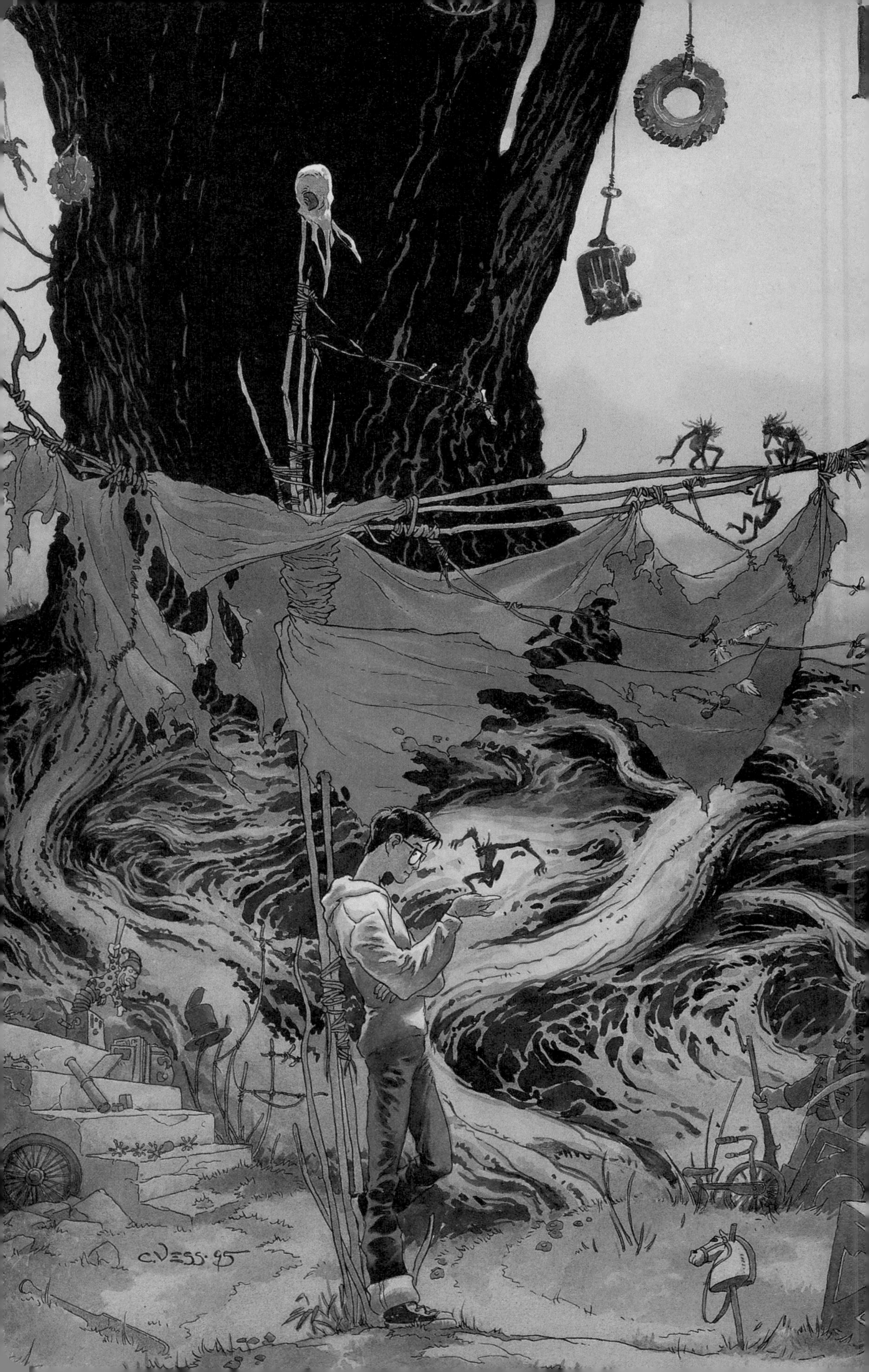
C.VESS·95

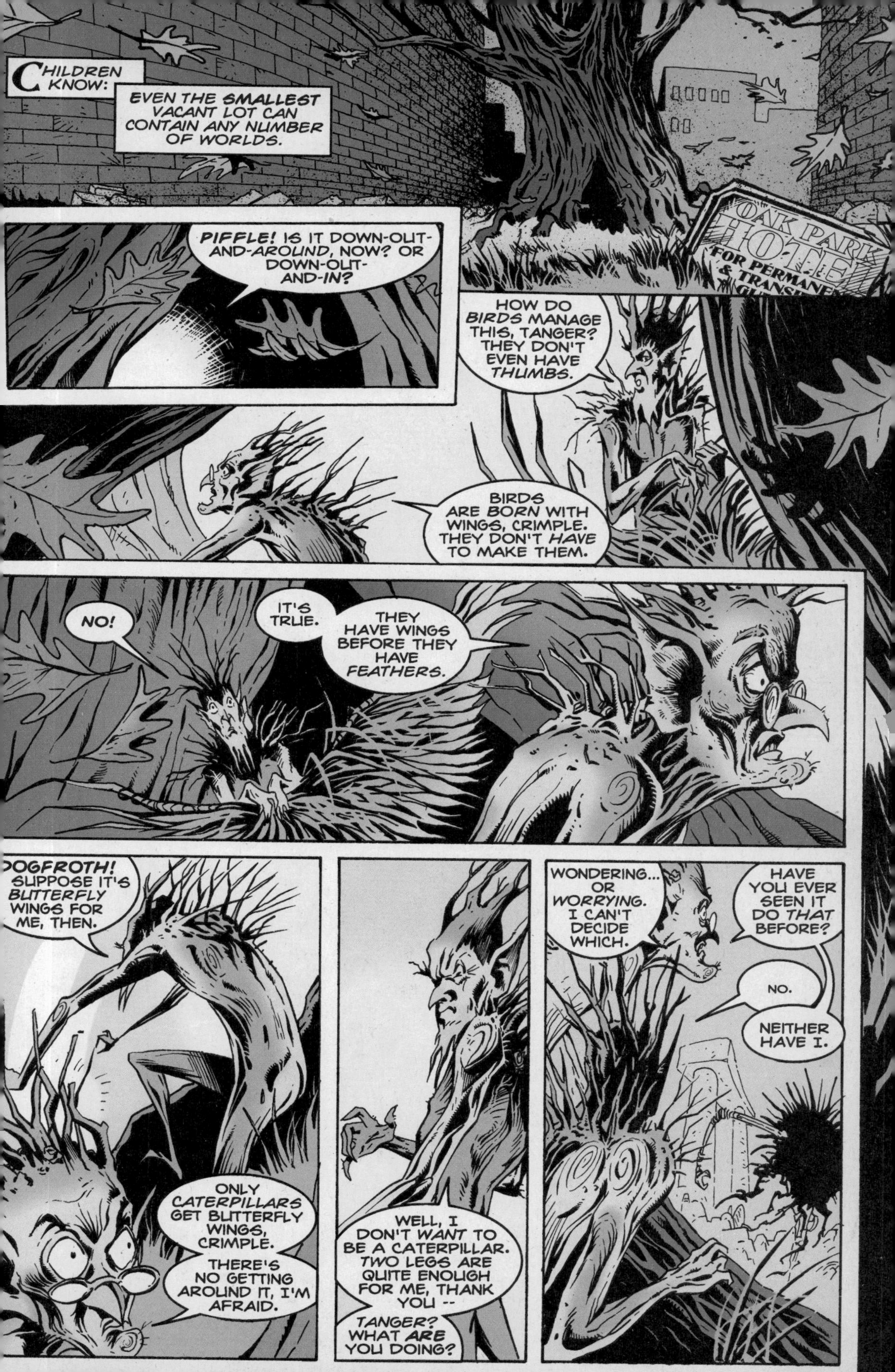
CHILDREN KNOW:
EVEN THE SMALLEST VACANT LOT CAN CONTAIN ANY NUMBER OF WORLDS.
OAK PARK HOTEL FOR PERMANE & TRANS
PIFFLE! IS IT DOWN-OUT-AND-AROUND, NOW? OR DOWN-OUT-AND-IN?
HOW DO BIRDS MANAGE THIS, TANGER? THEY DON'T EVEN HAVE THUMBS.
BIRDS ARE BORN WITH WINGS, CRIMPLE. THEY DON'T HAVE TO MAKE THEM.
NO!
IT'S TRUE.
THEY HAVE WINGS BEFORE THEY HAVE FEATHERS.
DOGFROTH! SUPPOSE IT'S BUTTERFLY WINGS FOR ME, THEN.
ONLY CATERPILLARS GET BUTTERFLY WINGS, CRIMPLE.
THERE'S NO GETTING AROUND IT, I'M AFRAID.
WELL, I DON'T WANT TO BE A CATERPILLAR. TWO LEGS ARE QUITE ENOUGH FOR ME, THANK YOU --
TANGER? WHAT ARE YOU DOING?
WONDERING... OR WORRYING. I CAN'T DECIDE WHICH.
HAVE YOU EVER SEEN IT DO THAT BEFORE?
NO.
NEITHER HAVE I.

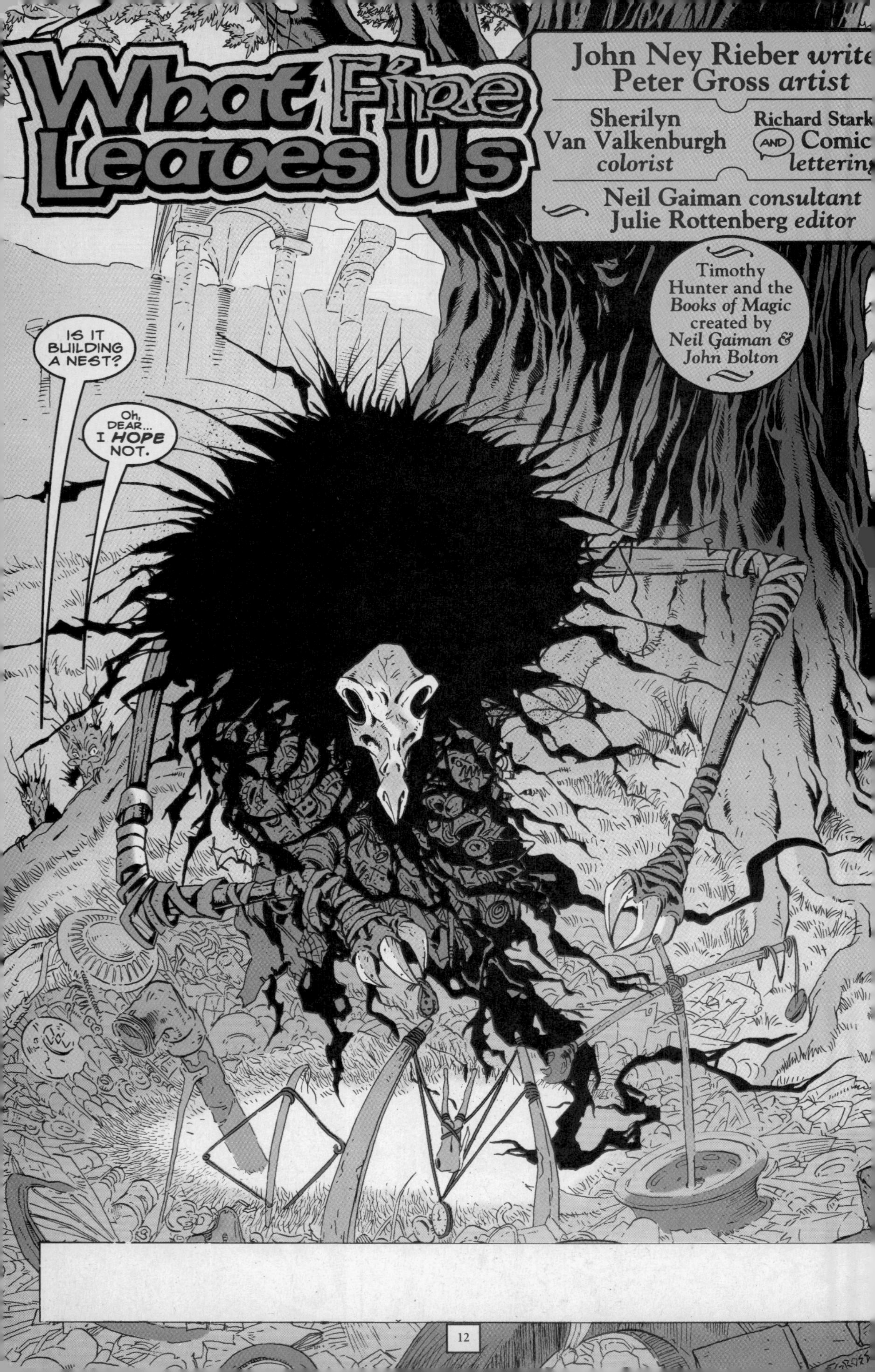
What Fire Leaves Us
John Ney Rieber writer
Peter Gross artist
Sherilyn Van Valkenburgh colorist
Richard Starkings AND Comicraft lettering
Neil Gaiman consultant
Julie Rottenberg editor
Timothy Hunter and the Books of Magic created by Neil Gaiman & John Bolton
IS IT BUILDING A NEST?
Oh, DEAR... I HOPE NOT.

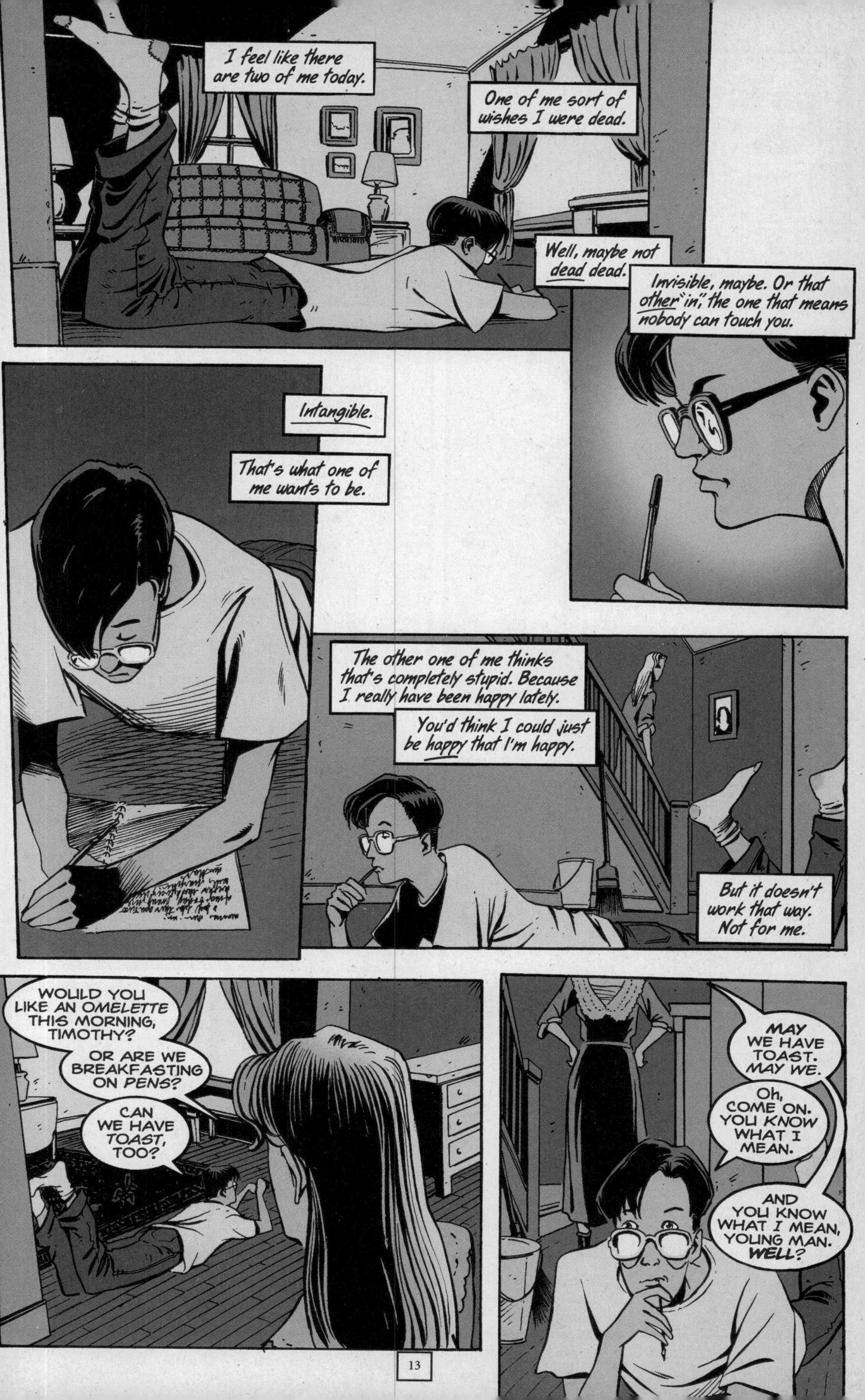
I feel like there are two of me today.
One of me sort of wishes I were dead.
Well, maybe not dead dead.
Invisible, maybe. Or that other "in," the one that means nobody can touch you.
Intangible.
That's what one of me wants to be.
The other one of me thinks that's completely stupid. Because I really have been happy lately.
You'd think I could just be happy that I'm happy.
But it doesn't work that way. Not for me.
WOULD YOU LIKE AN OMELETTE THIS MORNING, TIMOTHY?
OR ARE WE BREAKFASTING ON PENS?
CAN WE HAVE TOAST, TOO?
MAY WE HAVE TOAST. MAY WE.
Oh, COME ON. YOU KNOW WHAT I MEAN.
AND YOU KNOW WHAT I MEAN, YOUNG MAN. WELL?

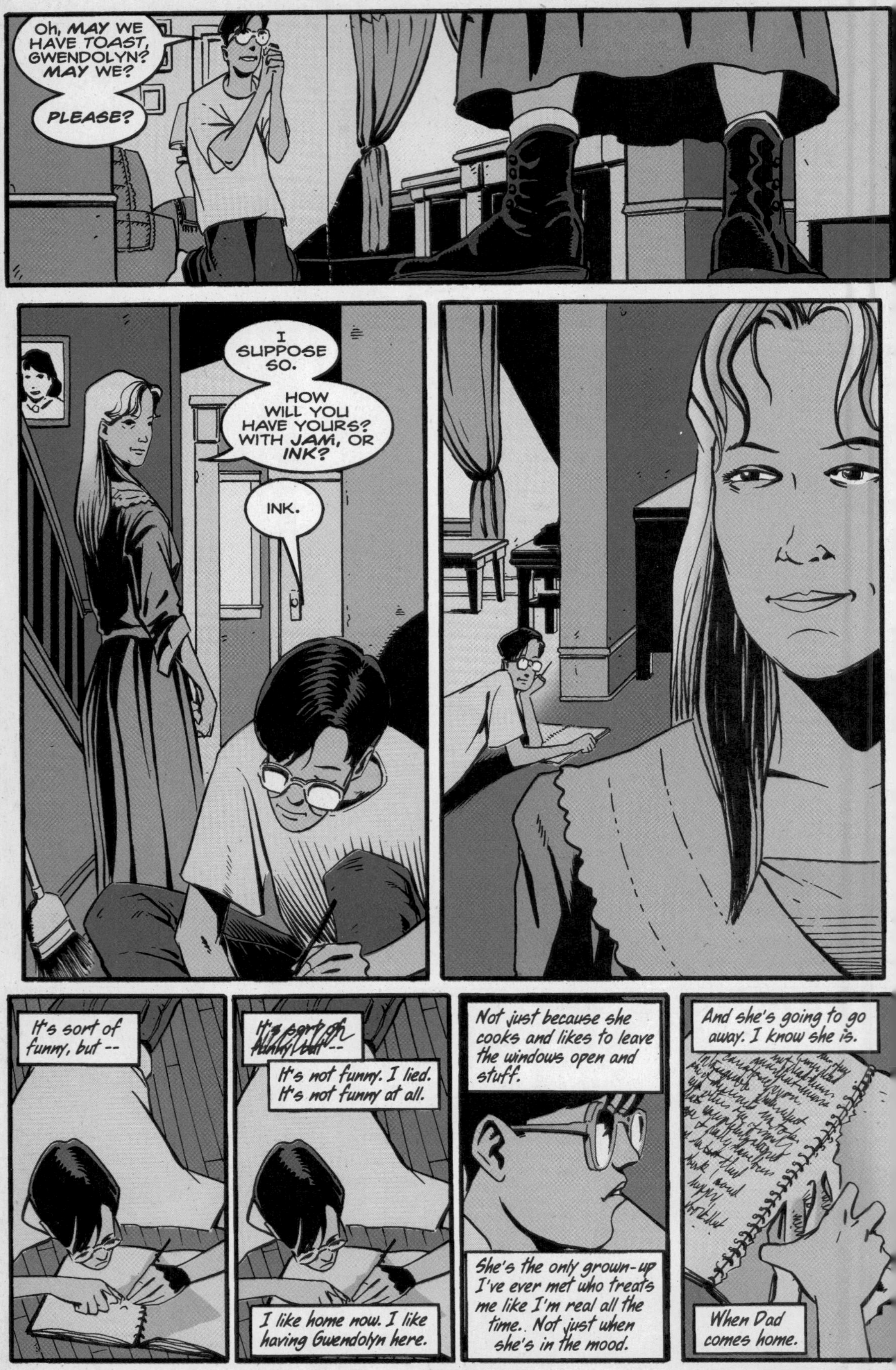
Oh, MAY WE HAVE TOAST, GWENDOLYN? MAY WE?
PLEASE?
I SUPPOSE SO.
HOW WILL YOU HAVE YOURS? WITH JAM, OR INK?
INK.
It's sort of funny, but --
~~It's sort of funny, but --~~
It's not funny. I lied. It's not funny at all.
I like home now. I like having Gwendolyn here.
Not just because she cooks and likes to leave the windows open and stuff.
She's the only grown-up I've ever met who treats me like I'm real all the time.. Not just when she's in the mood.
And she's going to go away. I know she is.
When Dad comes home.

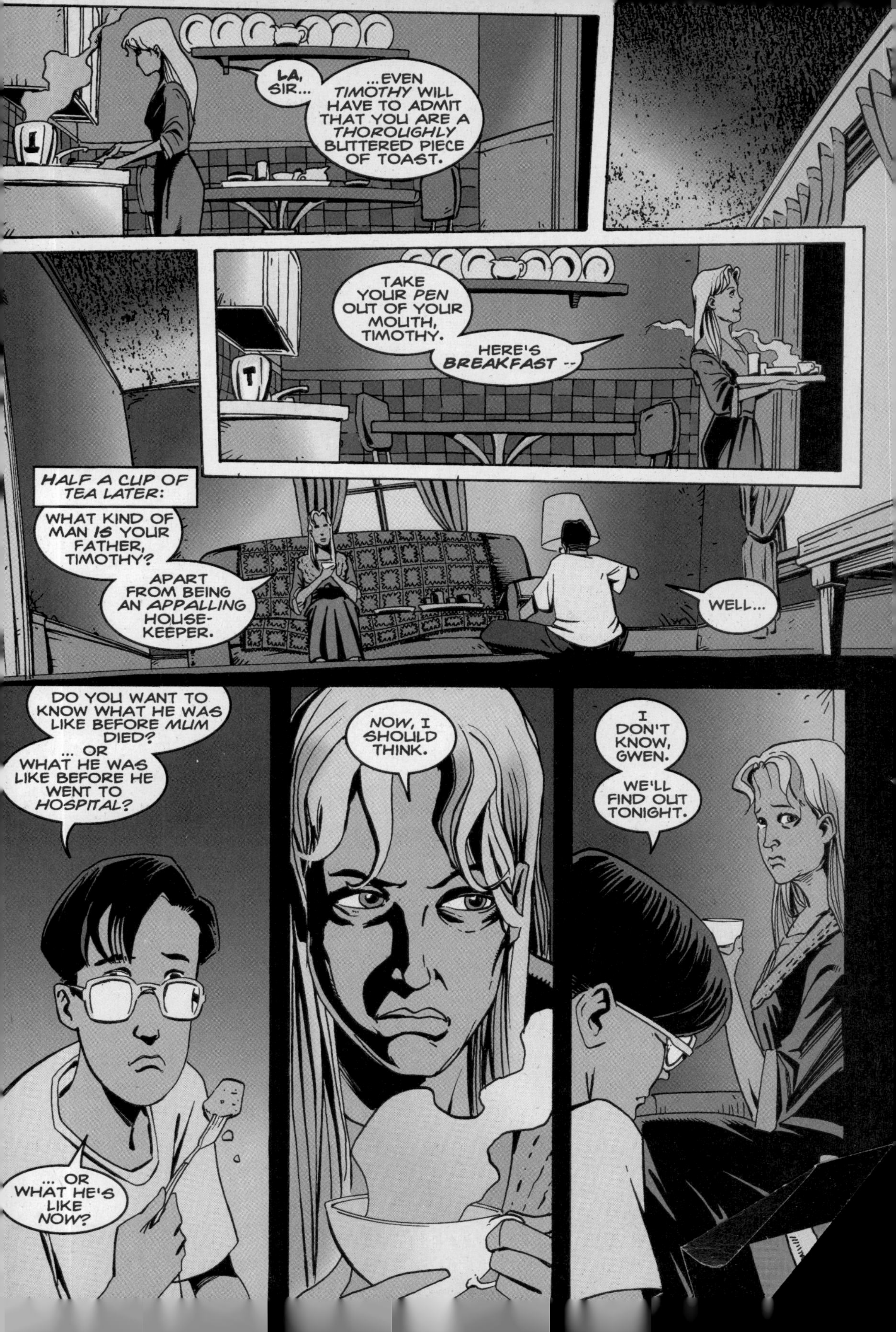
LA, SIR...
...EVEN TIMOTHY WILL HAVE TO ADMIT THAT YOU ARE A THOROUGHLY BUTTERED PIECE OF TOAST.
TAKE YOUR PEN OUT OF YOUR MOUTH, TIMOTHY.
HERE'S BREAKFAST --
HALF A CUP OF TEA LATER:
WHAT KIND OF MAN IS YOUR FATHER, TIMOTHY?
APART FROM BEING AN APPALLING HOUSE-KEEPER.
WELL...
DO YOU WANT TO KNOW WHAT HE WAS LIKE BEFORE MUM DIED?
... OR WHAT HE WAS LIKE BEFORE HE WENT TO HOSPITAL?
... OR WHAT HE'S LIKE NOW?
NOW, I SHOULD THINK.
I DON'T KNOW, GWEN.
WE'LL FIND OUT TONIGHT.

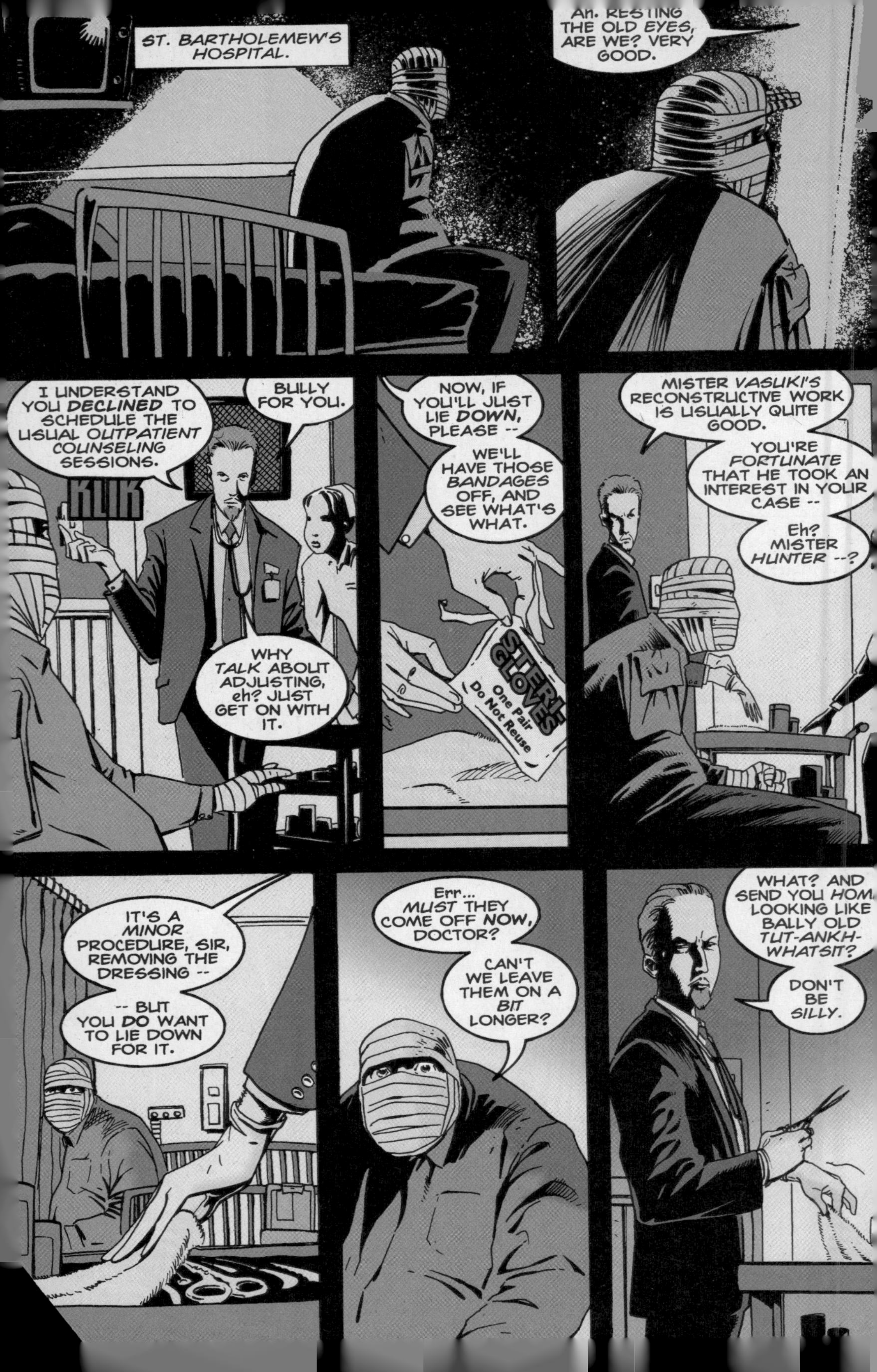
ST. BARTHOLEMEW'S HOSPITAL.
AH. RESTING THE OLD EYES, ARE WE? VERY GOOD.
I UNDERSTAND YOU DECLINED TO SCHEDULE THE USUAL OUTPATIENT COUNSELING SESSIONS.
KLIK
BULLY FOR YOU.
WHY TALK ABOUT ADJUSTING, eh? JUST GET ON WITH IT.
NOW, IF YOU'LL JUST LIE DOWN, PLEASE --
WE'LL HAVE THOSE BANDAGES OFF, AND SEE WHAT'S WHAT.
STERI-GLOVES One Pair Do Not Reuse
MISTER VASUKI'S RECONSTRUCTIVE WORK IS USUALLY QUITE GOOD.
YOU'RE FORTUNATE THAT HE TOOK AN INTEREST IN YOUR CASE --
Eh? MISTER HUNTER --?
IT'S A MINOR PROCEDURE, SIR, REMOVING THE DRESSING --
-- BUT YOU DO WANT TO LIE DOWN FOR IT.
Err... MUST THEY COME OFF NOW, DOCTOR?
CAN'T WE LEAVE THEM ON A BIT LONGER?
WHAT? AND SEND YOU HOM LOOKING LIKE BALLY OLD TUT-ANKH-WHATSIT?
DON'T BE SILLY.

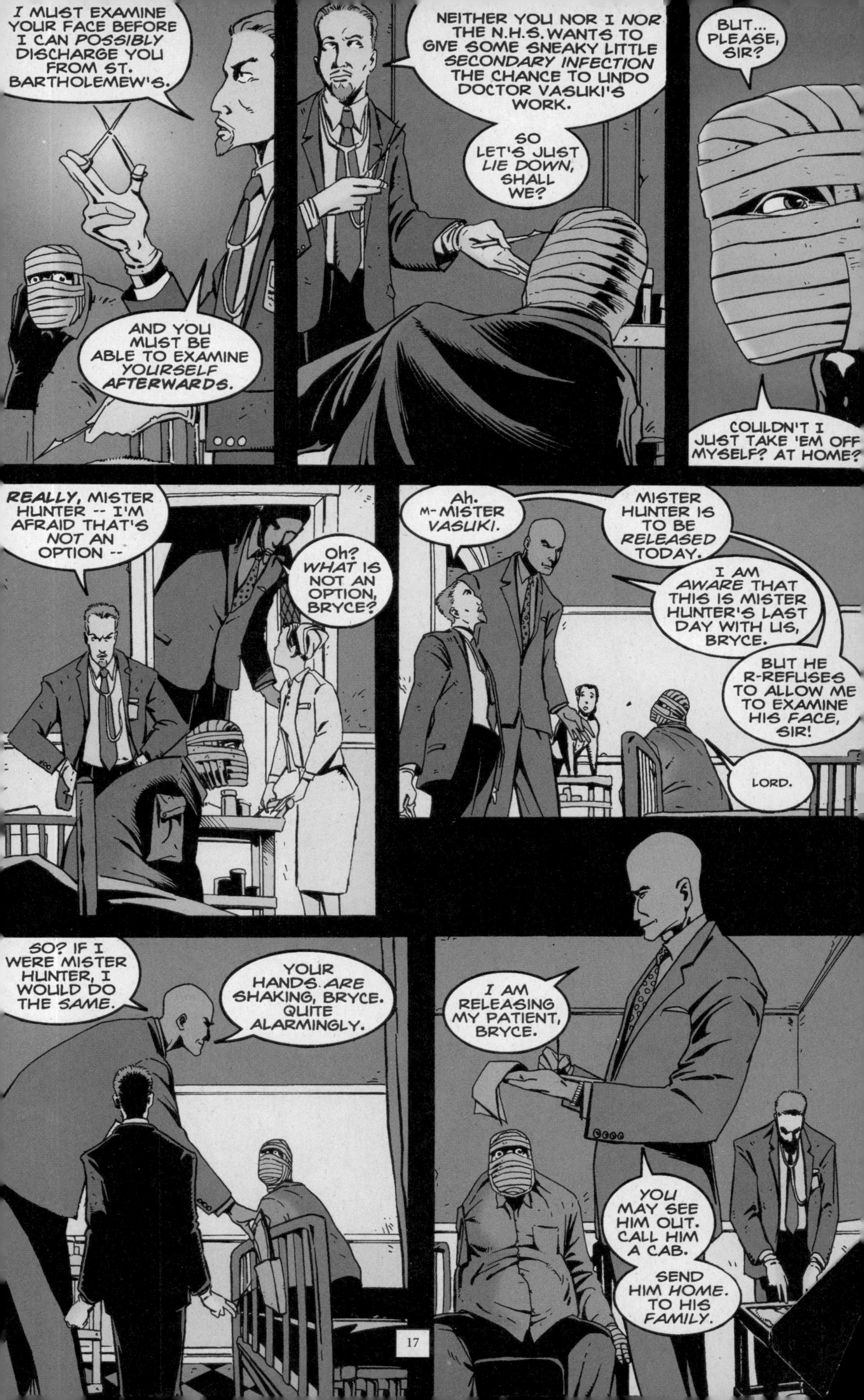
I MUST EXAMINE YOUR FACE BEFORE I CAN POSSIBLY DISCHARGE YOU FROM ST. BARTHOLEMEW'S.
AND YOU MUST BE ABLE TO EXAMINE YOURSELF AFTERWARDS.
NEITHER YOU NOR I NOR THE N.H.S. WANTS TO GIVE SOME SNEAKY LITTLE SECONDARY INFECTION THE CHANCE TO UNDO DOCTOR VASUKI'S WORK.
SO LET'S JUST LIE DOWN, SHALL WE?
BUT... PLEASE, SIR?
COULDN'T I JUST TAKE 'EM OFF MYSELF? AT HOME?
REALLY, MISTER HUNTER -- I'M AFRAID THAT'S NOT AN OPTION --
Oh? WHAT IS NOT AN OPTION, BRYCE?
Ah. M-MISTER VASUKI.
MISTER HUNTER IS TO BE RELEASED TODAY.
I AM AWARE THAT THIS IS MISTER HUNTER'S LAST DAY WITH US, BRYCE.
BUT HE R-REFUSES TO ALLOW ME TO EXAMINE HIS FACE, SIR!
LORD.
SO? IF I WERE MISTER HUNTER, I WOULD DO THE SAME.
YOUR HANDS ARE SHAKING, BRYCE. QUITE ALARMINGLY.
I AM RELEASING MY PATIENT, BRYCE.
YOU MAY SEE HIM OUT. CALL HIM A CAB.
SEND HIM HOME. TO HIS FAMILY.

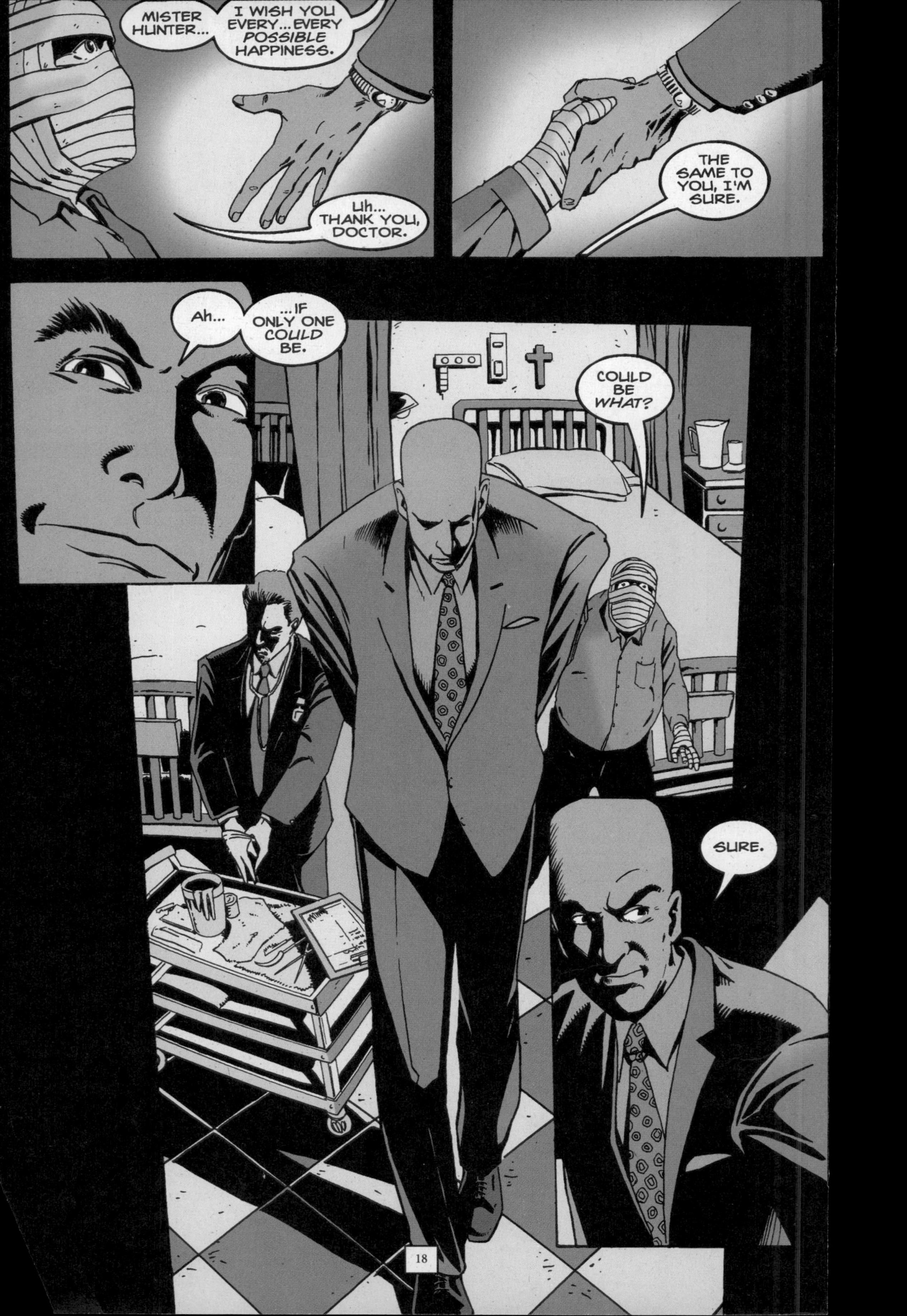
MISTER HUNTER...
I WISH YOU EVERY... EVERY POSSIBLE HAPPINESS.
Uh... THANK YOU, DOCTOR.
THE SAME TO YOU, I'M SURE.
Ah...
...IF ONLY ONE COULD BE.
COULD BE WHAT?
SURE.

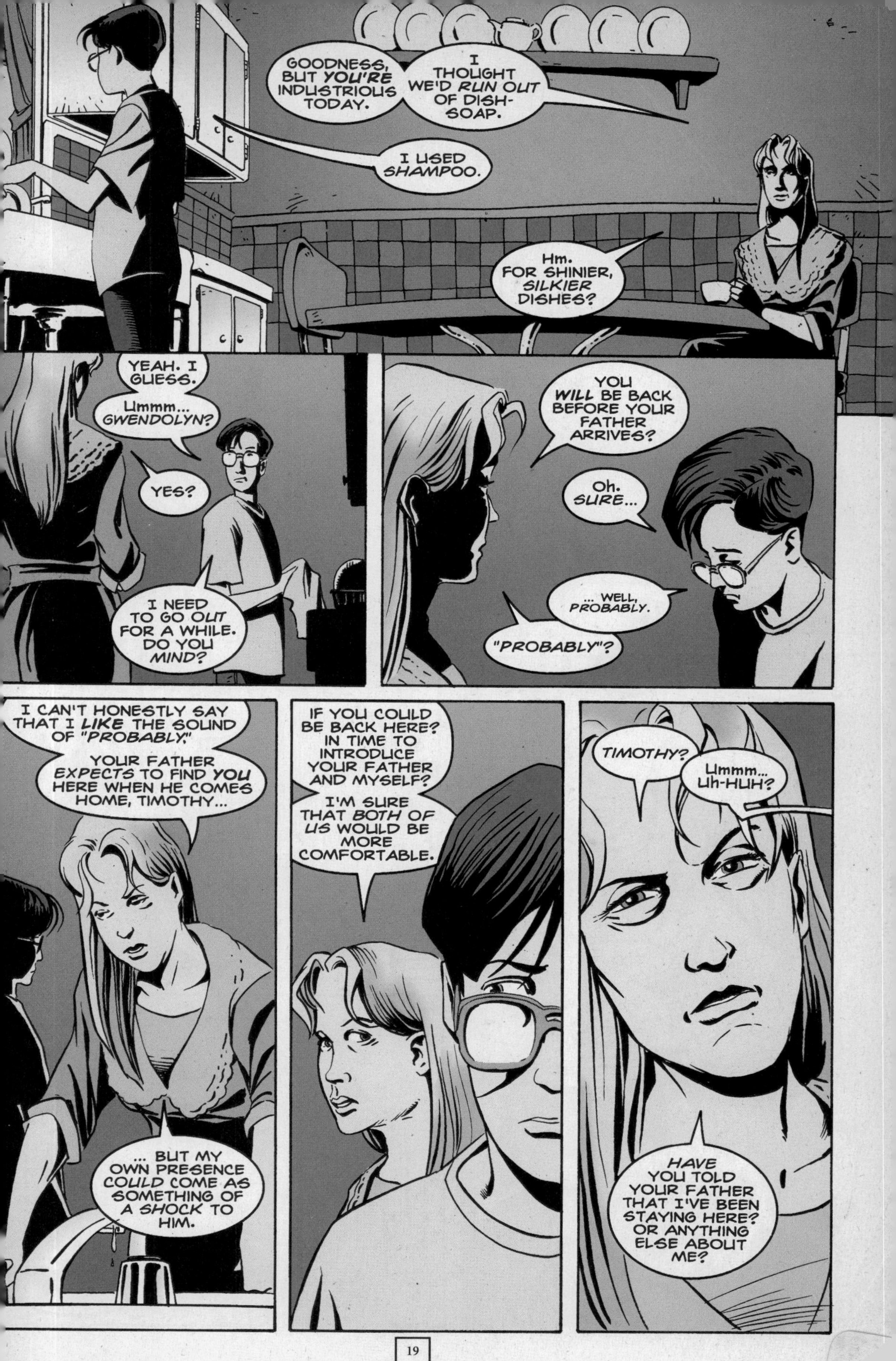

GOODNESS, BUT YOU'RE INDUSTRIOUS TODAY.
I THOUGHT WE'D RUN OUT OF DISH-SOAP.
I USED SHAMPOO.
Hm. FOR SHINIER, SILKIER DISHES?
YEAH. I GUESS.
Ummm... GWENDOLYN?
YES?
I NEED TO GO OUT FOR A WHILE. DO YOU MIND?
YOU WILL BE BACK BEFORE YOUR FATHER ARRIVES?
Oh. SURE...
... WELL, PROBABLY.
"PROBABLY"?
I CAN'T HONESTLY SAY THAT I LIKE THE SOUND OF "PROBABLY."
YOUR FATHER EXPECTS TO FIND YOU HERE WHEN HE COMES HOME, TIMOTHY...
... BUT MY OWN PRESENCE COULD COME AS SOMETHING OF A SHOCK TO HIM.
IF YOU COULD BE BACK HERE? IN TIME TO INTRODUCE YOUR FATHER AND MYSELF?
I'M SURE THAT BOTH OF US WOULD BE MORE COMFORTABLE.
TIMOTHY?
Ummm... Uh-HUH?
HAVE YOU TOLD YOUR FATHER THAT I'VE BEEN STAYING HERE? OR ANYTHING ELSE ABOUT ME?

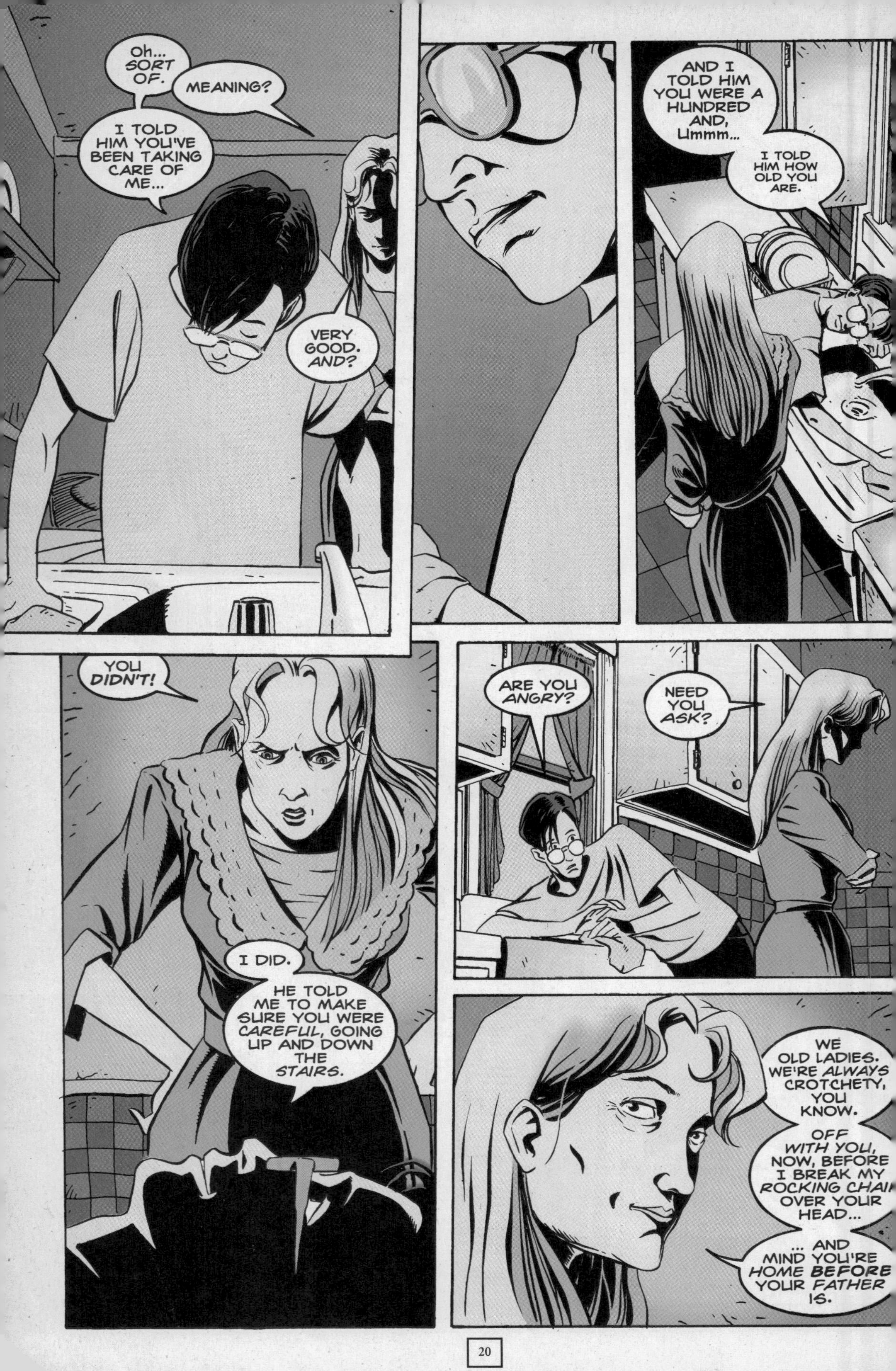
Oh... SORT OF.
MEANING?
I TOLD HIM YOU'VE BEEN TAKING CARE OF ME...
VERY GOOD. AND?
AND I TOLD HIM YOU WERE A HUNDRED AND, Ummm...
I TOLD HIM HOW OLD YOU ARE.
YOU DIDN'T!
I DID.
HE TOLD ME TO MAKE SURE YOU WERE CAREFUL, GOING UP AND DOWN THE STAIRS.
ARE YOU ANGRY?
NEED YOU ASK?
WE OLD LADIES. WE'RE ALWAYS CROTCHETY, YOU KNOW.
OFF WITH YOU, NOW, BEFORE I BREAK MY ROCKING CHAI OVER YOUR HEAD...
... AND MIND YOU'RE HOME BEFORE YOUR FATHER IS.

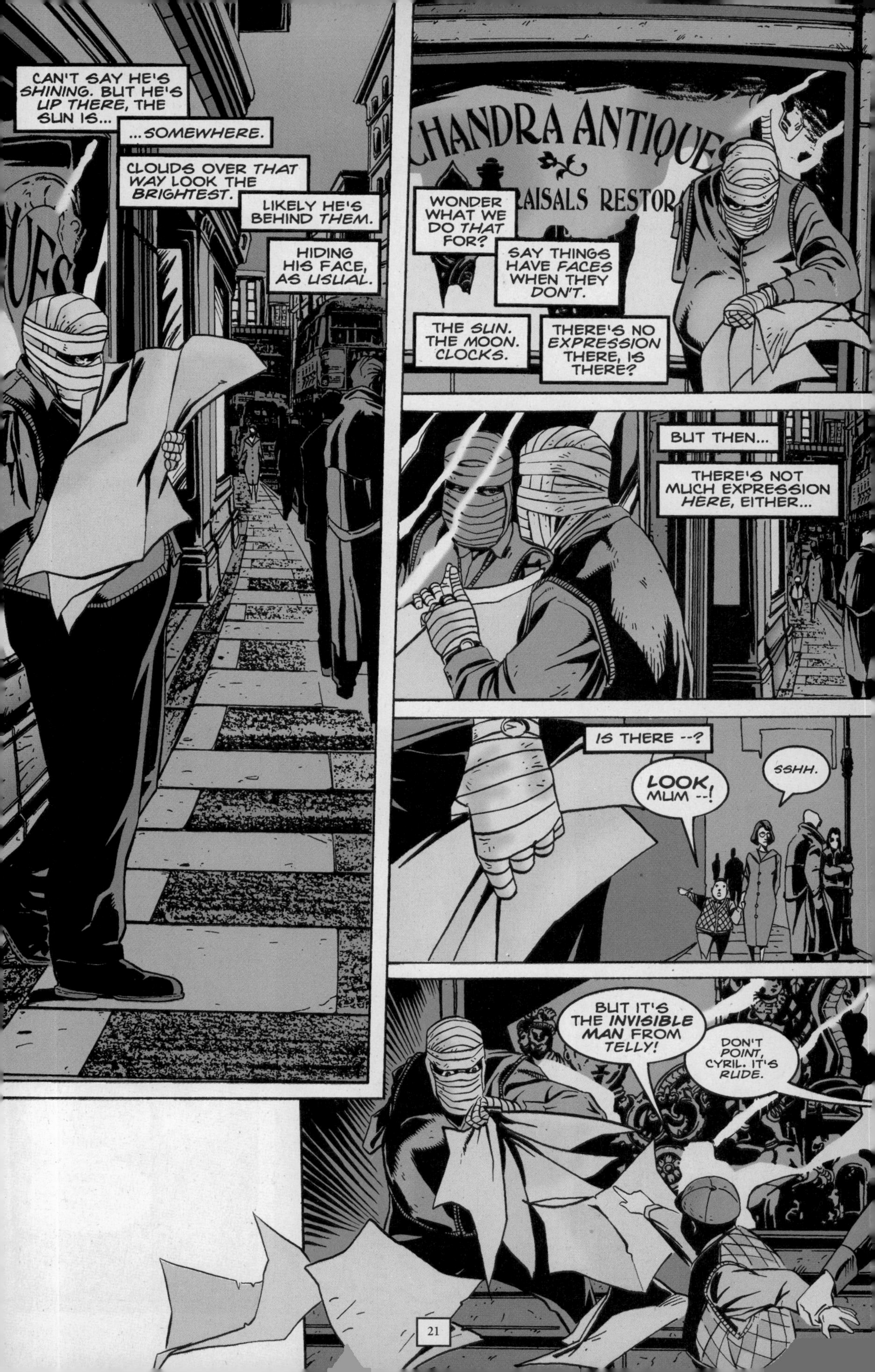
CAN'T SAY HE'S SHINING. BUT HE'S UP THERE, THE SUN IS...
...SOMEWHERE.
CLOUDS OVER THAT WAY LOOK THE BRIGHTEST.
LIKELY HE'S BEHIND THEM.
HIDING HIS FACE, AS USUAL.
CHANDRA ANTIQUE
RAISALS RESTOR
WONDER WHAT WE DO THAT FOR?
SAY THINGS HAVE FACES WHEN THEY DON'T.
THE SUN. THE MOON. CLOCKS.
THERE'S NO EXPRESSION THERE, IS THERE?
BUT THEN...
THERE'S NOT MUCH EXPRESSION HERE, EITHER...
IS THERE --?
LOOK, MUM --!
SSHH.
BUT IT'S THE INVISIBLE MAN FROM TELLY!
DON'T POINT, CYRIL. IT'S RUDE.

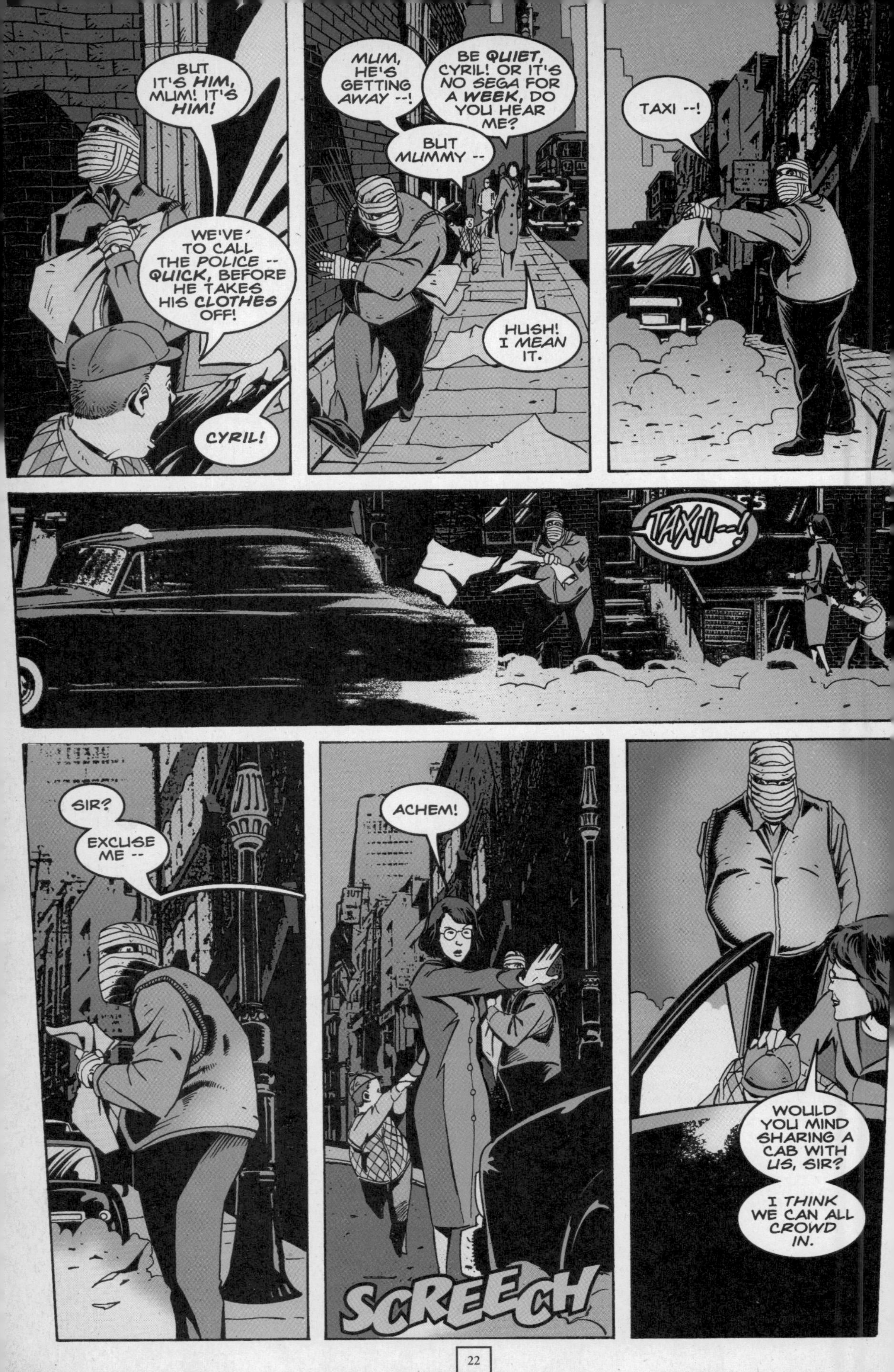
BUT IT'S *HIM*, MUM! IT'S *HIM*!
WE'VE TO CALL THE *POLICE* -- *QUICK*, BEFORE HE TAKES HIS *CLOTHES* OFF!
CYRIL!
MUM, HE'S GETTING *AWAY* --!
BE *QUIET*, CYRIL! OR IT'S NO SEGA FOR A *WEEK*, DO YOU HEAR ME?
BUT MUMMY --
HUSH! I *MEAN* IT.
TAXI --!
TAXIII--!
SIR?
EXCUSE ME --
ACHEM!
SCREECH
WOULD YOU MIND SHARING A CAB WITH US, SIR?
I *THINK* WE CAN ALL CROWD IN.

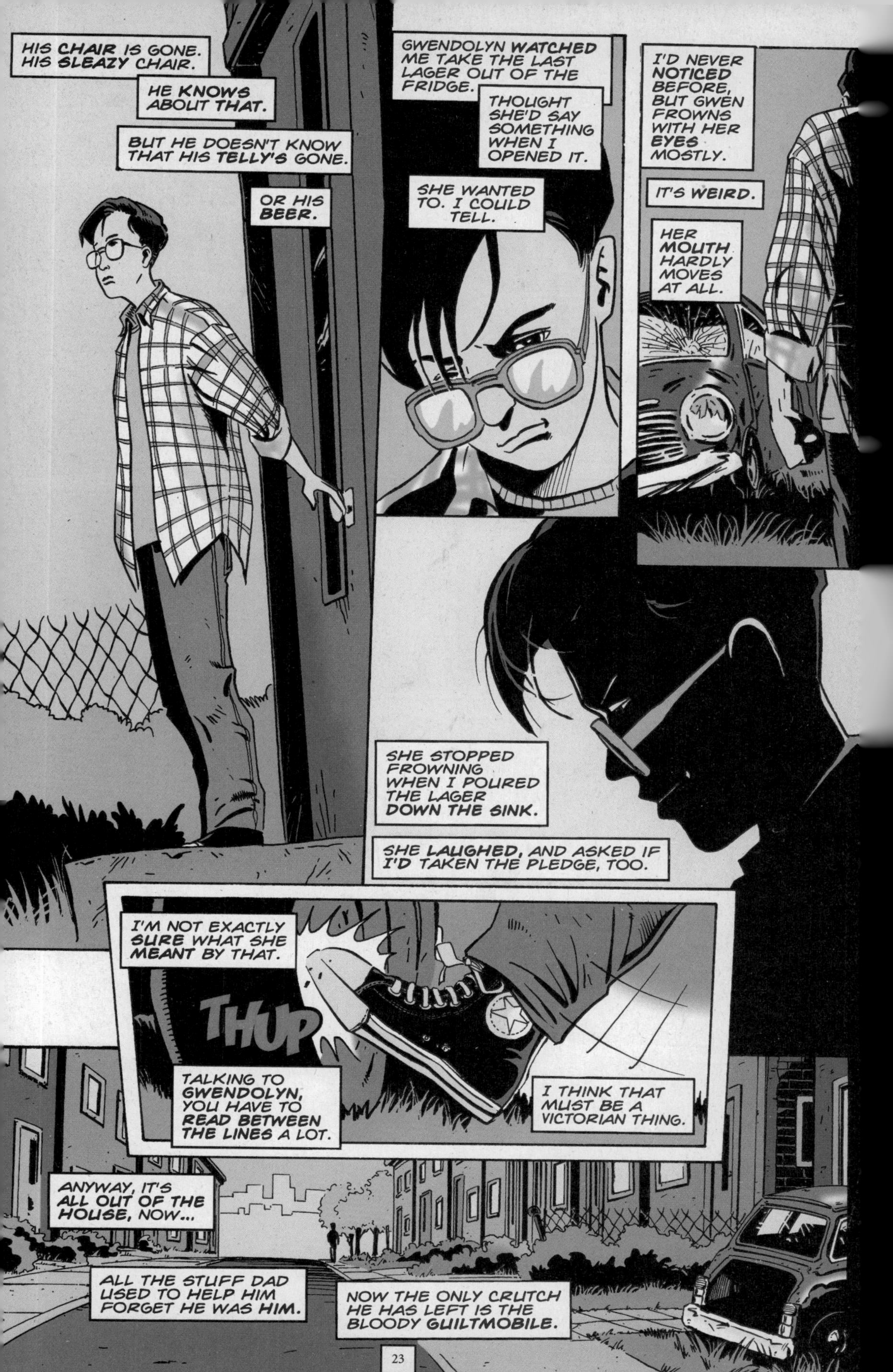
HIS CHAIR IS GONE. HIS SLEAZY CHAIR.
HE KNOWS ABOUT THAT.
BUT HE DOESN'T KNOW THAT HIS TELLY'S GONE.
OR HIS BEER.
GWENDOLYN WATCHED ME TAKE THE LAST LAGER OUT OF THE FRIDGE.
THOUGHT SHE'D SAY SOMETHING WHEN I OPENED IT.
SHE WANTED TO. I COULD TELL.
I'D NEVER NOTICED BEFORE, BUT GWEN FROWNS WITH HER EYES MOSTLY.
IT'S WEIRD.
HER MOUTH HARDLY MOVES AT ALL.
SHE STOPPED FROWNING WHEN I POURED THE LAGER DOWN THE SINK.
SHE LAUGHED, AND ASKED IF I'D TAKEN THE PLEDGE, TOO.
I'M NOT EXACTLY SURE WHAT SHE MEANT BY THAT.
THUP
TALKING TO GWENDOLYN, YOU HAVE TO READ BETWEEN THE LINES A LOT.
I THINK THAT MUST BE A VICTORIAN THING.
ANYWAY, IT'S ALL OUT OF THE HOUSE, NOW...
ALL THE STUFF DAD USED TO HELP HIM FORGET HE WAS HIM.
NOW THE ONLY CRUTCH HE HAS LEFT IS THE BLOODY GUILTMOBILE.

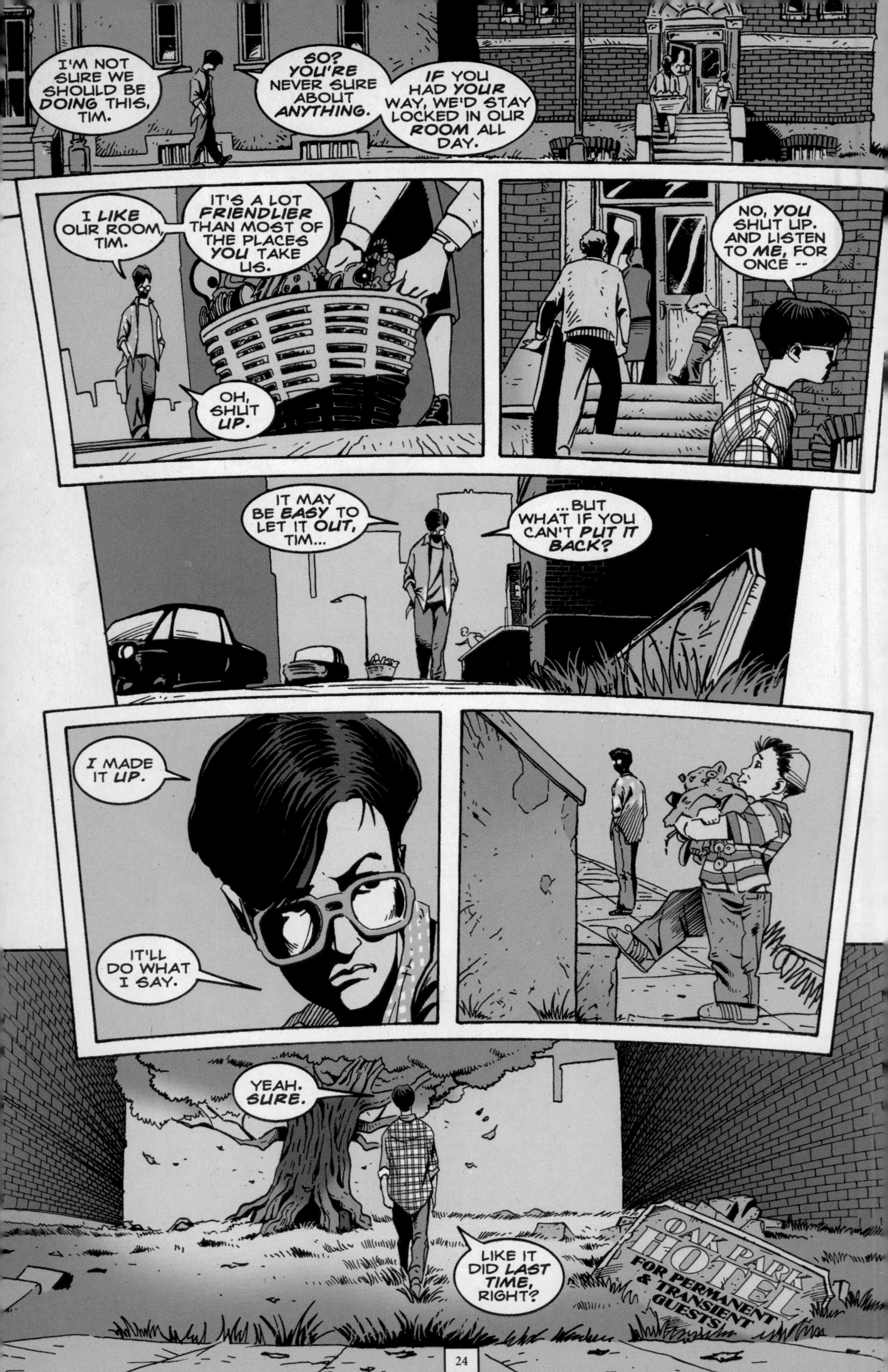
I'M NOT SURE WE SHOULD BE DOING THIS, TIM.
SO? YOU'RE NEVER SURE ABOUT ANYTHING.
IF YOU HAD YOUR WAY, WE'D STAY LOCKED IN OUR ROOM ALL DAY.
I LIKE OUR ROOM, TIM.
IT'S A LOT FRIENDLIER THAN MOST OF THE PLACES YOU TAKE US.
OH, SHUT UP.
NO, YOU SHUT UP. AND LISTEN TO ME, FOR ONCE --
IT MAY BE EASY TO LET IT OUT, TIM...
...BUT WHAT IF YOU CAN'T PUT IT BACK?
I MADE IT UP.
IT'LL DO WHAT I SAY.
YEAH. SURE.
LIKE IT DID LAST TIME, RIGHT?
OAK PARK HOTEL
FOR PERMANENT & TRANSIENT GUESTS

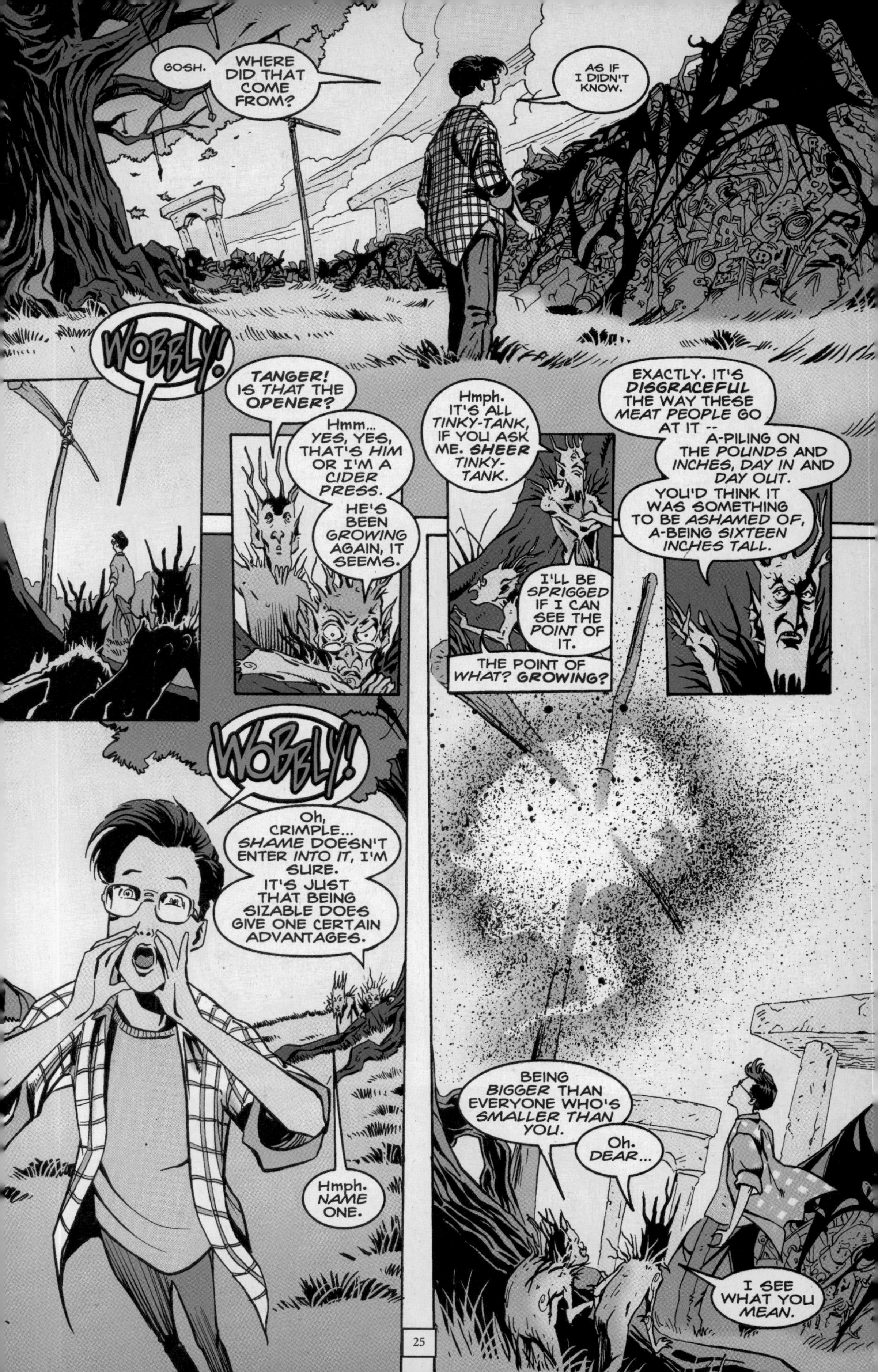
GOSH.
WHERE DID THAT COME FROM?
AS IF I DIDN'T KNOW.
WOBBLY!
TANGER! IS THAT THE OPENER?
Hmm... YES, YES, THAT'S HIM OR I'M A CIDER PRESS.
HE'S BEEN GROWING AGAIN, IT SEEMS.
Hmph. IT'S ALL TINKY-TANK, IF YOU ASK ME. SHEER TINKY-TANK.
I'LL BE SPRIGGED IF I CAN SEE THE POINT OF IT.
THE POINT OF WHAT? GROWING?
EXACTLY. IT'S DISGRACEFUL THE WAY THESE MEAT PEOPLE GO AT IT --
A-PILING ON THE POUNDS AND INCHES, DAY IN AND DAY OUT.
YOU'D THINK IT WAS SOMETHING TO BE ASHAMED OF, A-BEING SIXTEEN INCHES TALL.
WOBBLY!
Oh, CRIMPLE... SHAME DOESN'T ENTER INTO IT, I'M SURE.
IT'S JUST THAT BEING SIZABLE DOES GIVE ONE CERTAIN ADVANTAGES.
Hmph. NAME ONE.
BEING BIGGER THAN EVERYONE WHO'S SMALLER THAN YOU.
Oh. DEAR...
I SEE WHAT YOU MEAN.

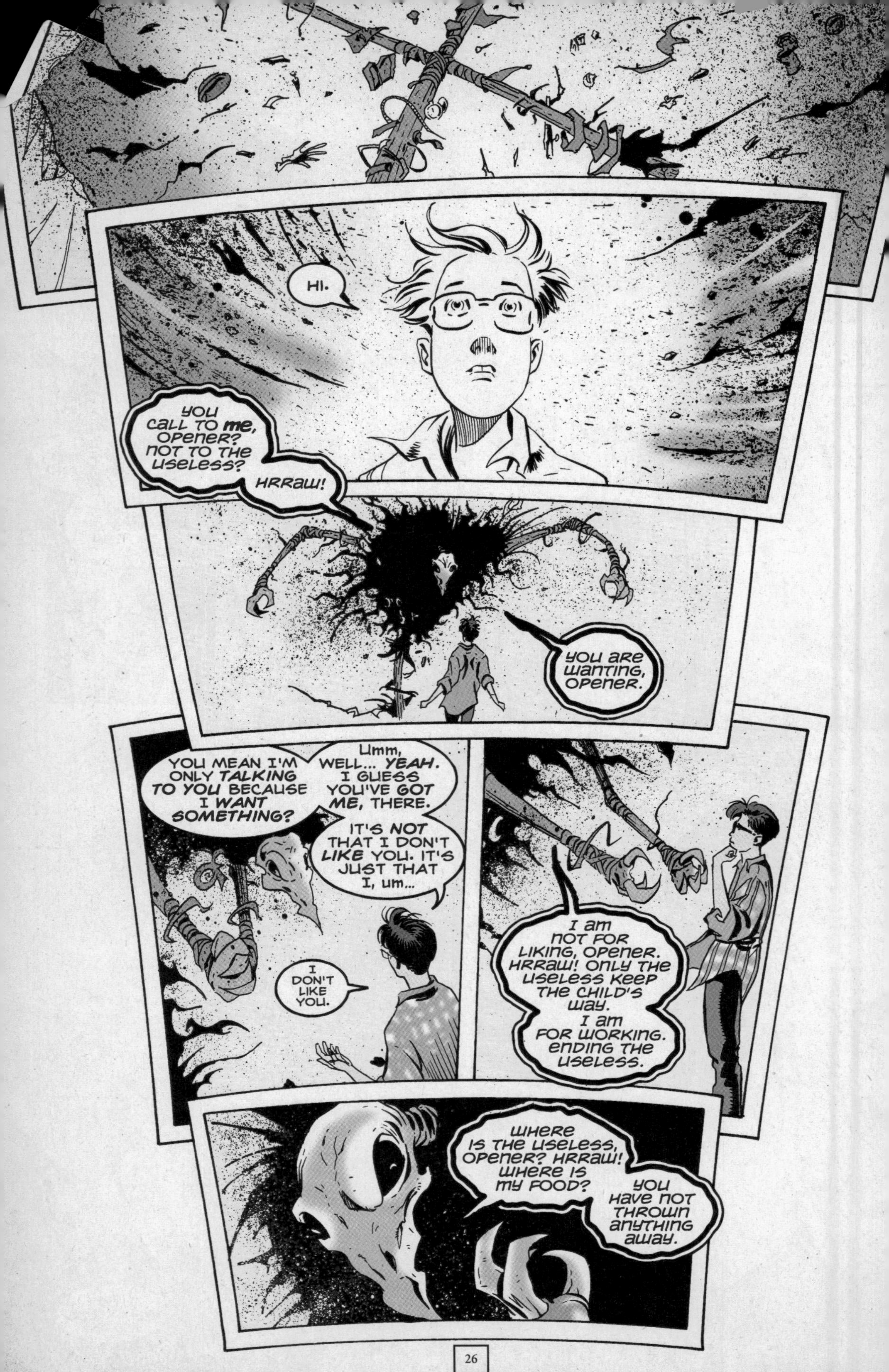
HI.
YOU CALL TO ME, OPENER? NOT TO THE USELESS?
HRRAW!
YOU ARE WANTING, OPENER.
YOU MEAN I'M ONLY TALKING TO YOU BECAUSE I WANT SOMETHING?
UMM, WELL... YEAH. I GUESS YOU'VE GOT ME, THERE.
IT'S NOT THAT I DON'T LIKE YOU. IT'S JUST THAT I, UM...
I DON'T LIKE YOU.
I AM NOT FOR LIKING, OPENER. HRRAW! ONLY THE USELESS KEEP THE CHILD'S WAY.
I AM FOR WORKING. ENDING THE USELESS.
WHERE IS THE USELESS, OPENER? HRRAW! WHERE IS MY FOOD?
YOU HAVE NOT THROWN ANYTHING AWAY.

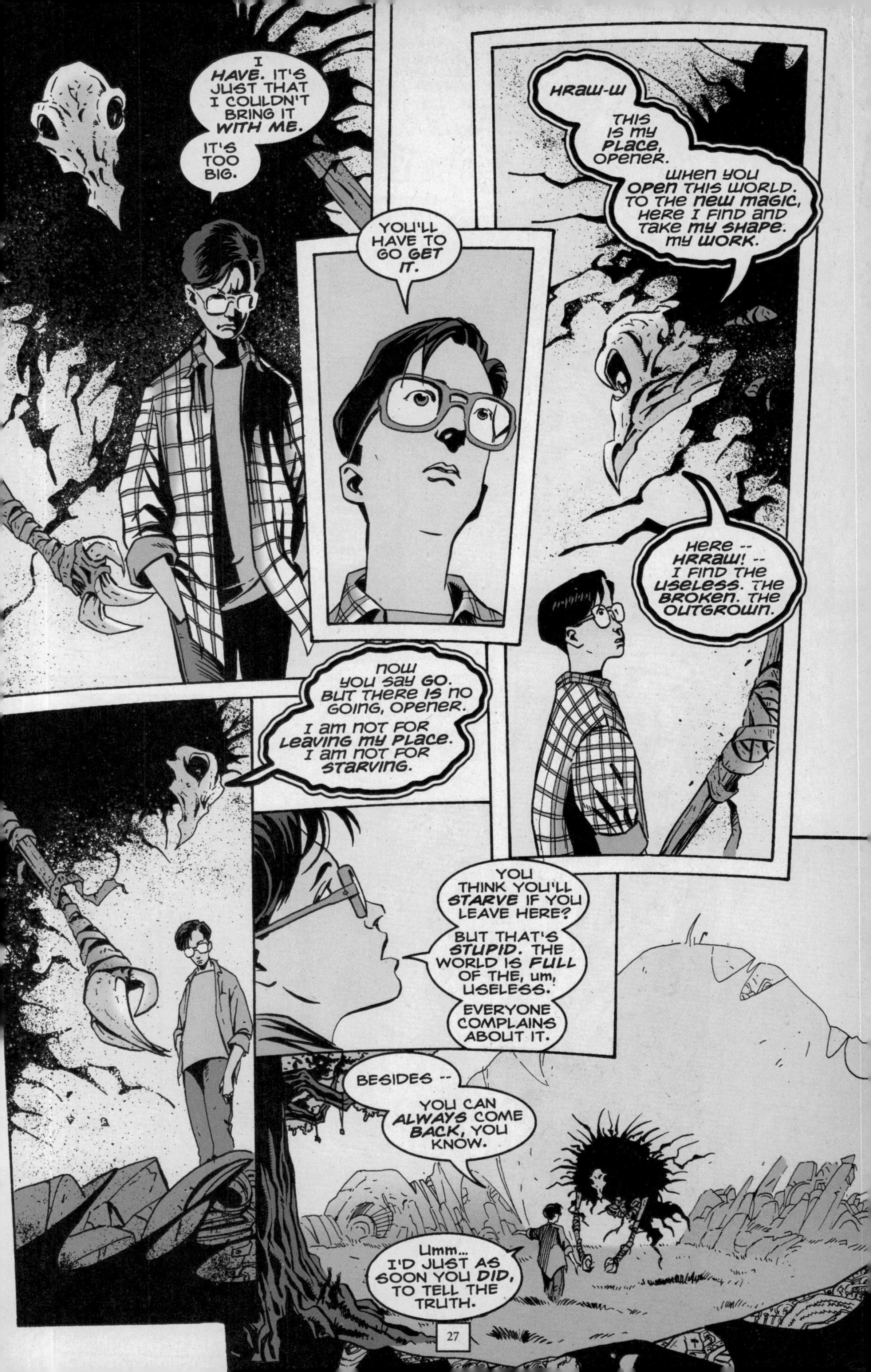
I HAVE. IT'S JUST THAT I COULDN'T BRING IT WITH ME.
IT'S TOO BIG.
YOU'LL HAVE TO GO GET IT.
HRAW-W
THIS IS MY PLACE, OPENER.
WHEN YOU OPEN THIS WORLD. TO THE NEW MAGIC, HERE I FIND AND TAKE MY SHAPE. MY WORK.
HERE -- HRRAW! -- I FIND THE USELESS. THE BROKEN. THE OUTGROWN.
NOW YOU SAY GO. BUT THERE IS NO GOING, OPENER.
I AM NOT FOR LEAVING MY PLACE. I AM NOT FOR STARVING.
YOU THINK YOU'LL STARVE IF YOU LEAVE HERE?
BUT THAT'S STUPID. THE WORLD IS FULL OF THE, UM, USELESS.
EVERYONE COMPLAINS ABOUT IT.
BESIDES --
YOU CAN ALWAYS COME BACK, YOU KNOW.
UMM... I'D JUST AS SOON YOU DID, TO TELL THE TRUTH.

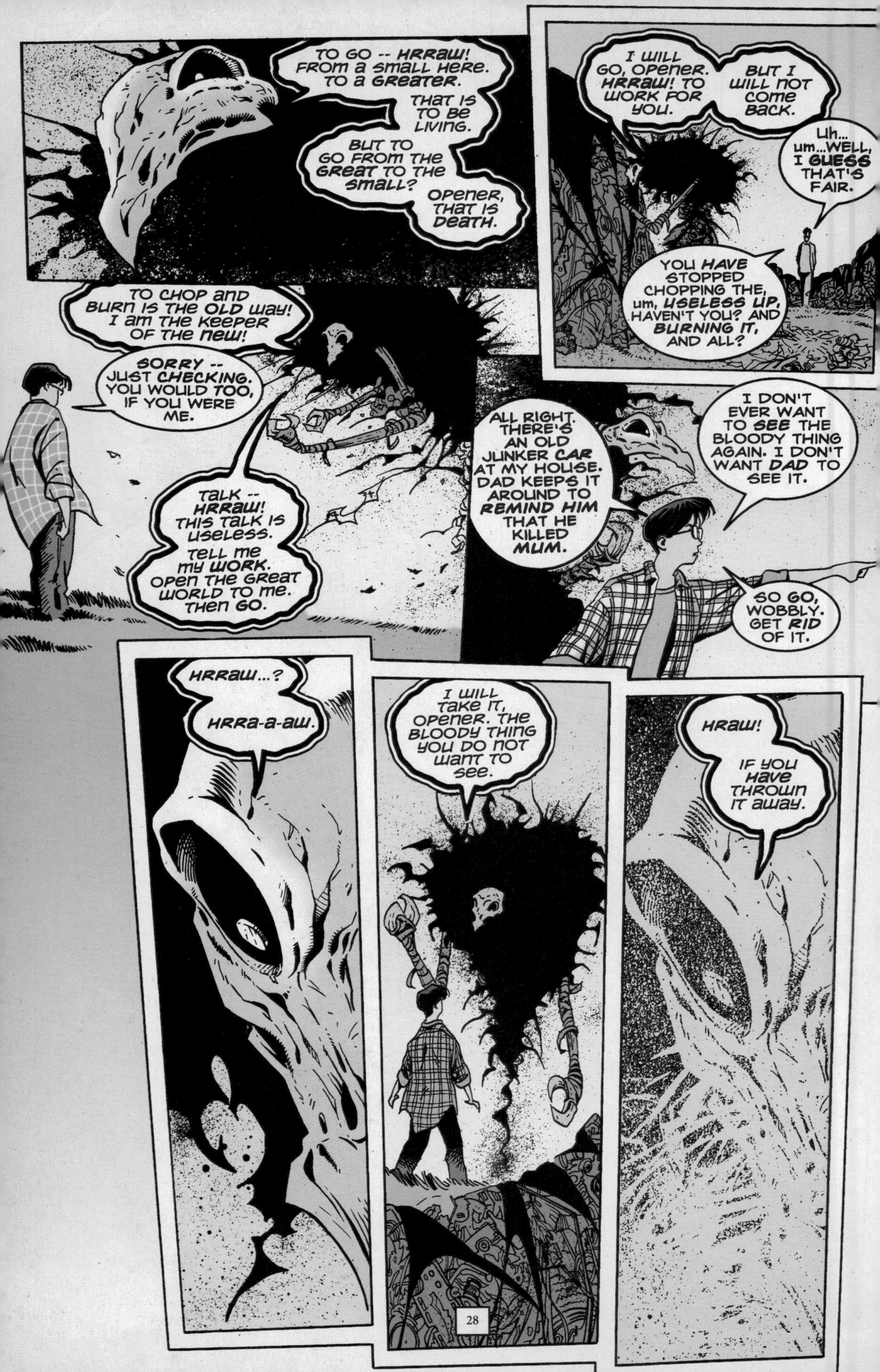
TO GO -- HRRAW! FROM A SMALL HERE. TO A GREATER.
THAT IS TO BE LIVING.
BUT TO GO FROM THE GREAT TO THE SMALL?
OPENER, THAT IS DEATH.
I WILL GO, OPENER. HRRAW! TO WORK FOR YOU.
BUT I WILL NOT COME BACK.
Uh... um...WELL, I GUESS THAT'S FAIR.
YOU HAVE STOPPED CHOPPING THE, um, USELESS UP, HAVEN'T YOU? AND BURNING IT, AND ALL?
TO CHOP AND BURN IS THE OLD WAY! I AM THE KEEPER OF THE NEW!
SORRY -- JUST CHECKING. YOU WOULD TOO, IF YOU WERE ME.
TALK -- HRRAW! THIS TALK IS USELESS. TELL ME MY WORK. OPEN THE GREAT WORLD TO ME. THEN GO.
ALL RIGHT. THERE'S AN OLD JUNKER CAR AT MY HOUSE. DAD KEEPS IT AROUND TO REMIND HIM THAT HE KILLED MUM.
I DON'T EVER WANT TO SEE THE BLOODY THING AGAIN. I DON'T WANT DAD TO SEE IT.
SO GO, WOBBLY. GET RID OF IT.
HRRAW...?
HRRA-A-AW.
I WILL TAKE IT, OPENER. THE BLOODY THING YOU DO NOT WANT TO SEE.
HRAW!
IF YOU HAVE THROWN IT AWAY.

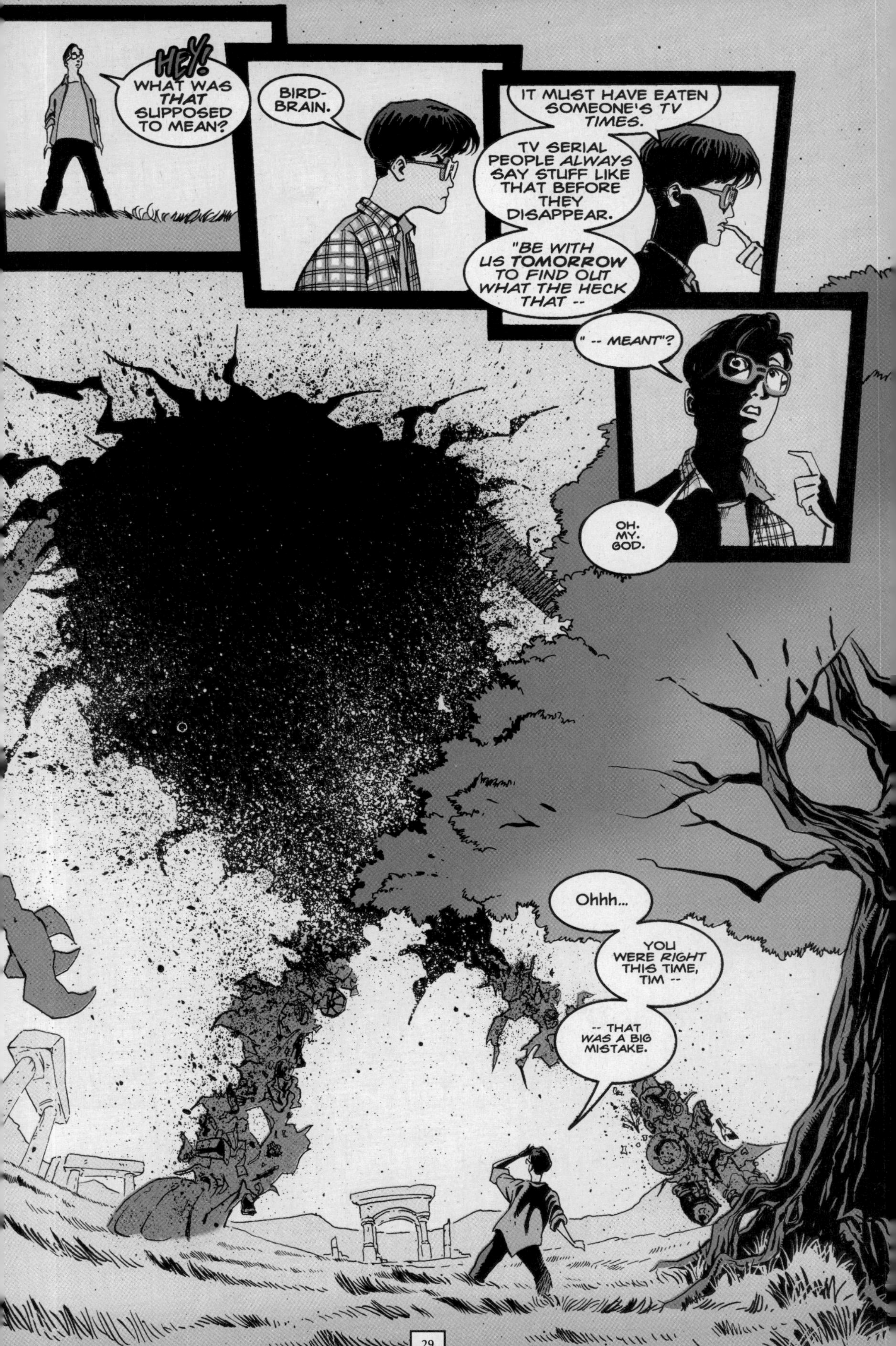
HEY!
WHAT WAS THAT SUPPOSED TO MEAN?
BIRD-BRAIN.
IT MUST HAVE EATEN SOMEONE'S TV TIMES.
TV SERIAL PEOPLE ALWAYS SAY STUFF LIKE THAT BEFORE THEY DISAPPEAR.
"BE WITH US TOMORROW TO FIND OUT WHAT THE HECK THAT --
" -- MEANT"?
OH. MY. GOD.
Ohhh...
YOU WERE RIGHT THIS TIME, TIM --
-- THAT WAS A BIG MISTAKE.

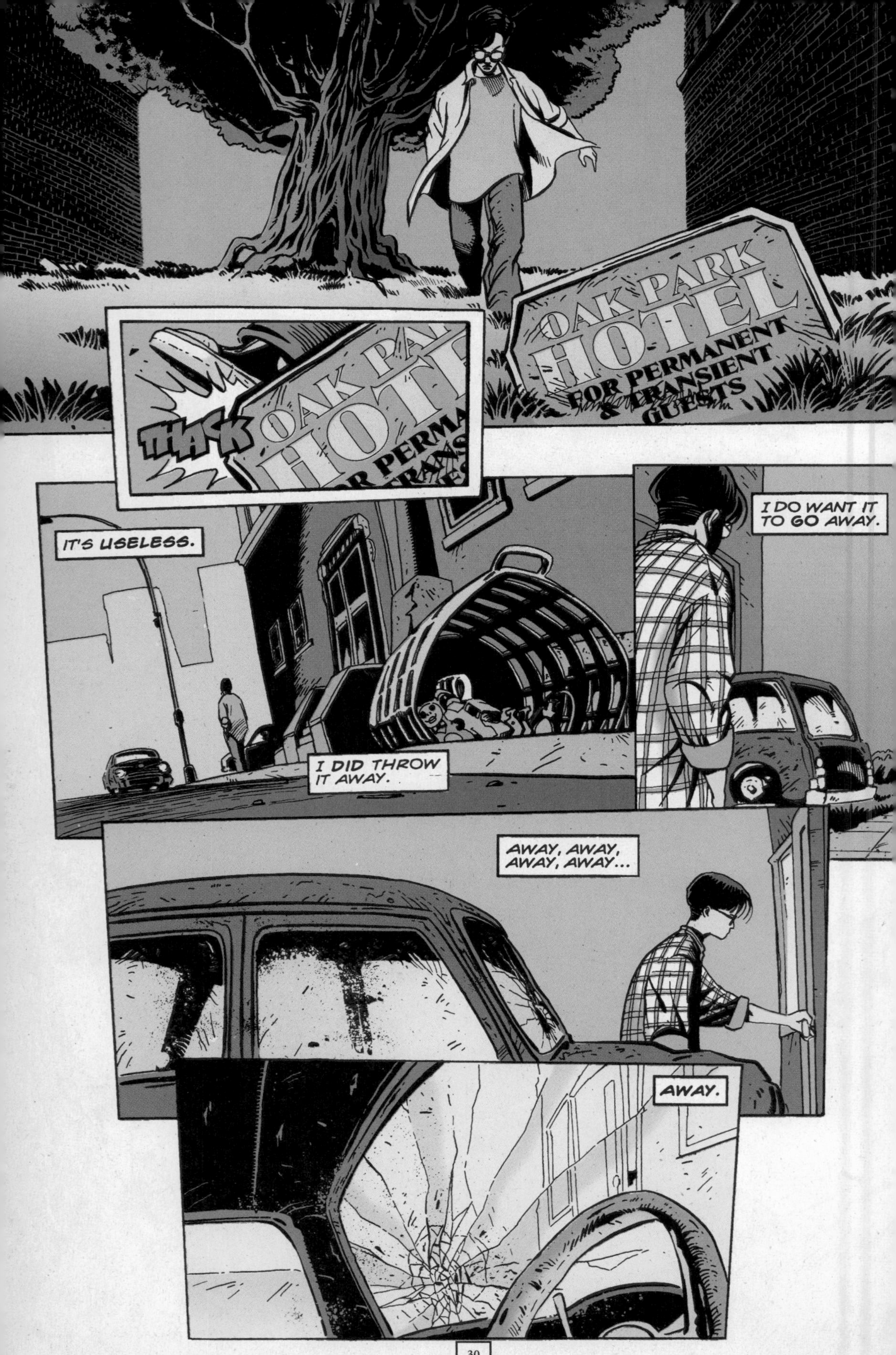
OAK PARK HOTEL FOR PERMANENT & TRANSIENT GUESTS
THACK
IT'S USELESS.
I DID THROW IT AWAY.
I DO WANT IT TO GO AWAY.
AWAY, AWAY, AWAY, AWAY...
AWAY.

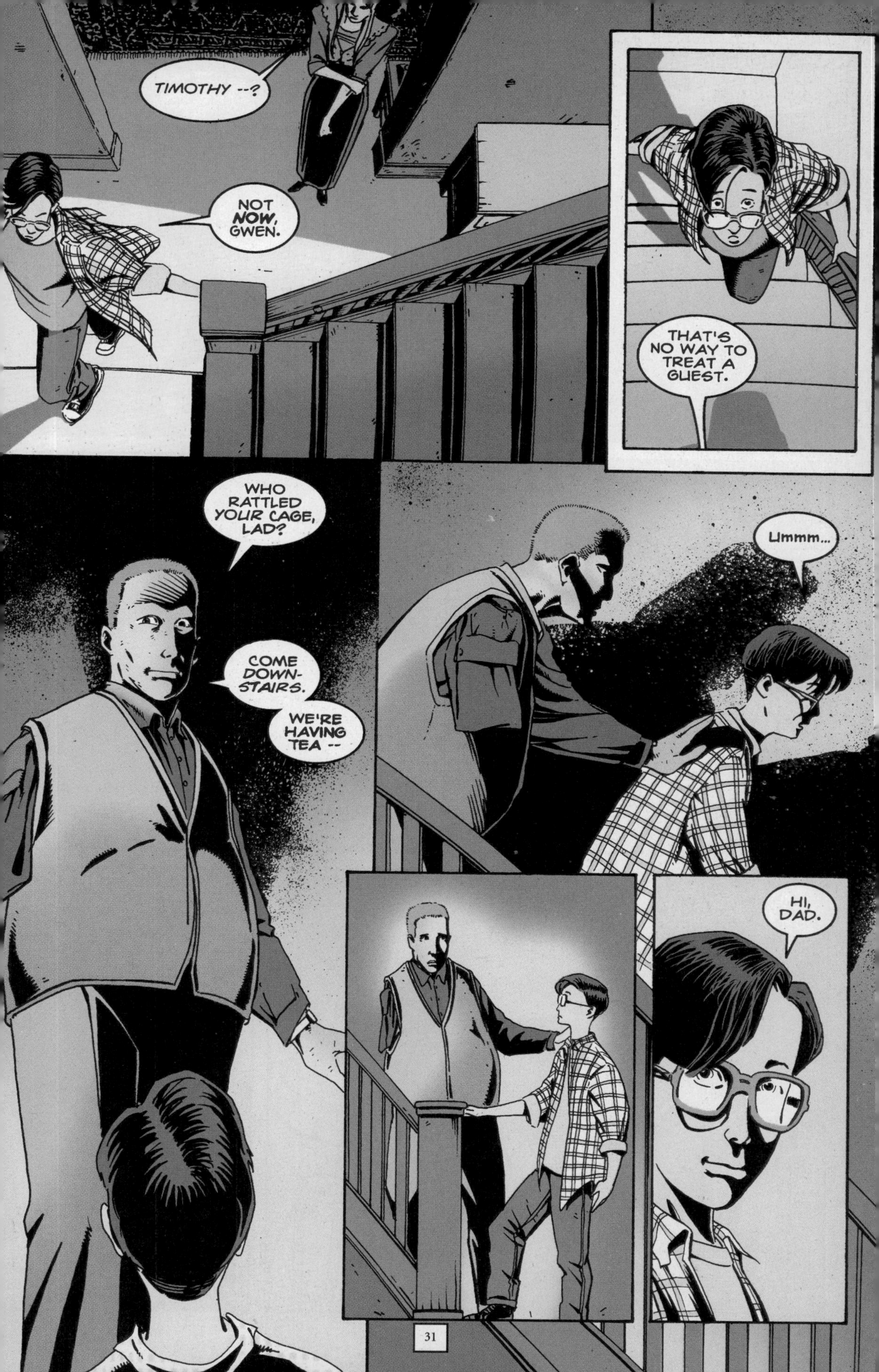
TIMOTHY --?
NOT NOW, GWEN.
THAT'S NO WAY TO TREAT A GUEST.
WHO RATTLED YOUR CAGE, LAD?
COME DOWN-STAIRS.
WE'RE HAVING TEA --
Ummm...
HI, DAD.

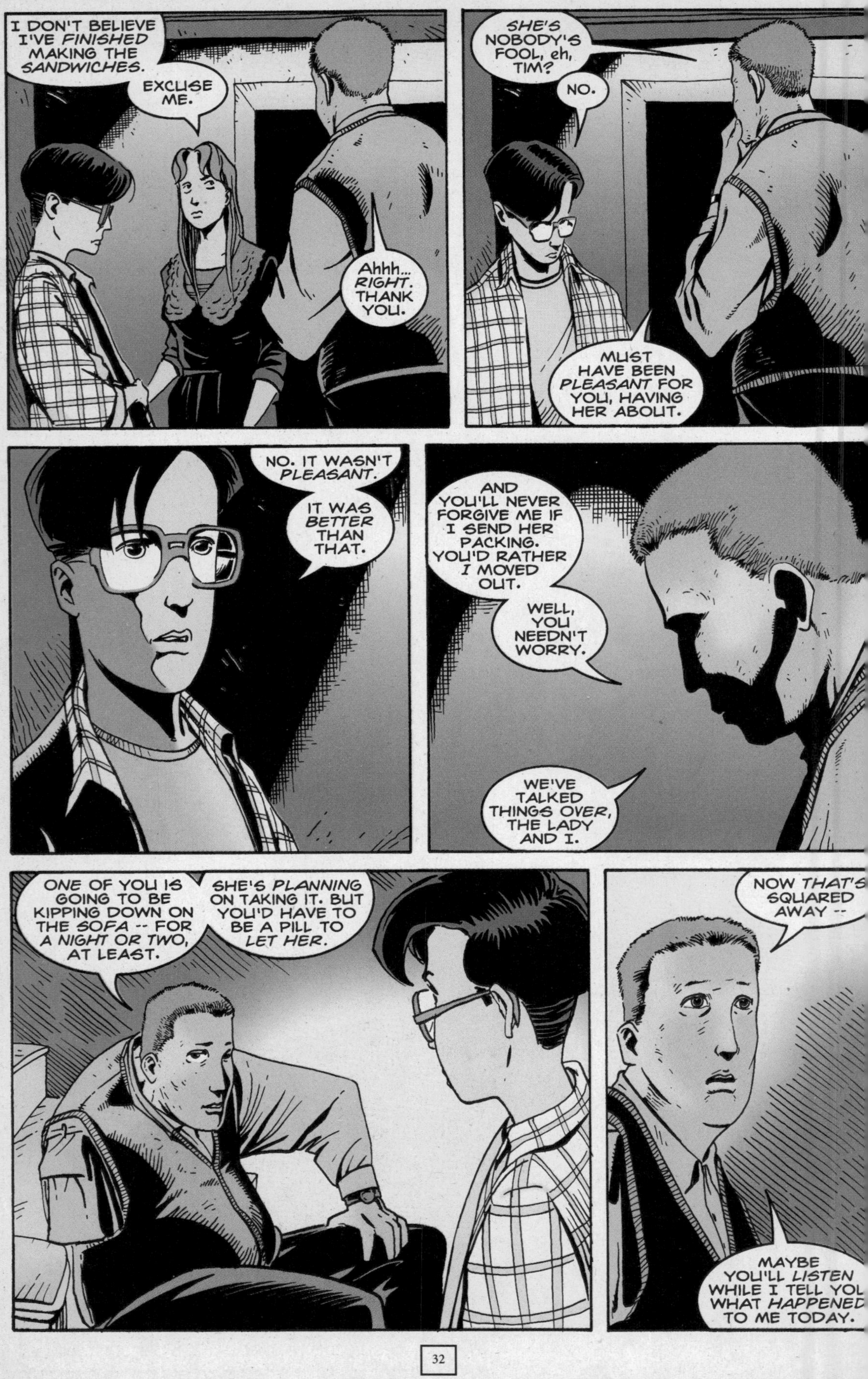
I DON'T BELIEVE I'VE *FINISHED* MAKING THE *SANDWICHES*.
EXCUSE ME.
Ahhh... *RIGHT*. THANK YOU.
SHE'S NOBODY'S FOOL, eh, TIM?
NO.
MUST HAVE BEEN *PLEASANT* FOR YOU, HAVING HER ABOUT.
NO. IT WASN'T *PLEASANT*.
IT WAS *BETTER* THAN THAT.
AND YOU'LL NEVER FORGIVE ME IF I SEND HER PACKING. YOU'D RATHER *I* MOVED OUT.
WELL, YOU NEEDN'T WORRY.
WE'VE TALKED THINGS *OVER*, THE LADY AND I.
ONE OF YOU IS GOING TO BE KIPPING DOWN ON THE *SOFA* -- FOR A *NIGHT OR TWO*, AT LEAST.
SHE'S *PLANNING* ON TAKING IT. BUT YOU'D HAVE TO BE A PILL TO *LET HER*.
NOW *THAT'S* SQUARED AWAY --
MAYBE YOU'LL *LISTEN* WHILE I TELL YOU WHAT *HAPPENED* TO ME TODAY.

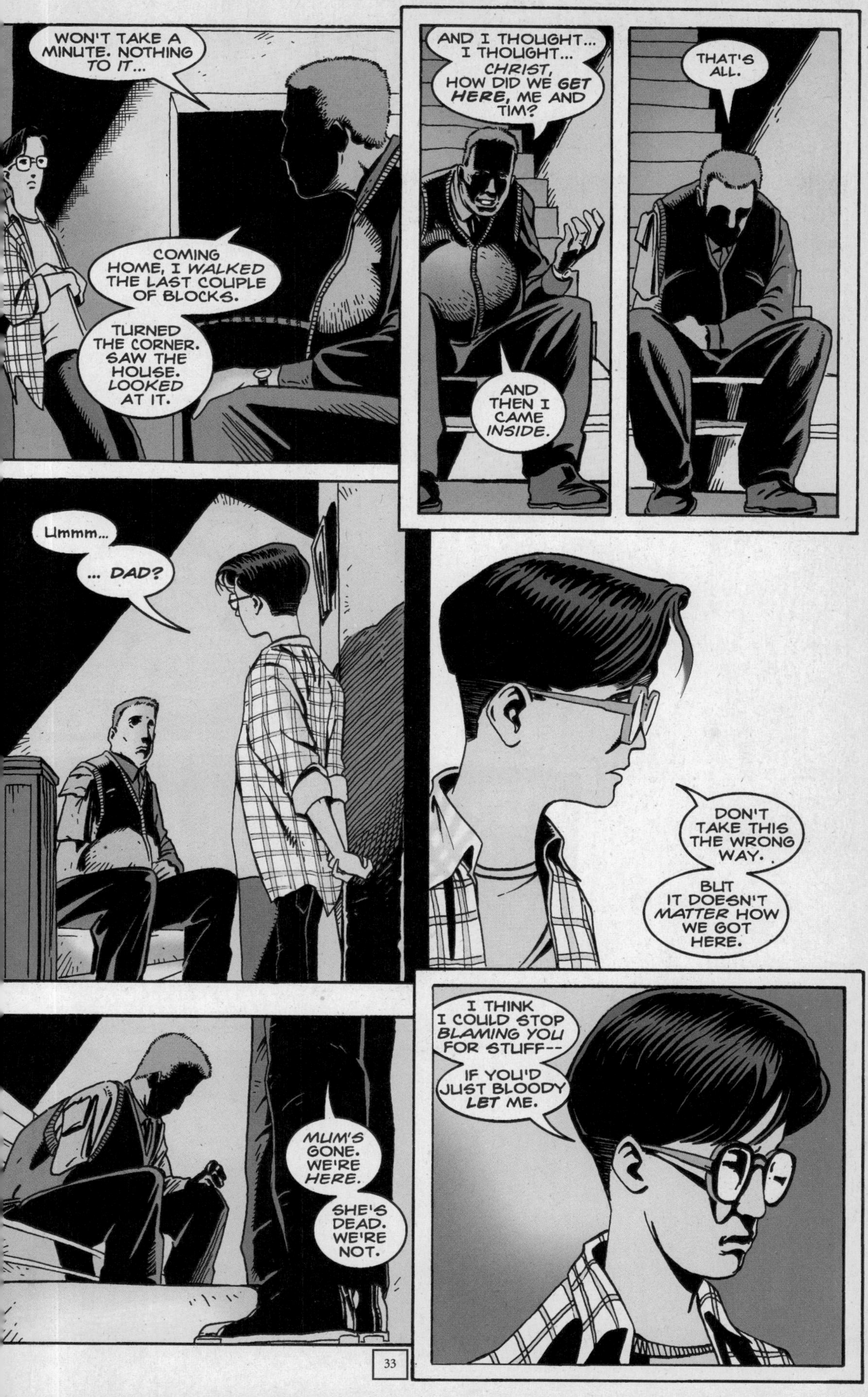
WON'T TAKE A MINUTE. NOTHING TO IT...
COMING HOME, I WALKED THE LAST COUPLE OF BLOCKS.
TURNED THE CORNER. SAW THE HOUSE. LOOKED AT IT.
AND I THOUGHT... I THOUGHT... CHRIST, HOW DID WE GET HERE, ME AND TIM?
AND THEN I CAME INSIDE.
THAT'S ALL.
Ummm...
... DAD?
DON'T TAKE THIS THE WRONG WAY.
BUT IT DOESN'T MATTER HOW WE GOT HERE.
MUM'S GONE. WE'RE HERE.
SHE'S DEAD. WE'RE NOT.
I THINK I COULD STOP BLAMING YOU FOR STUFF--
IF YOU'D JUST BLOODY LET ME.

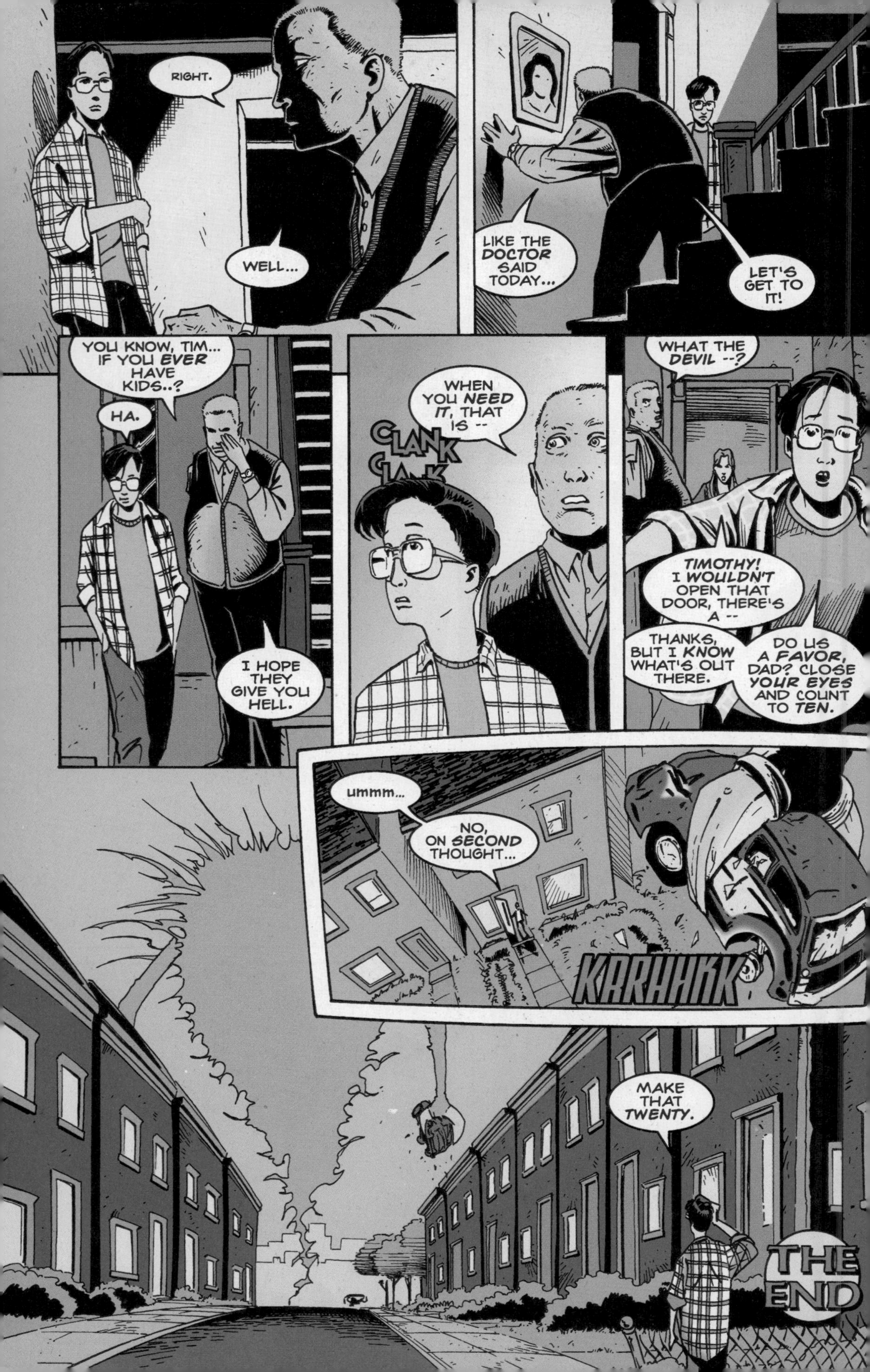
RIGHT.
WELL...
LIKE THE DOCTOR SAID TODAY...
LET'S GET TO IT!
YOU KNOW, TIM... IF YOU EVER HAVE KIDS..?
HA.
I HOPE THEY GIVE YOU HELL.
WHEN YOU NEED IT, THAT IS --
CLANK
CLANK
WHAT THE DEVIL --?
TIMOTHY! I WOULDN'T OPEN THAT DOOR, THERE'S A --
THANKS, BUT I KNOW WHAT'S OUT THERE.
DO US A FAVOR, DAD? CLOSE YOUR EYES AND COUNT TO TEN.
ummm...
NO, ON SECOND THOUGHT...
KRRAHKK
MAKE THAT TWENTY.
THE END

Hell
and
Back

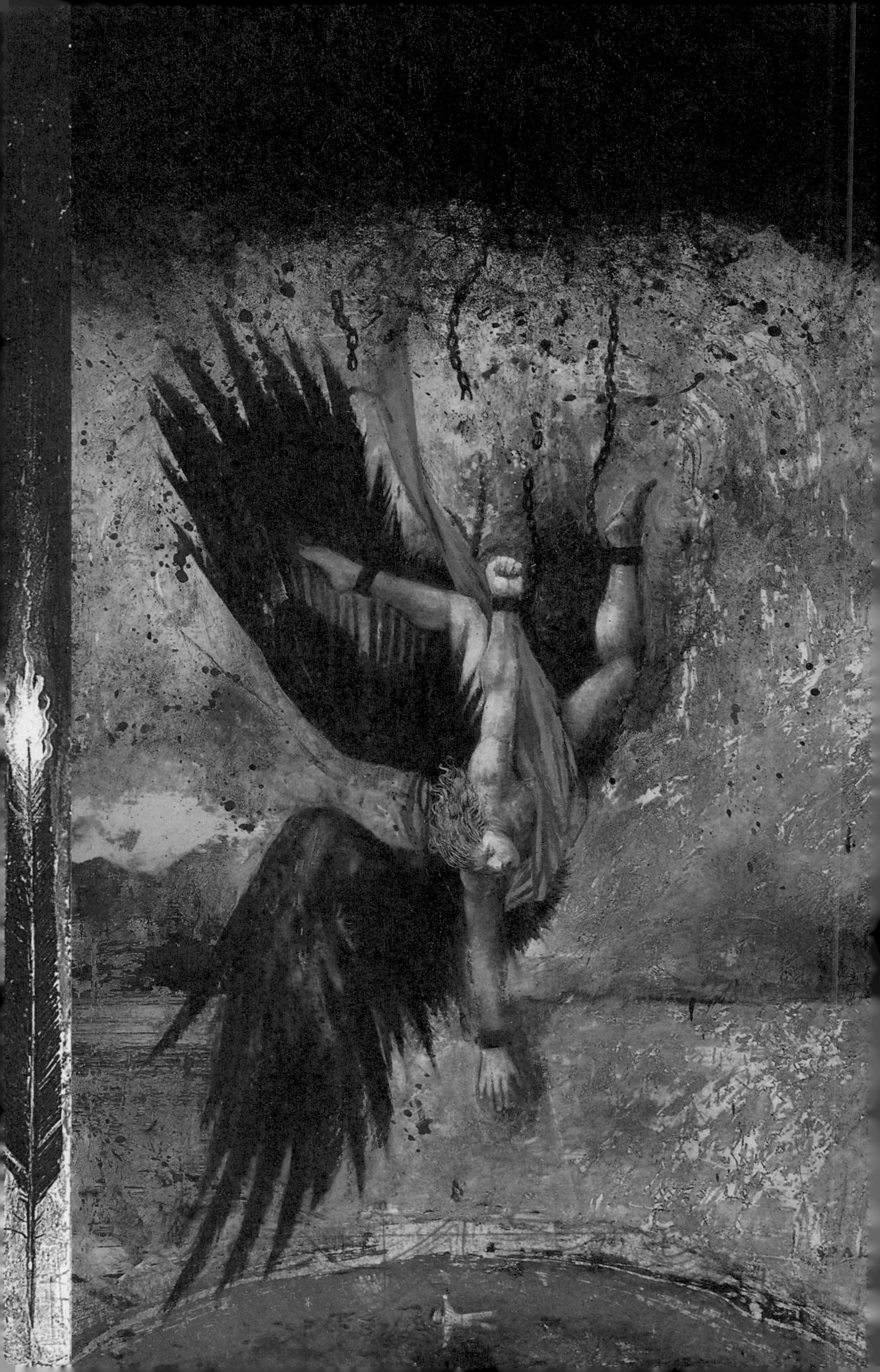

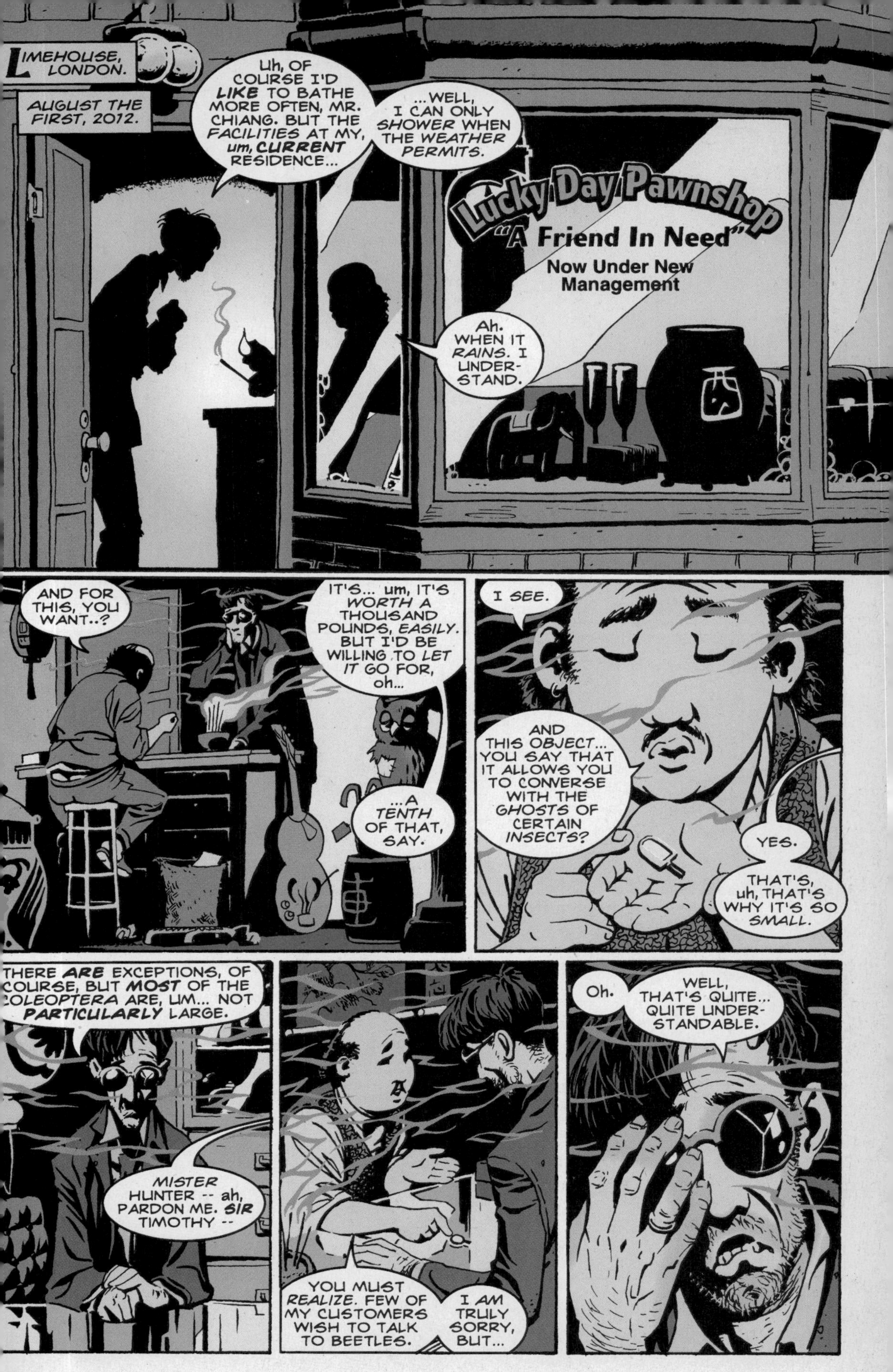
LIMEHOUSE, LONDON.
AUGUST THE FIRST, 2012.
Uh, OF COURSE I'D LIKE TO BATHE MORE OFTEN, MR. CHIANG. BUT THE FACILITIES AT MY, um, CURRENT RESIDENCE...
...WELL, I CAN ONLY SHOWER WHEN THE WEATHER PERMITS.
Lucky Day Pawnshop
"A Friend In Need"
Now Under New Management
Ah. WHEN IT RAINS. I UNDERSTAND.
AND FOR THIS, YOU WANT..?
IT'S... um, IT'S WORTH A THOUSAND POUNDS, EASILY. BUT I'D BE WILLING TO LET IT GO FOR, oh...
...A TENTH OF THAT, SAY.
I SEE.
AND THIS OBJECT... YOU SAY THAT IT ALLOWS YOU TO CONVERSE WITH THE GHOSTS OF CERTAIN INSECTS?
YES.
THAT'S, uh, THAT'S WHY IT'S SO SMALL.
THERE ARE EXCEPTIONS, OF COURSE, BUT MOST OF THE COLEOPTERA ARE, UM... NOT PARTICULARLY LARGE.
MISTER HUNTER -- ah, PARDON ME. SIR TIMOTHY --
YOU MUST REALIZE. FEW OF MY CUSTOMERS WISH TO TALK TO BEETLES.
I AM TRULY SORRY, BUT...
Oh.
WELL, THAT'S QUITE... QUITE UNDERSTANDABLE.

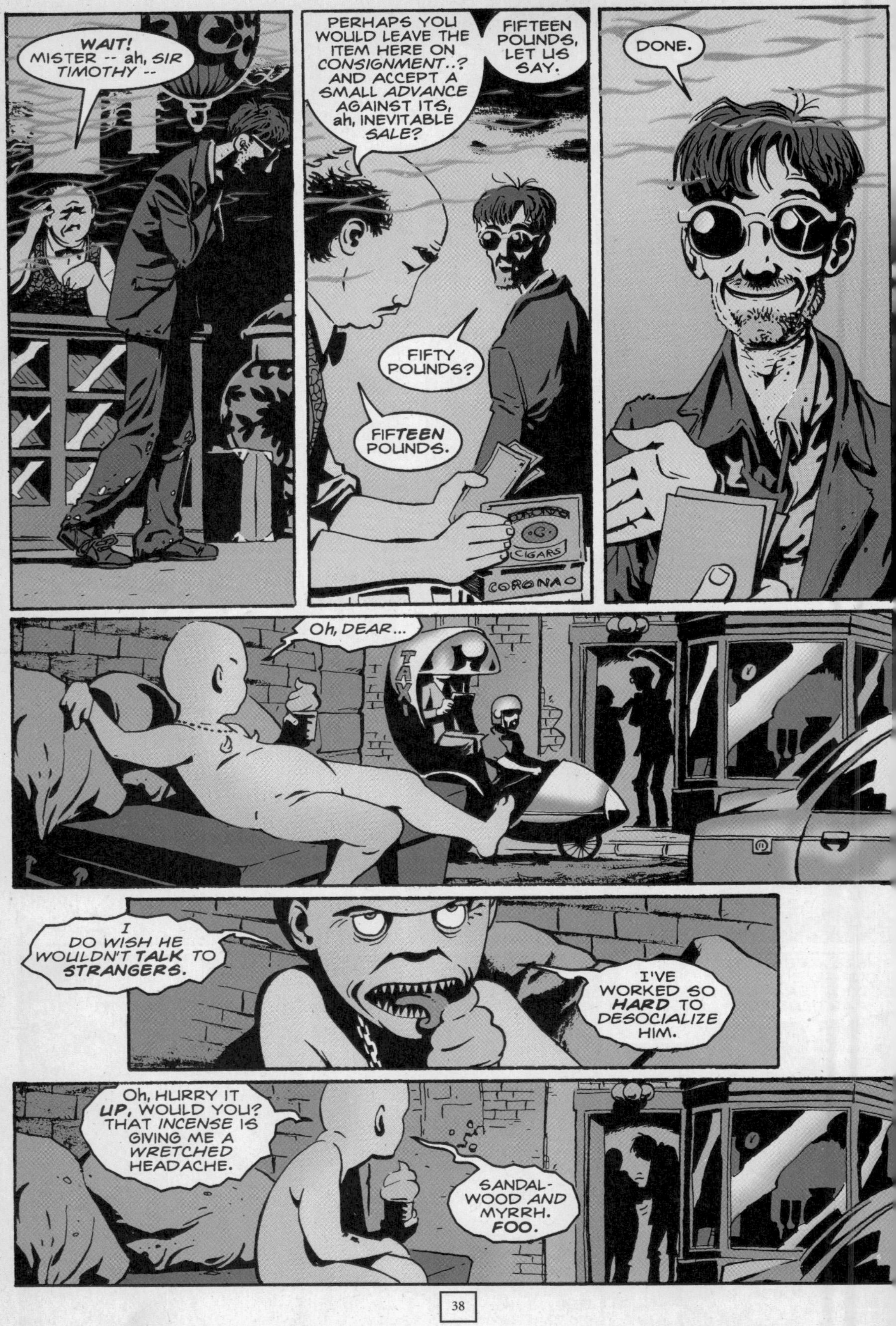
WAIT! MISTER -- ah, SIR TIMOTHY --
PERHAPS YOU WOULD LEAVE THE ITEM HERE ON CONSIGNMENT..? AND ACCEPT A SMALL ADVANCE AGAINST ITS, ah, INEVITABLE SALE?
FIFTEEN POUNDS, LET US SAY.
FIFTY POUNDS?
FIFTEEN POUNDS.
CIGARS
CORONAO
DONE.
Oh, DEAR...
TAXI
I DO WISH HE WOULDN'T TALK TO STRANGERS.
I'VE WORKED SO HARD TO DESOCIALIZE HIM.
Oh, HURRY IT UP, WOULD YOU? THAT INCENSE IS GIVING ME A WRETCHED HEADACHE.
SANDAL-WOOD AND MYRRH. FOO.

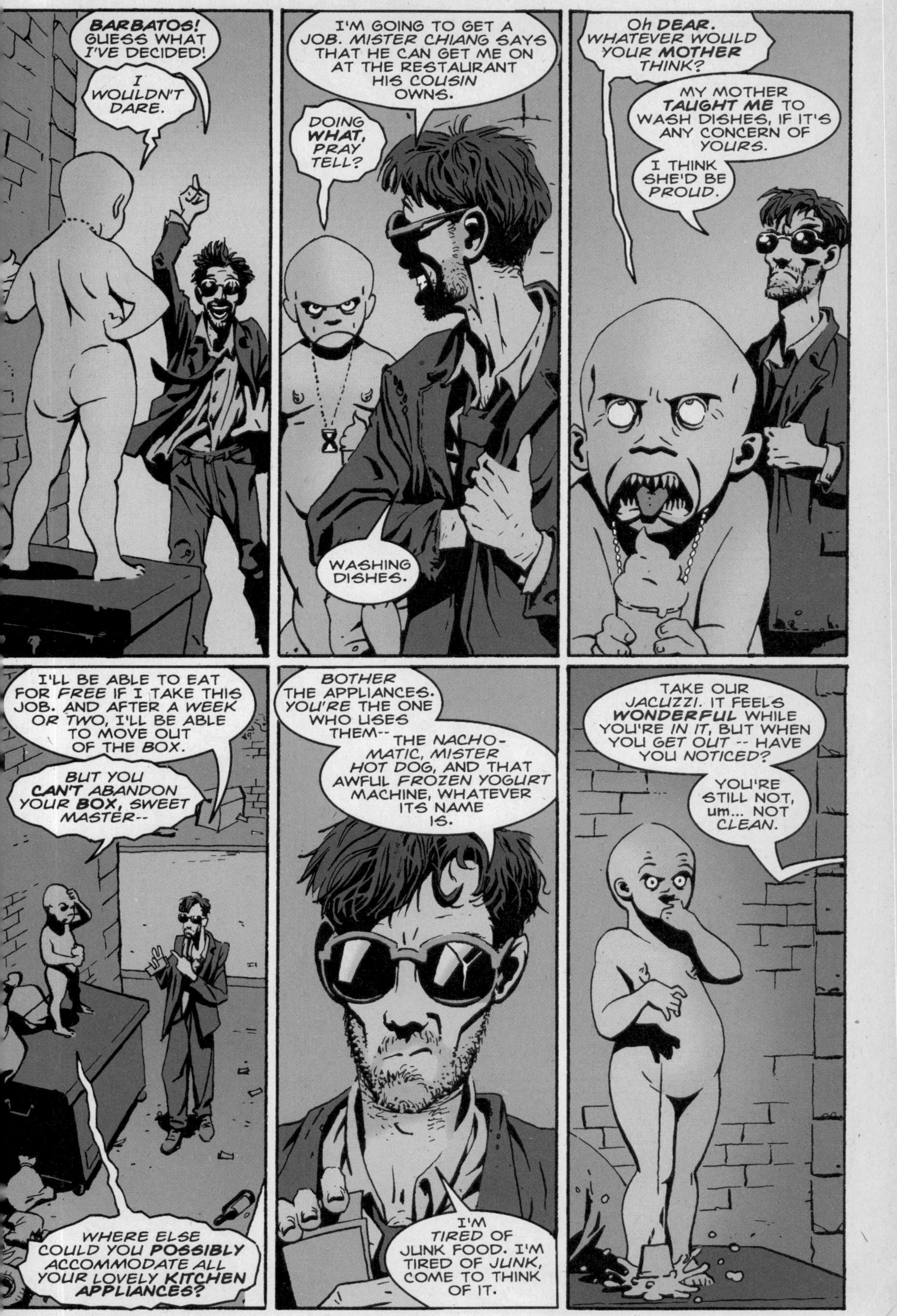
BARBATOS! GUESS WHAT I'VE DECIDED!
I WOULDN'T DARE.
I'M GOING TO GET A JOB. MISTER CHIANG SAYS THAT HE CAN GET ME ON AT THE RESTAURANT HIS COUSIN OWNS.
DOING WHAT, PRAY TELL?
WASHING DISHES.
Oh DEAR. WHATEVER WOULD YOUR MOTHER THINK?
MY MOTHER TAUGHT ME TO WASH DISHES, IF IT'S ANY CONCERN OF YOURS.
I THINK SHE'D BE PROUD.
I'LL BE ABLE TO EAT FOR FREE IF I TAKE THIS JOB. AND AFTER A WEEK OR TWO, I'LL BE ABLE TO MOVE OUT OF THE BOX.
BUT YOU CAN'T ABANDON YOUR BOX, SWEET MASTER--
WHERE ELSE COULD YOU POSSIBLY ACCOMMODATE ALL YOUR LOVELY KITCHEN APPLIANCES?
BOTHER THE APPLIANCES. YOU'RE THE ONE WHO USES THEM--
THE NACHO-MATIC, MISTER HOT DOG, AND THAT AWFUL FROZEN YOGURT MACHINE, WHATEVER ITS NAME IS.
I'M TIRED OF JUNK FOOD. I'M TIRED OF JUNK, COME TO THINK OF IT.
TAKE OUR JACUZZI. IT FEELS WONDERFUL WHILE YOU'RE IN IT, BUT WHEN YOU GET OUT -- HAVE YOU NOTICED?
YOU'RE STILL NOT, um... NOT CLEAN.

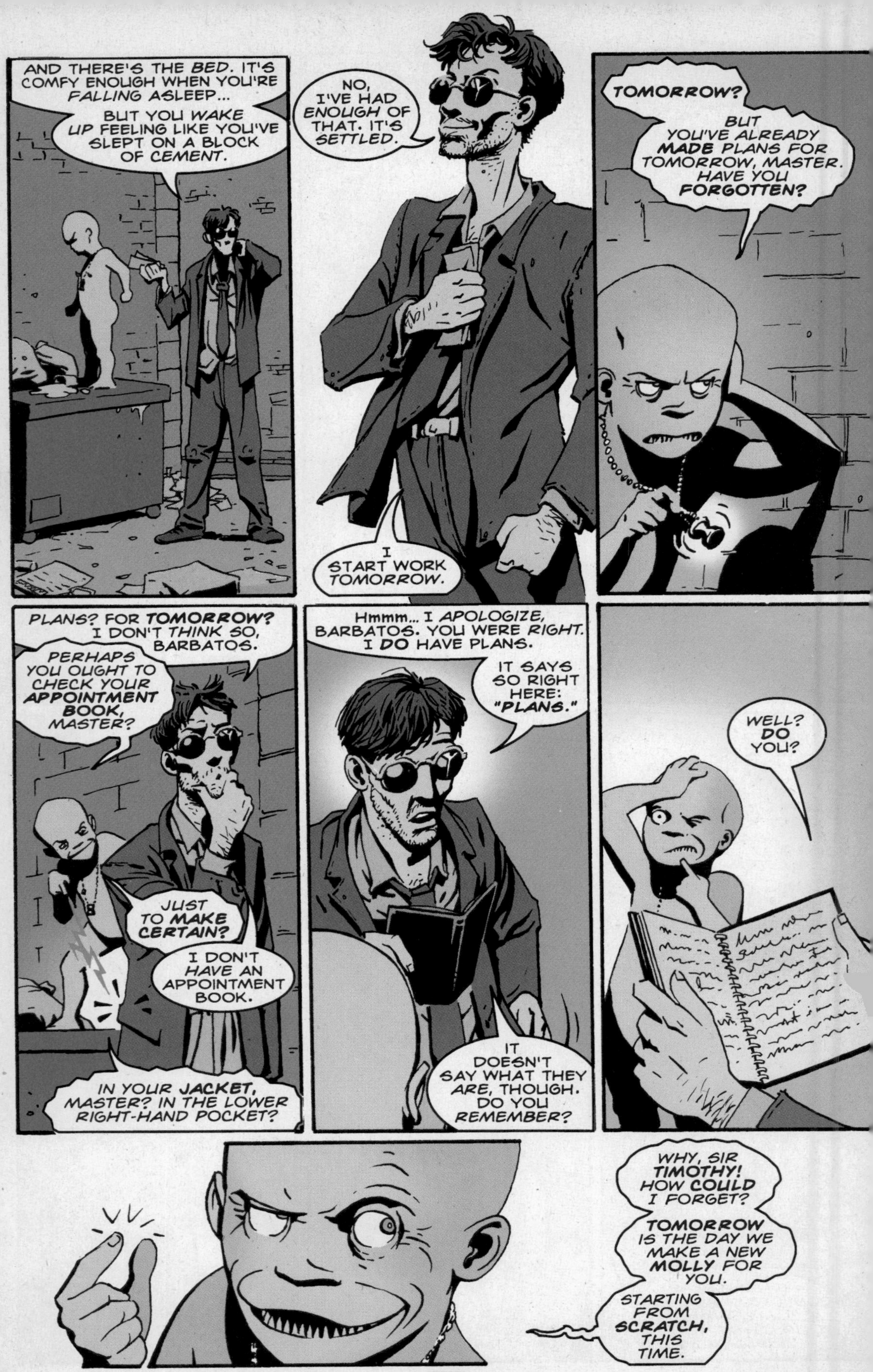
AND THERE'S THE BED. IT'S COMFY ENOUGH WHEN YOU'RE FALLING ASLEEP...
BUT YOU WAKE UP FEELING LIKE YOU'VE SLEPT ON A BLOCK OF CEMENT.
NO, I'VE HAD ENOUGH OF THAT. IT'S SETTLED.
I START WORK TOMORROW.
TOMORROW?
BUT YOU'VE ALREADY MADE PLANS FOR TOMORROW, MASTER. HAVE YOU FORGOTTEN?
PLANS? FOR TOMORROW? I DON'T THINK SO, BARBATOS.
PERHAPS YOU OUGHT TO CHECK YOUR APPOINTMENT BOOK, MASTER?
JUST TO MAKE CERTAIN?
I DON'T HAVE AN APPOINTMENT BOOK.
IN YOUR JACKET, MASTER? IN THE LOWER RIGHT-HAND POCKET?
Hmmm... I APOLOGIZE, BARBATOS. YOU WERE RIGHT. I DO HAVE PLANS.
IT SAYS SO RIGHT HERE: "PLANS."
IT DOESN'T SAY WHAT THEY ARE, THOUGH. DO YOU REMEMBER?
WELL? DO YOU?
WHY, SIR TIMOTHY! HOW COULD I FORGET?
TOMORROW IS THE DAY WE MAKE A NEW MOLLY FOR YOU.
STARTING FROM SCRATCH, THIS TIME.

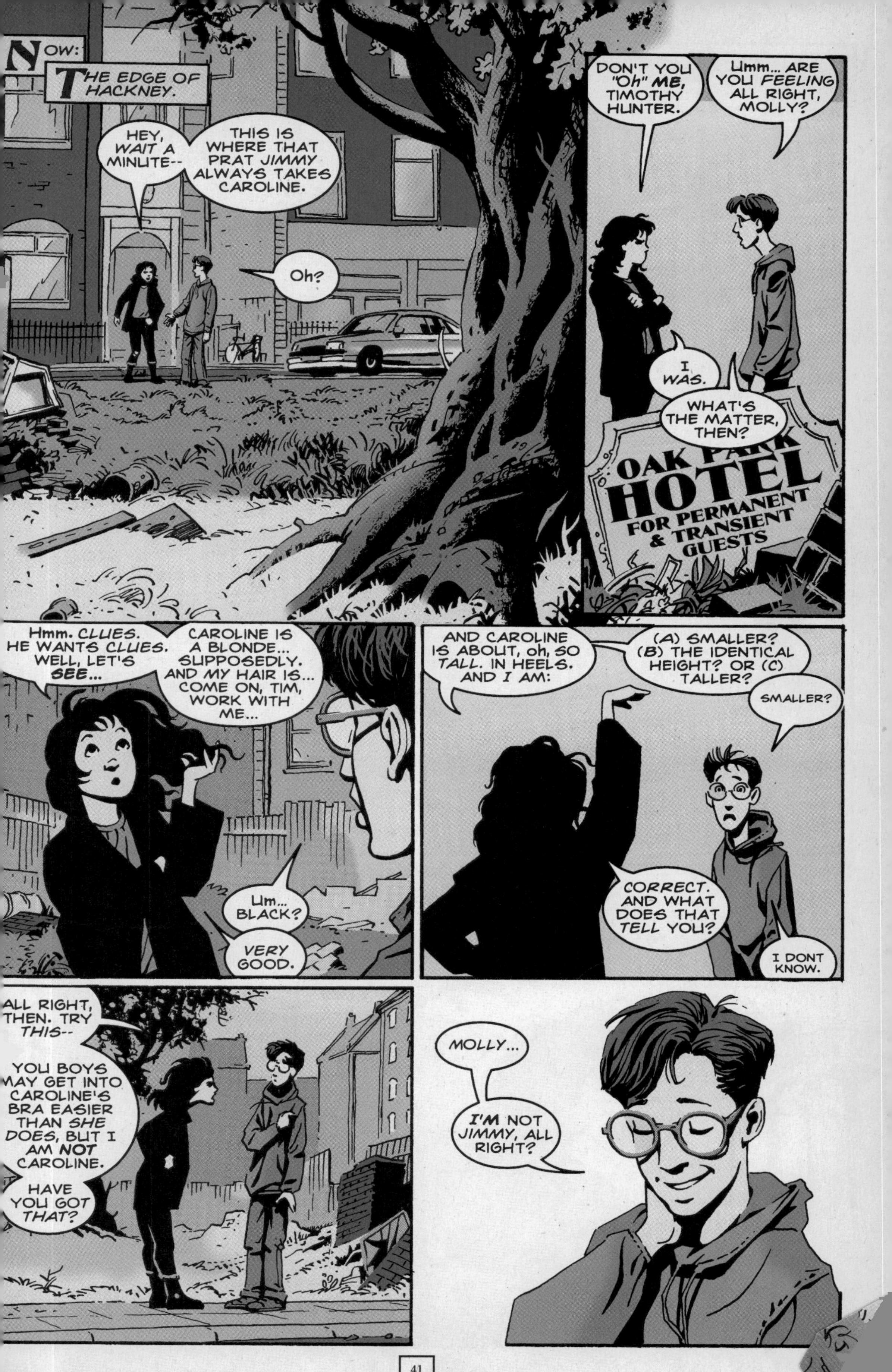
NOW:
THE EDGE OF HACKNEY.
HEY, WAIT A MINUTE--
THIS IS WHERE THAT PRAT JIMMY ALWAYS TAKES CAROLINE.
Oh?
DON'T YOU "Oh" ME, TIMOTHY HUNTER.
Umm... ARE YOU FEELING ALL RIGHT, MOLLY?
I WAS.
WHAT'S THE MATTER, THEN?
OAK PARK HOTEL FOR PERMANENT & TRANSIENT GUESTS
Hmm. CLUES. HE WANTS CLUES. WELL, LET'S SEE...
CAROLINE IS A BLONDE... SUPPOSEDLY. AND MY HAIR IS... COME ON, TIM, WORK WITH ME...
Um... BLACK?
VERY GOOD.
AND CAROLINE IS ABOUT, oh, SO TALL. IN HEELS. AND I AM:
(A) SMALLER? (B) THE IDENTICAL HEIGHT? OR (C) TALLER?
SMALLER?
CORRECT. AND WHAT DOES THAT TELL YOU?
I DONT KNOW.
ALL RIGHT, THEN. TRY THIS--
YOU BOYS MAY GET INTO CAROLINE'S BRA EASIER THAN SHE DOES, BUT I AM NOT CAROLINE.
HAVE YOU GOT THAT?
MOLLY...
I'M NOT JIMMY, ALL RIGHT?

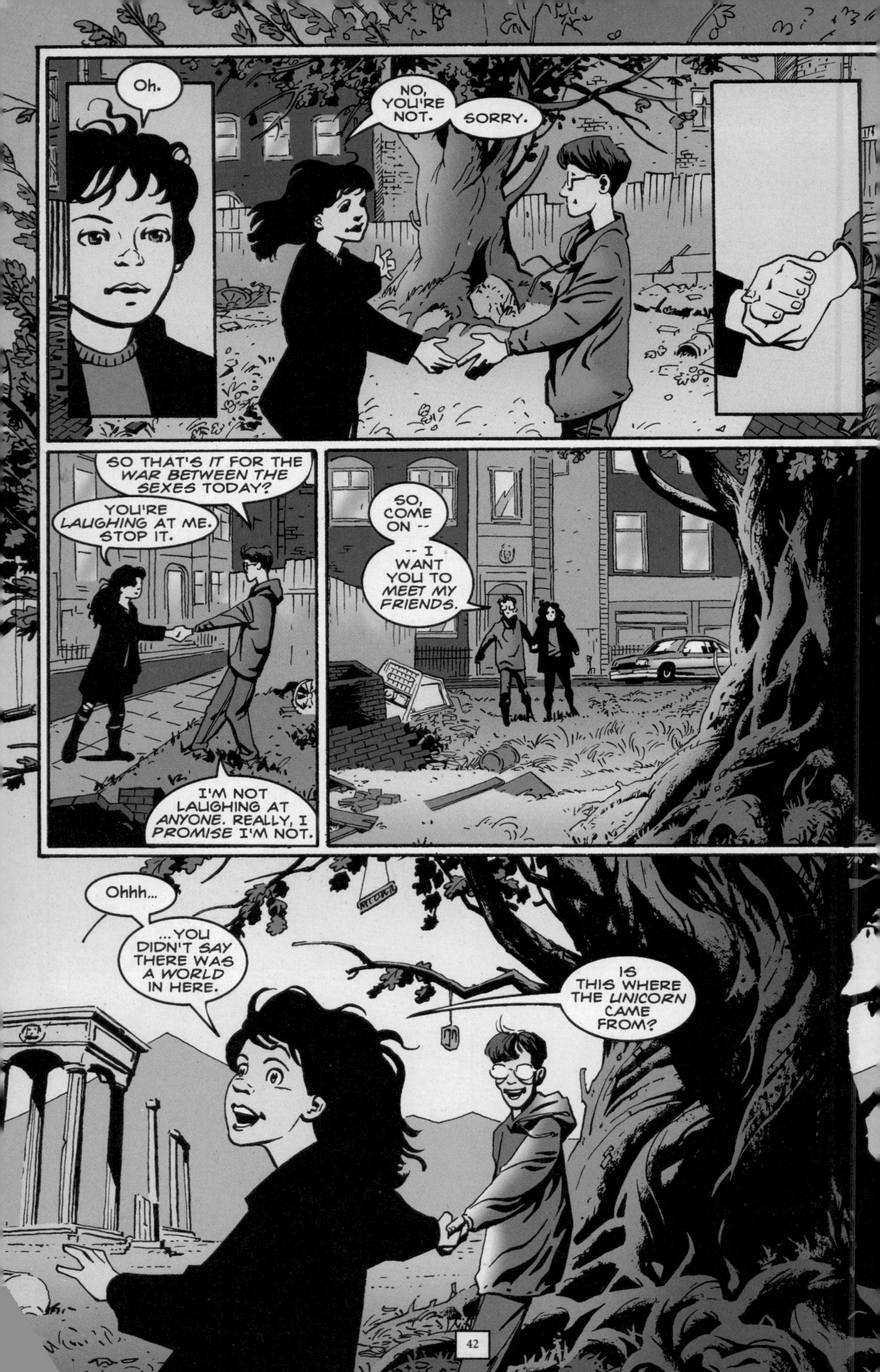

Oh.
NO, YOU'RE NOT.
SORRY.
SO THAT'S *IT* FOR THE *WAR BETWEEN THE SEXES* TODAY?
YOU'RE *LAUGHING AT ME.* STOP IT.
I'M NOT LAUGHING AT *ANYONE.* REALLY, I *PROMISE* I'M NOT.
SO, COME ON --
-- I WANT YOU TO *MEET MY FRIENDS.*
Ohhh...
...YOU DIDN'T *SAY* THERE WAS A *WORLD* IN HERE.
IS THIS WHERE THE *UNICORN* CAME FROM?

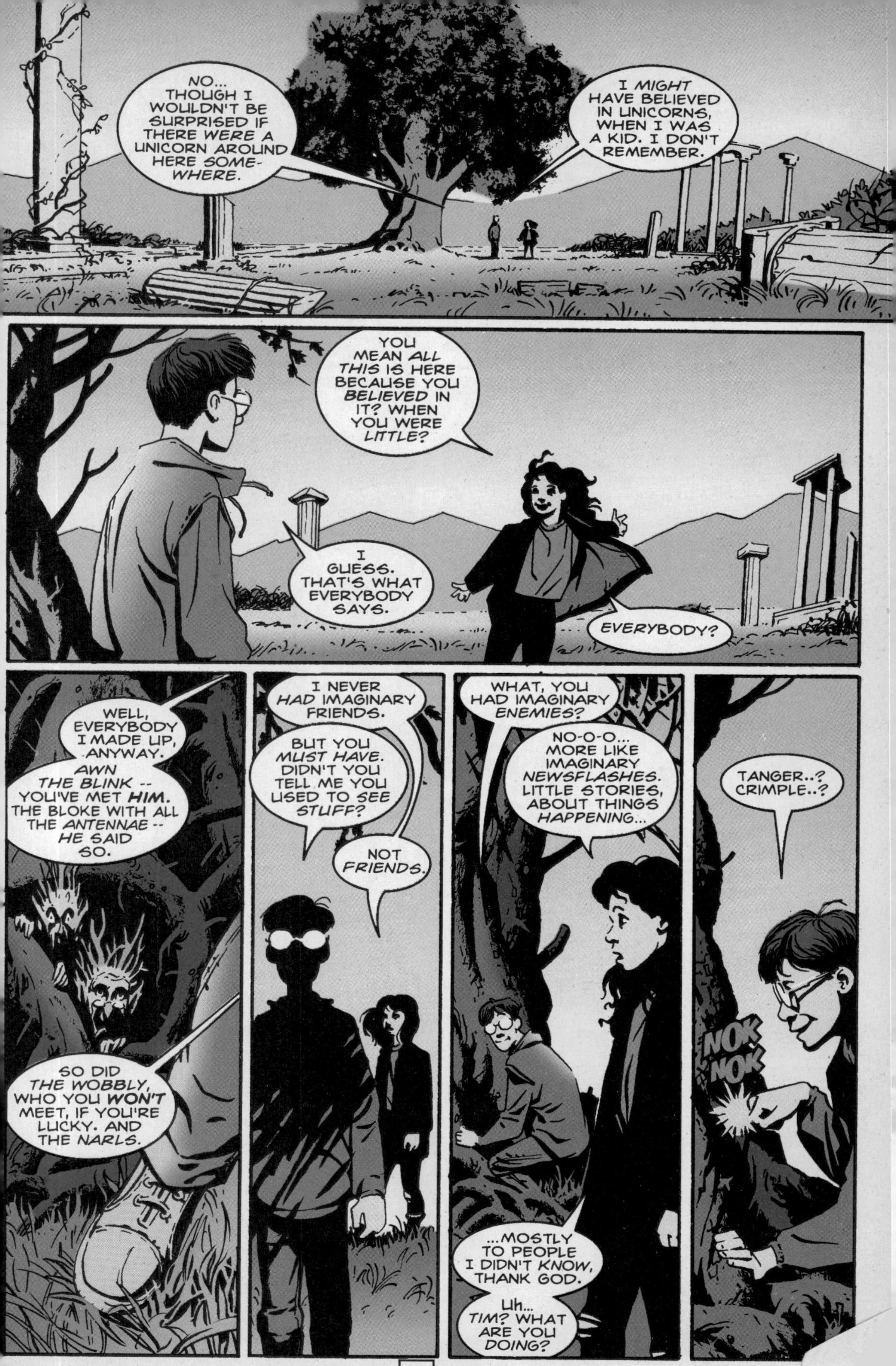
NO... THOUGH I WOULDN'T BE SURPRISED IF THERE WERE A UNICORN AROUND HERE SOME-WHERE.
I MIGHT HAVE BELIEVED IN UNICORNS, WHEN I WAS A KID. I DON'T REMEMBER.
YOU MEAN ALL THIS IS HERE BECAUSE YOU BELIEVED IN IT? WHEN YOU WERE LITTLE?
I GUESS. THAT'S WHAT EVERYBODY SAYS.
EVERYBODY?
WELL, EVERYBODY I MADE UP, ANYWAY.
AWN THE BLINK -- YOU'VE MET HIM. THE BLOKE WITH ALL THE ANTENNAE -- HE SAID SO.
SO DID THE WOBBLY, WHO YOU WON'T MEET, IF YOU'RE LUCKY. AND THE NARLS.
I NEVER HAD IMAGINARY FRIENDS.
BUT YOU MUST HAVE. DIDN'T YOU TELL ME YOU USED TO SEE STUFF?
NOT FRIENDS.
WHAT, YOU HAD IMAGINARY ENEMIES?
NO-O-O... MORE LIKE IMAGINARY NEWSFLASHES. LITTLE STORIES, ABOUT THINGS HAPPENING...
...MOSTLY TO PEOPLE I DIDN'T KNOW, THANK GOD.
Uh... TIM? WHAT ARE YOU DOING?
TANGER..? CRIMPLE..?
NOK NOK

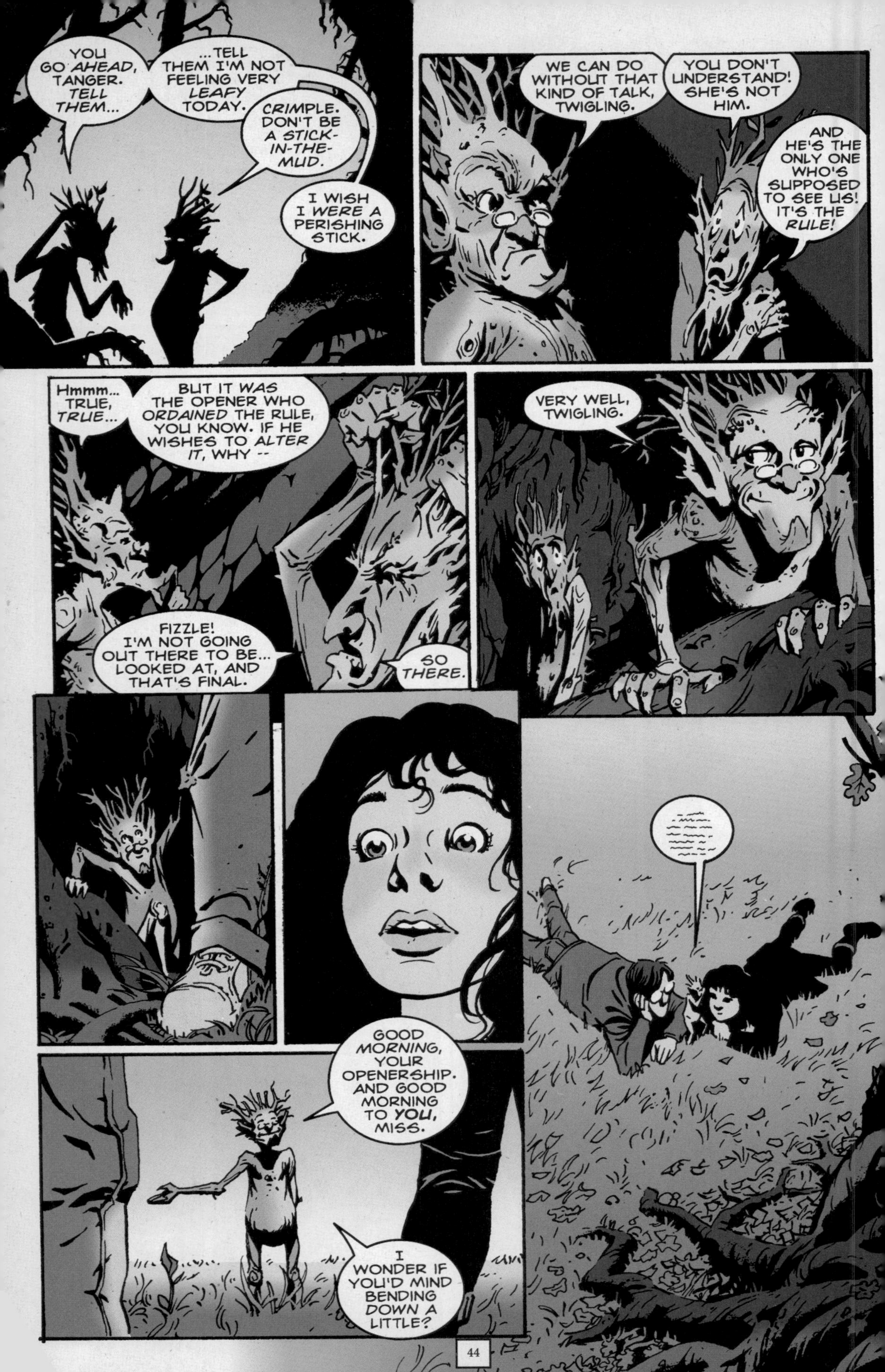
YOU GO AHEAD, TANGER. TELL THEM...
...TELL THEM I'M NOT FEELING VERY LEAFY TODAY.
CRIMPLE. DON'T BE A STICK-IN-THE-MUD.
I WISH I WERE A PERISHING STICK.
WE CAN DO WITHOUT THAT KIND OF TALK, TWIGLING.
YOU DON'T UNDERSTAND! SHE'S NOT HIM.
AND HE'S THE ONLY ONE WHO'S SUPPOSED TO SEE US! IT'S THE RULE!
Hmmm... TRUE, TRUE...
BUT IT WAS THE OPENER WHO ORDAINED THE RULE, YOU KNOW. IF HE WISHES TO ALTER IT, WHY --
FIZZLE! I'M NOT GOING OUT THERE TO BE... LOOKED AT, AND THAT'S FINAL.
SO THERE.
VERY WELL, TWIGLING.
GOOD MORNING, YOUR OPENERSHIP. AND GOOD MORNING TO YOU, MISS.
I WONDER IF YOU'D MIND BENDING DOWN A LITTLE?

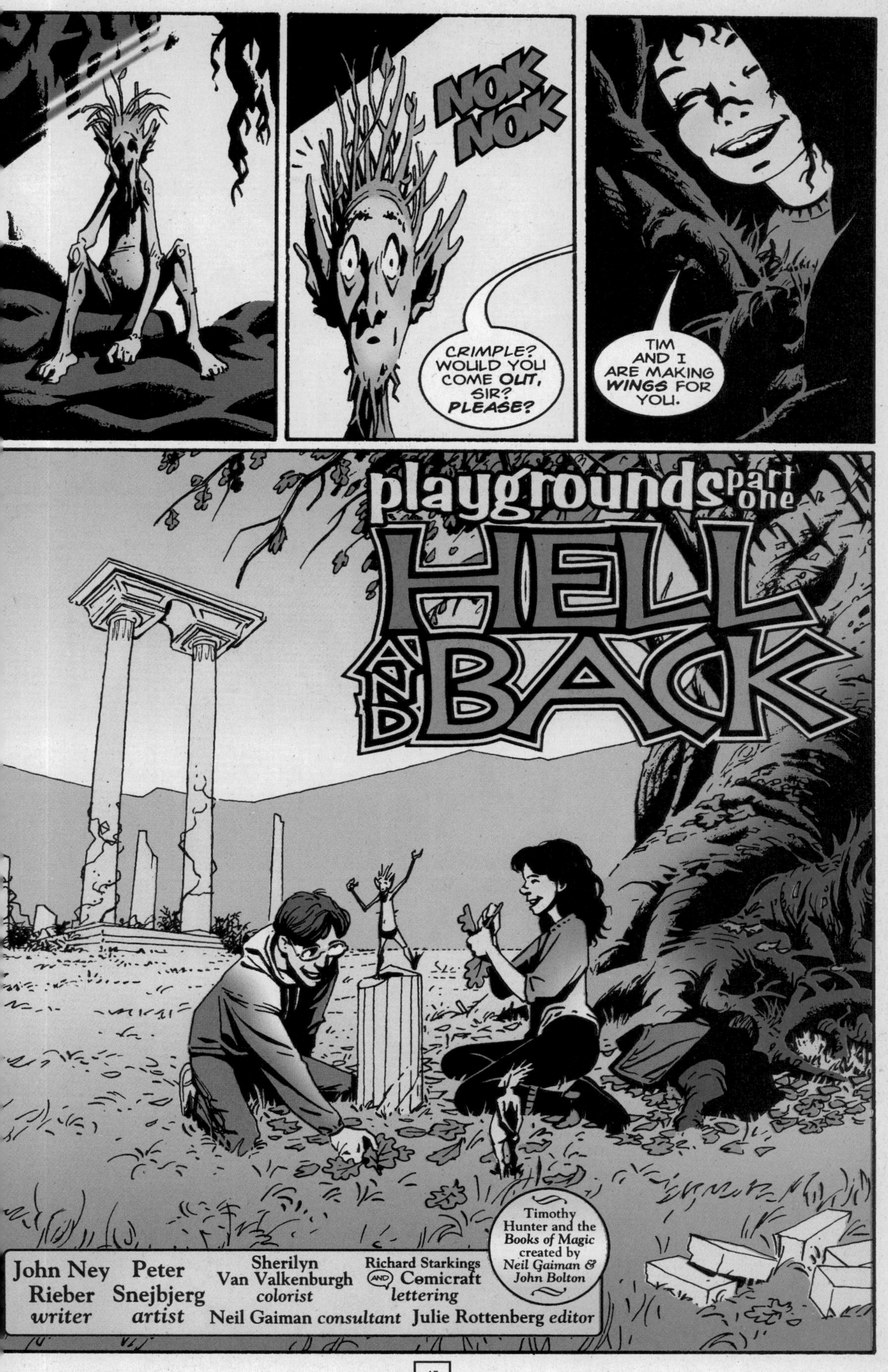
NOK NOK
CRIMPLE? WOULD YOU COME OUT, SIR? PLEASE?
TIM AND I ARE MAKING WINGS FOR YOU.
playgrounds part one
HELL AND BACK
Timothy Hunter and the Books of Magic created by Neil Gaiman & John Bolton
John Ney Rieber writer
Peter Snejbjerg artist
Sherilyn Van Valkenburgh colorist
Richard Starkings and Comicraft lettering
Neil Gaiman consultant
Julie Rottenberg editor

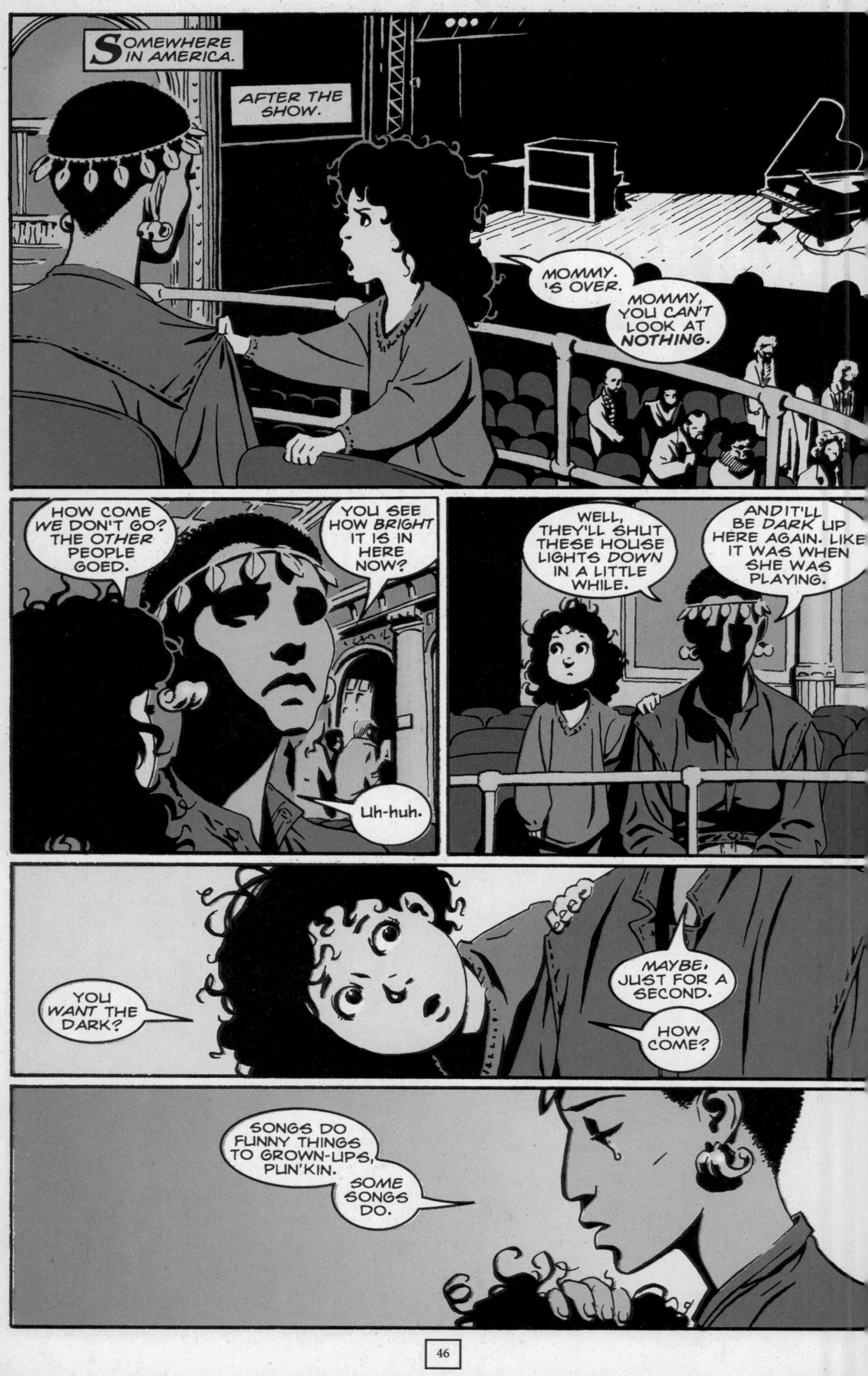
SOMEWHERE IN AMERICA.
AFTER THE SHOW.
MOMMY. 'S OVER.
MOMMY, YOU CAN'T LOOK AT NOTHING.
HOW COME WE DON'T GO? THE OTHER PEOPLE GOED.
YOU SEE HOW BRIGHT IT IS IN HERE NOW?
Uh-huh.
WELL, THEY'LL SHUT THESE HOUSE LIGHTS DOWN IN A LITTLE WHILE.
AND IT'LL BE DARK UP HERE AGAIN. LIKE IT WAS WHEN SHE WAS PLAYING.
YOU WANT THE DARK?
MAYBE. JUST FOR A SECOND.
HOW COME?
SONGS DO FUNNY THINGS TO GROWN-UPS, PUN'KIN.
SOME SONGS DO.

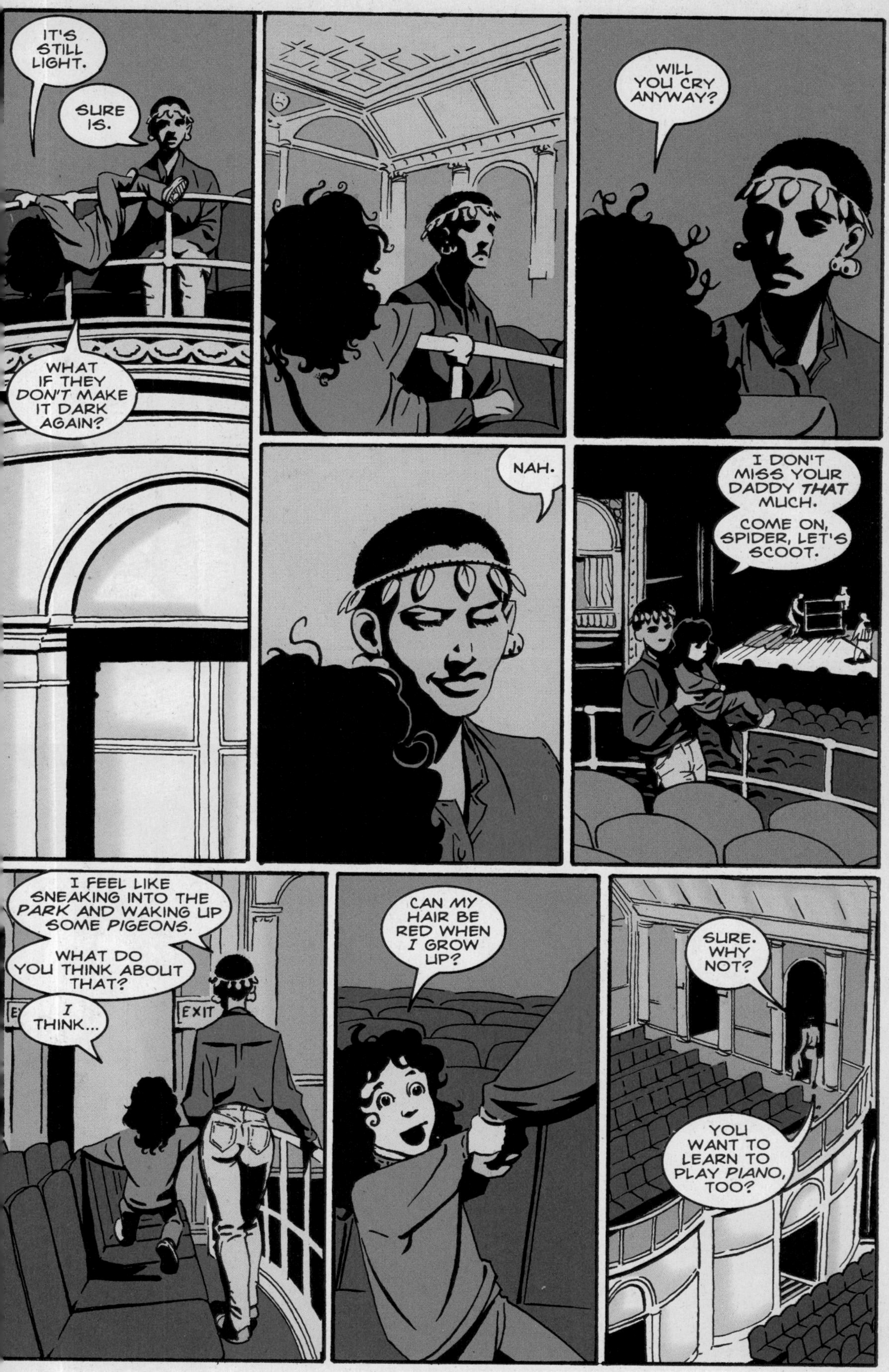
IT'S STILL LIGHT.
SURE IS.
WHAT IF THEY *DON'T* MAKE IT DARK AGAIN?
WILL YOU CRY ANYWAY?
NAH.
I DON'T MISS YOUR DADDY *THAT* MUCH.
COME ON, SPIDER, LET'S SCOOT.
I FEEL LIKE SNEAKING INTO THE *PARK* AND WAKING UP SOME *PIGEONS*.
WHAT DO YOU THINK ABOUT THAT?
EXIT
I THINK...
CAN *MY* HAIR BE RED WHEN *I* GROW UP?
SURE. WHY NOT?
YOU WANT TO LEARN TO PLAY *PIANO*, TOO?

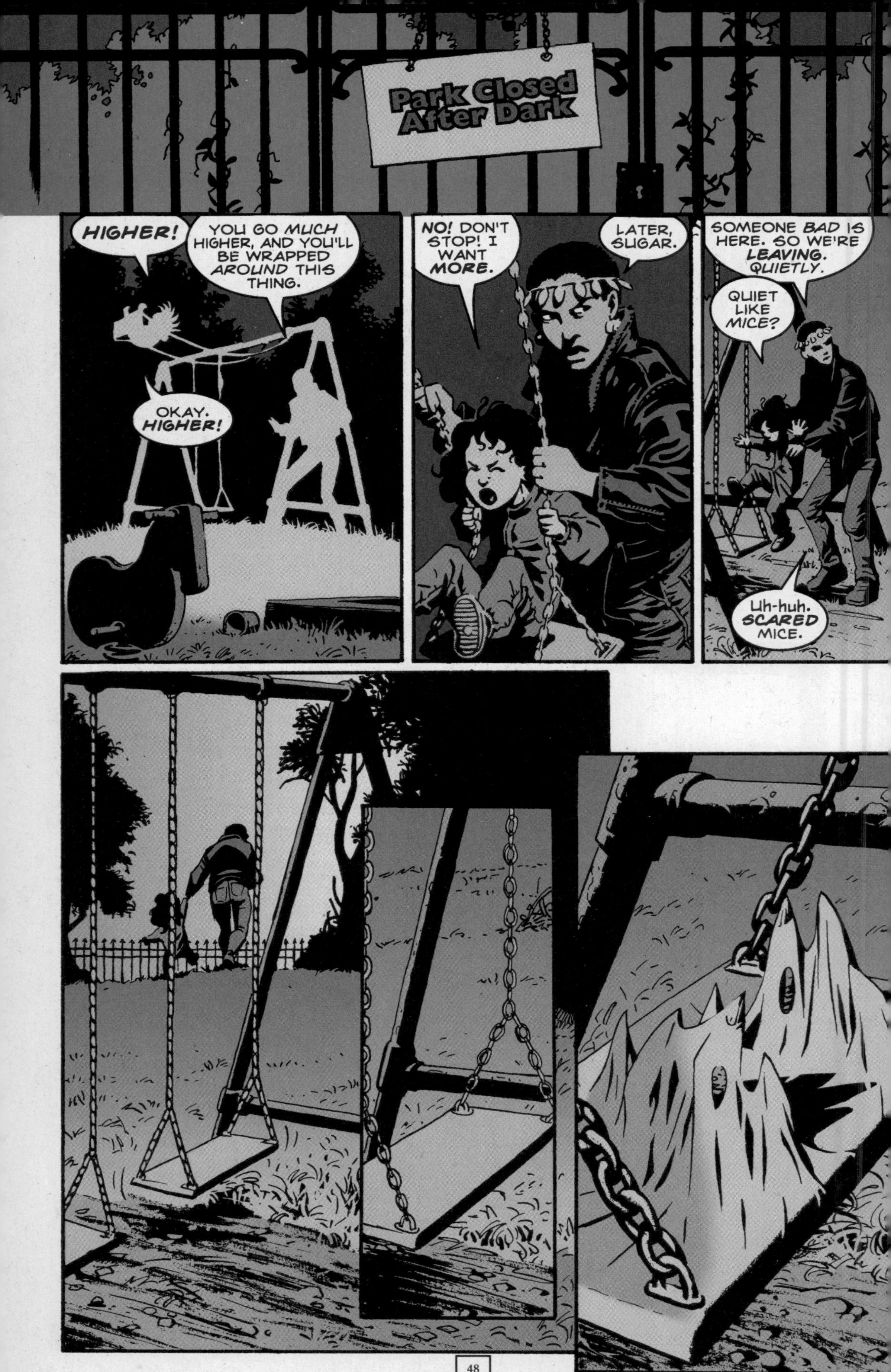
Park Closed After Dark
HIGHER!
YOU GO MUCH HIGHER, AND YOU'LL BE WRAPPED AROUND THIS THING.
OKAY. HIGHER!
NO! DON'T STOP! I WANT MORE.
LATER, SUGAR.
SOMEONE BAD IS HERE. SO WE'RE LEAVING. QUIETLY.
QUIET LIKE MICE?
Uh-huh. SCARED MICE.

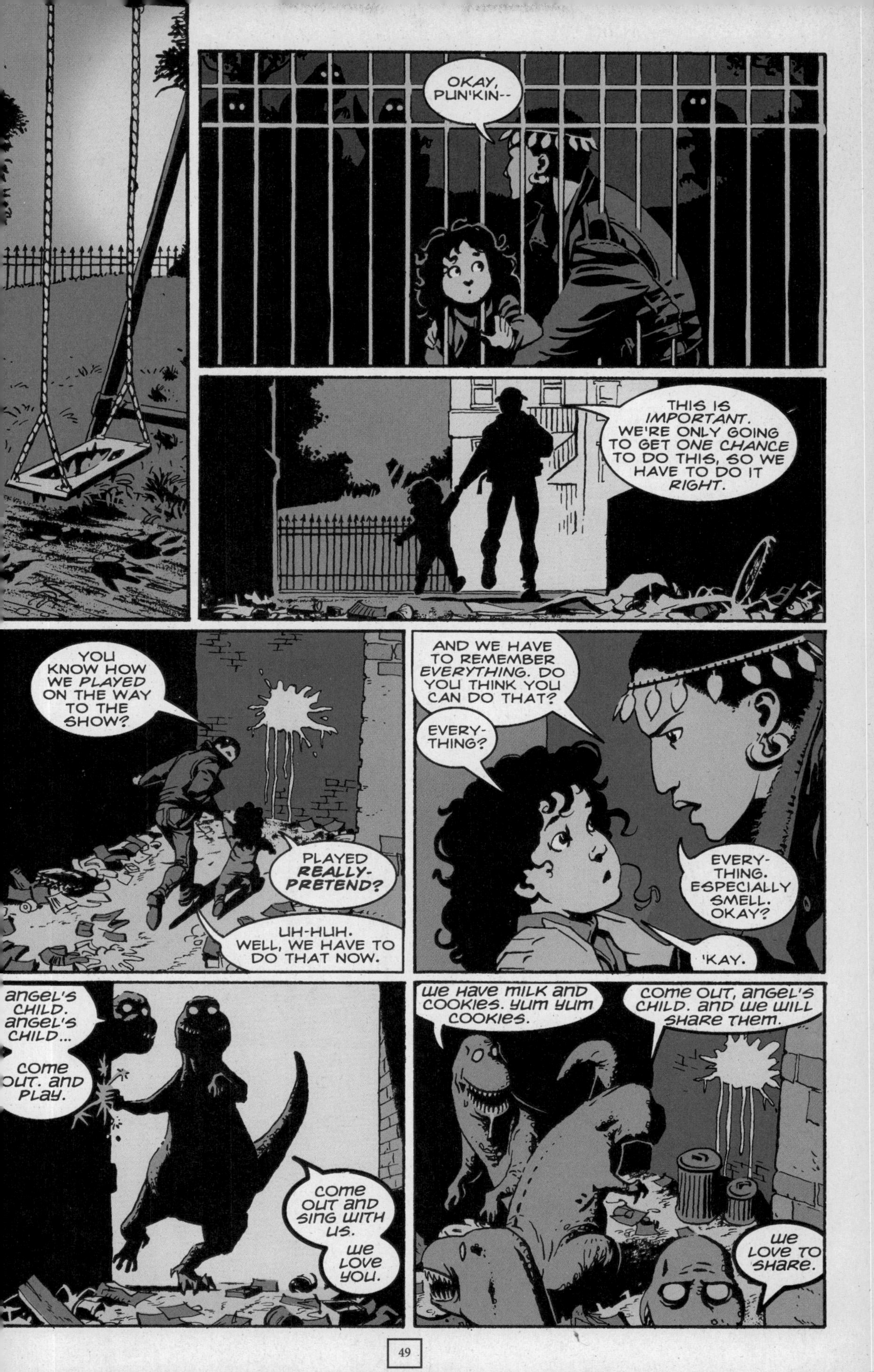
OKAY, PUN'KIN--
THIS IS IMPORTANT. WE'RE ONLY GOING TO GET ONE CHANCE TO DO THIS, SO WE HAVE TO DO IT RIGHT.
YOU KNOW HOW WE PLAYED ON THE WAY TO THE SHOW?
PLAYED REALLY-PRETEND?
UH-HUH. WELL, WE HAVE TO DO THAT NOW.
AND WE HAVE TO REMEMBER EVERYTHING. DO YOU THINK YOU CAN DO THAT?
EVERY-THING?
EVERY-THING. ESPECIALLY SMELL. OKAY?
'KAY.
ANGEL'S CHILD. ANGEL'S CHILD...
COME OUT. AND PLAY.
COME OUT AND SING WITH US.
WE LOVE YOU.
WE HAVE MILK AND COOKIES. YUM YUM COOKIES.
COME OUT, ANGEL'S CHILD. AND WE WILL SHARE THEM.
WE LOVE TO SHARE.

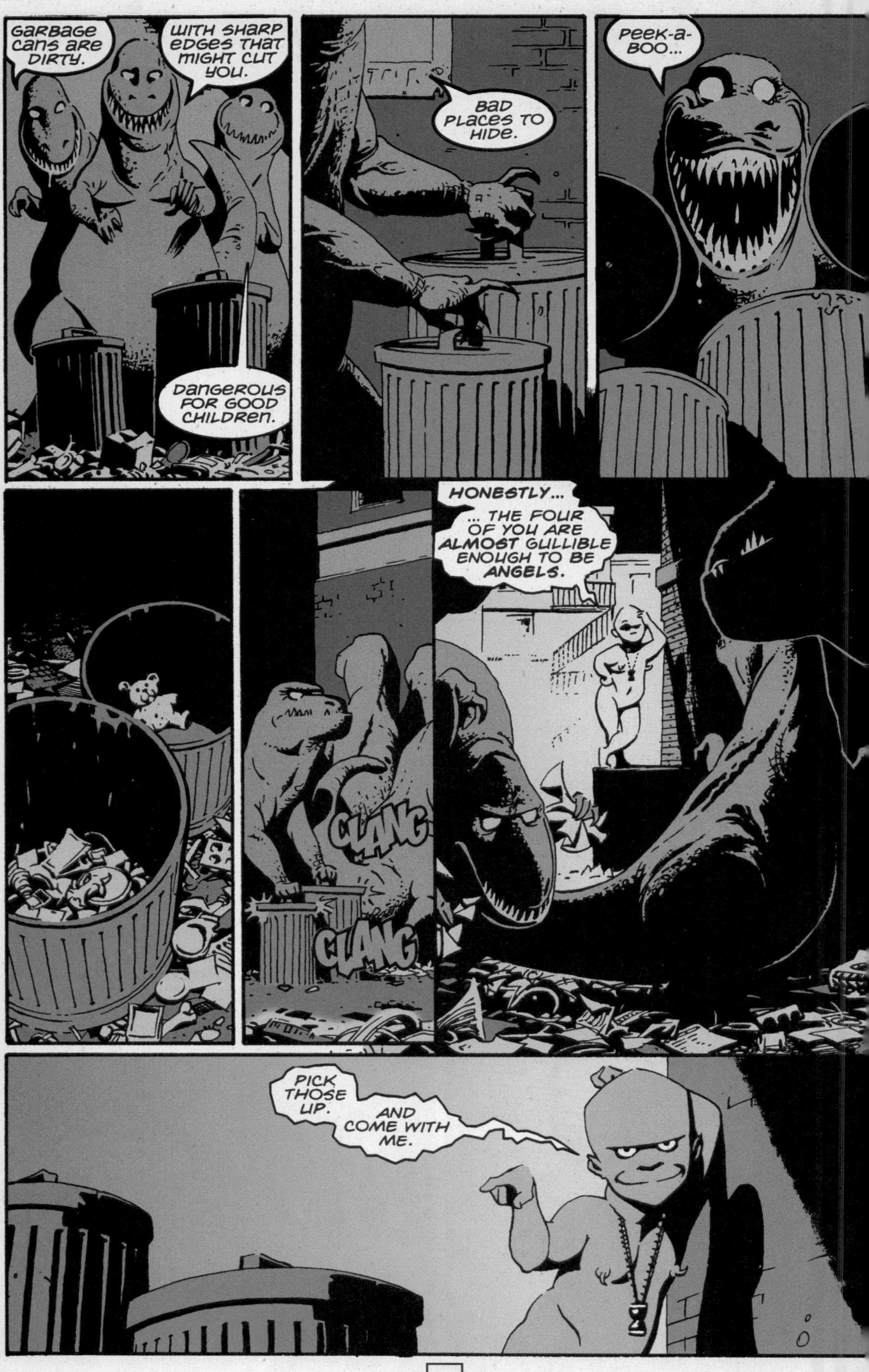
GARBAGE CANS ARE DIRTY.
WITH SHARP EDGES THAT MIGHT CUT YOU.
DANGEROUS FOR GOOD CHILDREN.
BAD PLACES TO HIDE.
PEEK-A-BOO...
HONESTLY...
... THE FOUR OF YOU ARE ALMOST GULLIBLE ENOUGH TO BE ANGELS.
CLANG
CLANG
PICK THOSE UP.
AND COME WITH ME.

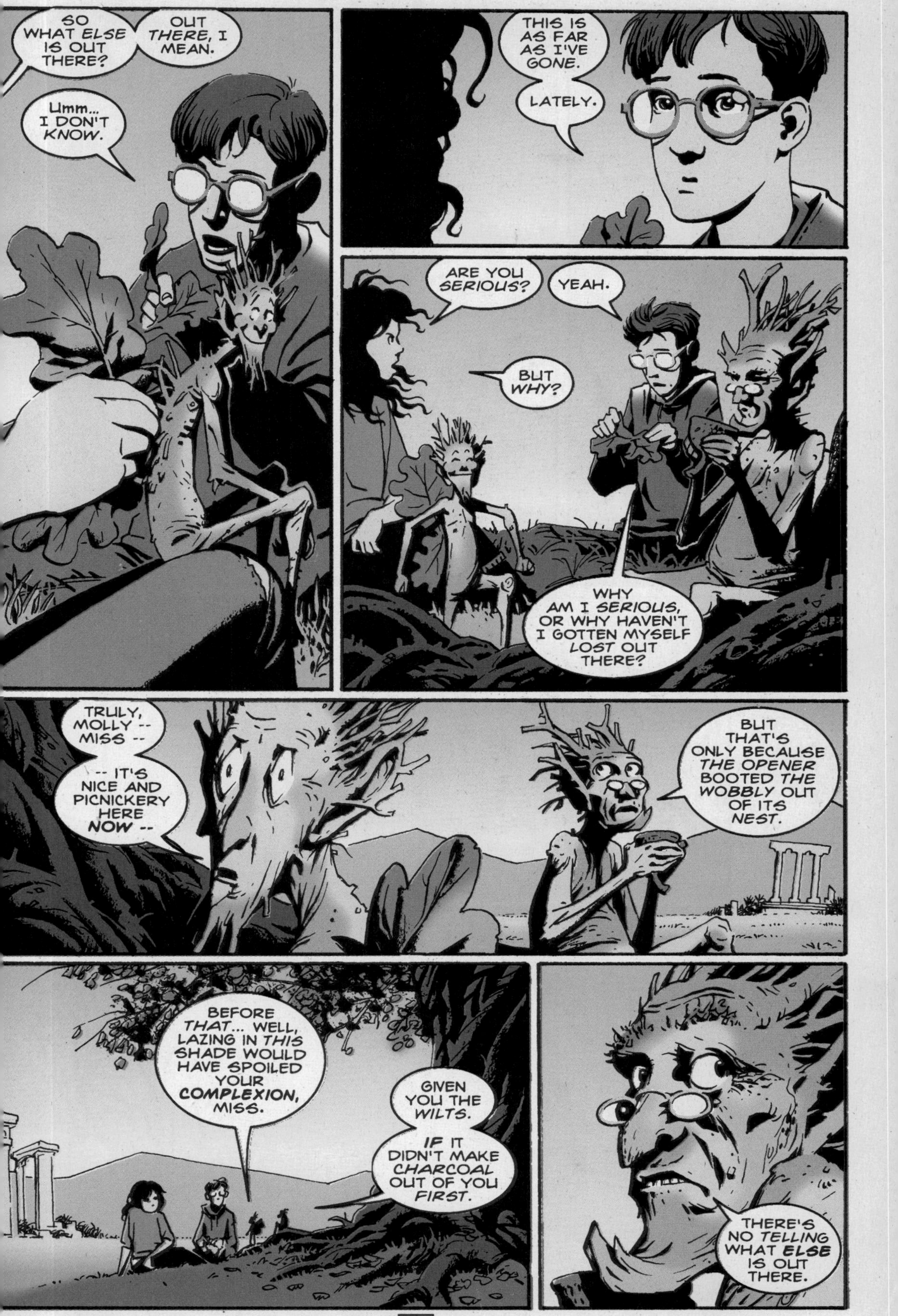
SO WHAT ELSE IS OUT THERE?
OUT THERE, I MEAN.
Umm... I DON'T KNOW.
THIS IS AS FAR AS I'VE GONE.
LATELY.
ARE YOU SERIOUS?
YEAH.
BUT WHY?
WHY AM I SERIOUS, OR WHY HAVEN'T I GOTTEN MYSELF LOST OUT THERE?
TRULY, MOLLY MISS --
-- IT'S NICE AND PICNICKERY HERE NOW --
BUT THAT'S ONLY BECAUSE THE OPENER BOOTED THE WOBBLY OUT OF ITS NEST.
BEFORE THAT... WELL, LAZING IN THIS SHADE WOULD HAVE SPOILED YOUR COMPLEXION, MISS.
GIVEN YOU THE WILTS.
IF IT DIDN'T MAKE CHARCOAL OUT OF YOU FIRST.
THERE'S NO TELLING WHAT ELSE IS OUT THERE.

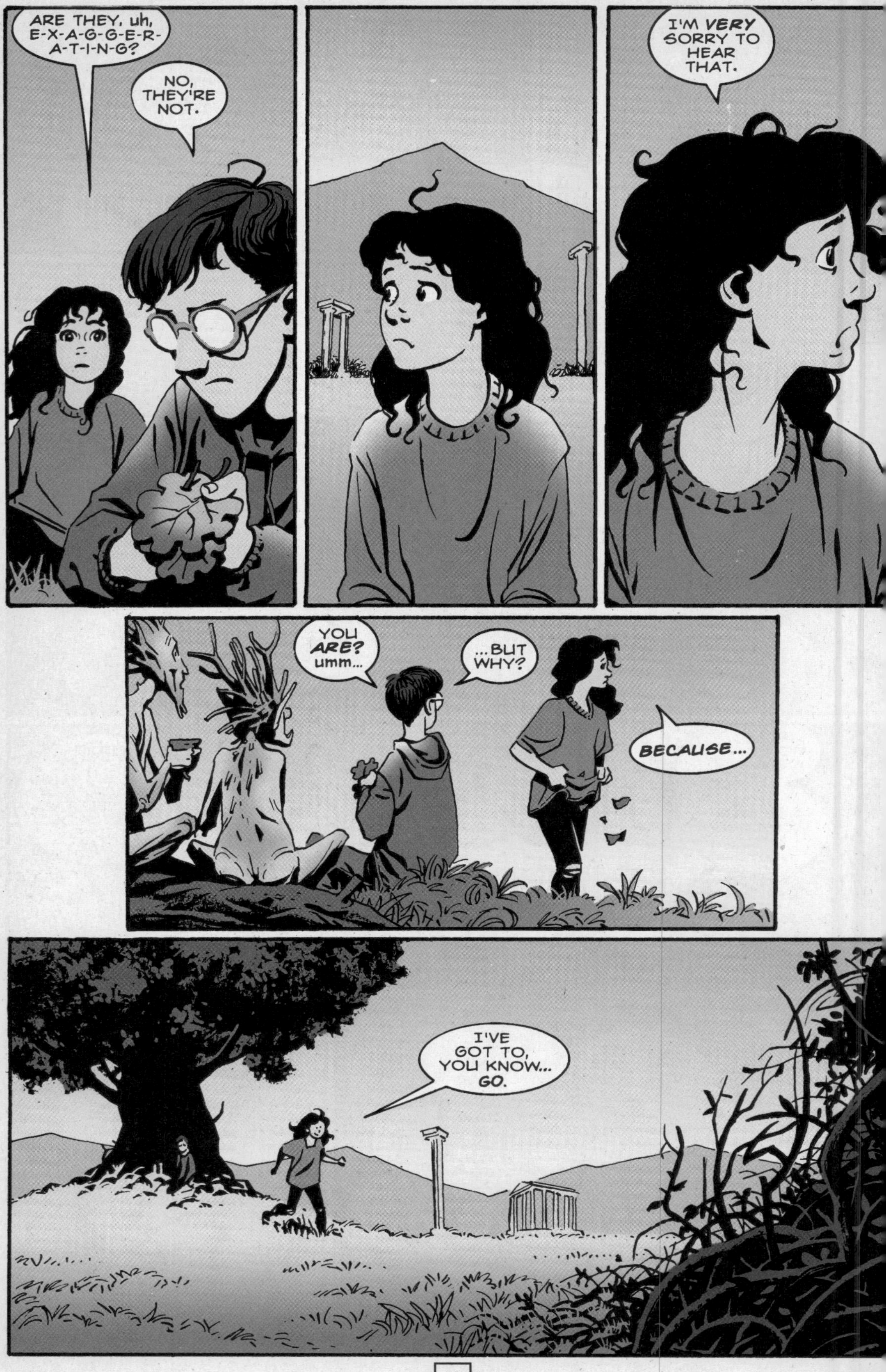
ARE THEY, uh, E-X-A-G-G-E-R-A-T-I-N-G?
NO, THEY'RE NOT.
I'M VERY SORRY TO HEAR THAT.
YOU ARE? umm...
...BUT WHY?
BECAUSE...
I'VE GOT TO, YOU KNOW... GO.

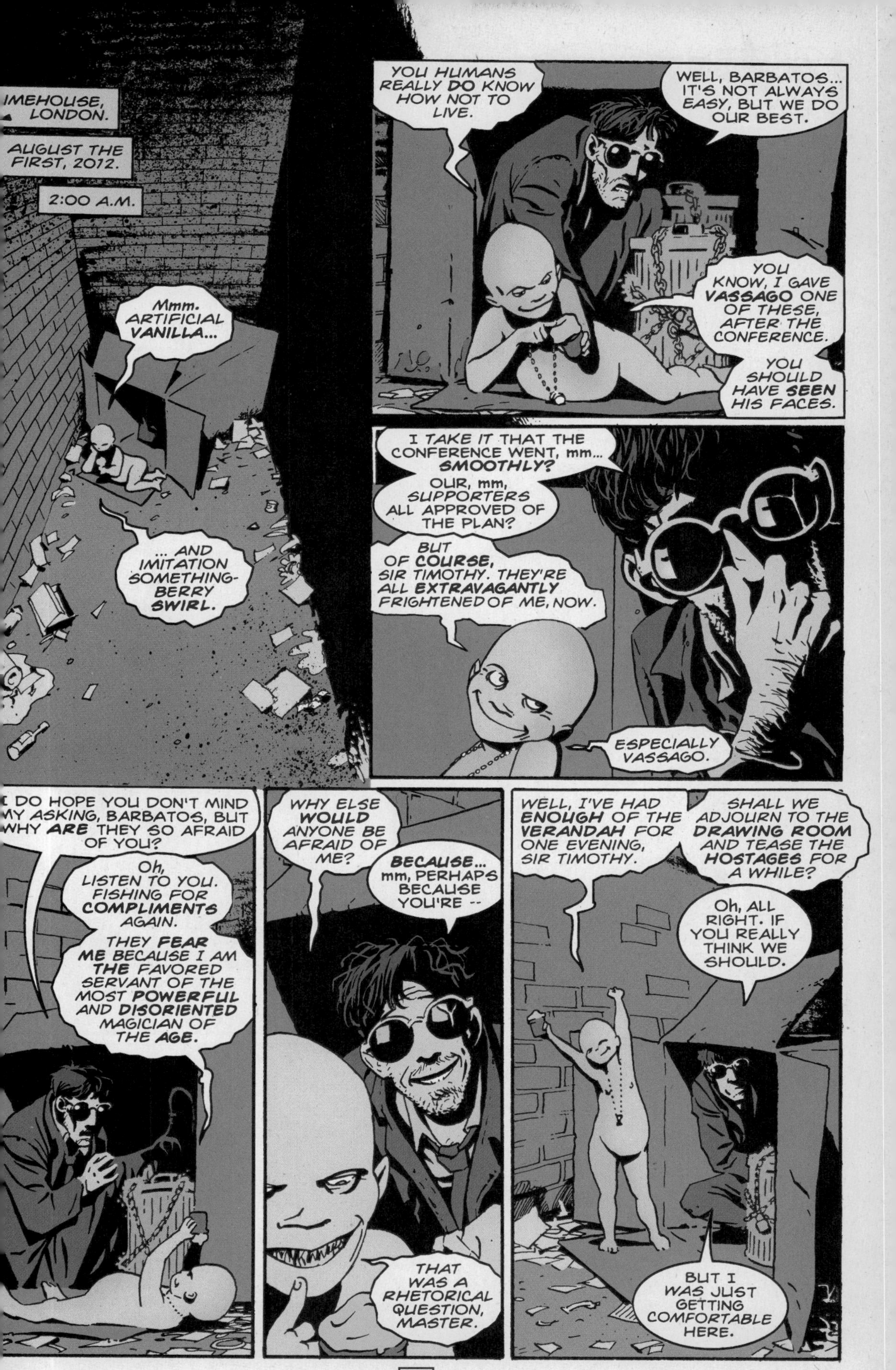

IMEHOUSE, LONDON.
AUGUST THE FIRST, 2012.
2:00 A.M.
Mmm. ARTIFICIAL VANILLA...
... AND IMITATION SOMETHING-BERRY SWIRL.
YOU HUMANS REALLY DO KNOW HOW NOT TO LIVE.
WELL, BARBATOS... IT'S NOT ALWAYS EASY, BUT WE DO OUR BEST.
YOU KNOW, I GAVE VASSAGO ONE OF THESE, AFTER THE CONFERENCE.
YOU SHOULD HAVE SEEN HIS FACES.
I TAKE IT THAT THE CONFERENCE WENT, mm... SMOOTHLY?
OUR, mm, SUPPORTERS ALL APPROVED OF THE PLAN?
BUT OF COURSE, SIR TIMOTHY. THEY'RE ALL EXTRAVAGANTLY FRIGHTENED OF ME, NOW.
ESPECIALLY VASSAGO.
I DO HOPE YOU DON'T MIND MY ASKING, BARBATOS, BUT WHY ARE THEY SO AFRAID OF YOU?
Oh, LISTEN TO YOU. FISHING FOR COMPLIMENTS AGAIN.
THEY FEAR ME BECAUSE I AM THE FAVORED SERVANT OF THE MOST POWERFUL AND DISORIENTED MAGICIAN OF THE AGE.
WHY ELSE WOULD ANYONE BE AFRAID OF ME?
BECAUSE... mm, PERHAPS BECAUSE YOU'RE --
THAT WAS A RHETORICAL QUESTION, MASTER.
WELL, I'VE HAD ENOUGH OF THE VERANDAH FOR ONE EVENING, SIR TIMOTHY.
SHALL WE ADJOURN TO THE DRAWING ROOM AND TEASE THE HOSTAGES FOR A WHILE?
Oh, ALL RIGHT. IF YOU REALLY THINK WE SHOULD.
BUT I WAS JUST GETTING COMFORTABLE HERE.

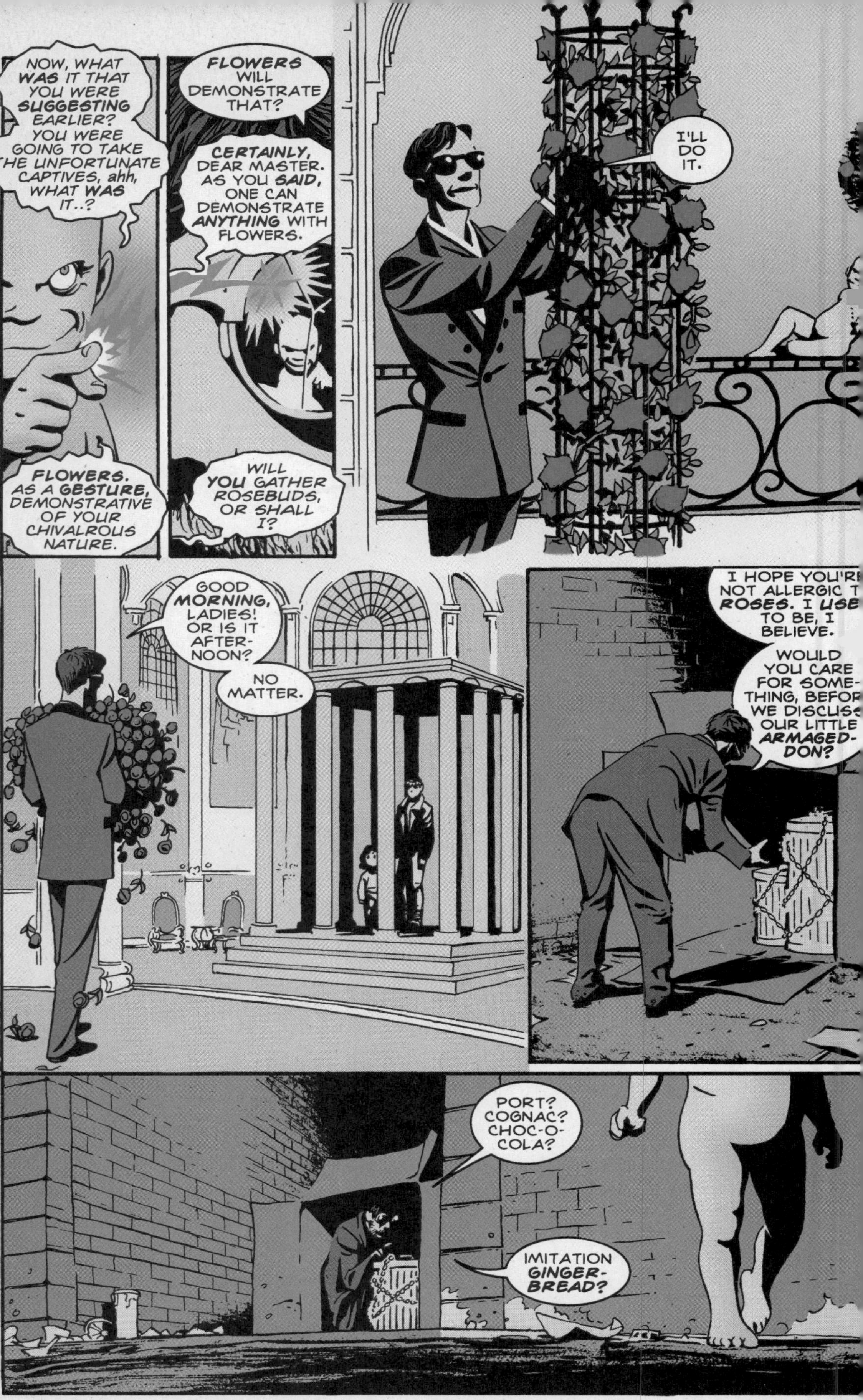
NOW, WHAT WAS IT THAT YOU WERE SUGGESTING EARLIER? YOU WERE GOING TO TAKE THE UNFORTUNATE CAPTIVES, AHH, WHAT WAS IT..?
FLOWERS. AS A GESTURE, DEMONSTRATIVE OF YOUR CHIVALROUS NATURE.
FLOWERS WILL DEMONSTRATE THAT?
CERTAINLY, DEAR MASTER. AS YOU SAID, ONE CAN DEMONSTRATE ANYTHING WITH FLOWERS.
WILL YOU GATHER ROSEBUDS, OR SHALL I?
I'LL DO IT.
GOOD MORNING, LADIES! OR IS IT AFTER-NOON?
NO MATTER.
I HOPE YOU'R NOT ALLERGIC T ROSES. I USE TO BE, I BELIEVE.
WOULD YOU CARE FOR SOME-THING, BEFOR WE DISCUS OUR LITTLE ARMAGED-DON?
PORT? COGNAC? CHOC-O-COLA?
IMITATION GINGER-BREAD?

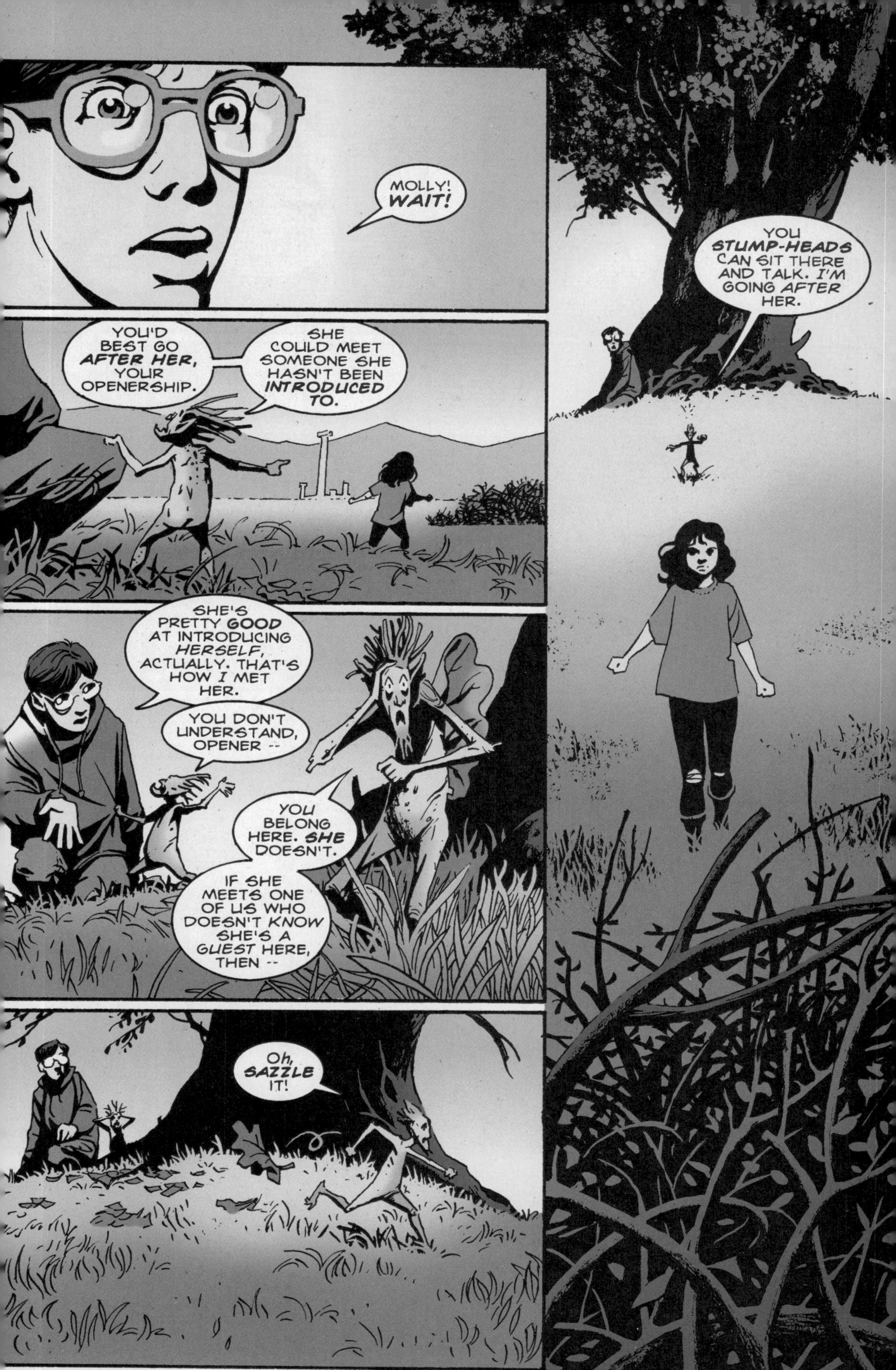
MOLLY! WAIT!
YOU'D BEST GO AFTER HER, YOUR OPENERSHIP.
SHE COULD MEET SOMEONE SHE HASN'T BEEN INTRODUCED TO.
SHE'S PRETTY GOOD AT INTRODUCING HERSELF, ACTUALLY. THAT'S HOW I MET HER.
YOU DON'T UNDERSTAND, OPENER --
YOU BELONG HERE. SHE DOESN'T.
IF SHE MEETS ONE OF US WHO DOESN'T KNOW SHE'S A GUEST HERE, THEN --
Oh, SAZZLE IT!
YOU STUMP-HEADS CAN SIT THERE AND TALK. I'M GOING AFTER HER.

HE LEFT THE TREE.

LOOK, IS HE OVER-REACTING, OR DO WE NEED TO DO SOMETHING?

HE'S LEAVING THE MEADOW.

THEY'VE *BOTH* GONE IN THE BUSHES.

COME ON. WE DON'T WANT TO *LOSE* THEM.

NO...

NO, WE DON'T.

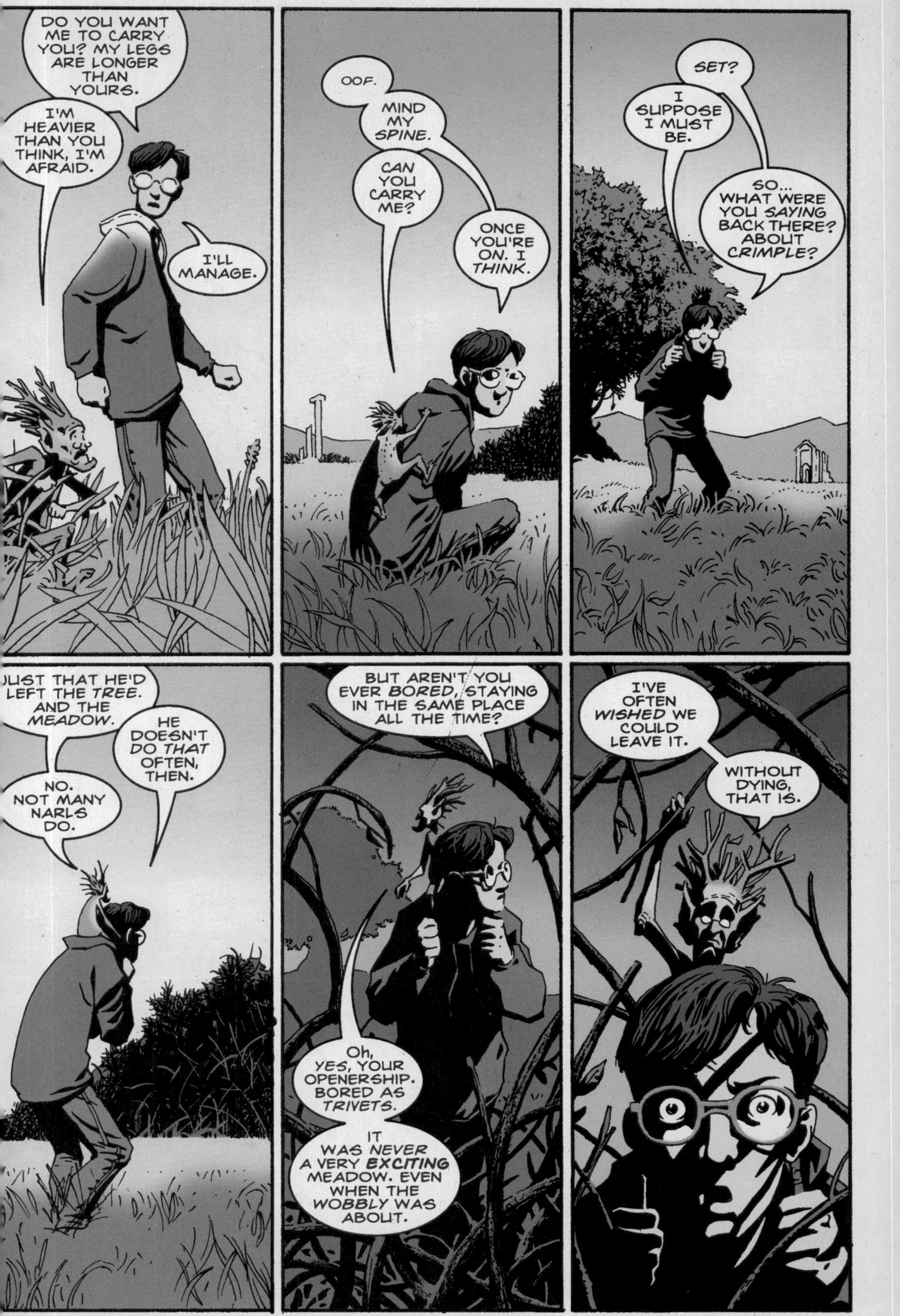
DO YOU WANT ME TO CARRY YOU? MY LEGS ARE LONGER THAN YOURS.
I'M HEAVIER THAN YOU THINK, I'M AFRAID.
I'LL MANAGE.
OOF.
MIND MY *SPINE*.
CAN YOU CARRY ME?
ONCE YOU'RE ON. I *THINK*.
SET?
I SUPPOSE I MUST BE.
SO... WHAT WERE YOU *SAYING* BACK THERE? ABOUT *CRIMPLE?*
JUST THAT HE'D LEFT THE *TREE*. AND THE *MEADOW*.
HE DOESN'T *DO THAT* OFTEN, THEN.
NO. NOT MANY NARLS DO.
BUT AREN'T YOU EVER *BORED*, STAYING IN THE SAME PLACE ALL THE TIME?
Oh, *YES*, YOUR OPENERSHIP. BORED AS *TRIVETS*.
IT WAS *NEVER* A VERY ***EXCITING*** MEADOW. EVEN WHEN THE *WOBBLY* WAS ABOUT.
I'VE OFTEN *WISHED* WE COULD LEAVE IT.
WITHOUT DYING, THAT IS.

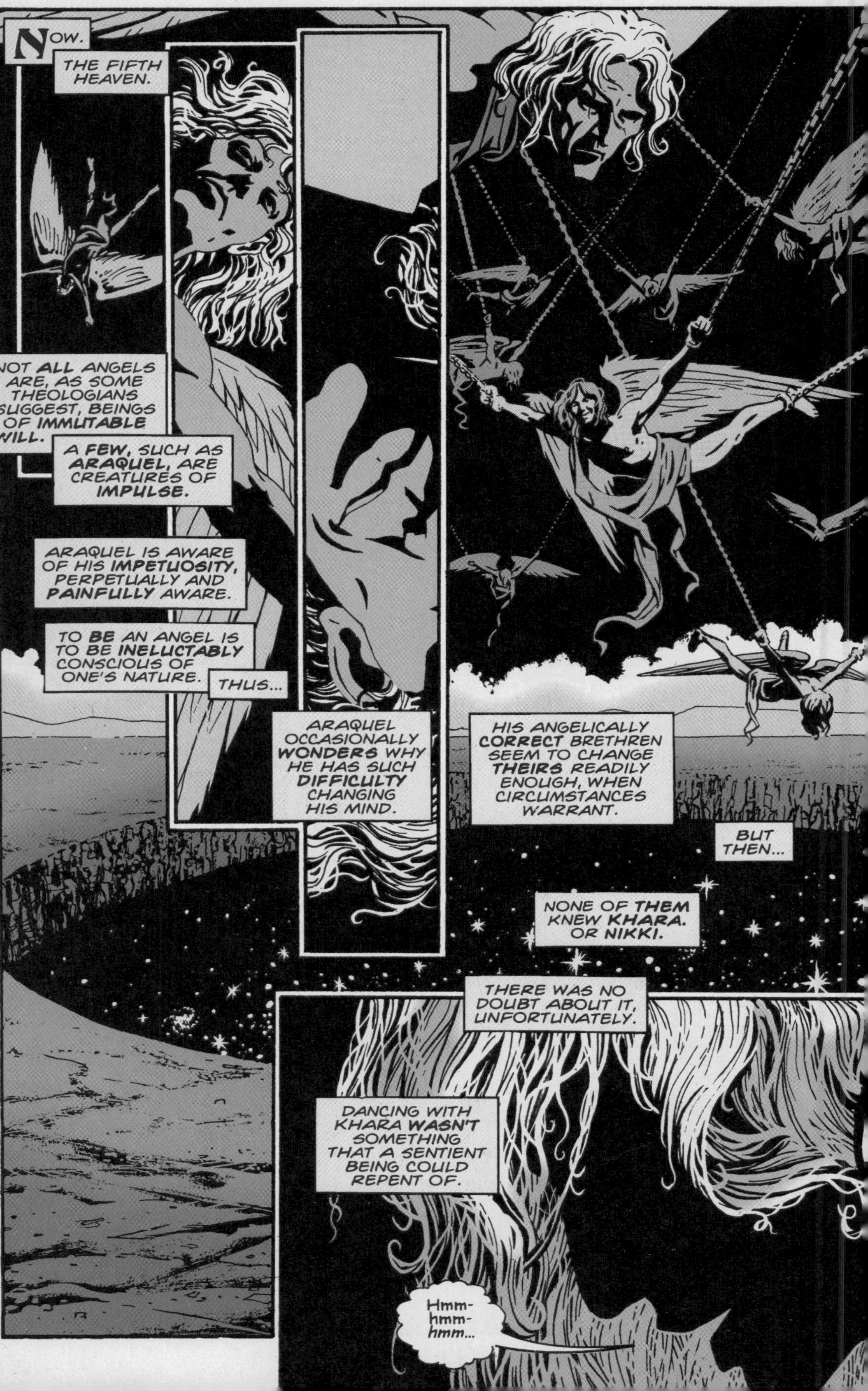
NOW.
THE FIFTH HEAVEN.
NOT ALL ANGELS ARE, AS SOME THEOLOGIANS SUGGEST, BEINGS OF IMMUTABLE WILL.
A FEW, SUCH AS ARAQUEL, ARE CREATURES OF IMPULSE.
ARAQUEL IS AWARE OF HIS IMPETUOSITY, PERPETUALLY AND PAINFULLY AWARE.
TO BE AN ANGEL IS TO BE INELUCTABLY CONSCIOUS OF ONE'S NATURE.
THUS...
ARAQUEL OCCASIONALLY WONDERS WHY HE HAS SUCH DIFFICULTY CHANGING HIS MIND.
HIS ANGELICALLY CORRECT BRETHREN SEEM TO CHANGE THEIRS READILY ENOUGH, WHEN CIRCUMSTANCES WARRANT.
BUT THEN...
NONE OF THEM KNEW KHARA. OR NIKKI.
THERE WAS NO DOUBT ABOUT IT, UNFORTUNATELY.
DANCING WITH KHARA WASN'T SOMETHING THAT A SENTIENT BEING COULD REPENT OF.
Hmm-hmm-hmm...

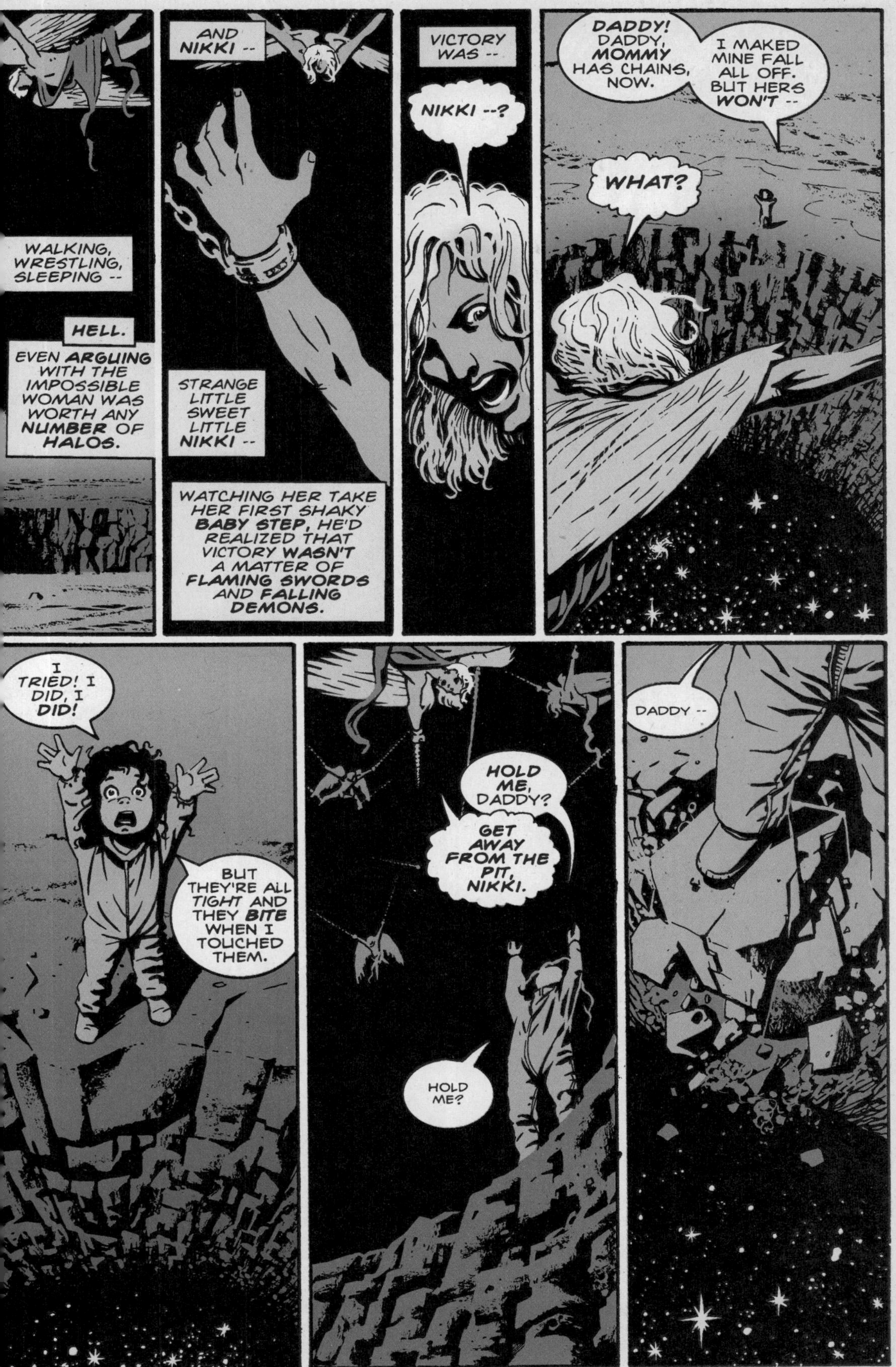
WALKING, WRESTLING, SLEEPING --
HELL.
EVEN ARGUING WITH THE IMPOSSIBLE WOMAN WAS WORTH ANY NUMBER OF HALOS.
AND NIKKI --
STRANGE LITTLE SWEET LITTLE NIKKI --
WATCHING HER TAKE HER FIRST SHAKY BABY STEP, HE'D REALIZED THAT VICTORY WASN'T A MATTER OF FLAMING SWORDS AND FALLING DEMONS.
VICTORY WAS --
NIKKI --?
DADDY! DADDY, MOMMY HAS CHAINS, NOW.
I MAKED MINE FALL ALL OFF. BUT HERS WON'T --
WHAT?
I TRIED! I DID, I DID!
BUT THEY'RE ALL TIGHT AND THEY BITE WHEN I TOUCHED THEM.
HOLD ME, DADDY?
GET AWAY FROM THE PIT, NIKKI.
HOLD ME?
DADDY --

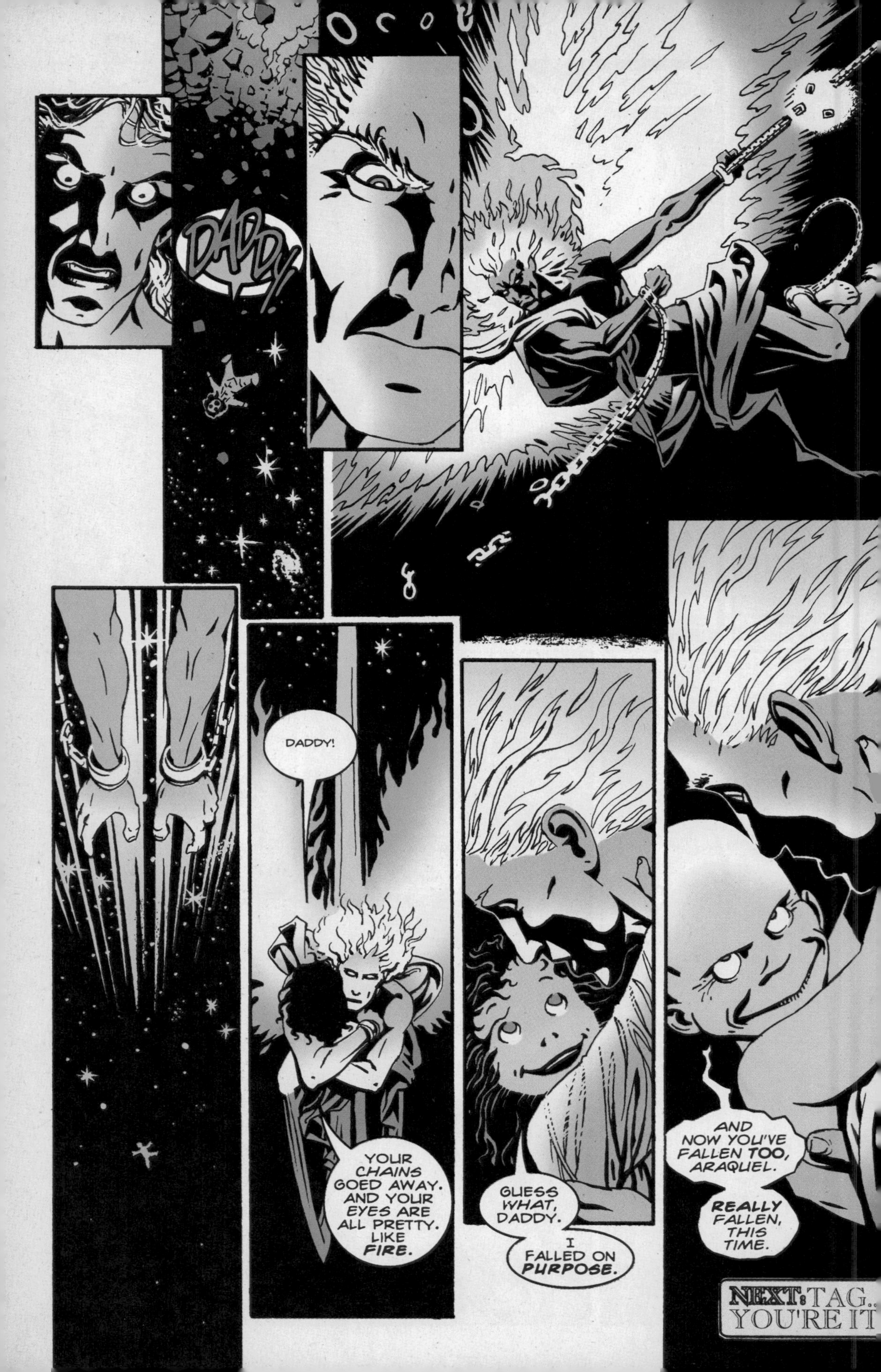
DADDY!
DADDY!
YOUR CHAINS GOED AWAY. AND YOUR EYES ARE ALL PRETTY. LIKE FIRE.
GUESS WHAT, DADDY.
I FALLED ON PURPOSE.
AND NOW YOU'VE FALLEN TOO, ARAQUEL.
REALLY FALLEN, THIS TIME.
NEXT: TAG... YOU'RE IT

Tag...
You're
It.

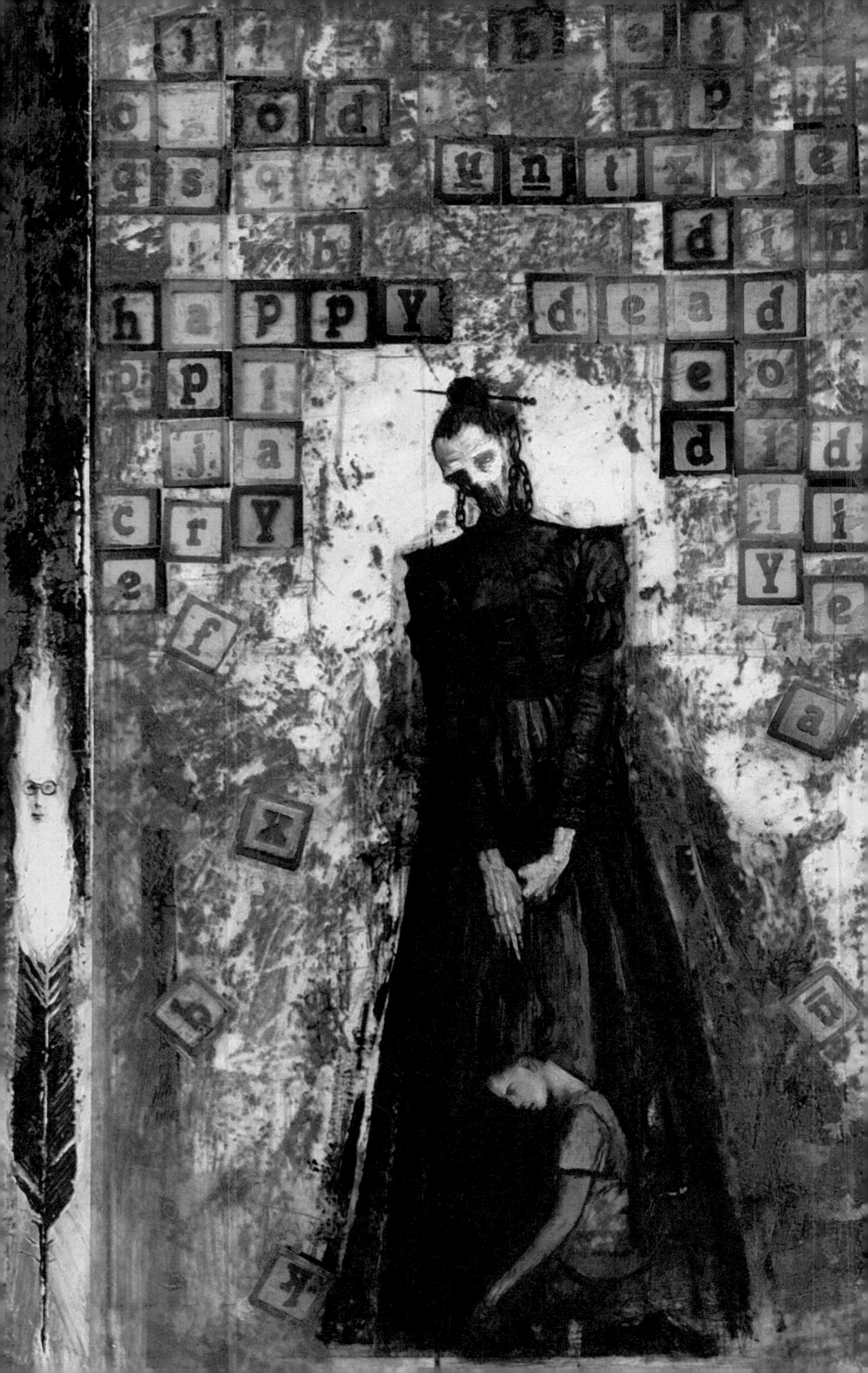
happy
dead
cry

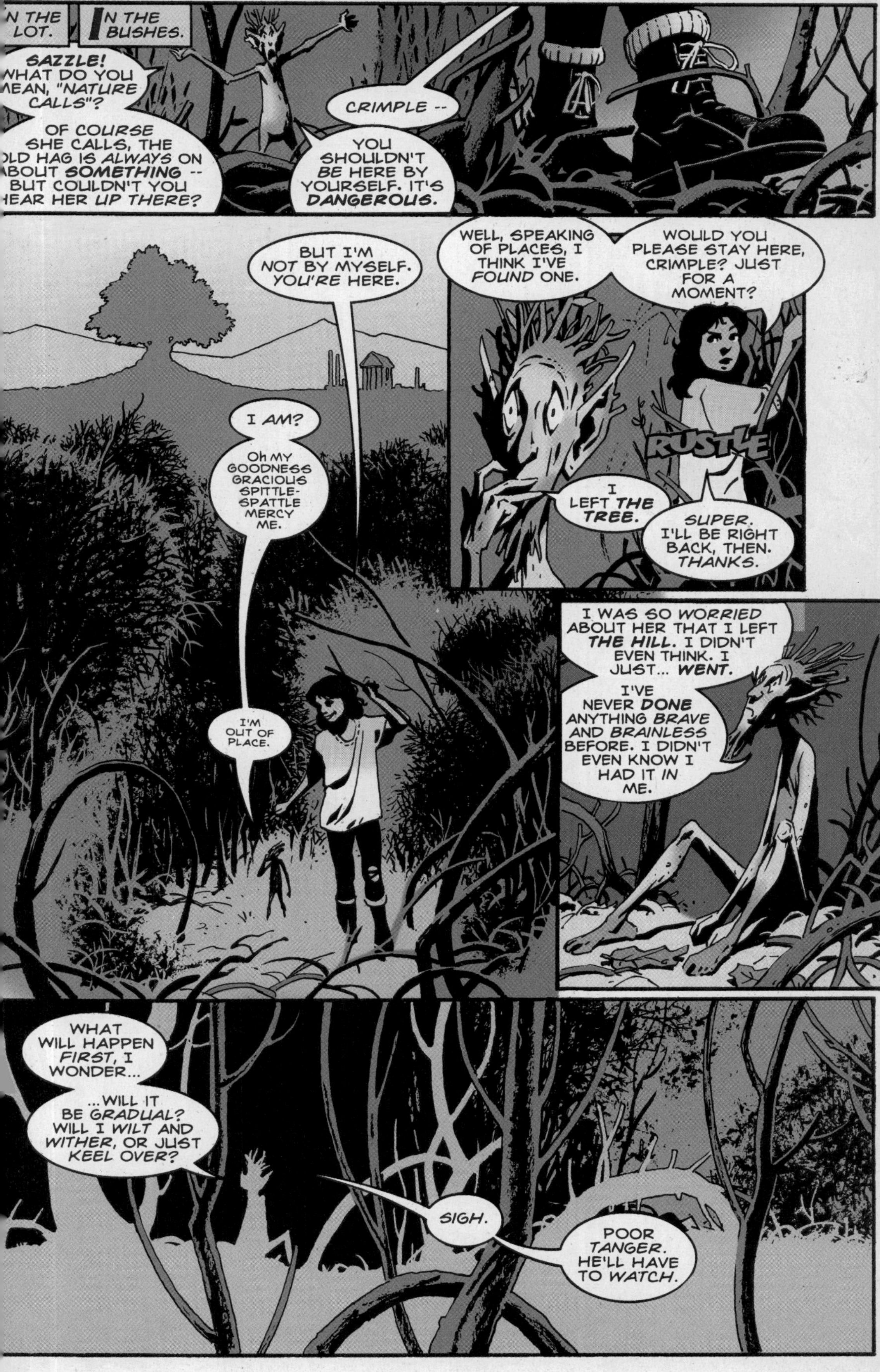
N THE LOT.
IN THE BUSHES.
SAZZLE! WHAT DO YOU EAN, "NATURE CALLS"?
OF COURSE SHE CALLS, THE LD HAG IS ALWAYS ON BOUT SOMETHING -- BUT COULDN'T YOU HEAR HER UP THERE?
CRIMPLE --
YOU SHOULDN'T BE HERE BY YOURSELF. IT'S DANGEROUS.
BUT I'M NOT BY MYSELF. YOU'RE HERE.
I AM?
Oh MY GOODNESS GRACIOUS SPITTLE-SPATTLE MERCY ME.
I'M OUT OF PLACE.
WELL, SPEAKING OF PLACES, I THINK I'VE FOUND ONE.
WOULD YOU PLEASE STAY HERE, CRIMPLE? JUST FOR A MOMENT?
RUSTLE
I LEFT THE TREE.
SUPER. I'LL BE RIGHT BACK, THEN. THANKS.
I WAS SO WORRIED ABOUT HER THAT I LEFT THE HILL. I DIDN'T EVEN THINK. I JUST... WENT.
I'VE NEVER DONE ANYTHING BRAVE AND BRAINLESS BEFORE. I DIDN'T EVEN KNOW I HAD IT IN ME.
WHAT WILL HAPPEN FIRST, I WONDER...
...WILL IT BE GRADUAL? WILL I WILT AND WITHER, OR JUST KEEL OVER?
SIGH.
POOR TANGER. HE'LL HAVE TO WATCH.

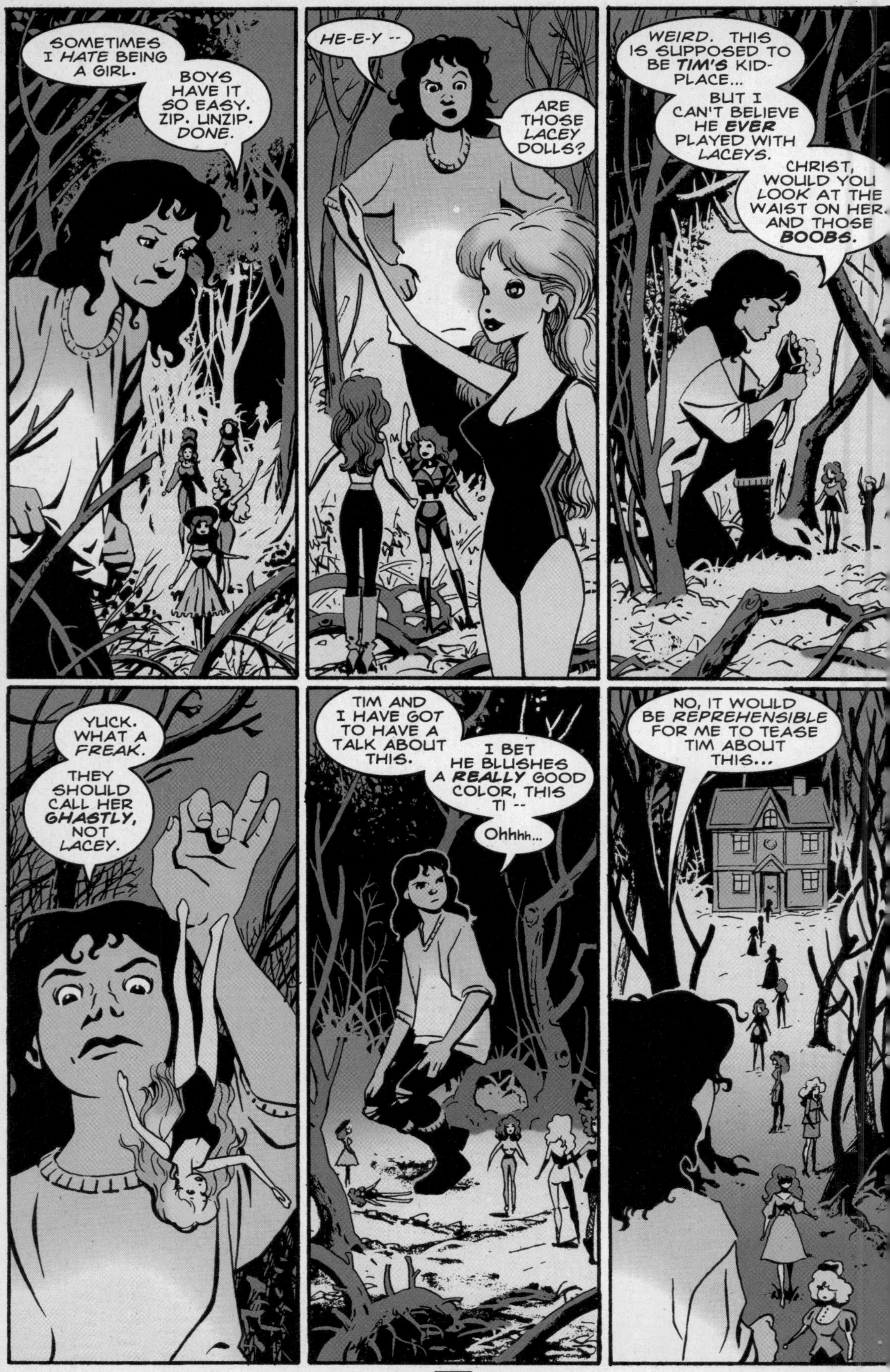
SOMETIMES I HATE BEING A GIRL.
BOYS HAVE IT SO EASY. ZIP. UNZIP. DONE.
HE-E-Y --
ARE THOSE LACEY DOLLS?
WEIRD. THIS IS SUPPOSED TO BE TIM'S KID-PLACE...
BUT I CAN'T BELIEVE HE EVER PLAYED WITH LACEYS.
CHRIST, WOULD YOU LOOK AT THE WAIST ON HER. AND THOSE BOOBS.
YUCK. WHAT A FREAK.
THEY SHOULD CALL HER GHASTLY, NOT LACEY.
TIM AND I HAVE GOT TO HAVE A TALK ABOUT THIS.
I BET HE BLUSHES A REALLY GOOD COLOR, THIS TI --
Ohhhh...
NO, IT WOULD BE REPREHENSIBLE FOR ME TO TEASE TIM ABOUT THIS...

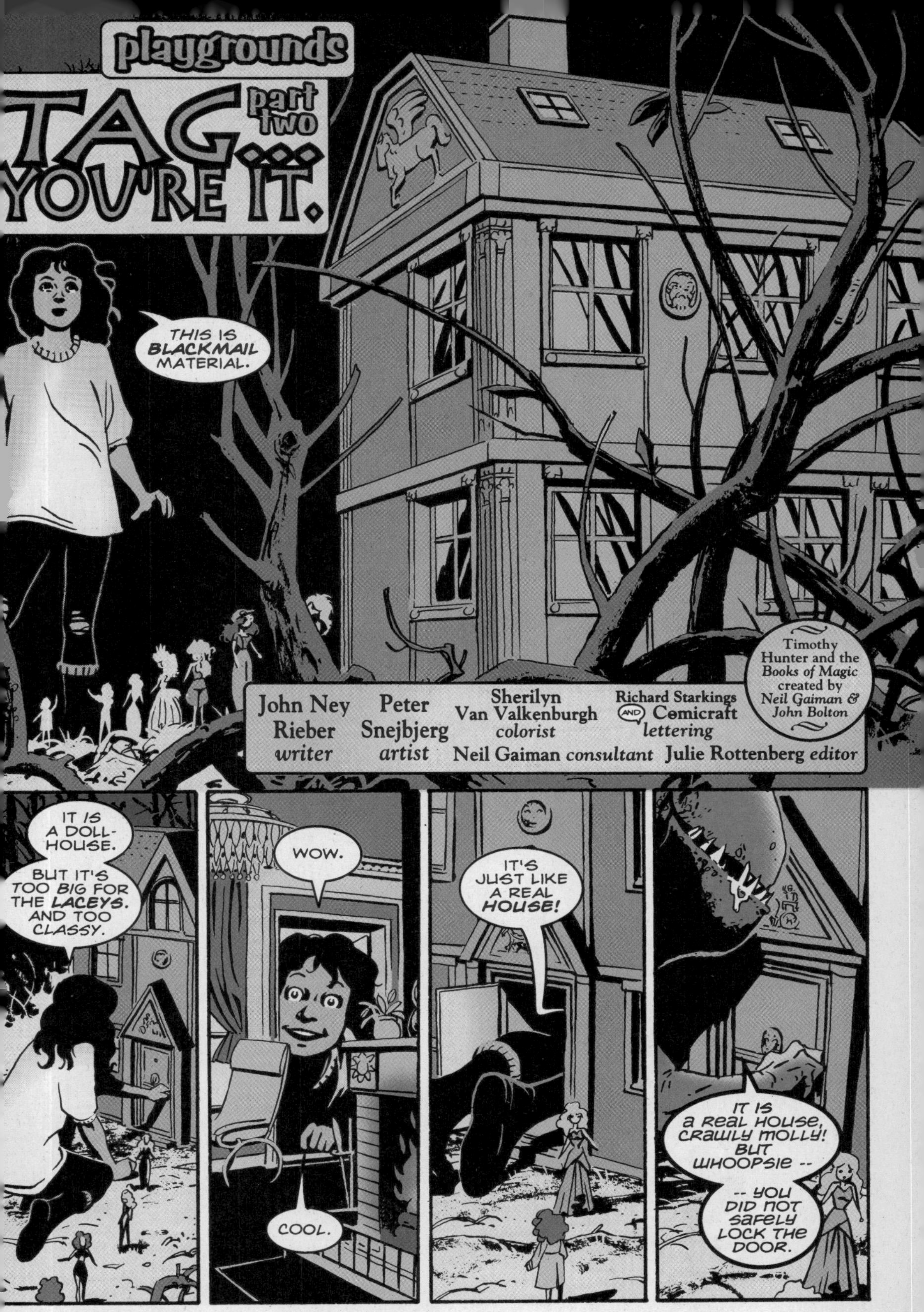
playgrounds
TAG part two... YOU'RE IT.
THIS IS BLACKMAIL MATERIAL.
John Ney Rieber writer
Peter Snejbjerg artist
Sherilyn Van Valkenburgh colorist
Richard Starkings AND Comicraft lettering
Neil Gaiman consultant
Julie Rottenberg editor
Timothy Hunter and the Books of Magic created by Neil Gaiman & John Bolton
IT IS A DOLL-HOUSE.
BUT IT'S TOO BIG FOR THE LACEYS. AND TOO CLASSY.
WOW.
COOL.
IT'S JUST LIKE A REAL HOUSE!
IT IS A REAL HOUSE, CRAWLY MOLLY! BUT WHOOPSIE --
-- YOU DID NOT SAFELY LOCK THE DOOR.

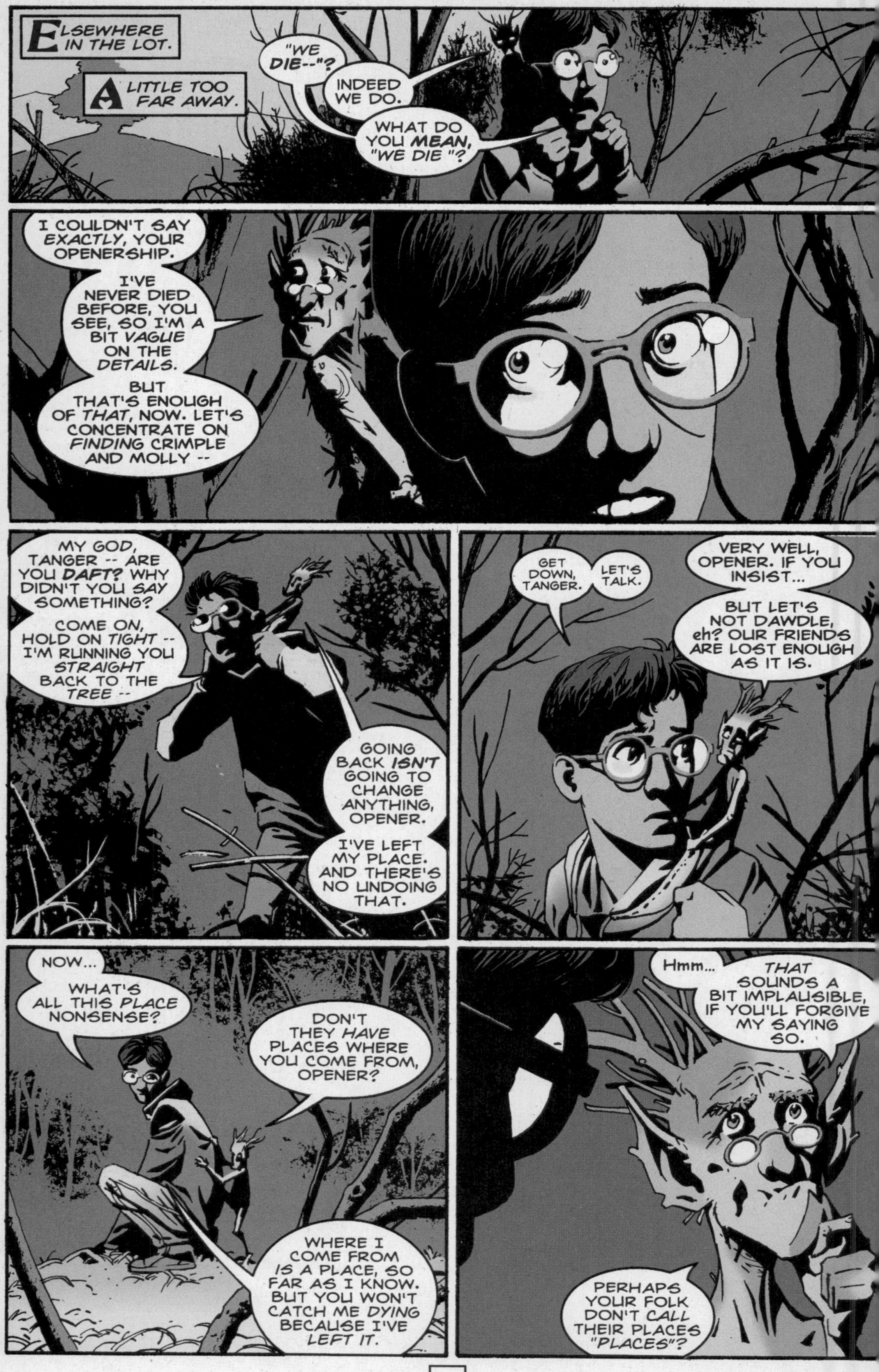
ELSEWHERE IN THE LOT.
A LITTLE TOO FAR AWAY.
"WE DIE--"?
INDEED WE DO.
WHAT DO YOU MEAN, "WE DIE"?
I COULDN'T SAY EXACTLY, YOUR OPENERSHIP.
I'VE NEVER DIED BEFORE, YOU SEE, SO I'M A BIT VAGUE ON THE DETAILS.
BUT THAT'S ENOUGH OF THAT, NOW. LET'S CONCENTRATE ON FINDING CRIMPLE AND MOLLY --
MY GOD, TANGER -- ARE YOU DAFT? WHY DIDN'T YOU SAY SOMETHING?
COME ON, HOLD ON TIGHT -- I'M RUNNING YOU STRAIGHT BACK TO THE TREE --
GOING BACK ISN'T GOING TO CHANGE ANYTHING, OPENER.
I'VE LEFT MY PLACE. AND THERE'S NO UNDOING THAT.
GET DOWN, TANGER.
LET'S TALK.
VERY WELL, OPENER. IF YOU INSIST...
BUT LET'S NOT DAWDLE, eh? OUR FRIENDS ARE LOST ENOUGH AS IT IS.
NOW...
WHAT'S ALL THIS PLACE NONSENSE?
DON'T THEY HAVE PLACES WHERE YOU COME FROM, OPENER?
WHERE I COME FROM IS A PLACE, SO FAR AS I KNOW. BUT YOU WON'T CATCH ME DYING BECAUSE I'VE LEFT IT.
Hmm...
THAT SOUNDS A BIT IMPLAUSIBLE, IF YOU'LL FORGIVE MY SAYING SO.
PERHAPS YOUR FOLK DON'T CALL THEIR PLACES "PLACES"?

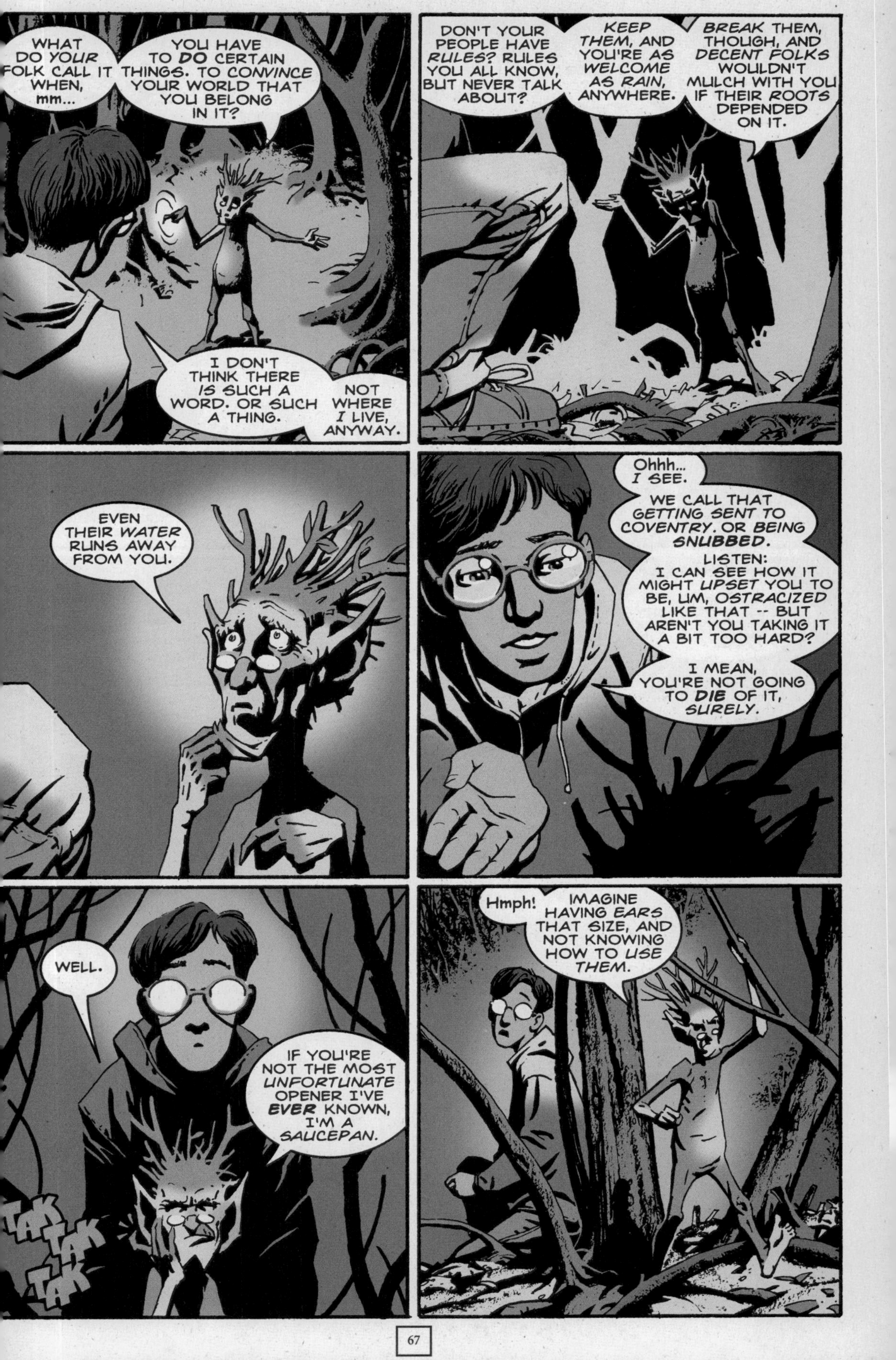

WHAT DO YOUR FOLK CALL IT WHEN, mm...
YOU HAVE TO DO CERTAIN THINGS. TO CONVINCE YOUR WORLD THAT YOU BELONG IN IT?
I DON'T THINK THERE IS SUCH A WORD. OR SUCH A THING.
NOT WHERE I LIVE, ANYWAY.
DON'T YOUR PEOPLE HAVE RULES? RULES YOU ALL KNOW, BUT NEVER TALK ABOUT?
KEEP THEM, AND YOU'RE AS WELCOME AS RAIN, ANYWHERE.
BREAK THEM, THOUGH, AND DECENT FOLKS WOULDN'T MULCH WITH YOU IF THEIR ROOTS DEPENDED ON IT.
EVEN THEIR WATER RUNS AWAY FROM YOU.
Ohhh... I SEE.
WE CALL THAT GETTING SENT TO COVENTRY. OR BEING SNUBBED.
LISTEN: I CAN SEE HOW IT MIGHT UPSET YOU TO BE, UM, OSTRACIZED LIKE THAT -- BUT AREN'T YOU TAKING IT A BIT TOO HARD?
I MEAN, YOU'RE NOT GOING TO DIE OF IT, SURELY.
WELL.
IF YOU'RE NOT THE MOST UNFORTUNATE OPENER I'VE EVER KNOWN, I'M A SAUCEPAN.
TAK TAK TAK
Hmph!
IMAGINE HAVING EARS THAT SIZE, AND NOT KNOWING HOW TO USE THEM.

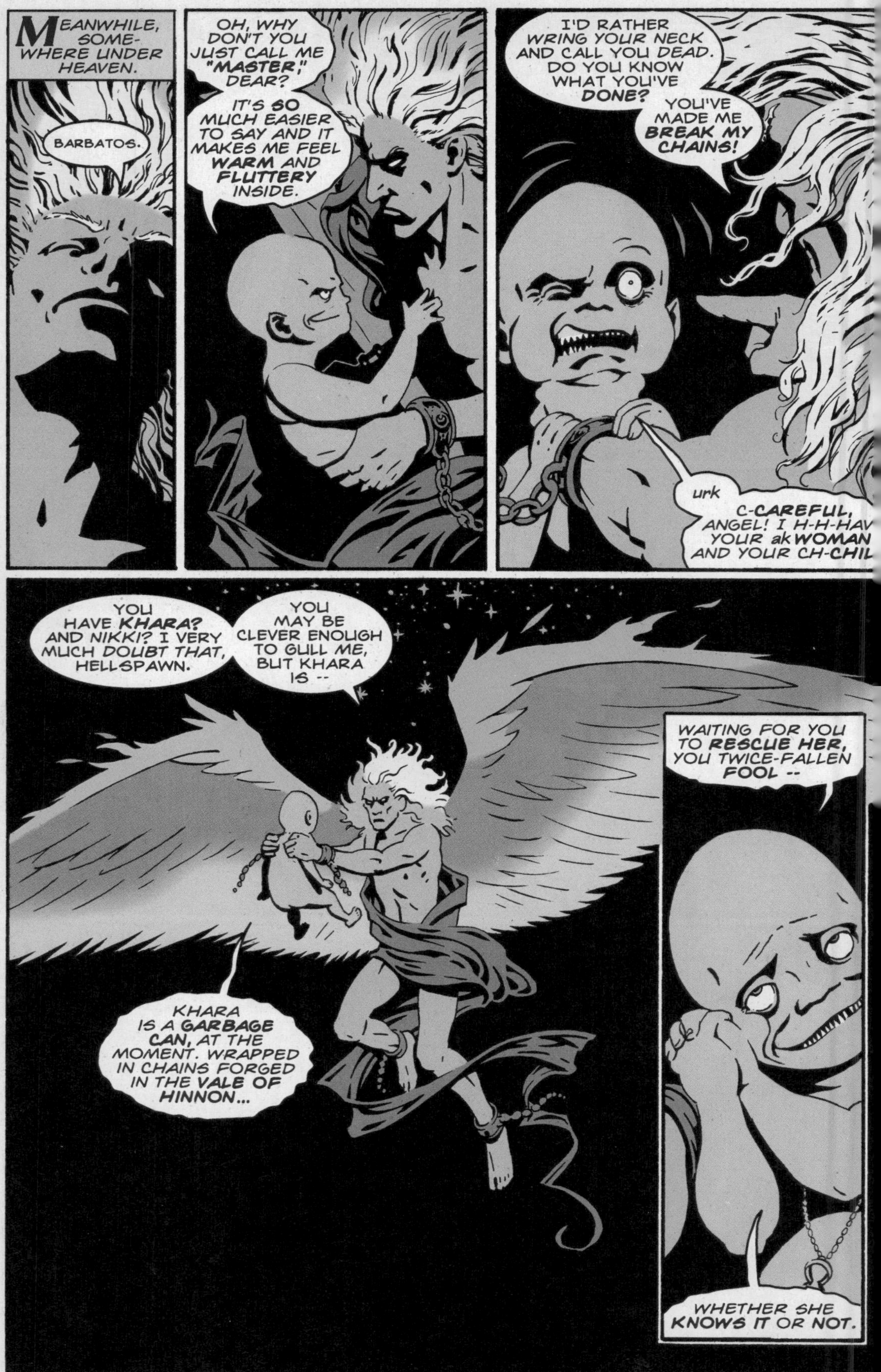
MEANWHILE, SOME-WHERE UNDER HEAVEN.
BARBATOS.
OH, WHY DON'T YOU JUST CALL ME "MASTER," DEAR?
IT'S SO MUCH EASIER TO SAY AND IT MAKES ME FEEL WARM AND FLUTTERY INSIDE.
I'D RATHER WRING YOUR NECK AND CALL YOU DEAD. DO YOU KNOW WHAT YOU'VE DONE?
YOU'VE MADE ME BREAK MY CHAINS!
urk
C-CAREFUL, ANGEL! I H-H-HAV YOUR akWOMAN AND YOUR CH-CHIL
YOU HAVE KHARA? AND NIKKI? I VERY MUCH DOUBT THAT, HELLSPAWN.
YOU MAY BE CLEVER ENOUGH TO GULL ME, BUT KHARA IS --
KHARA IS A GARBAGE CAN, AT THE MOMENT. WRAPPED IN CHAINS FORGED IN THE VALE OF HINNON...
WAITING FOR YOU TO RESCUE HER, YOU TWICE-FALLEN FOOL --
WHETHER SHE KNOWS IT OR NOT.

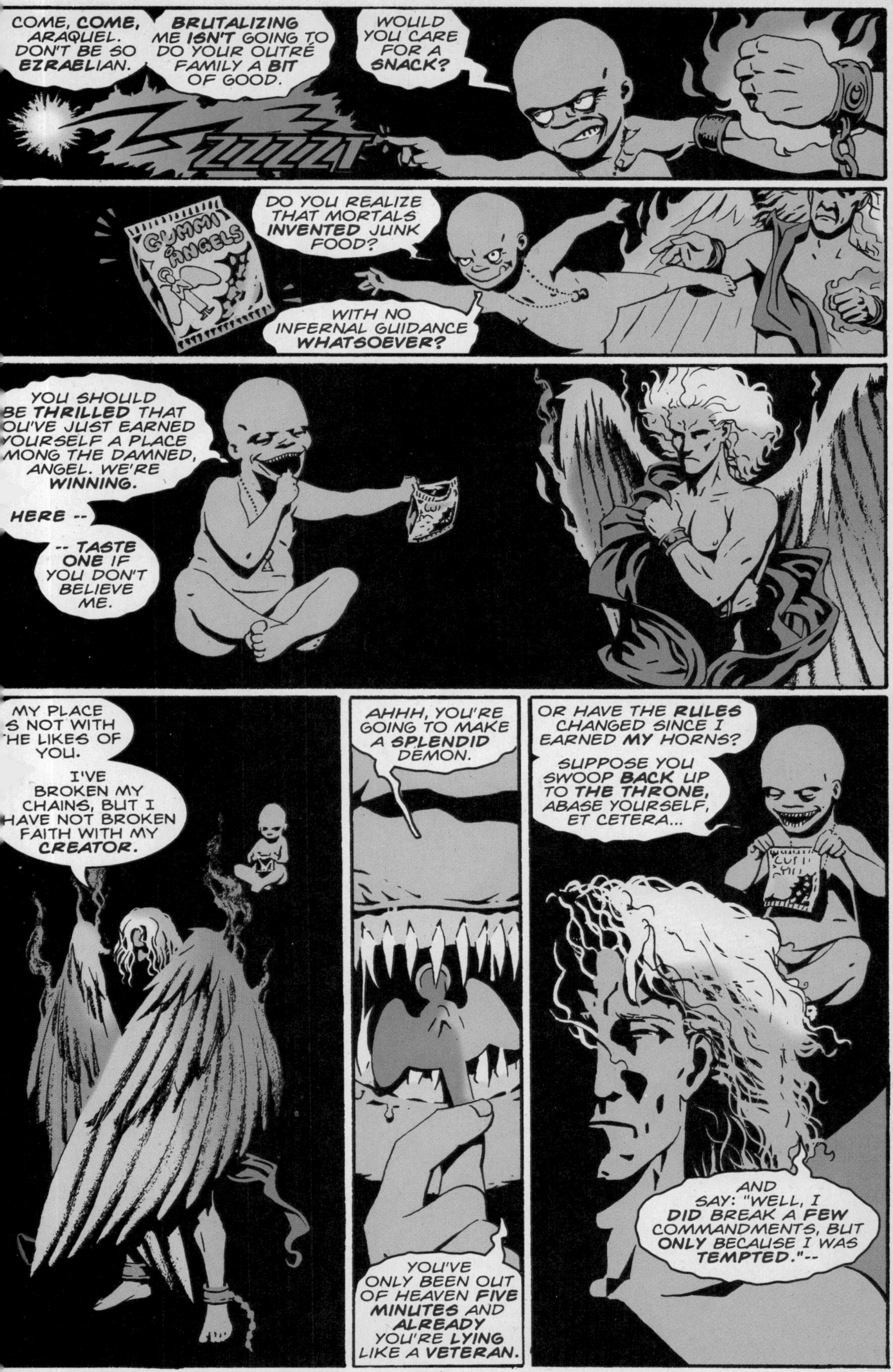
COME, COME, ARAQUEL. DON'T BE SO EZRABLIAN.
BRUTALIZING ME ISN'T GOING TO DO YOUR OUTRÉ FAMILY A BIT OF GOOD.
WOULD YOU CARE FOR A SNACK?
ZZZZZZZT
GUMMI ANGELS
DO YOU REALIZE THAT MORTALS INVENTED JUNK FOOD?
WITH NO INFERNAL GUIDANCE WHATSOEVER?
YOU SHOULD BE THRILLED THAT OU'VE JUST EARNED YOURSELF A PLACE MONG THE DAMNED, ANGEL. WE'RE WINNING.
HERE --
-- TASTE ONE IF YOU DON'T BELIEVE ME.
MY PLACE S NOT WITH HE LIKES OF YOU.
I'VE BROKEN MY CHAINS, BUT I HAVE NOT BROKEN FAITH WITH MY CREATOR.
AHHH, YOU'RE GOING TO MAKE A SPLENDID DEMON.
YOU'VE ONLY BEEN OUT OF HEAVEN FIVE MINUTES AND ALREADY YOU'RE LYING LIKE A VETERAN.
OR HAVE THE RULES CHANGED SINCE I EARNED MY HORNS?
SUPPOSE YOU SWOOP BACK UP TO THE THRONE, ABASE YOURSELF, ET CETERA...
AND SAY: "WELL, I DID BREAK A FEW COMMANDMENTS, BUT ONLY BECAUSE I WAS TEMPTED."--

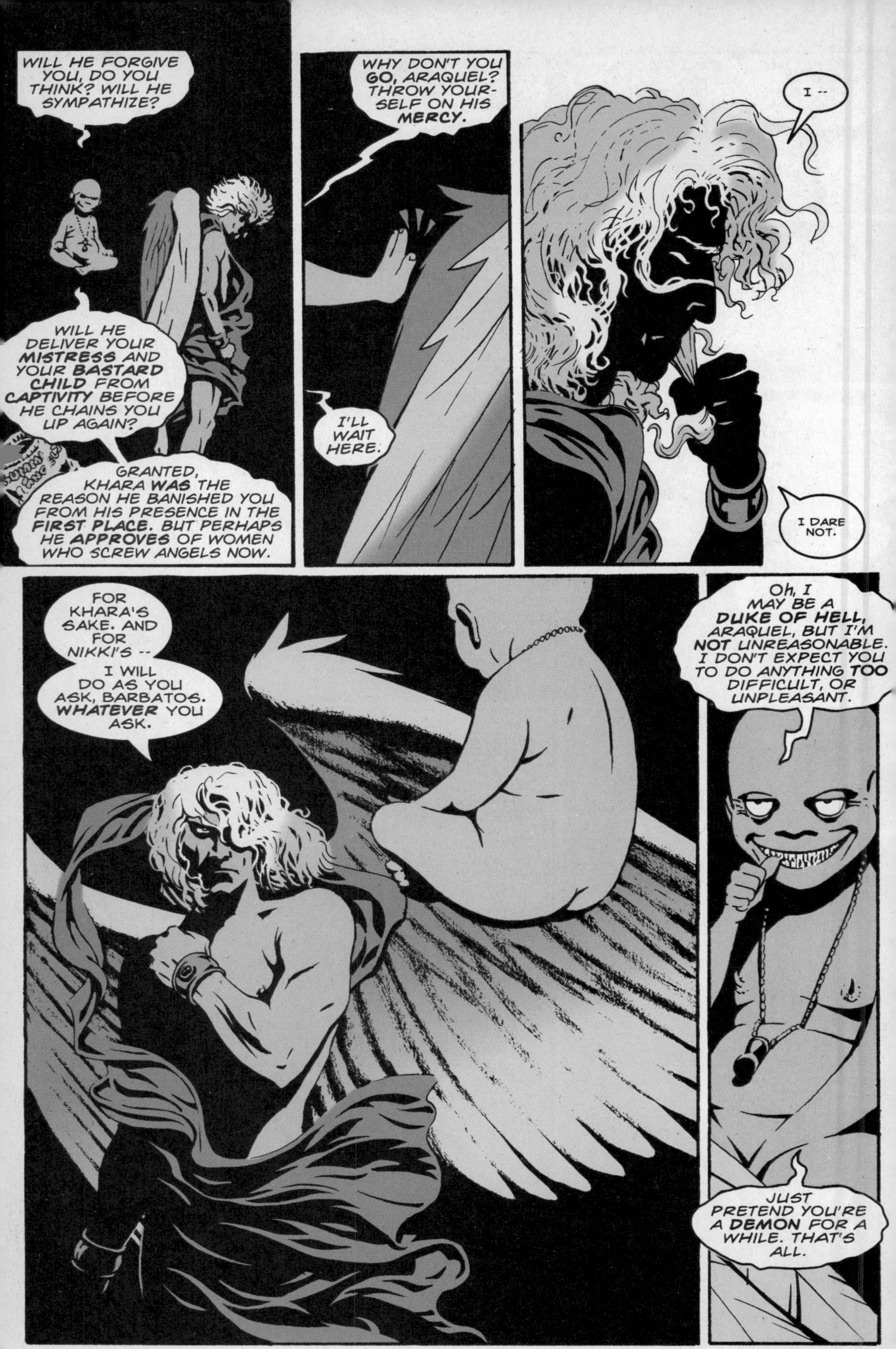
WILL HE FORGIVE YOU, DO YOU THINK? WILL HE SYMPATHIZE?
WILL HE DELIVER YOUR **MISTRESS** AND YOUR **BASTARD CHILD** FROM **CAPTIVITY** BEFORE HE CHAINS YOU UP AGAIN?
GRANTED, KHARA **WAS** THE REASON HE BANISHED YOU FROM HIS PRESENCE IN THE **FIRST PLACE**. BUT PERHAPS HE **APPROVES** OF WOMEN WHO SCREW ANGELS NOW.
WHY DON'T YOU **GO**, ARAQUEL? THROW YOURSELF ON HIS **MERCY**.
I'LL WAIT HERE.
I --
I DARE NOT.
FOR KHARA'S SAKE. AND FOR NIKKI'S --
I WILL DO AS YOU ASK, BARBATOS. **WHATEVER** YOU ASK.
Oh, I MAY BE A **DUKE OF HELL**, ARAQUEL, BUT I'M **NOT** UNREASONABLE. I DON'T EXPECT YOU TO DO ANYTHING **TOO** DIFFICULT, OR UNPLEASANT.
JUST PRETEND YOU'RE A **DEMON** FOR A WHILE. THAT'S ALL.

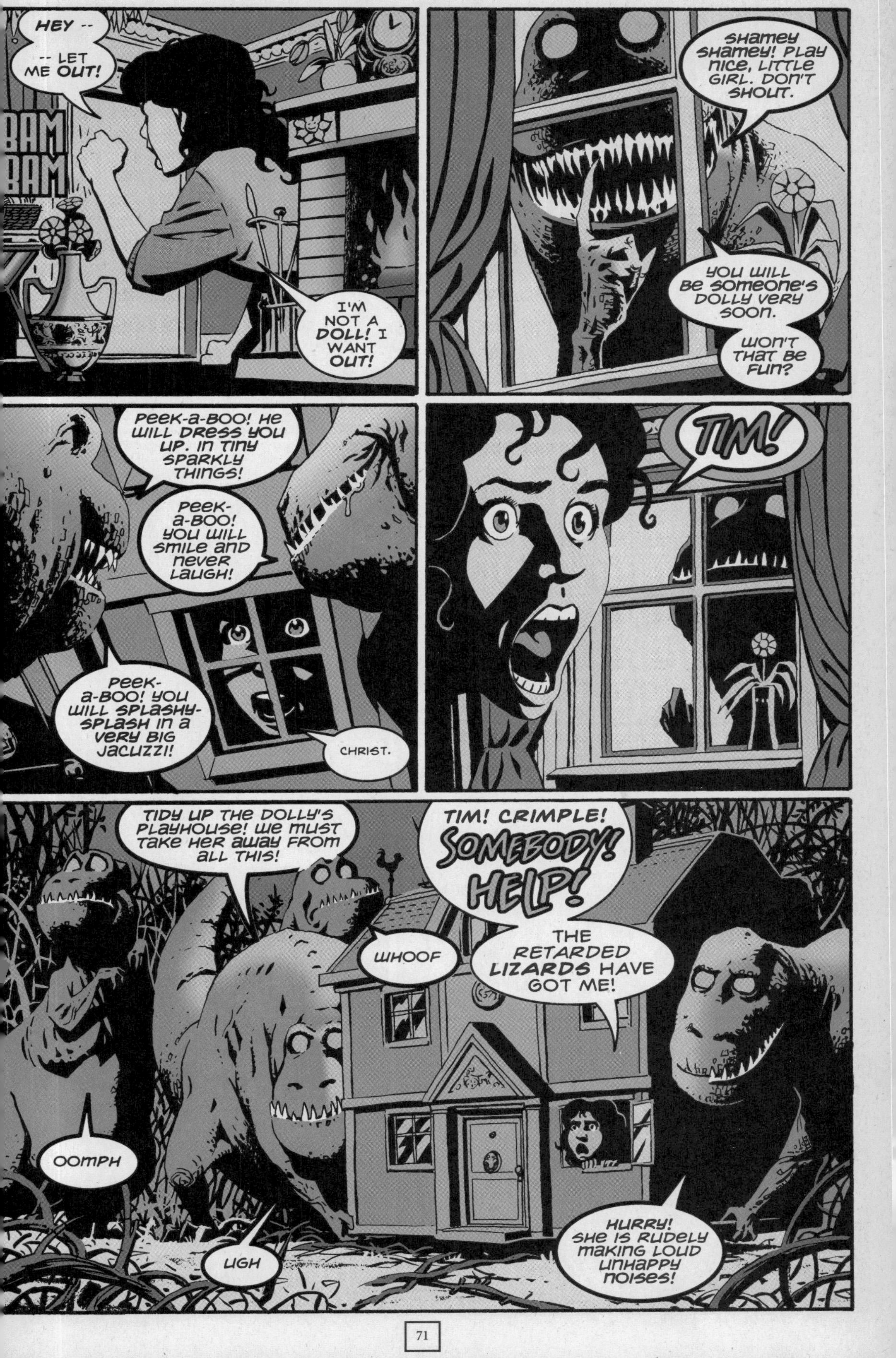
HEY --
-- LET ME OUT!
BAM BAM
I'M NOT A DOLL! I WANT OUT!
SHAMEY SHAMEY! PLAY NICE, LITTLE GIRL. DON'T SHOUT.
YOU WILL BE SOMEONE'S DOLLY VERY SOON.
WON'T THAT BE FUN?
PEEK-A-BOO! HE WILL DRESS YOU UP. IN TINY SPARKLY THINGS!
PEEK-A-BOO! YOU WILL SMILE AND NEVER LAUGH!
PEEK-A-BOO! YOU WILL SPLASHY-SPLASH IN A VERY BIG JACUZZI!
CHRIST.
TIM!
TIDY UP THE DOLLY'S PLAYHOUSE! WE MUST TAKE HER AWAY FROM ALL THIS!
TIM! CRIMPLE! SOMEBODY! HELP!
THE RETARDED LIZARDS HAVE GOT ME!
WHOOF
OOMPH
UGH
HURRY! SHE IS RUDELY MAKING LOUD UNHAPPY NOISES!

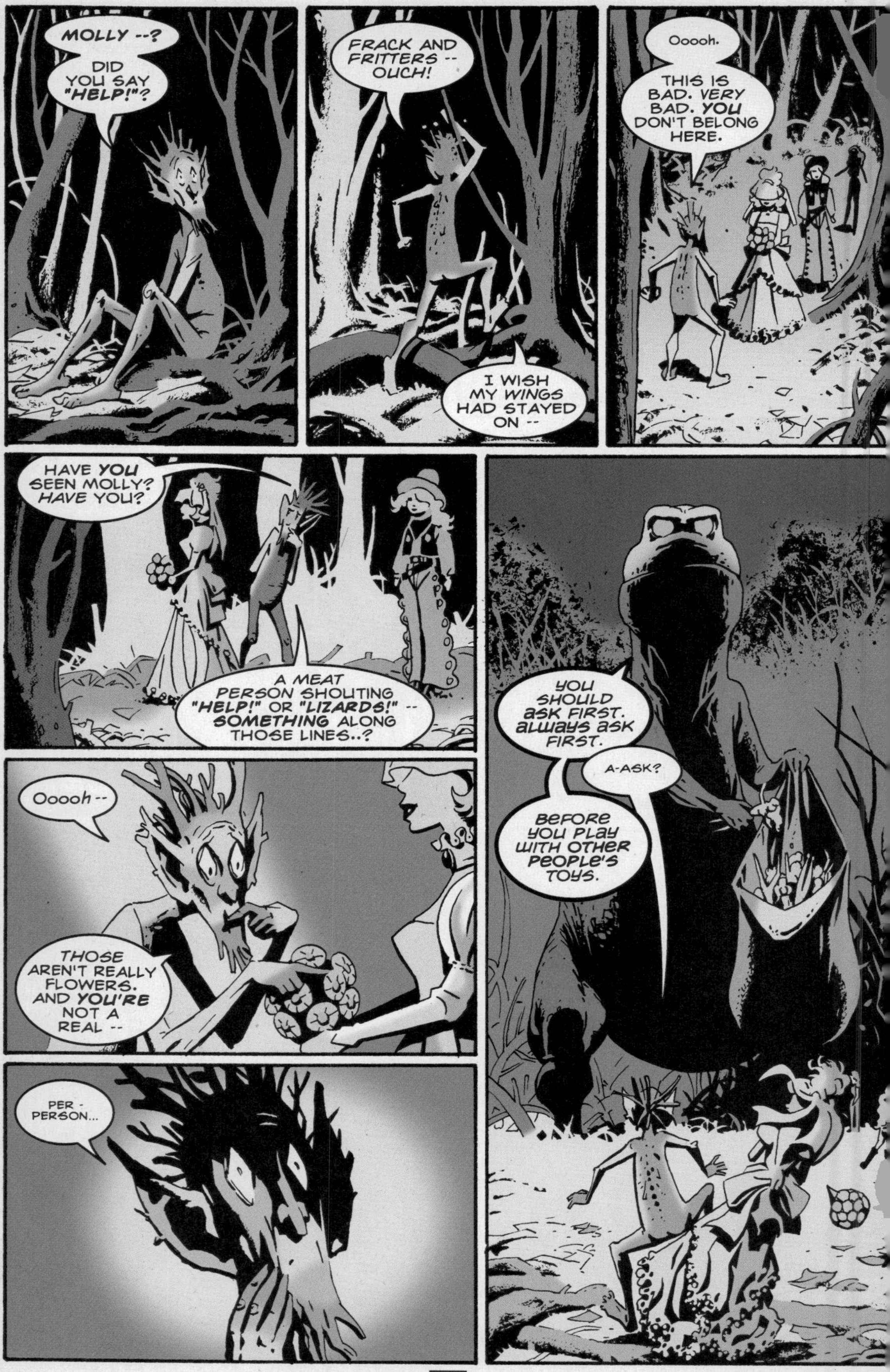
MOLLY --?
DID YOU SAY "HELP!"?
FRACK AND FRITTERS -- OUCH!
I WISH MY WINGS HAD STAYED ON --
Ooooh.
THIS IS BAD. VERY BAD. YOU DON'T BELONG HERE.
HAVE YOU SEEN MOLLY? HAVE YOU?
A MEAT PERSON SHOUTING "HELP!" OR "LIZARDS!" -- SOMETHING ALONG THOSE LINES..?
Ooooh --
THOSE AREN'T REALLY FLOWERS. AND YOU'RE NOT A REAL --
PER - PERSON...
YOU SHOULD ASK FIRST. ALWAYS ASK FIRST.
A-ASK?
BEFORE YOU PLAY WITH OTHER PEOPLE'S TOYS.

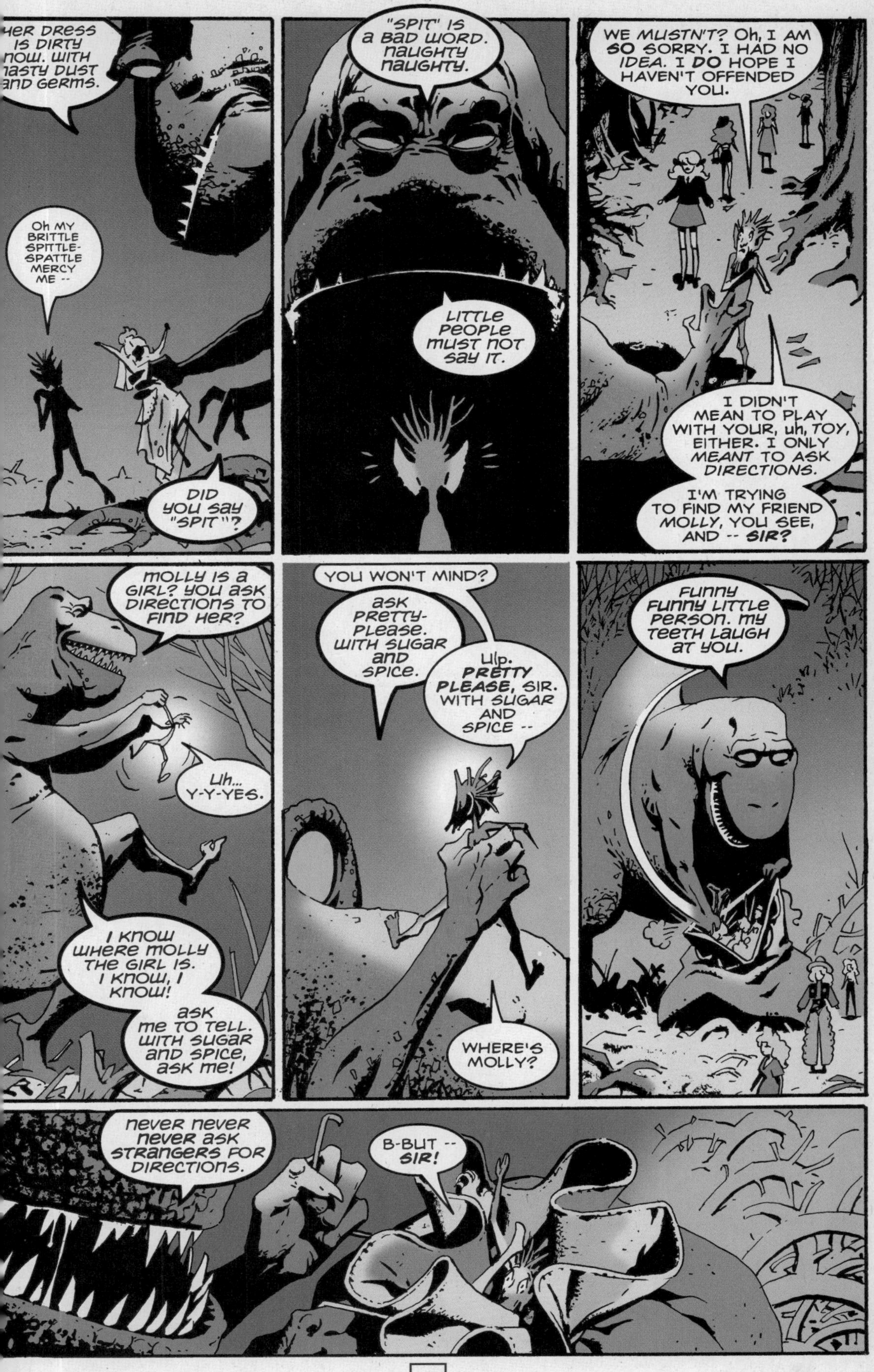
HER DRESS IS DIRTY NOW. WITH NASTY DUST AND GERMS.
Oh MY BRITTLE SPITTLE-SPATTLE MERCY ME --
DID YOU SAY "SPIT"?
"SPIT" IS A BAD WORD. NAUGHTY NAUGHTY.
LITTLE PEOPLE MUST NOT SAY IT.
WE MUSTN'T? Oh, I AM SO SORRY. I HAD NO IDEA. I DO HOPE I HAVEN'T OFFENDED YOU.
I DIDN'T MEAN TO PLAY WITH YOUR, uh, TOY, EITHER. I ONLY MEANT TO ASK DIRECTIONS.
I'M TRYING TO FIND MY FRIEND MOLLY, YOU SEE, AND -- SIR?
MOLLY IS A GIRL? YOU ASK DIRECTIONS TO FIND HER?
Uh... Y-Y-YES.
I KNOW WHERE MOLLY THE GIRL IS. I KNOW, I KNOW!
ASK ME TO TELL. WITH SUGAR AND SPICE, ASK ME!
YOU WON'T MIND?
ASK PRETTY-PLEASE. WITH SUGAR AND SPICE.
Ulp. PRETTY PLEASE, SIR. WITH SUGAR AND SPICE --
WHERE'S MOLLY?
FUNNY FUNNY LITTLE PERSON. MY TEETH LAUGH AT YOU.
NEVER NEVER NEVER ASK STRANGERS FOR DIRECTIONS.
B-BUT -- SIR!

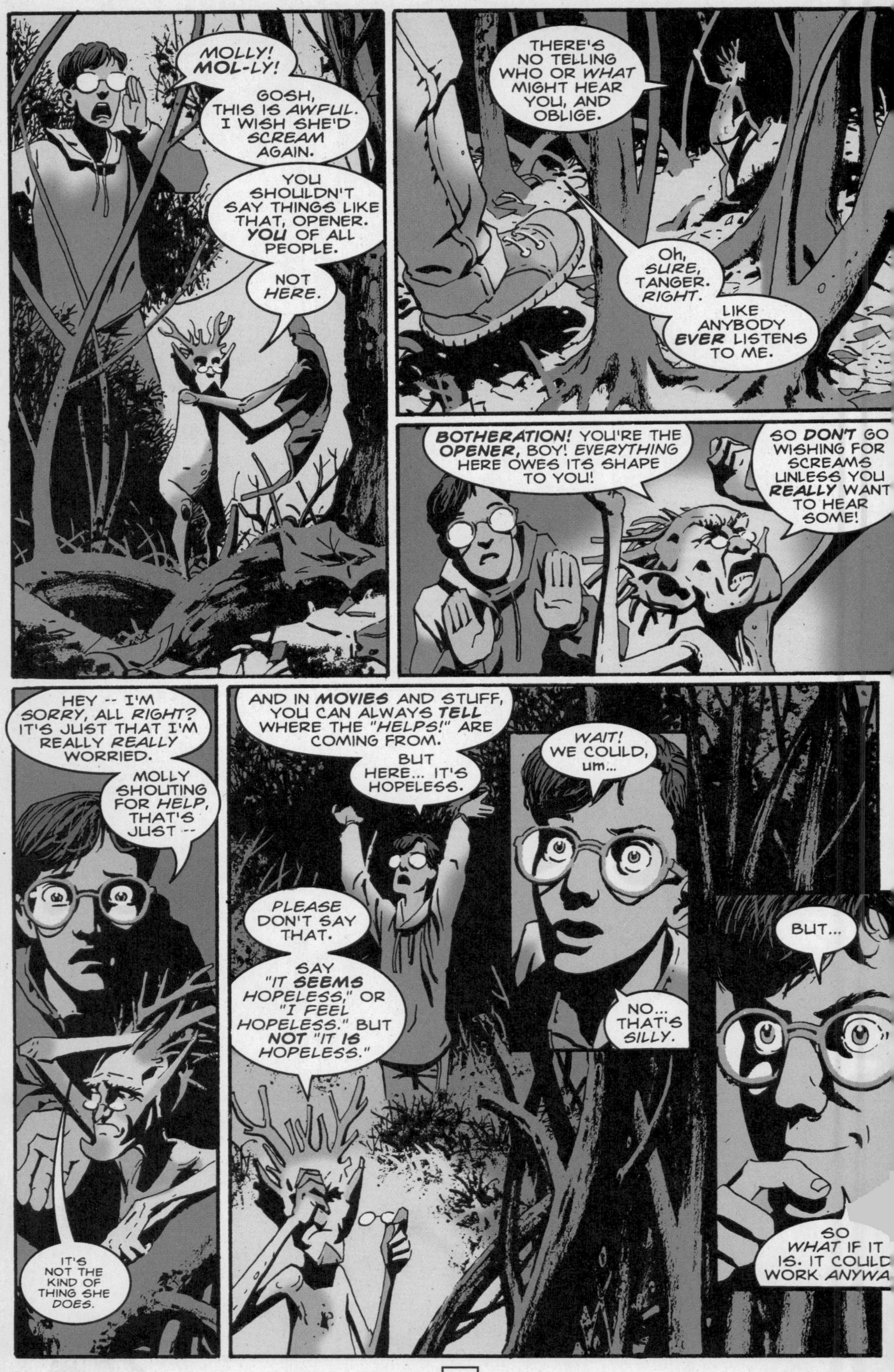
MOLLY! MOL-LY!
GOSH, THIS IS AWFUL. I WISH SHE'D SCREAM AGAIN.
YOU SHOULDN'T SAY THINGS LIKE THAT, OPENER. YOU OF ALL PEOPLE.
NOT HERE.
THERE'S NO TELLING WHO OR WHAT MIGHT HEAR YOU, AND OBLIGE.
Oh, SURE, TANGER. RIGHT.
LIKE ANYBODY EVER LISTENS TO ME.
BOTHERATION! YOU'RE THE OPENER, BOY! EVERYTHING HERE OWES ITS SHAPE TO YOU!
SO DON'T GO WISHING FOR SCREAMS UNLESS YOU REALLY WANT TO HEAR SOME!
HEY -- I'M SORRY, ALL RIGHT? IT'S JUST THAT I'M REALLY REALLY WORRIED.
MOLLY SHOUTING FOR HELP, THAT'S JUST --
IT'S NOT THE KIND OF THING SHE DOES.
AND IN MOVIES AND STUFF, YOU CAN ALWAYS TELL WHERE THE "HELPS!" ARE COMING FROM.
BUT HERE... IT'S HOPELESS.
PLEASE DON'T SAY THAT.
SAY "IT SEEMS HOPELESS," OR "I FEEL HOPELESS." BUT NOT "IT IS HOPELESS."
WAIT! WE COULD, um...
NO... THAT'S SILLY.
BUT...
SO WHAT IF IT IS. IT COULD WORK ANYWA

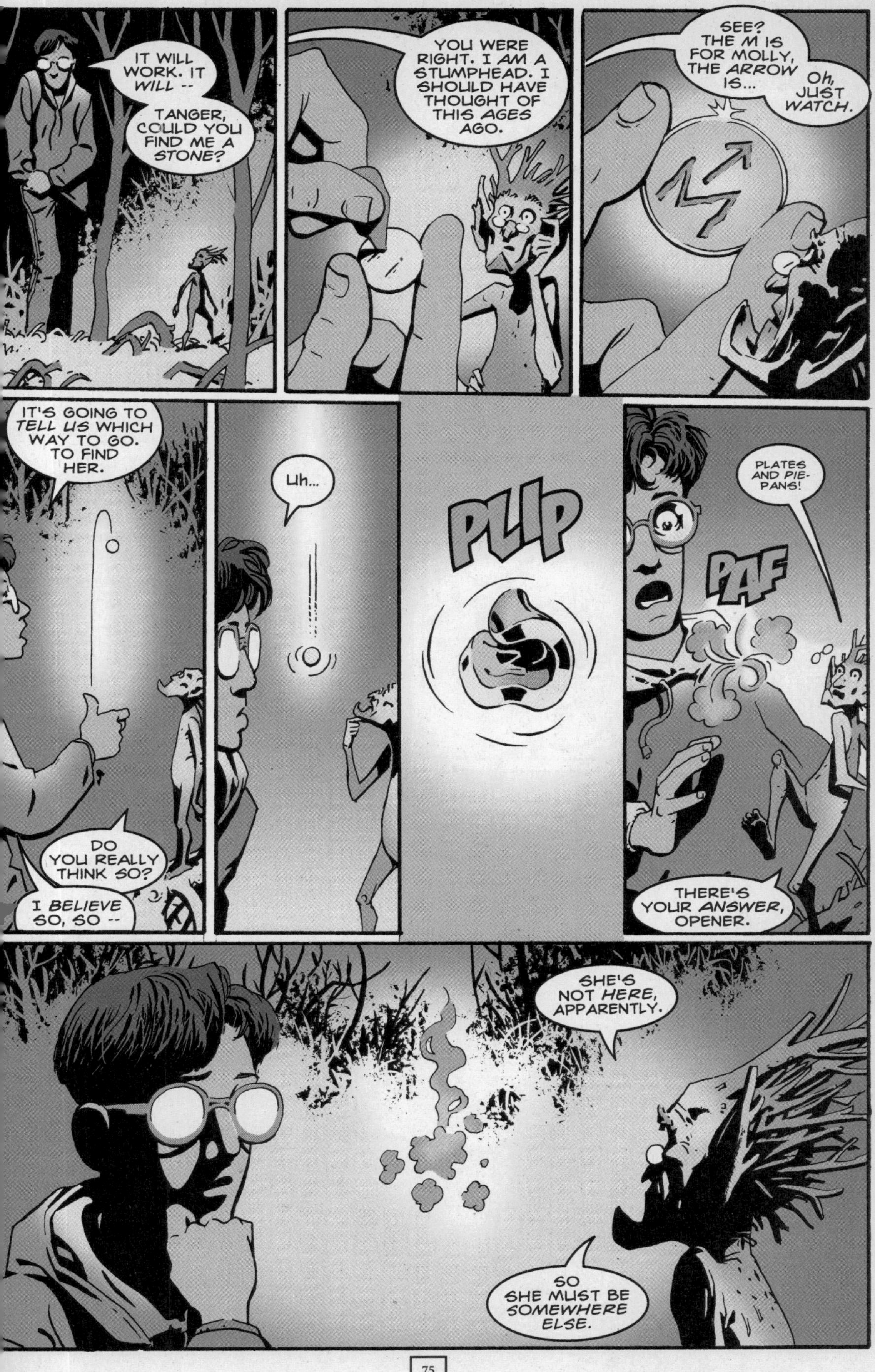
IT WILL WORK. IT WILL --
TANGER, COULD YOU FIND ME A STONE?
YOU WERE RIGHT. I AM A STUMPHEAD. I SHOULD HAVE THOUGHT OF THIS AGES AGO.
SEE? THE M IS FOR MOLLY, THE ARROW IS...
Oh, JUST WATCH.
IT'S GOING TO TELL US WHICH WAY TO GO. TO FIND HER.
DO YOU REALLY THINK SO?
I BELIEVE SO, SO --
Uh...
PLIP
PLATES AND PIE-PANS!
PAF
THERE'S YOUR ANSWER, OPENER.
SHE'S NOT HERE, APPARENTLY.
SO SHE MUST BE SOMEWHERE ELSE.

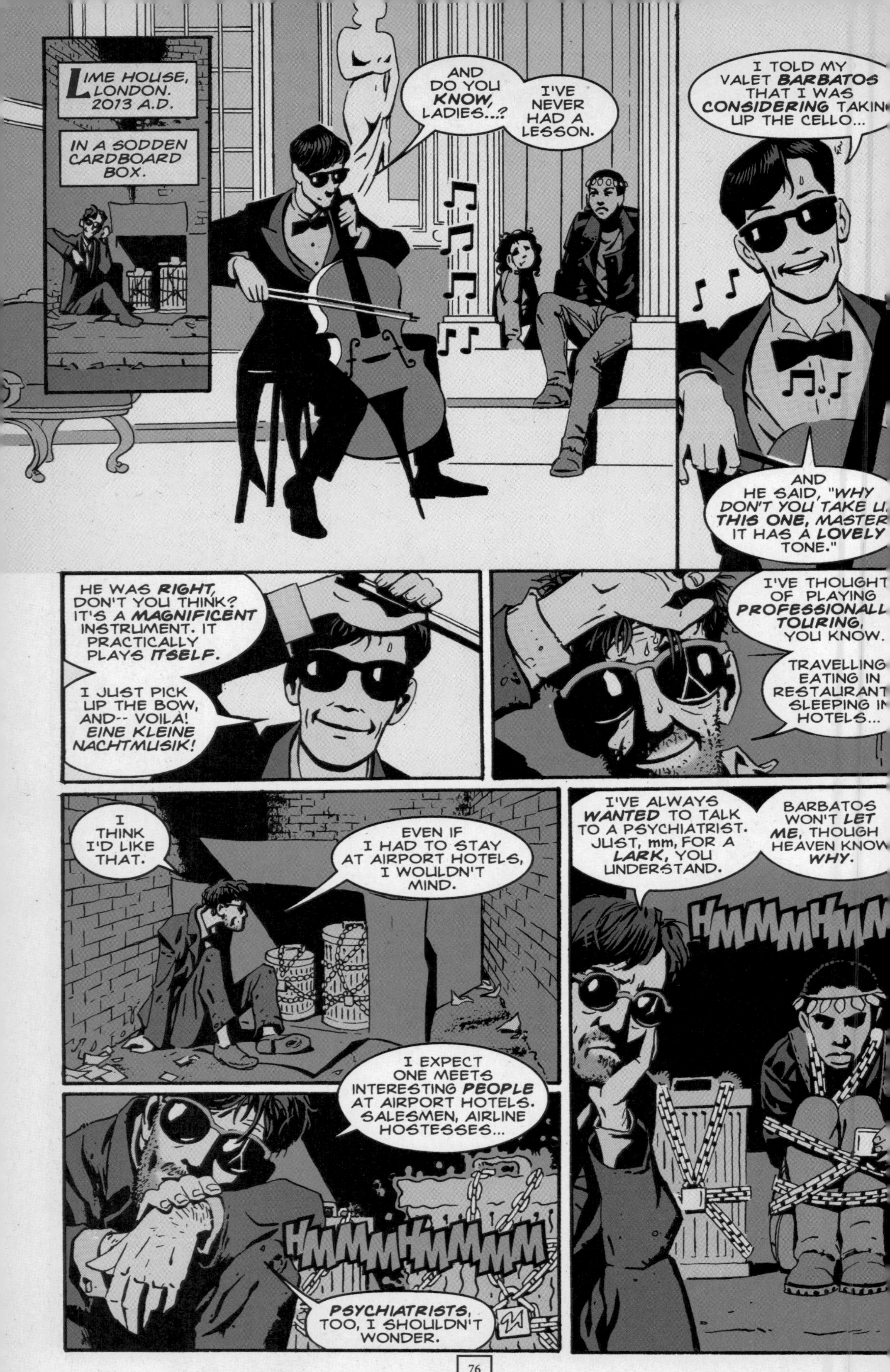
LIME HOUSE, LONDON. 2013 A.D.
IN A SODDEN CARDBOARD BOX.
AND DO YOU KNOW, LADIES...?
I'VE NEVER HAD A LESSON.
I TOLD MY VALET BARBATOS THAT I WAS CONSIDERING TAKIN UP THE CELLO...
AND HE SAID, "WHY DON'T YOU TAKE U THIS ONE, MASTER IT HAS A LOVELY TONE."
HE WAS RIGHT, DON'T YOU THINK? IT'S A MAGNIFICENT INSTRUMENT. IT PRACTICALLY PLAYS ITSELF.
I JUST PICK UP THE BOW, AND-- VOILÀ! EINE KLEINE NACHTMUSIK!
I'VE THOUGHT OF PLAYING PROFESSIONALL TOURING, YOU KNOW.
TRAVELLING EATING IN RESTAURANT SLEEPING IN HOTELS...
I THINK I'D LIKE THAT.
EVEN IF I HAD TO STAY AT AIRPORT HOTELS, I WOULDN'T MIND.
I EXPECT ONE MEETS INTERESTING PEOPLE AT AIRPORT HOTELS. SALESMEN, AIRLINE HOSTESSES...
HMMMHMMMM
PSYCHIATRISTS, TOO, I SHOULDN'T WONDER.
I'VE ALWAYS WANTED TO TALK TO A PSYCHIATRIST. JUST, mm, FOR A LARK, YOU UNDERSTAND.
BARBATOS WON'T LET ME, THOUGH HEAVEN KNOW WHY.
HMMMHMM

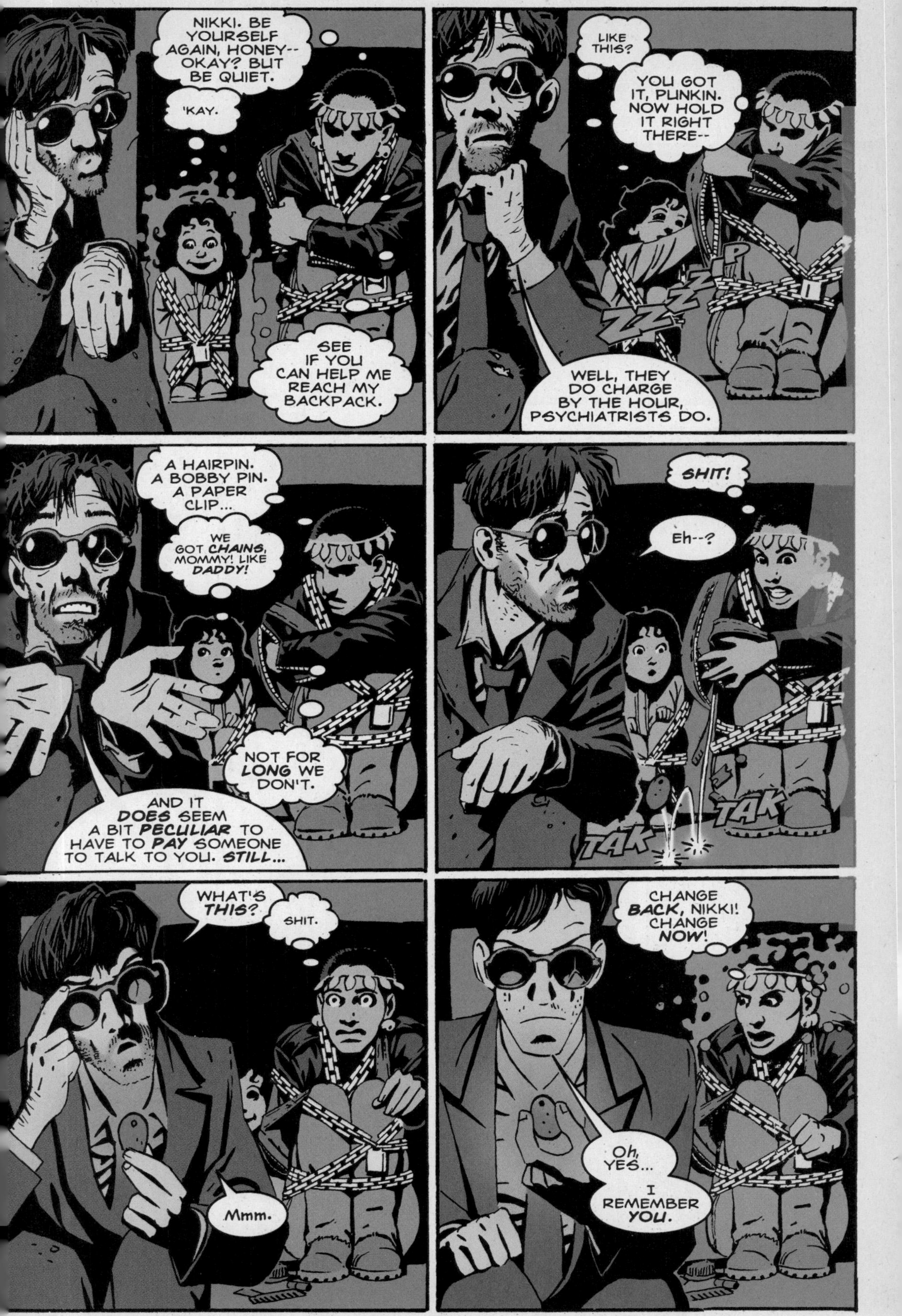
NIKKI. BE YOURSELF AGAIN, HONEY--OKAY? BUT BE QUIET.
'KAY.
SEE IF YOU CAN HELP ME REACH MY BACKPACK.
LIKE THIS?
YOU GOT IT, PUNKIN. NOW HOLD IT RIGHT THERE--
ZZZZIP
WELL, THEY DO CHARGE BY THE HOUR, PSYCHIATRISTS DO.
A HAIRPIN. A BOBBY PIN. A PAPER CLIP...
WE GOT CHAINS, MOMMY! LIKE DADDY!
NOT FOR LONG WE DON'T.
AND IT DOES SEEM A BIT PECULIAR TO HAVE TO PAY SOMEONE TO TALK TO YOU. STILL...
SHIT!
Eh--?
TAK
TAK
WHAT'S THIS?
SHIT.
Mmm.
CHANGE BACK, NIKKI! CHANGE NOW!
Oh, YES... I REMEMBER YOU.

FAUGH. A CARDBOARD BOX FOR A HOME. *RUBBISH* BINS FOR FURNITURE...

Ahhhh. NO, NO, NO...*NOT* FURNITURE. COMPANY.

WELL, LADIES. WE *PART* COMPANY HERE.

YOU WON'T OBJECT IF I KEEP THE STONE?

IT *IS* MINE, OR SO IT TELLS ME.

SHISHHH

SHISHHH

MOMMY! MOMMY, *LOOK!*

IT'S NOT *BAD FIRE*. IT LETS US GO.

HE LET US GO, SUGAR. MISTER *WRONG* OVER THERE.

AND I'LL BE *DAMNED* IF I KNOW WHY.

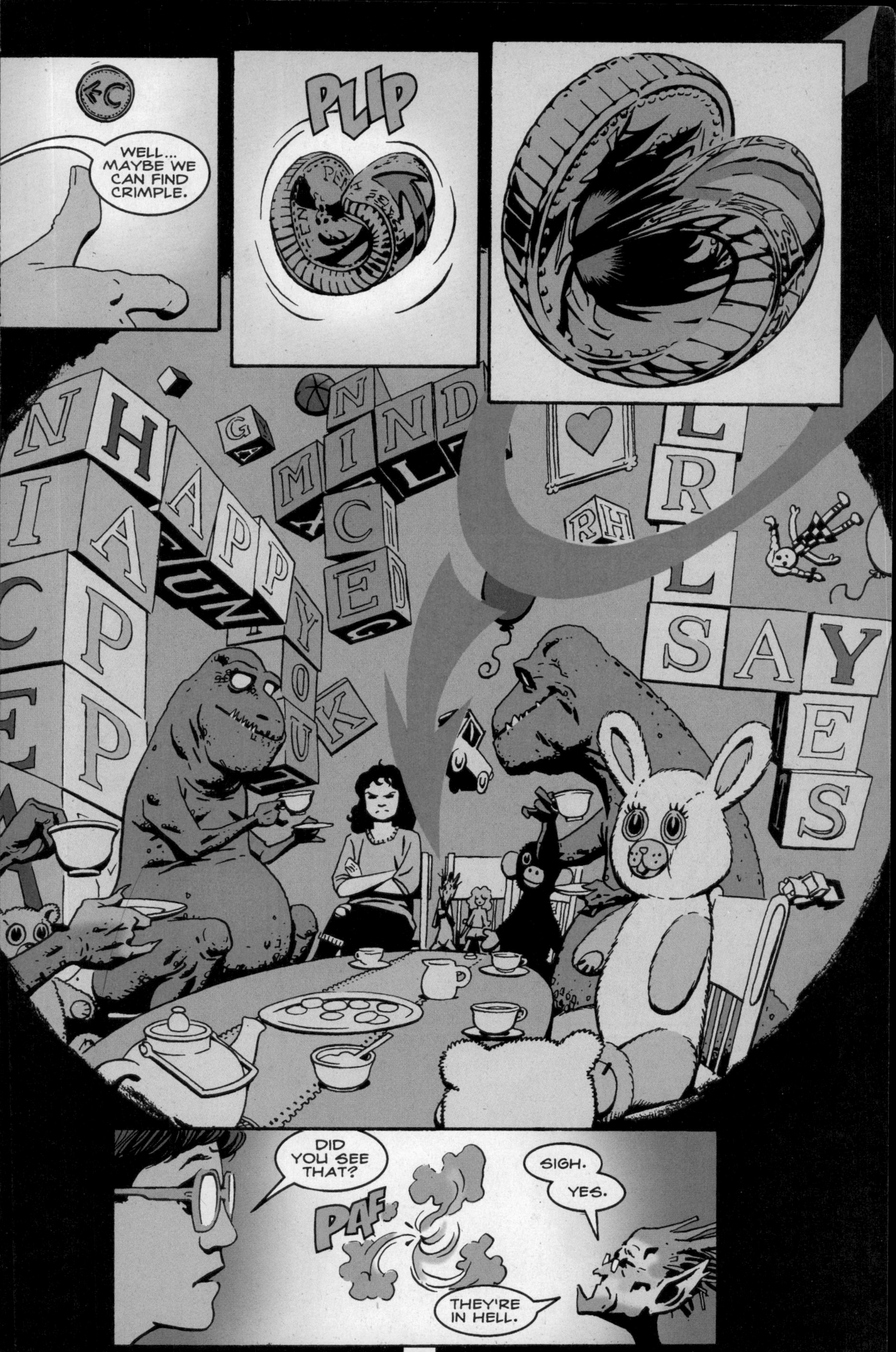
WELL... MAYBE WE CAN FIND CRIMPLE.
PLIP
DID YOU SEE THAT?
PAF
SIGH.
YES.
THEY'RE IN HELL.

SO THOSE **LIZARD** THINGS... THEY WERE **DEMONS?**

UNMISTAKABLY.

ALTHOUGH I DIDN'T KNOW THEY CAME IN PINK.

YOU'VE SEEN **DEMONS** BEFORE?

ARE YOU **SERIOUS?** WHEN?

WHY, WHEN MY PLACE WAS DIFFERENT, OPENER. WHEN ELSE?

I HAVEN'T ALWAYS BEEN A NARL, YOU KNOW.

YOU'RE NOT THE **ONLY** OPENER I'VE HAD DEALINGS WITH. AND EVERY **ONE** OF YOU HAS IMAGINED THINGS DIFFERENTLY-- **QUITE** DIFFERENTLY.

I'VE HAD **MANY** PLACES, IN MY TIME.

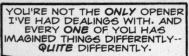

AND **TENANTED** MANY SHAPES.

BUT THAT'S NEITHER HERE NOR THERE. SO--

SHALL WE GO TO HELL **NOW,** OPENER? WHILE I'M STILL MORE OR LESS **ALIVE?**

I WOULD LIKE TO SPEND A LITTLE MORE TIME WITH CRIMPLE BEFORE I DIE.

I EXPECT YOU FEEL THE SAME WAY ABOUT MOLLY.

YEAH... I DO.

LET'S GO.

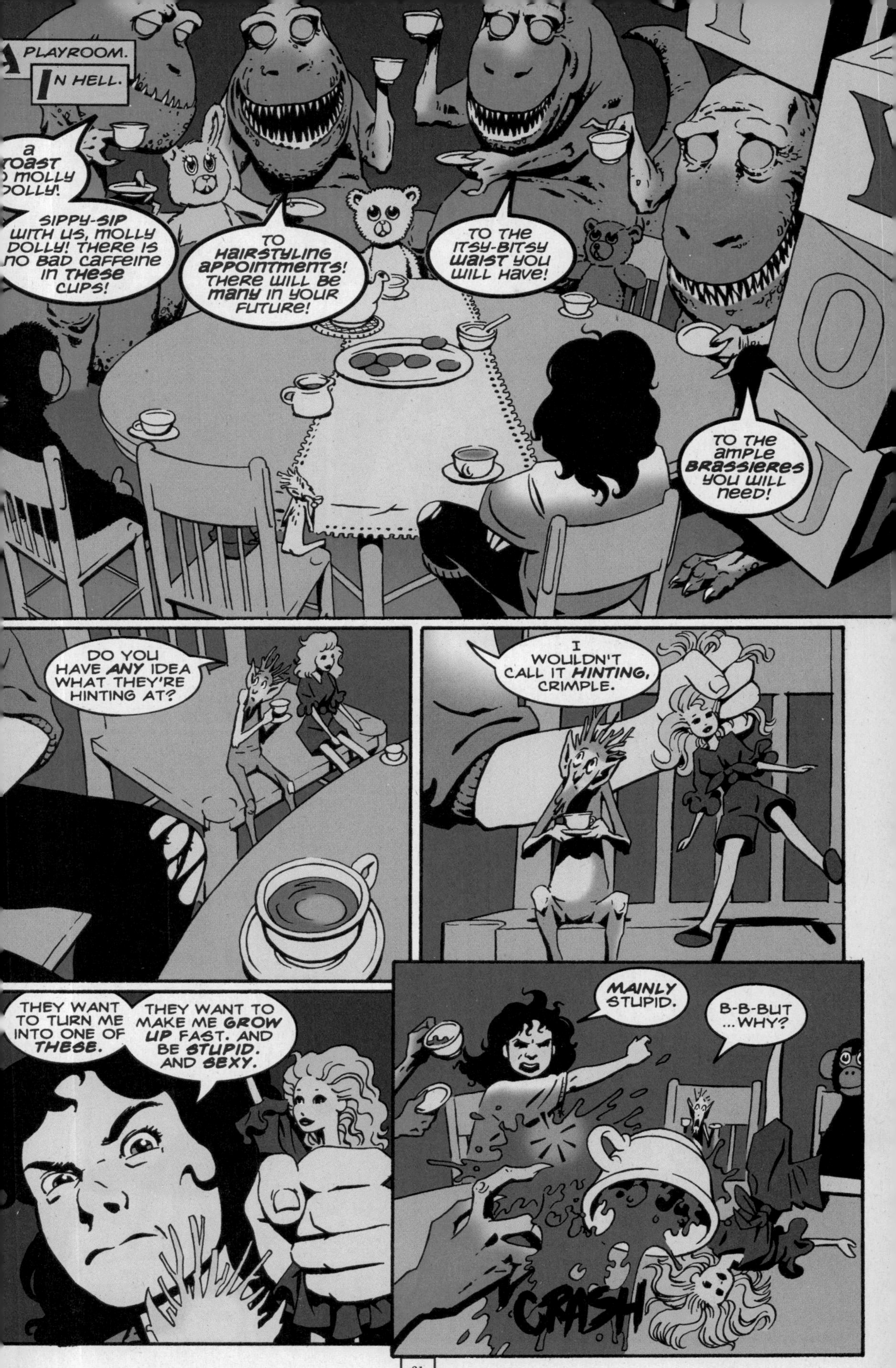
A PLAYROOM.
IN HELL.
a toast to molly dolly!
sippy-sip with us, molly dolly! there is no bad caffeine in these cups!
TO hairstyling appointments! there will be many in your future!
TO THE itsy-bitsy waist you will have!
TO THE ample brassieres you will need!
DO YOU HAVE ANY IDEA WHAT THEY'RE HINTING AT?
I WOULDN'T CALL IT HINTING, CRIMPLE.
THEY WANT TO TURN ME INTO ONE OF THESE.
THEY WANT TO MAKE ME GROW UP FAST. AND BE STUPID. AND SEXY.
MAINLY STUPID.
B-B-BUT ...WHY?
CRASH

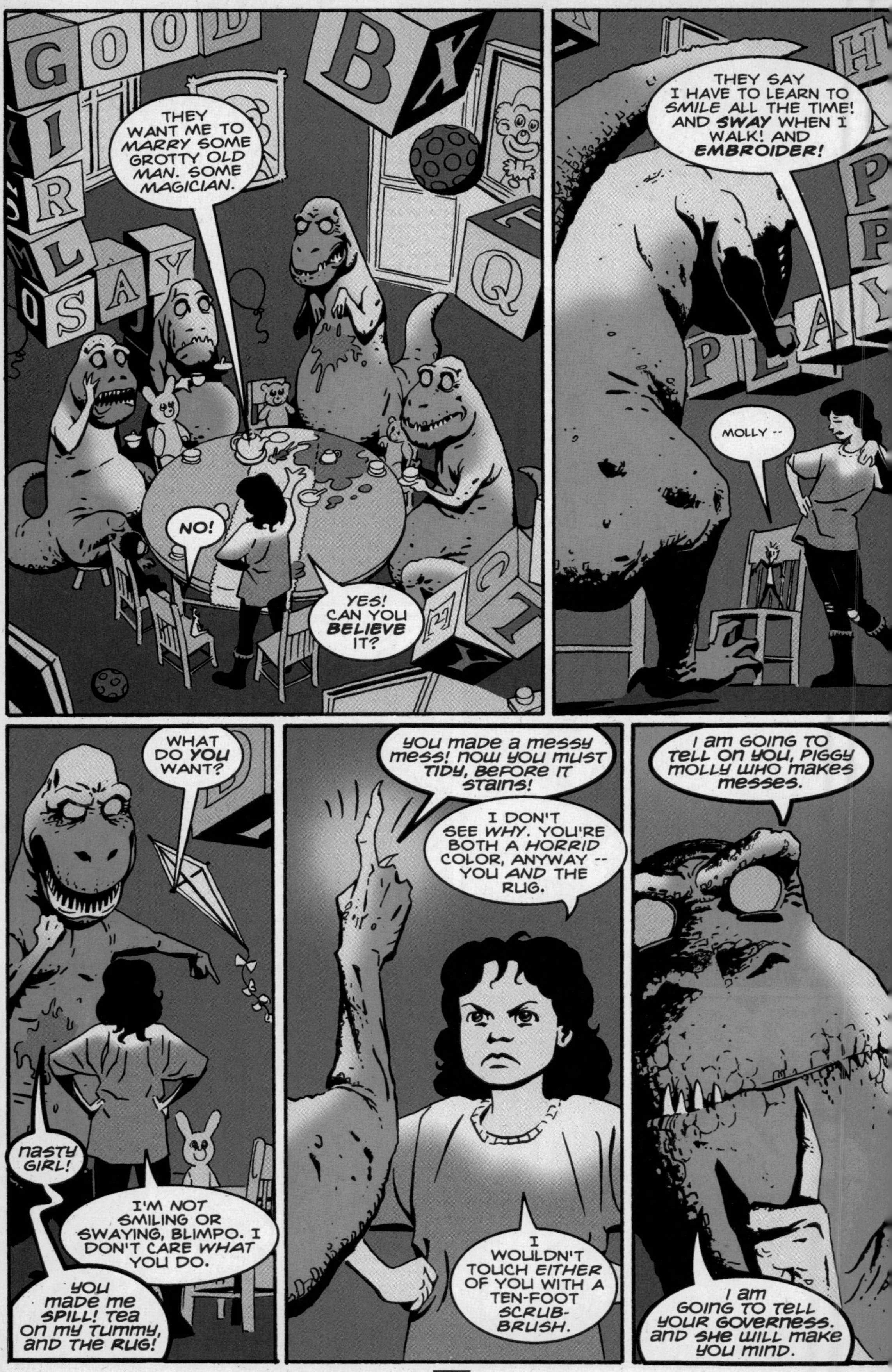
THEY WANT ME TO MARRY SOME GROTTY OLD MAN. SOME MAGICIAN.
NO!
YES! CAN YOU BELIEVE IT?
THEY SAY I HAVE TO LEARN TO SMILE ALL THE TIME! AND SWAY WHEN I WALK! AND EMBROIDER!
MOLLY --
WHAT DO YOU WANT?
NASTY GIRL!
I'M NOT SMILING OR SWAYING, BLIMPO. I DON'T CARE WHAT YOU DO.
YOU MADE ME SPILL! TEA ON MY TUMMY, AND THE RUG!
YOU MADE A MESSY MESS! NOW YOU MUST TIDY, BEFORE IT STAINS!
I DON'T SEE WHY. YOU'RE BOTH A HORRID COLOR, ANYWAY -- YOU AND THE RUG.
I WOULDN'T TOUCH EITHER OF YOU WITH A TEN-FOOT SCRUB-BRUSH.
I AM GOING TO TELL ON YOU, PIGGY MOLLY WHO MAKES MESSES.
I AM GOING TO TELL YOUR GOVERNESS. AND SHE WILL MAKE YOU MIND.

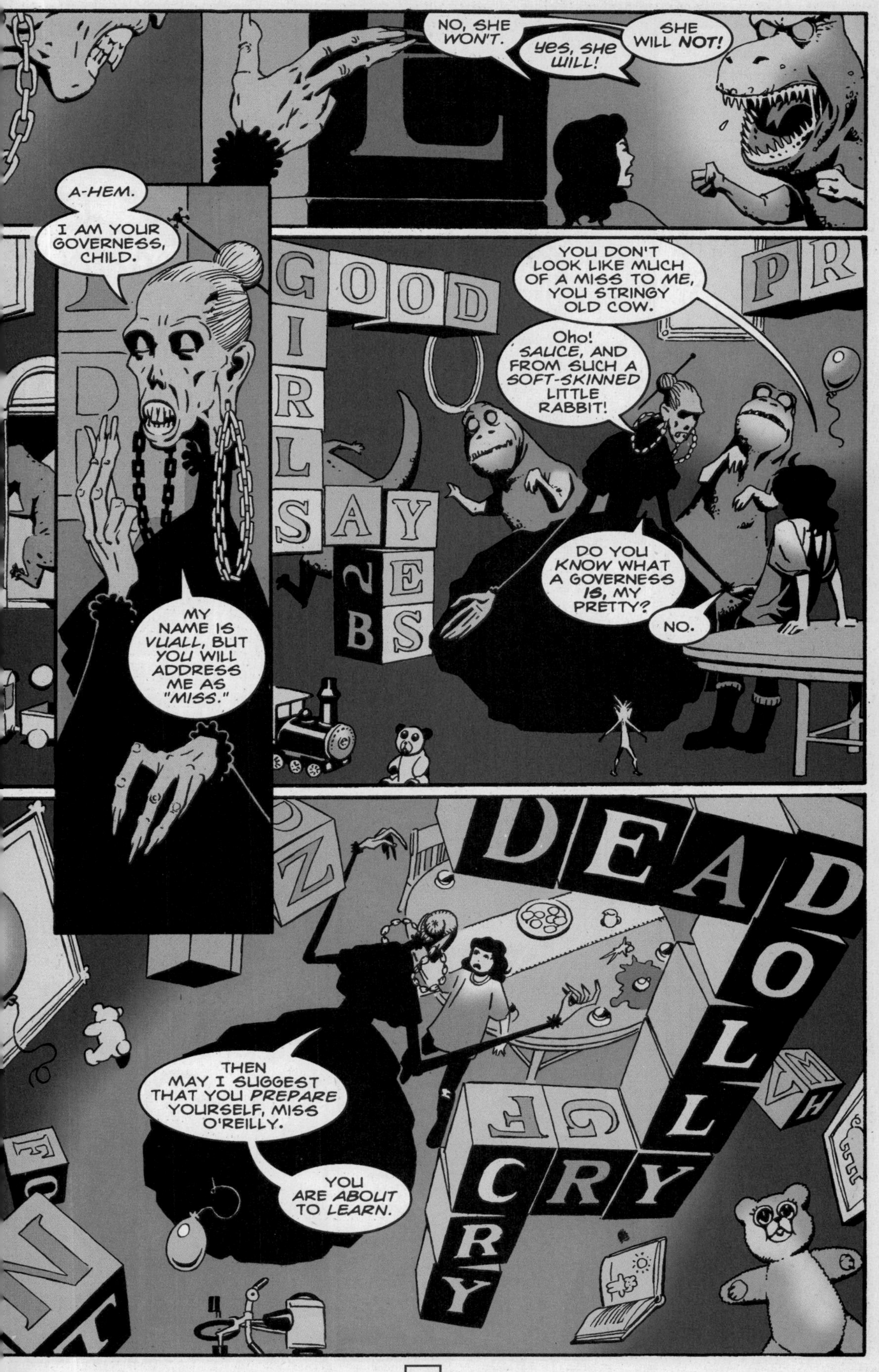
NO, SHE WON'T.
yes, SHE WILL!
SHE WILL NOT!
A-HEM.
I AM YOUR GOVERNESS, CHILD.
MY NAME IS VUALL, BUT YOU WILL ADDRESS ME AS "MISS."
YOU DON'T LOOK LIKE MUCH OF A MISS TO ME, YOU STRINGY OLD COW.
Oho! SAUCE, AND FROM SUCH A SOFT-SKINNED LITTLE RABBIT!
DO YOU KNOW WHAT A GOVERNESS IS, MY PRETTY?
NO.
THEN MAY I SUGGEST THAT YOU PREPARE YOURSELF, MISS O'REILLY.
YOU ARE ABOUT TO LEARN.

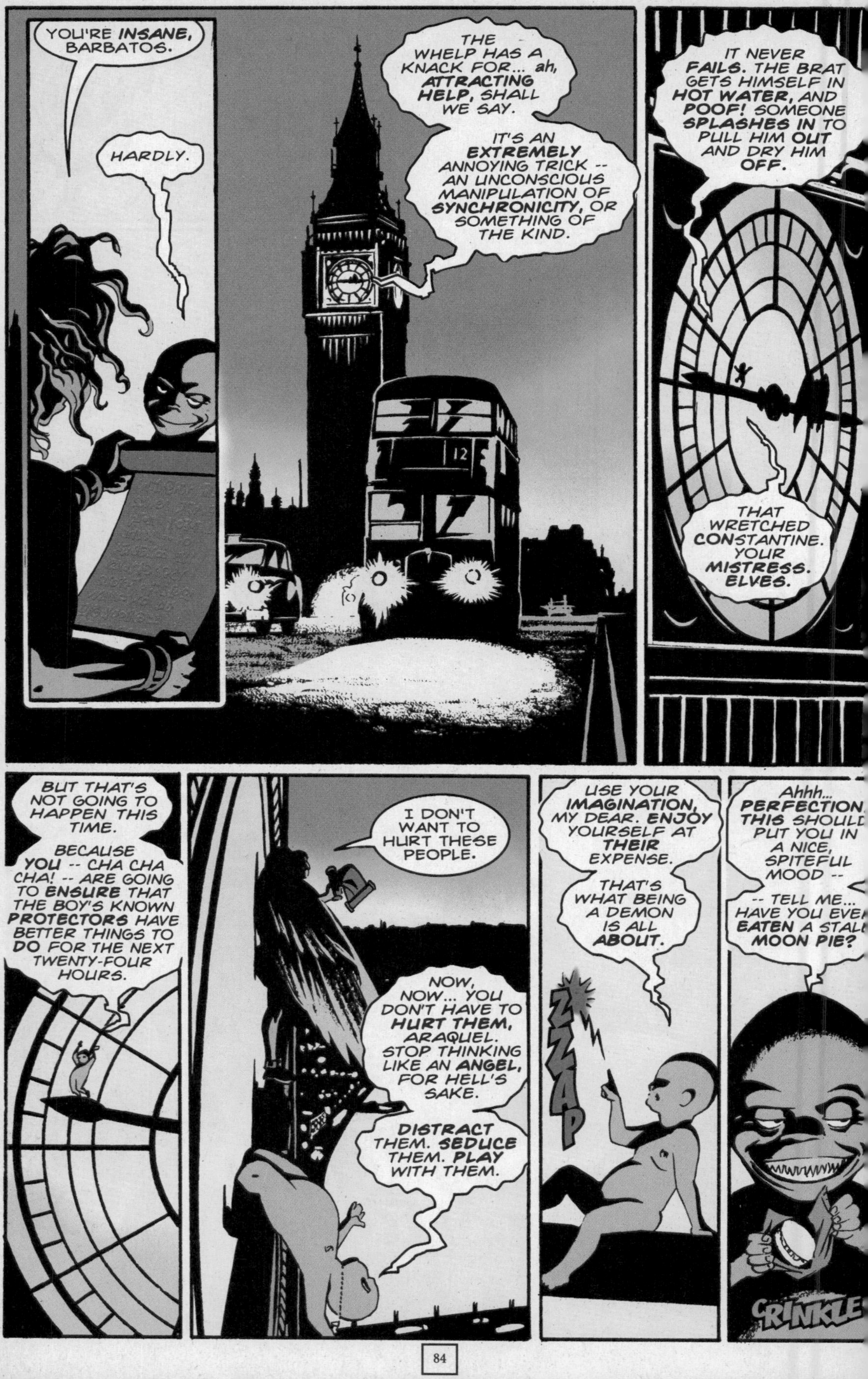
YOU'RE INSANE, BARBATOS.
HARDLY.
THE WHELP HAS A KNACK FOR... ah, ATTRACTING HELP, SHALL WE SAY.
IT'S AN EXTREMELY ANNOYING TRICK -- AN UNCONSCIOUS MANIPULATION OF SYNCHRONICITY, OR SOMETHING OF THE KIND.
12
IT NEVER FAILS. THE BRAT GETS HIMSELF IN HOT WATER, AND POOF! SOMEONE SPLASHES IN TO PULL HIM OUT AND DRY HIM OFF.
THAT WRETCHED CONSTANTINE. YOUR MISTRESS. ELVES.
BUT THAT'S NOT GOING TO HAPPEN THIS TIME.
BECAUSE YOU -- CHA CHA CHA! -- ARE GOING TO ENSURE THAT THE BOY'S KNOWN PROTECTORS HAVE BETTER THINGS TO DO FOR THE NEXT TWENTY-FOUR HOURS.
I DON'T WANT TO HURT THESE PEOPLE.
NOW, NOW... YOU DON'T HAVE TO HURT THEM, ARAQUEL. STOP THINKING LIKE AN ANGEL, FOR HELL'S SAKE.
DISTRACT THEM. SEDUCE THEM. PLAY WITH THEM.
USE YOUR IMAGINATION, MY DEAR. ENJOY YOURSELF AT THEIR EXPENSE.
THAT'S WHAT BEING A DEMON IS ALL ABOUT.
ZZZAP
Ahhh... PERFECTION. THIS SHOULD PUT YOU IN A NICE, SPITEFUL MOOD --
-- TELL ME... HAVE YOU EVER EATEN A STALE MOON PIE?
CRINKLE

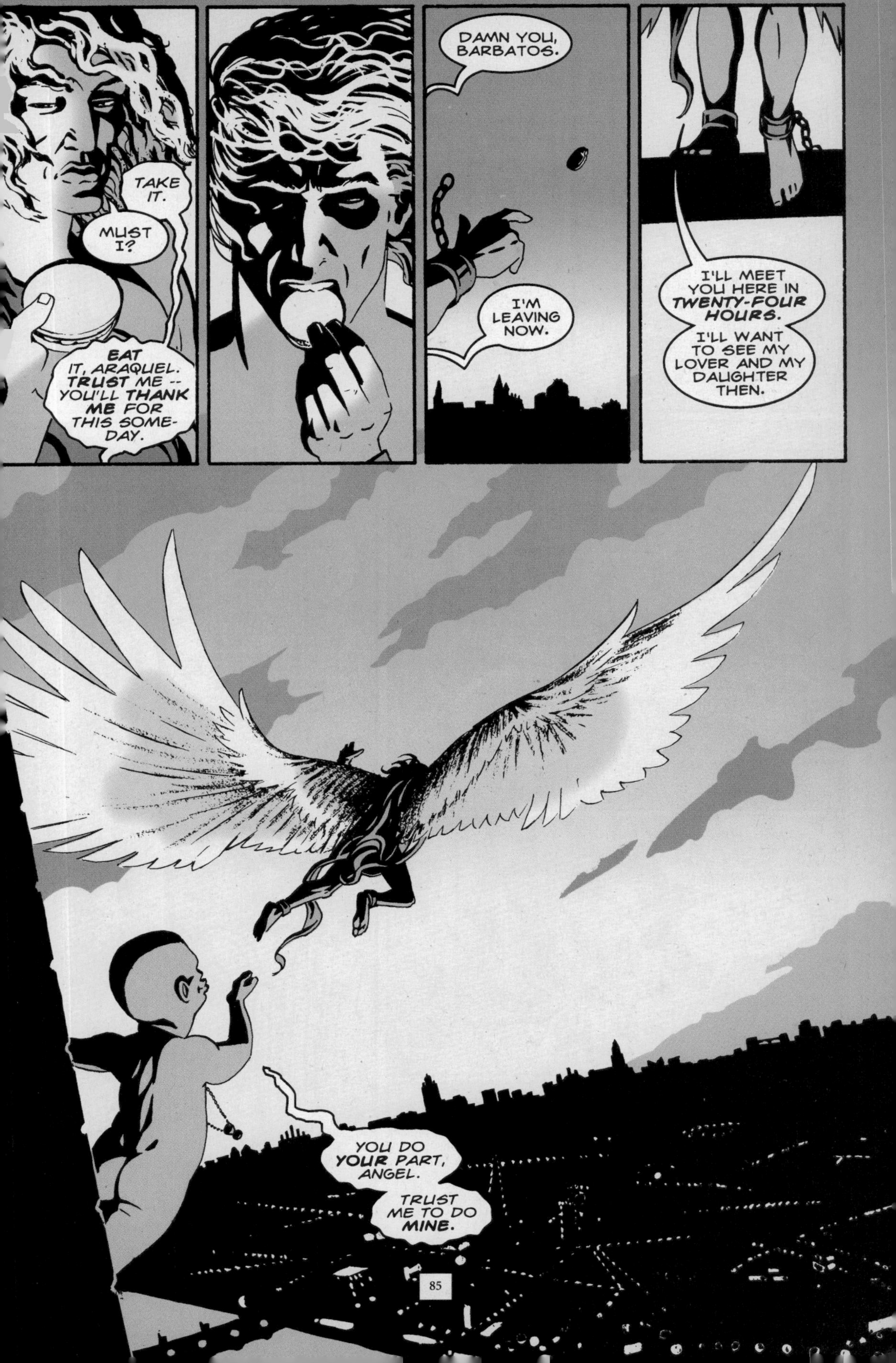
TAKE IT.
MUST I?
EAT IT, ARAQUEL. TRUST ME -- YOU'LL THANK ME FOR THIS SOME-DAY.
DAMN YOU, BARBATOS.
I'M LEAVING NOW.
I'LL MEET YOU HERE IN TWENTY-FOUR HOURS.
I'LL WANT TO SEE MY LOVER AND MY DAUGHTER THEN.
YOU DO YOUR PART, ANGEL.
TRUST ME TO DO MINE.

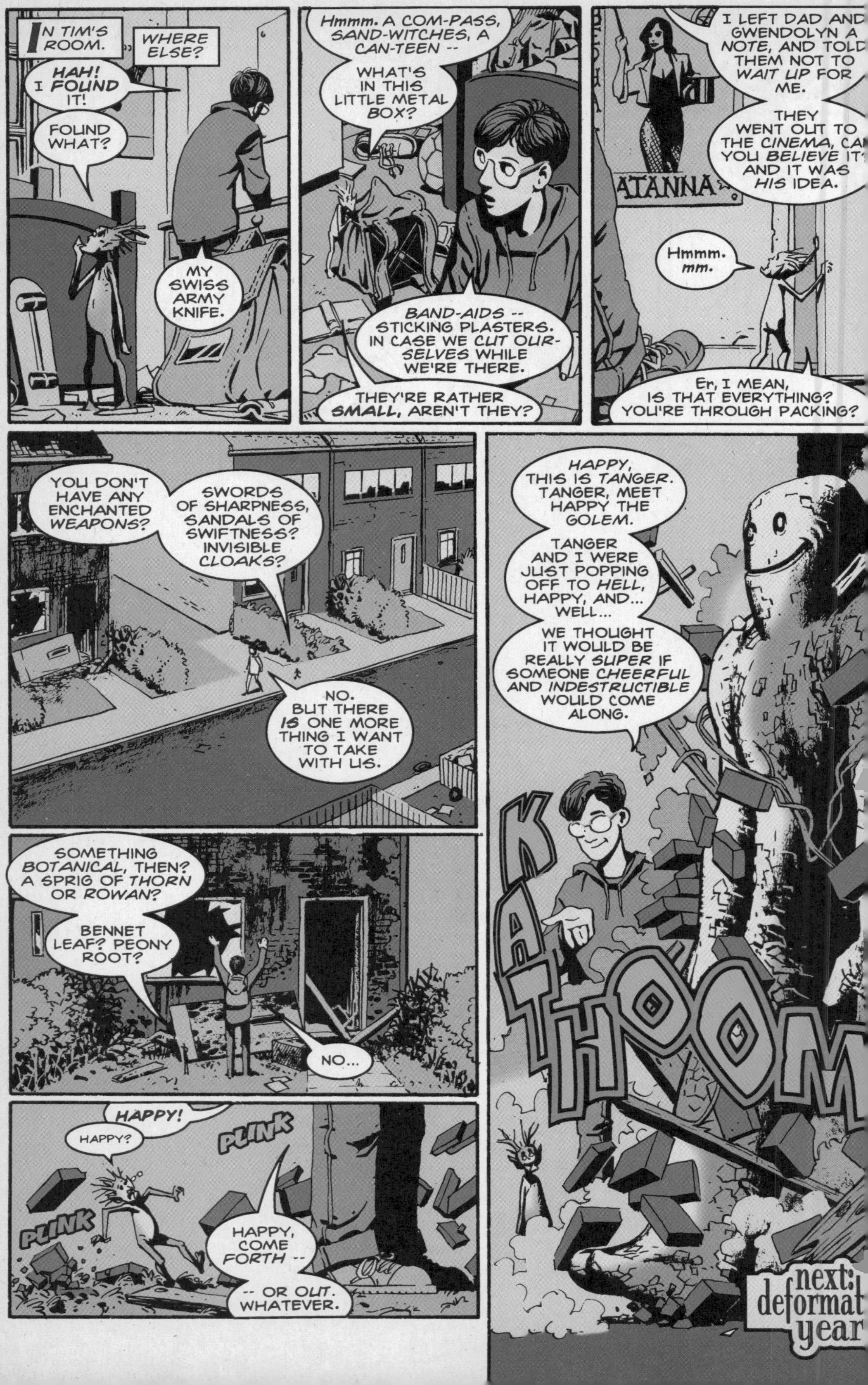
IN TIM'S ROOM.
WHERE ELSE?
HAH! I FOUND IT!
FOUND WHAT?
MY SWISS ARMY KNIFE.
Hmmm. A COM-PASS, SAND-WITCHES, A CAN-TEEN --
WHAT'S IN THIS LITTLE METAL BOX?
BAND-AIDS -- STICKING PLASTERS. IN CASE WE CUT OUR-SELVES WHILE WE'RE THERE.
THEY'RE RATHER SMALL, AREN'T THEY?
ATANNA
I LEFT DAD AND GWENDOLYN A NOTE, AND TOLD THEM NOT TO WAIT UP FOR ME.
THEY WENT OUT TO THE CINEMA, CA YOU BELIEVE IT AND IT WAS HIS IDEA.
Hmmm. mm.
Er, I MEAN, IS THAT EVERYTHING? YOU'RE THROUGH PACKING?
YOU DON'T HAVE ANY ENCHANTED WEAPONS?
SWORDS OF SHARPNESS, SANDALS OF SWIFTNESS? INVISIBLE CLOAKS?
NO. BUT THERE IS ONE MORE THING I WANT TO TAKE WITH US.
SOMETHING BOTANICAL, THEN? A SPRIG OF THORN OR ROWAN?
BENNET LEAF? PEONY ROOT?
NO...
HAPPY!
HAPPY?
PLINK
PLINK
HAPPY, COME FORTH --
-- OR OUT. WHATEVER.
HAPPY, THIS IS TANGER. TANGER, MEET HAPPY THE GOLEM.
TANGER AND I WERE JUST POPPING OFF TO HELL, HAPPY, AND... WELL...
WE THOUGHT IT WOULD BE REALLY SUPER IF SOMEONE CHEERFUL AND INDESTRUCTIBLE WOULD COME ALONG.
KATHOOM
next: deformat year

Deformative
Years

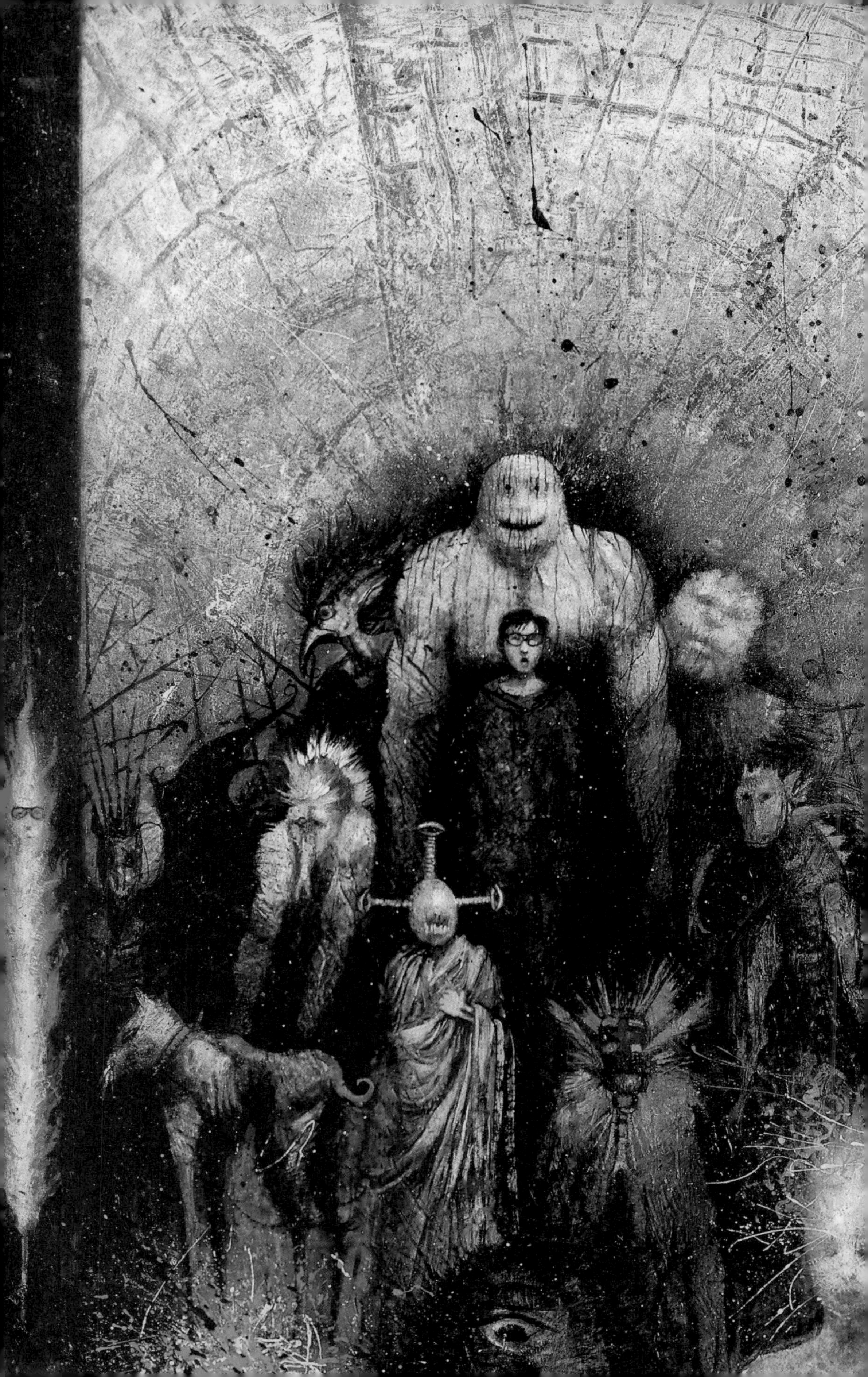

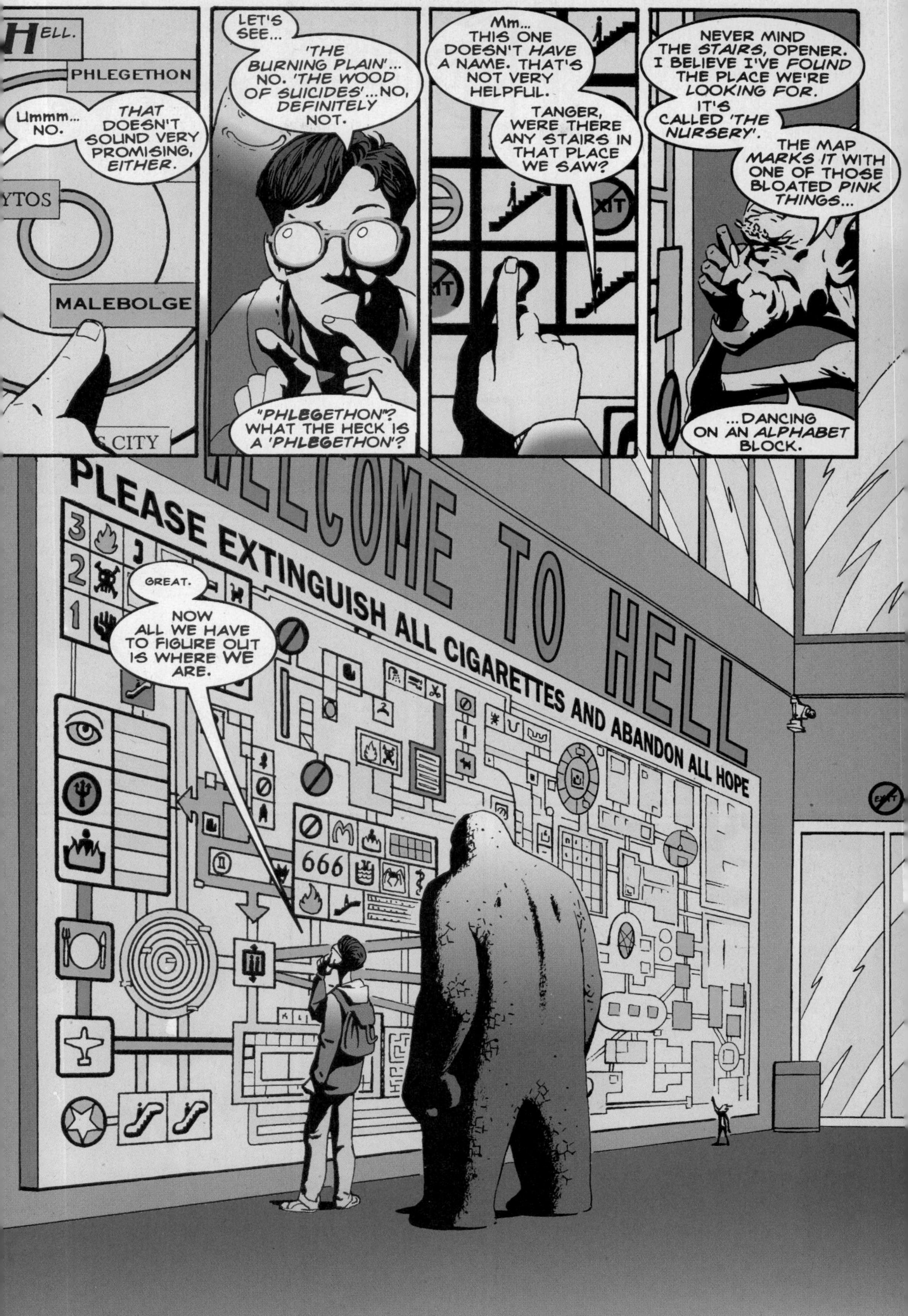
HELL.
PHLEGETHON
Ummm... NO.
THAT DOESN'T SOUND VERY PROMISING, EITHER.
MALEBOLGE
LET'S SEE...
'THE BURNING PLAIN'... NO. 'THE WOOD OF SUICIDES'...NO, DEFINITELY NOT.
"PHLEGETHON"? WHAT THE HECK IS A 'PHLEGETHON'?
Mm... THIS ONE DOESN'T HAVE A NAME. THAT'S NOT VERY HELPFUL.
TANGER, WERE THERE ANY STAIRS IN THAT PLACE WE SAW?
NEVER MIND THE STAIRS, OPENER. I BELIEVE I'VE FOUND THE PLACE WE'RE LOOKING FOR.
IT'S CALLED 'THE NURSERY'.
THE MAP MARKS IT WITH ONE OF THOSE BLOATED PINK THINGS...
...DANCING ON AN ALPHABET BLOCK.
PLEASE EXTINGUISH ALL CIGARETTES AND ABANDON ALL HOPE
GREAT.
NOW ALL WE HAVE TO FIGURE OUT IS WHERE WE ARE.
666

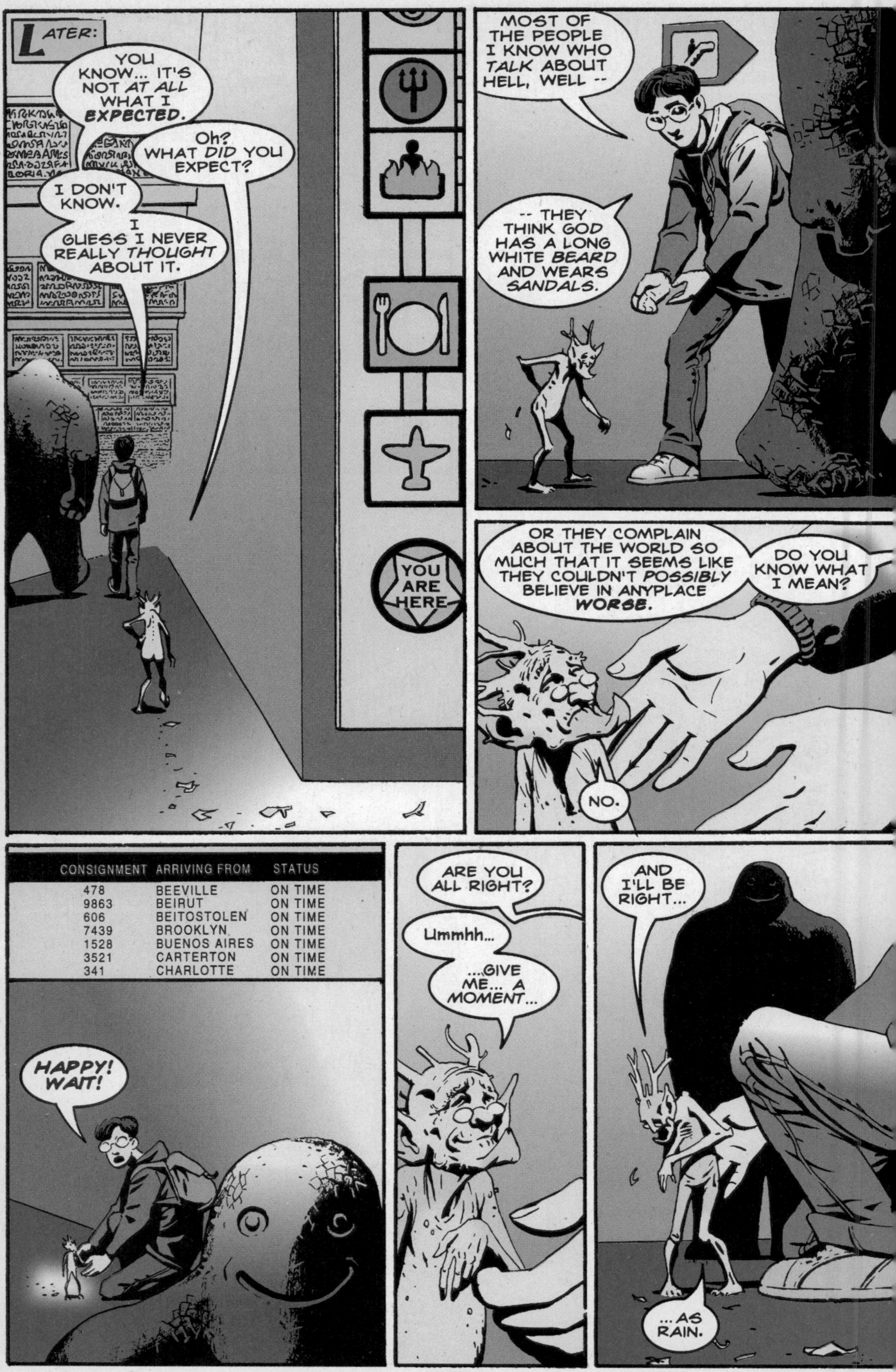
LATER:
YOU KNOW... IT'S NOT AT ALL WHAT I EXPECTED.
Oh? WHAT DID YOU EXPECT?
I DON'T KNOW.
I GUESS I NEVER REALLY THOUGHT ABOUT IT.
YOU ARE HERE
MOST OF THE PEOPLE I KNOW WHO TALK ABOUT HELL, WELL --
-- THEY THINK GOD HAS A LONG WHITE BEARD AND WEARS SANDALS.
OR THEY COMPLAIN ABOUT THE WORLD SO MUCH THAT IT SEEMS LIKE THEY COULDN'T POSSIBLY BELIEVE IN ANYPLACE WORSE.
DO YOU KNOW WHAT I MEAN?
NO.
CONSIGNMENT ARRIVING FROM STATUS
478 BEEVILLE ON TIME
9863 BEIRUT ON TIME
606 BEITOSTOLEN ON TIME
7439 BROOKLYN ON TIME
1528 BUENOS AIRES ON TIME
3521 CARTERTON ON TIME
341 CHARLOTTE ON TIME
HAPPY! WAIT!
ARE YOU ALL RIGHT?
Ummhh...
...GIVE ME... A MOMENT...
AND I'LL BE RIGHT...
...AS RAIN.

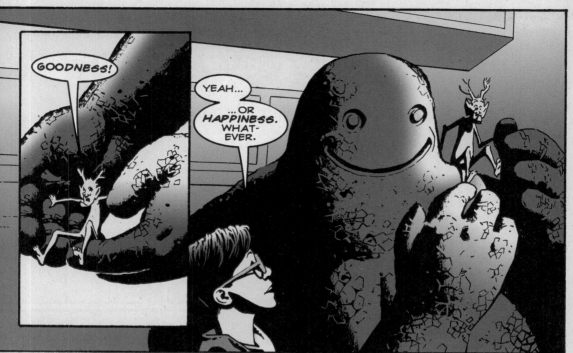

GOODNESS!

YEAH... ...OR *HAPPINESS*. WHAT-EVER.

OPENER..?

ARE *YOU* DOING THIS?

UMM... NO. I THINK *HAPPY* IS.

DO YOU *FEEL* BETTER? YOU *LOOK* BETTER.

I'VE NEVER FELT *BETTER.*

WOULD YOU, *ah*, HAPPEN TO KNOW WHAT *KIND* OF CLAY OUR FRIEND IS MADE OF?

Uh-uh. BUT IT SEEMS TO BE JUST THE *THING* FOR *TREE DEPRIVATION*, DOESN'T IT?

OR MAYBE IT'S *NOT* THE CLAY. MAYBE IT'S JUST *HIM.*

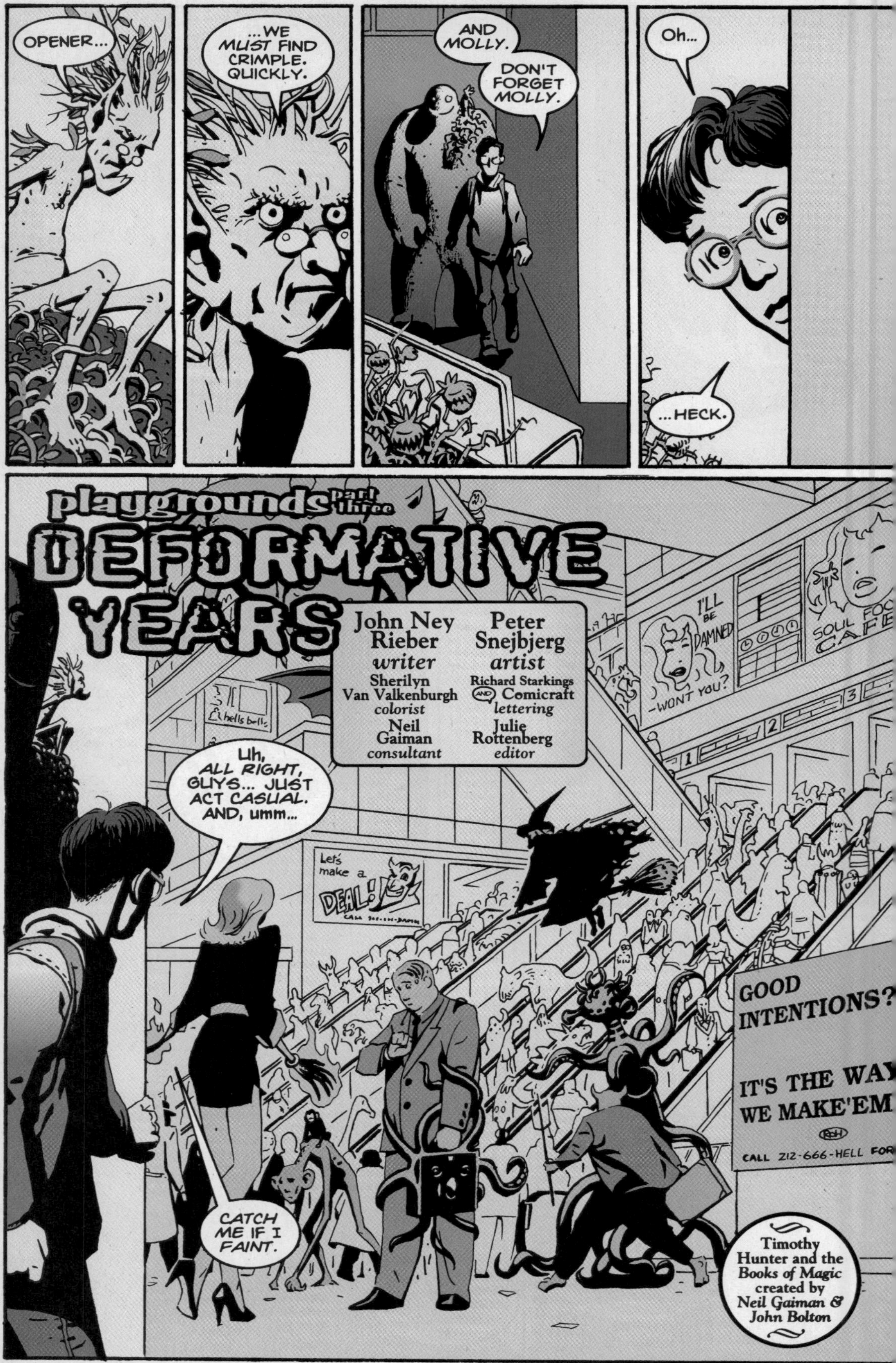
OPENER...
...WE MUST FIND CRIMPLE. QUICKLY.
AND MOLLY.
DON'T FORGET MOLLY.
Oh...
...HECK.
playgrounds part three
DEFORMATIVE YEARS
John Ney Rieber writer
Peter Snejbjerg artist
Sherilyn Van Valkenburgh colorist
Richard Starkings AND Comicraft lettering
Neil Gaiman consultant
Julie Rottenberg editor
I'LL BE DAMNED -WON'T YOU?
SOUL FOOD CAFE
hells bells
Uh, ALL RIGHT, GUYS... JUST ACT CASUAL. AND, umm...
Let's make a DEAL!
GOOD INTENTIONS?
IT'S THE WAY WE MAKE'EM
CALL 212-666-HELL FOR
CATCH ME IF I FAINT.
Timothy Hunter and the Books of Magic created by Neil Gaiman & John Bolton

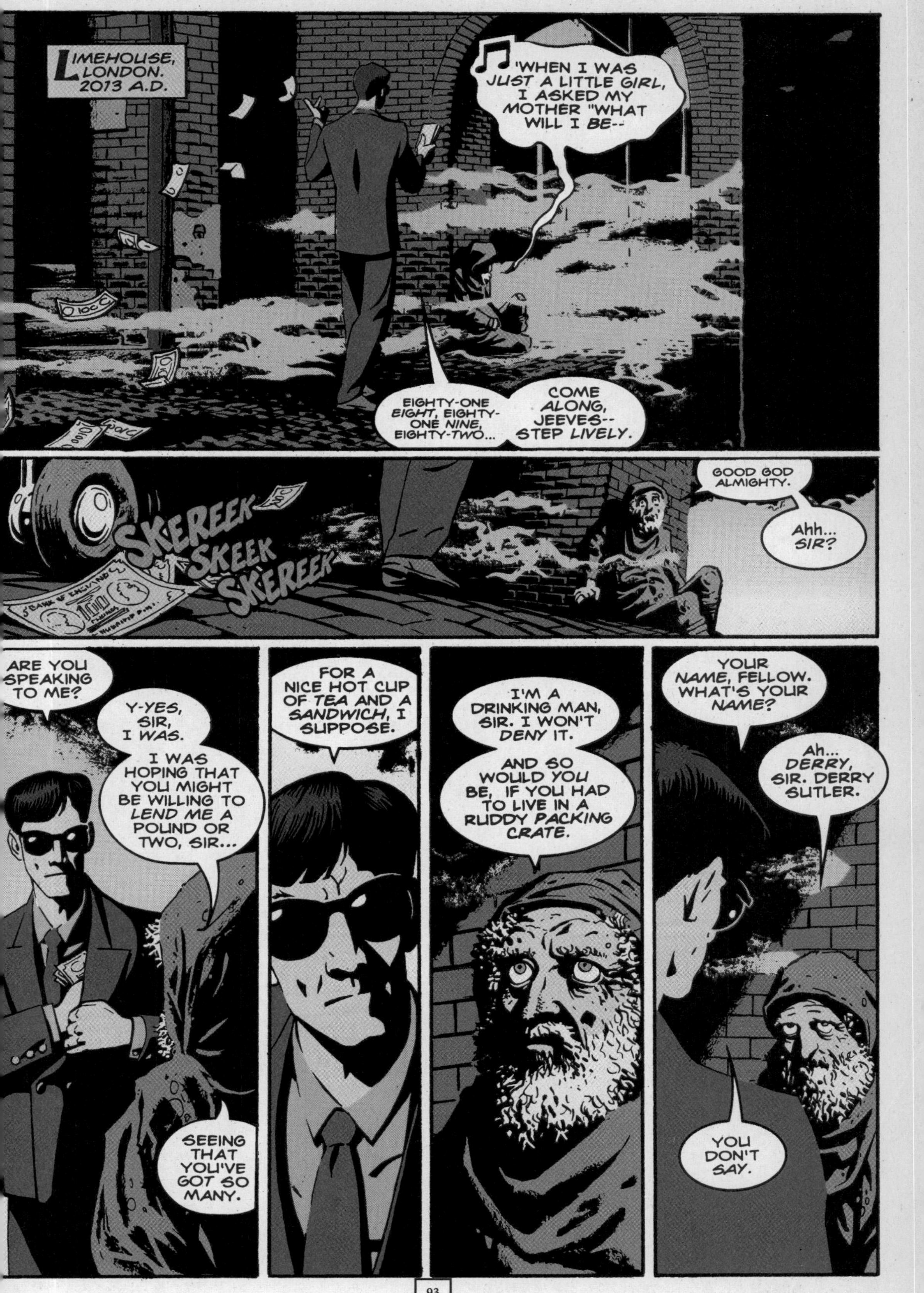
LIMEHOUSE, LONDON. 2013 A.D.
'WHEN I WAS JUST A LITTLE GIRL, I ASKED MY MOTHER "WHAT WILL I BE--
EIGHTY-ONE EIGHT, EIGHTY-ONE NINE, EIGHTY-TWO...
COME ALONG, JEEVES-- STEP LIVELY.
SKEREEK SKEEK SKEREEK
GOOD GOD ALMIGHTY.
Ahh... SIR?
ARE YOU SPEAKING TO ME?
Y-YES, SIR, I WAS.
I WAS HOPING THAT YOU MIGHT BE WILLING TO LEND ME A POUND OR TWO, SIR...
SEEING THAT YOU'VE GOT SO MANY.
FOR A NICE HOT CUP OF TEA AND A SANDWICH, I SUPPOSE.
I'M A DRINKING MAN, SIR. I WON'T DENY IT.
AND SO WOULD YOU BE, IF YOU HAD TO LIVE IN A RUDDY PACKING CRATE.
YOUR NAME, FELLOW. WHAT'S YOUR NAME?
Ah... DERRY, SIR. DERRY SUTLER.
YOU DON'T SAY.

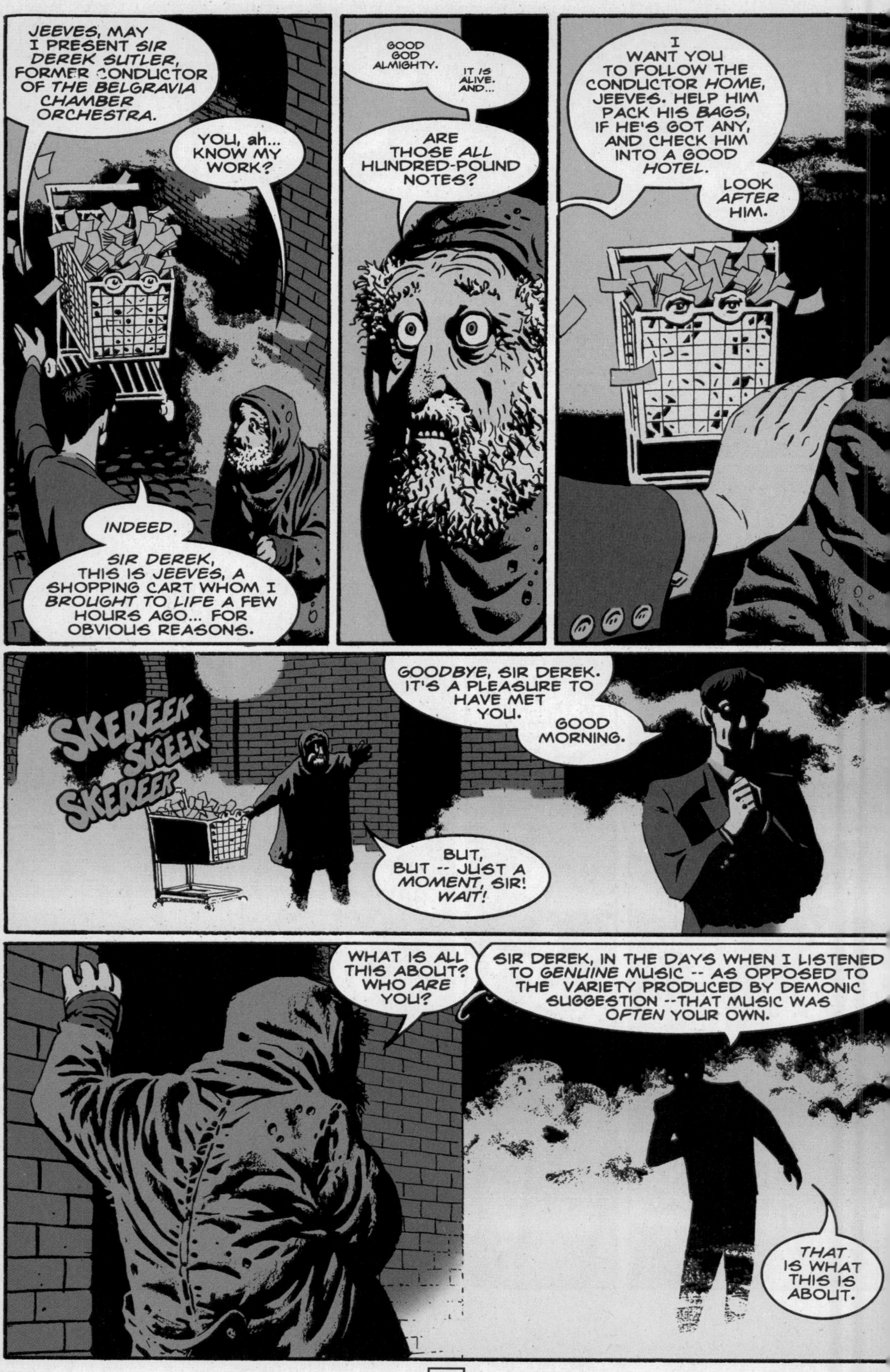
JEEVES, MAY I PRESENT SIR DEREK SUTLER, FORMER CONDUCTOR OF THE BELGRAVIA CHAMBER ORCHESTRA.
YOU, ah... KNOW MY WORK?
INDEED.
SIR DEREK, THIS IS JEEVES, A SHOPPING CART WHOM I BROUGHT TO LIFE A FEW HOURS AGO... FOR OBVIOUS REASONS.
GOOD GOD ALMIGHTY.
IT IS ALIVE. AND...
ARE THOSE ALL HUNDRED-POUND NOTES?
I WANT YOU TO FOLLOW THE CONDUCTOR HOME, JEEVES. HELP HIM PACK HIS BAGS, IF HE'S GOT ANY, AND CHECK HIM INTO A GOOD HOTEL.
LOOK AFTER HIM.
SKEREEK SKEEK SKEREEK
GOODBYE, SIR DEREK. IT'S A PLEASURE TO HAVE MET YOU.
GOOD MORNING.
BUT, BUT -- JUST A MOMENT, SIR! WAIT!
WHAT IS ALL THIS ABOUT? WHO ARE YOU?
SIR DEREK, IN THE DAYS WHEN I LISTENED TO GENUINE MUSIC -- AS OPPOSED TO THE VARIETY PRODUCED BY DEMONIC SUGGESTION --THAT MUSIC WAS OFTEN YOUR OWN.
THAT IS WHAT THIS IS ABOUT.

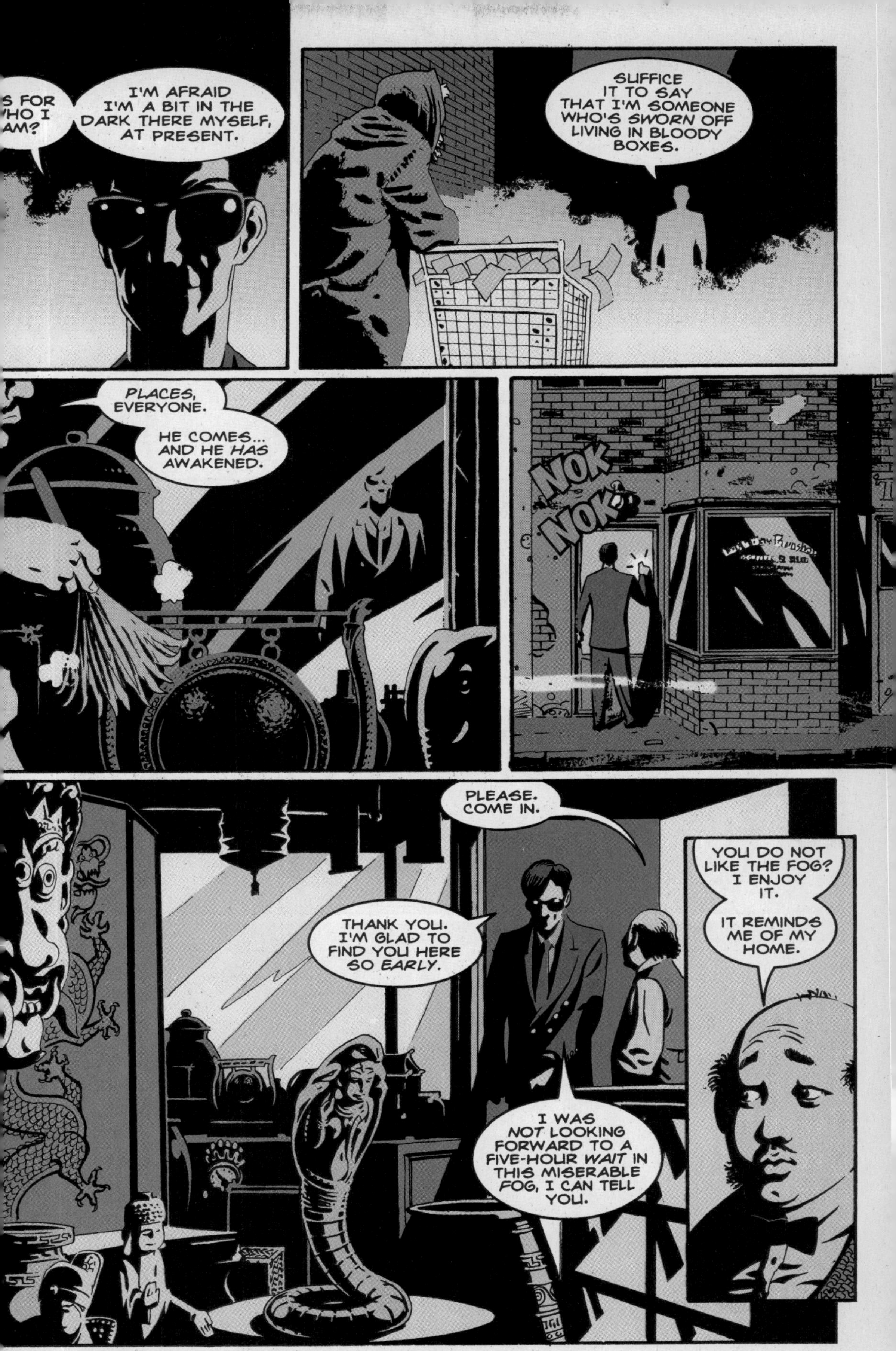
I'M AFRAID I'M A BIT IN THE DARK THERE MYSELF, AT PRESENT.
SUFFICE IT TO SAY THAT I'M SOMEONE WHO'S SWORN OFF LIVING IN BLOODY BOXES.
PLACES, EVERYONE.
HE COMES... AND HE HAS AWAKENED.
NOK
NOK
PLEASE. COME IN.
THANK YOU. I'M GLAD TO FIND YOU HERE SO EARLY.
I WAS NOT LOOKING FORWARD TO A FIVE-HOUR WAIT IN THIS MISERABLE FOG, I CAN TELL YOU.
YOU DO NOT LIKE THE FOG? I ENJOY IT.
IT REMINDS ME OF MY HOME.

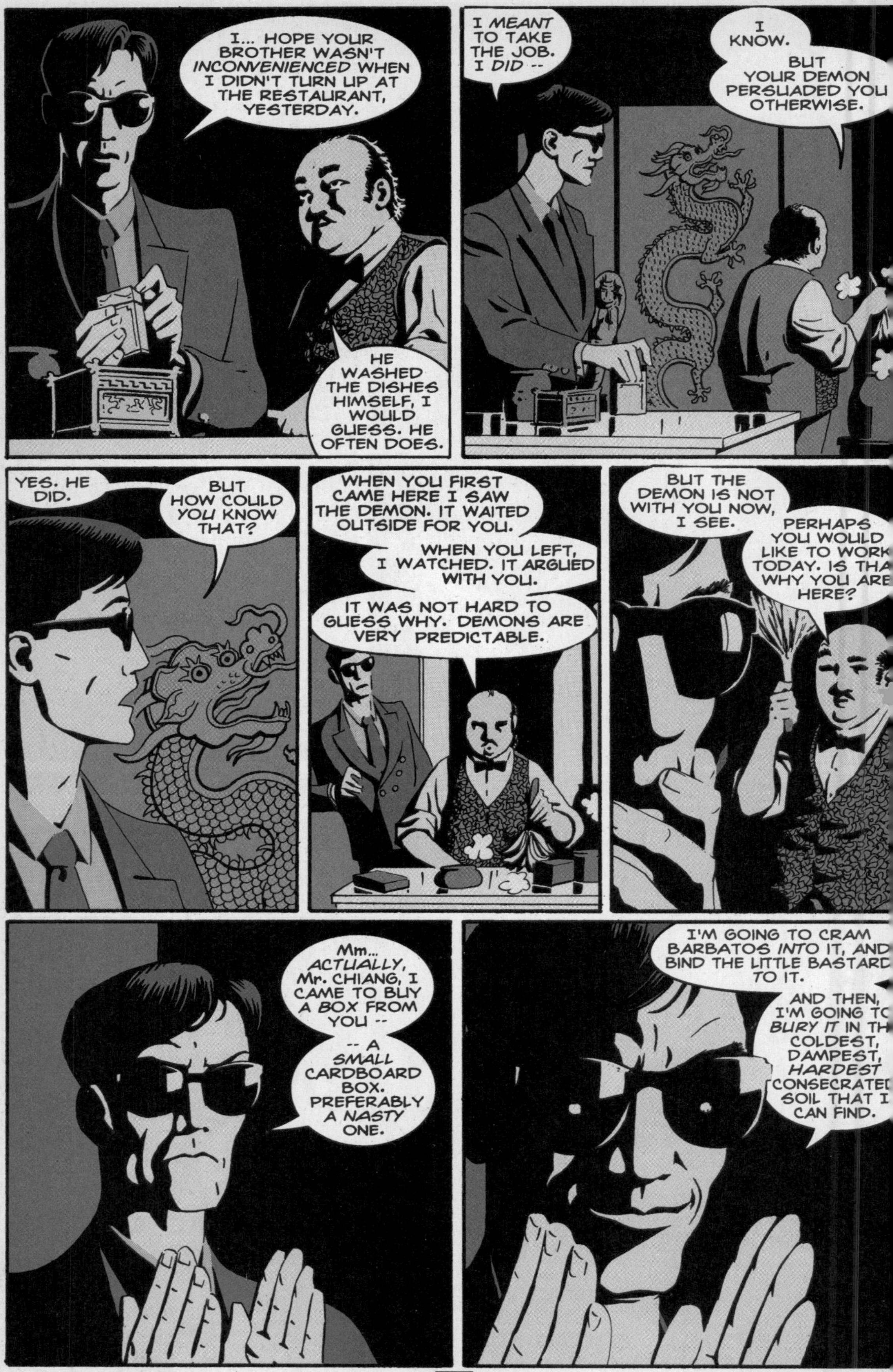

I... HOPE YOUR BROTHER WASN'T *INCONVENIENCED* WHEN I DIDN'T TURN UP AT THE RESTAURANT, YESTERDAY.
HE WASHED THE DISHES HIMSELF, I WOULD GUESS. HE OFTEN DOES.
I *MEANT* TO TAKE THE JOB. I *DID* --
I KNOW.
BUT YOUR DEMON PERSUADED YOU OTHERWISE.
YES. HE DID.
BUT HOW COULD *YOU* KNOW THAT?
WHEN YOU FIRST CAME HERE I SAW THE DEMON. IT WAITED OUTSIDE FOR YOU.
WHEN YOU LEFT, I WATCHED. IT ARGUED WITH YOU.
IT WAS NOT HARD TO GUESS WHY. DEMONS ARE VERY PREDICTABLE.
BUT THE DEMON IS NOT WITH YOU NOW, I SEE.
PERHAPS YOU WOULD LIKE TO WORK TODAY. IS THA WHY YOU ARE HERE?
Mm... *ACTUALLY,* Mr. CHIANG, I CAME TO BUY A *BOX* FROM YOU --
-- A *SMALL* CARDBOARD BOX. PREFERABLY A *NASTY* ONE.
I'M GOING TO CRAM BARBATOS *INTO* IT, AND BIND THE LITTLE BASTARD TO IT.
AND THEN, I'M GOING TO *BURY IT* IN TH COLDEST, DAMPEST, *HARDEST* CONSECRATED SOIL THAT I CAN FIND.

ARE YOU SURE IT WOULD NOT DO YOU MORE GOOD TO GET A JOB?

CONSIDER THIS, SIR TIMOTHY:

IF YOU SUCCEED IN MASTERING THE DEMON, WHAT WILL YOU DO THEN?

YOU ARE EXTREMELY POWERFUL, YES, BUT YOU ARE ALSO QUITE HOPELESSLY NEUROTIC.

APART FROM YOUR DESIRE TO LIVE IN OPULENCE, AND TO BE WORSHIPPED BY A WOMAN WHO LOATHES YOU, YOU HAVE NO AIM IN LIFE.

YOU DO NOT KNOW HOW TO INTERACT WITH OTHERS --

IN SHORT, YOU ARE NOT BY NATURE *QUALIFIED* TO ENJOY LIFE AS A HUMAN BEING.

HOWEVER --

I BELIEVE THAT YOU WOULD MAKE AN *EXCELLENT* DRAGON.

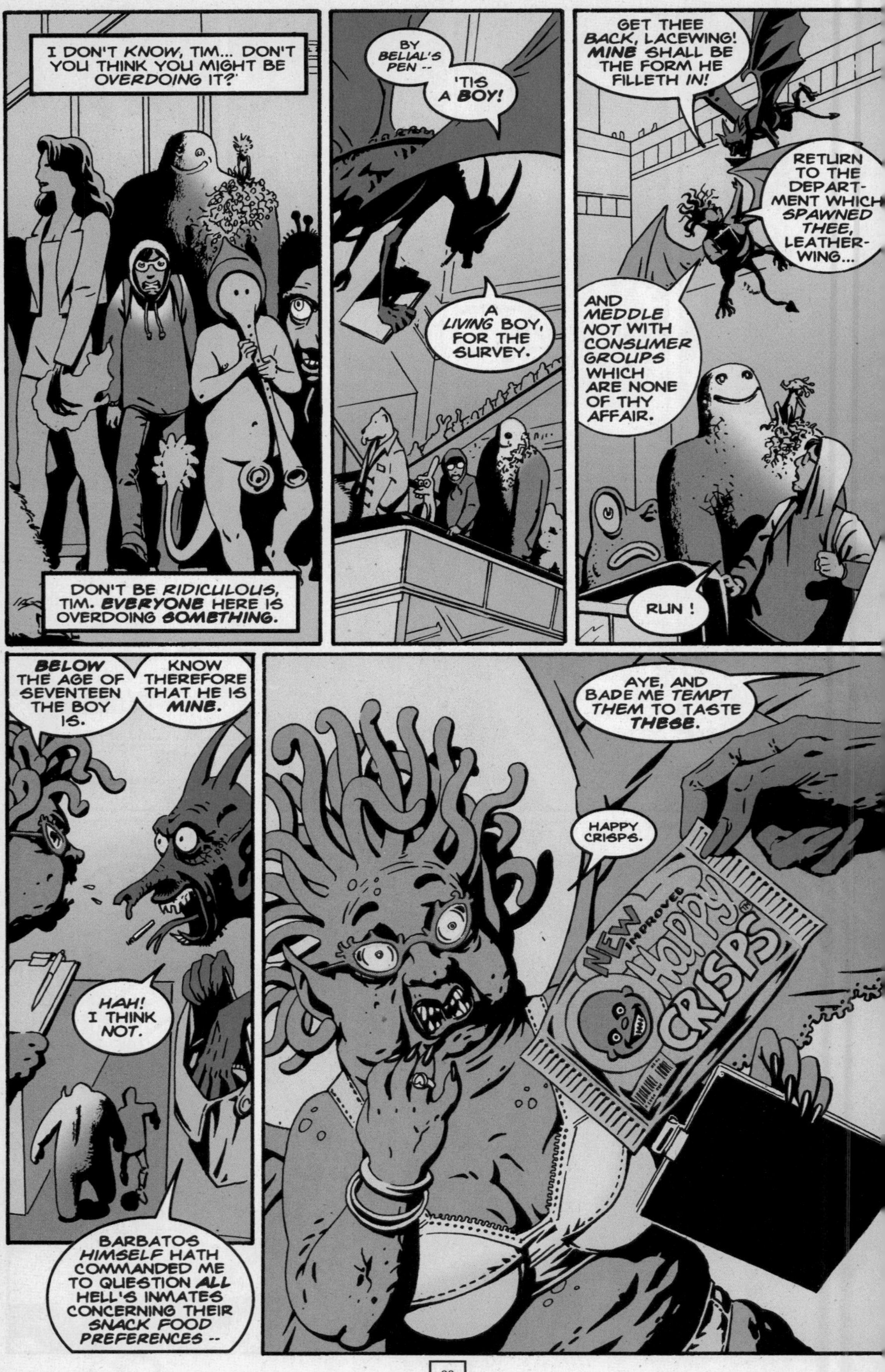

I DON'T KNOW, TIM... DON'T YOU THINK YOU MIGHT BE OVERDOING IT?'
DON'T BE RIDICULOUS, TIM. EVERYONE HERE IS OVERDOING SOMETHING.
BY BELIAL'S PEN --
'TIS A BOY!
A LIVING BOY, FOR THE SURVEY.
GET THEE BACK, LACEWING! MINE SHALL BE THE FORM HE FILLETH IN!
RETURN TO THE DEPART-MENT WHICH SPAWNED THEE, LEATHER-WING...
AND MEDDLE NOT WITH CONSUMER GROUPS WHICH ARE NONE OF THY AFFAIR.
RUN !
BELOW THE AGE OF SEVENTEEN THE BOY IS.
KNOW THEREFORE THAT HE IS MINE.
HAH! I THINK NOT.
BARBATOS HIMSELF HATH COMMANDED ME TO QUESTION ALL HELL'S INMATES CONCERNING THEIR SNACK FOOD PREFERENCES --
AYE, AND BADE ME TEMPT THEM TO TASTE THESE.
HAPPY CRISPS.
NEW IMPROVED Happy CRISPS

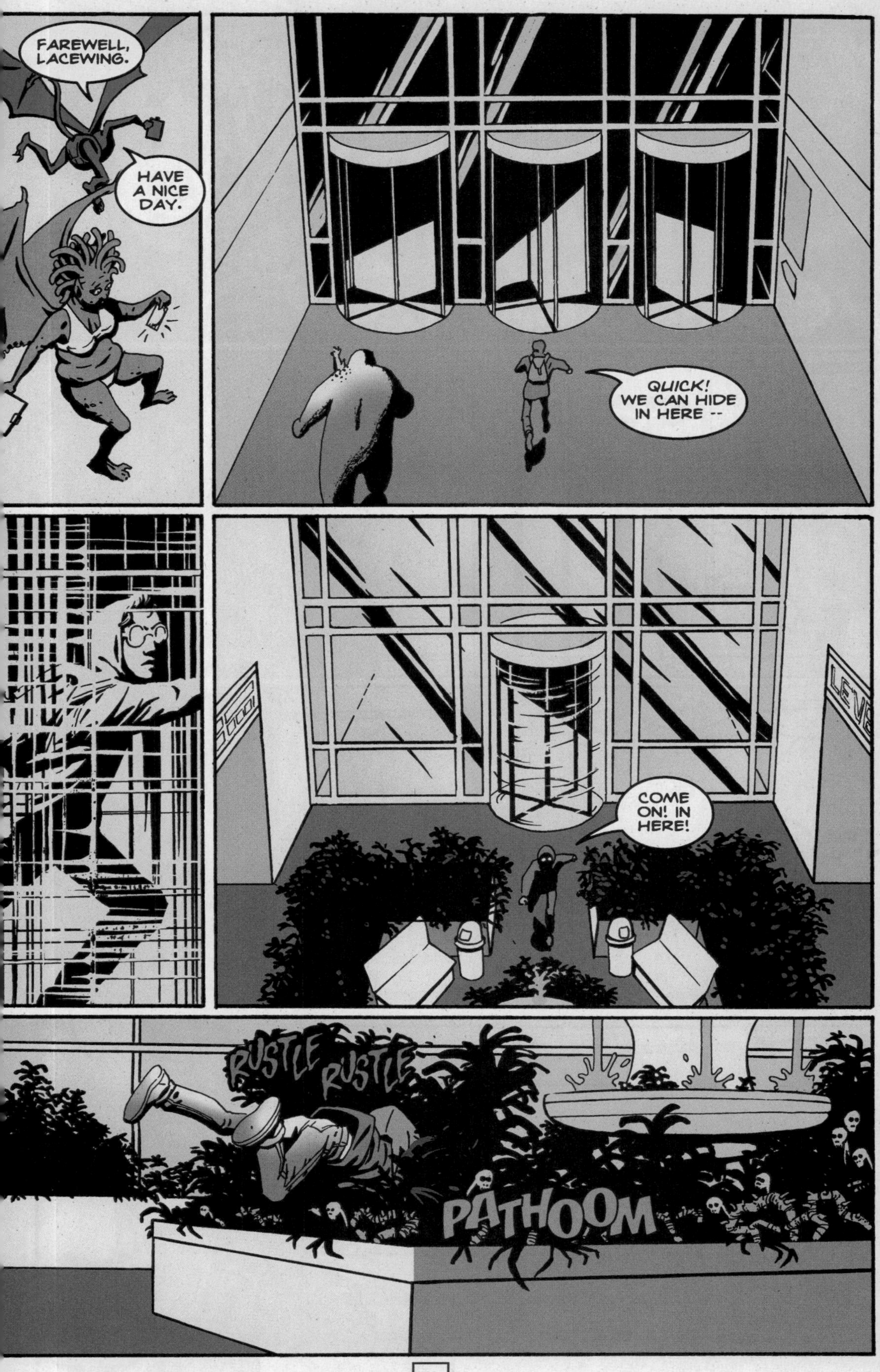
FAREWELL, LACEWING.
HAVE A NICE DAY.
QUICK! WE CAN HIDE IN HERE --
COME ON! IN HERE!
RUSTLE RUSTLE
PATHOOM

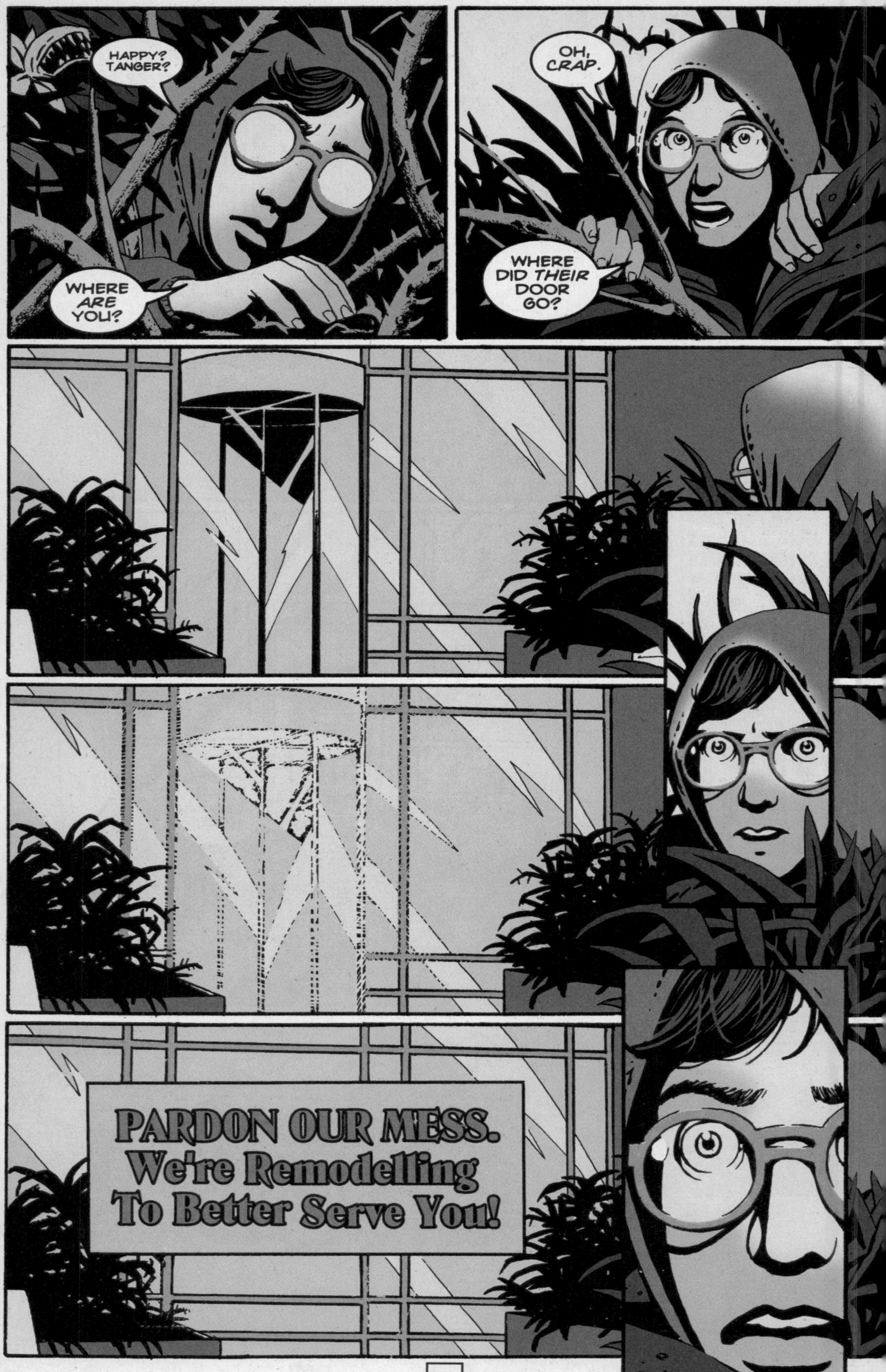

HAPPY? TANGER?
WHERE ARE YOU!?
OH, CRAP.
WHERE DID THEIR DOOR GO?
PARDON OUR MESS.
We're Remodelling
To Better Serve You!

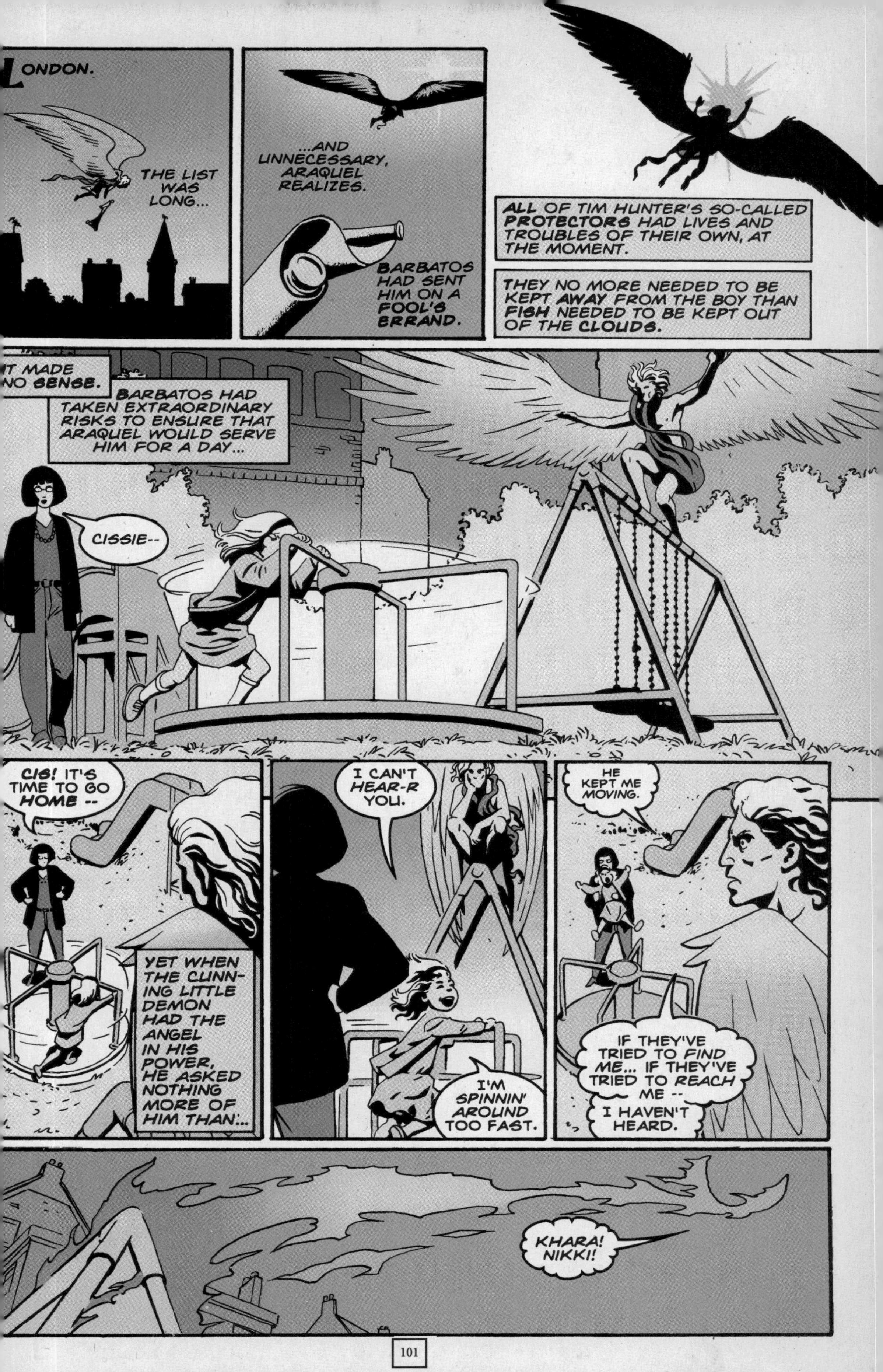
LONDON.
THE LIST WAS LONG...
...AND UNNECESSARY, ARAQUEL REALIZES.
BARBATOS HAD SENT HIM ON A FOOL'S ERRAND.
ALL OF TIM HUNTER'S SO-CALLED PROTECTORS HAD LIVES AND TROUBLES OF THEIR OWN, AT THE MOMENT.
THEY NO MORE NEEDED TO BE KEPT AWAY FROM THE BOY THAN FISH NEEDED TO BE KEPT OUT OF THE CLOUDS.
IT MADE NO SENSE.
BARBATOS HAD TAKEN EXTRAORDINARY RISKS TO ENSURE THAT ARAQUEL WOULD SERVE HIM FOR A DAY...
CISSIE--
CIS! IT'S TIME TO GO HOME --
YET WHEN THE CUNNING LITTLE DEMON HAD THE ANGEL IN HIS POWER, HE ASKED NOTHING MORE OF HIM THAN...
I CAN'T HEAR-R YOU.
I'M SPINNIN' AROUND TOO FAST.
HE KEPT ME MOVING.
IF THEY'VE TRIED TO FIND ME... IF THEY'VE TRIED TO REACH ME --
I HAVEN'T HEARD.
KHARA! NIKKI!

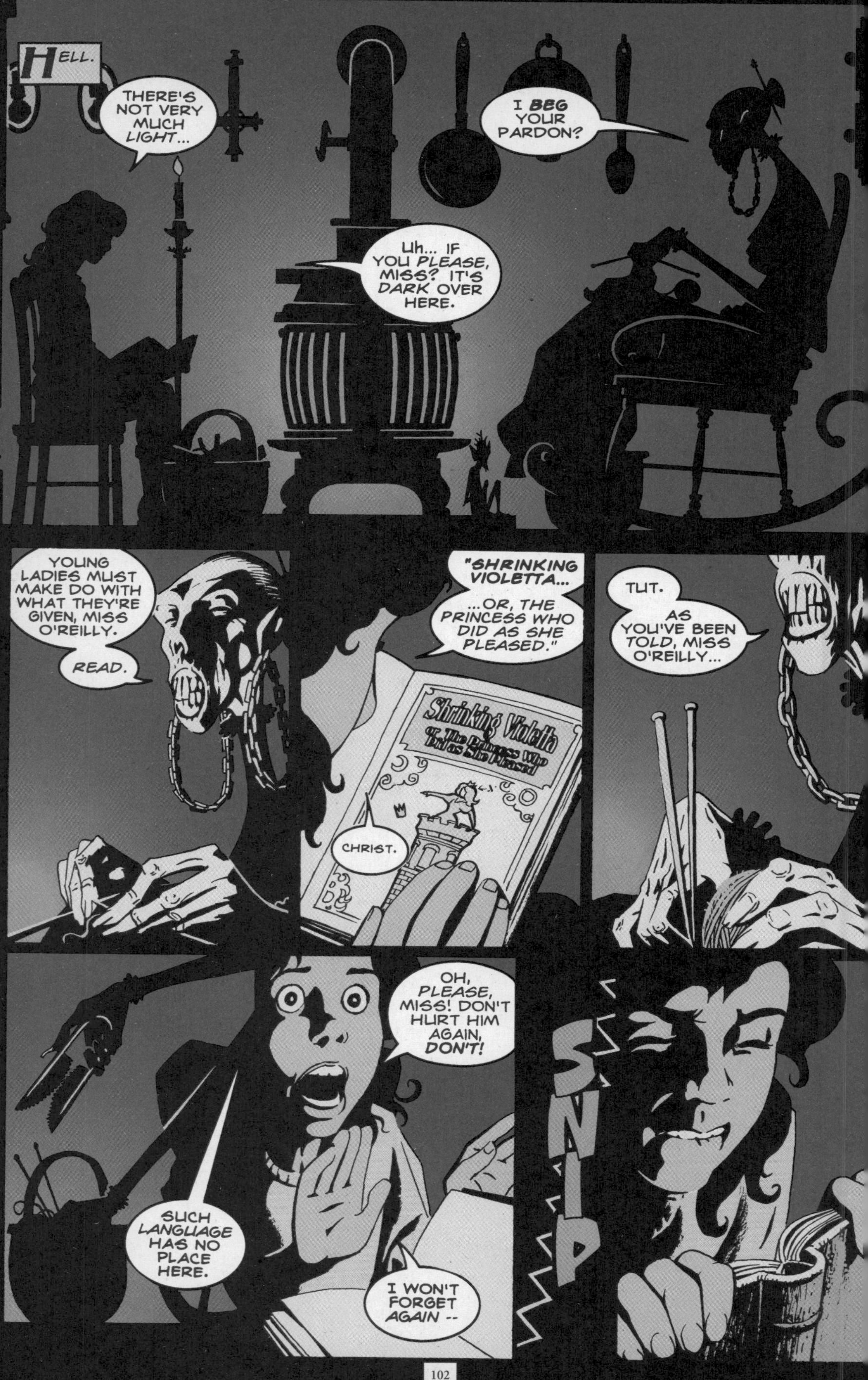
HELL.
THERE'S NOT VERY MUCH LIGHT...
I BEG YOUR PARDON?
Uh... IF YOU PLEASE, MISS? IT'S DARK OVER HERE.
YOUNG LADIES MUST MAKE DO WITH WHAT THEY'RE GIVEN, MISS O'REILLY.
READ.
"SHRINKING VIOLETTA...
...OR, THE PRINCESS WHO DID AS SHE PLEASED."
Shrinking Violetta
or The Princess Who Did as She Pleased
CHRIST.
TUT.
AS YOU'VE BEEN TOLD, MISS O'REILLY...
SUCH LANGUAGE HAS NO PLACE HERE.
OH, PLEASE, MISS! DON'T HURT HIM AGAIN, DON'T!
I WON'T FORGET AGAIN --
SNIP

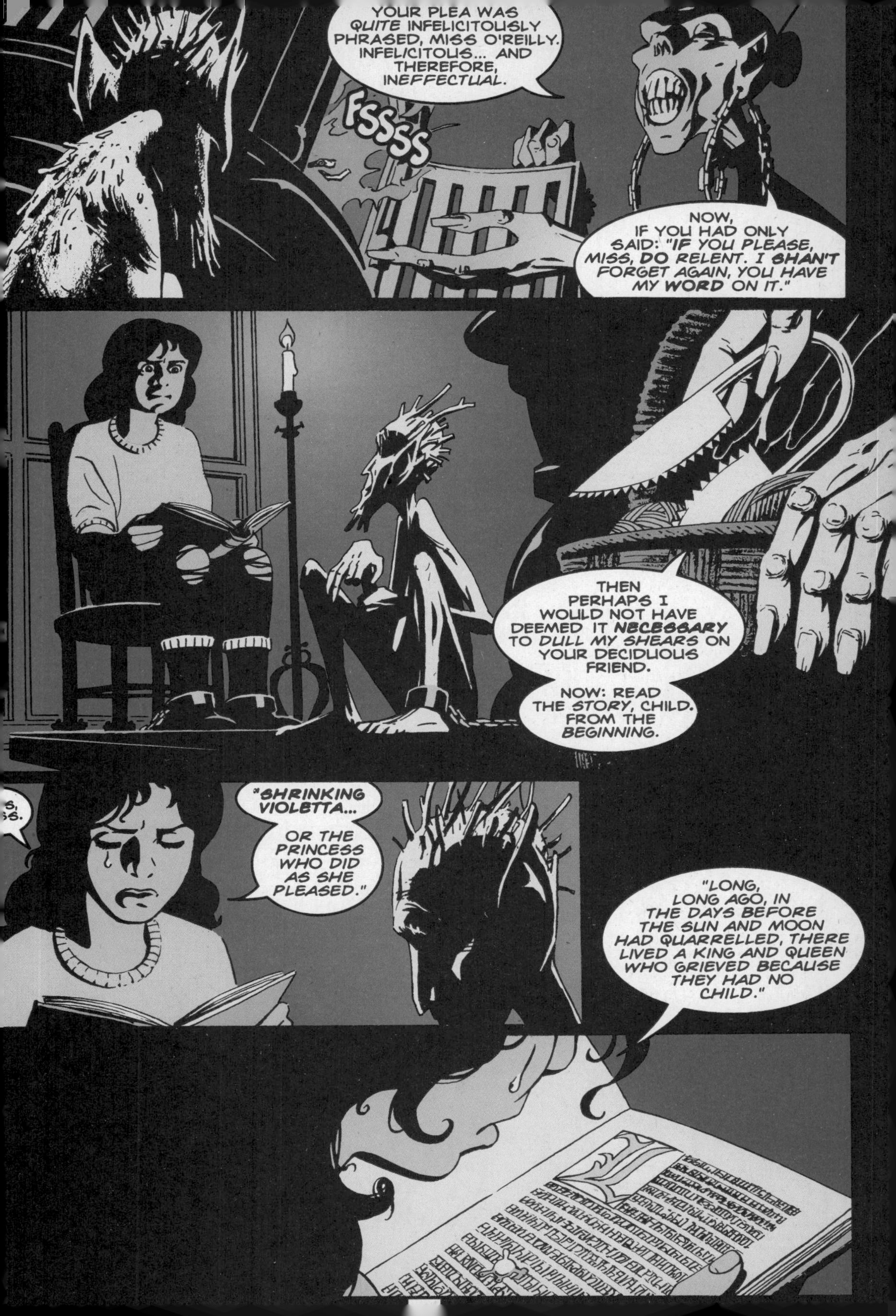
YOUR PLEA WAS *QUITE* INFELICITOUSLY PHRASED, MISS O'REILLY. INFELICITOUS... AND THEREFORE, *INEFFECTUAL*.
FSSSS
NOW, IF YOU HAD ONLY SAID: "*IF YOU PLEASE,* MISS, **DO** RELENT. I **SHAN'T** FORGET AGAIN, YOU HAVE MY **WORD** ON IT."
THEN PERHAPS I WOULD NOT HAVE DEEMED IT ***NECESSARY*** TO *DULL MY SHEARS* ON YOUR DECIDUOUS FRIEND.
NOW: READ THE *STORY*, CHILD. FROM THE *BEGINNING*.
"SHRINKING VIOLETTA...
OR THE PRINCESS WHO DID AS SHE PLEASED."
"LONG, LONG AGO, IN THE DAYS BEFORE THE SUN AND MOON HAD QUARRELLED, THERE LIVED A KING AND QUEEN WHO GRIEVED BECAUSE THEY HAD NO CHILD."

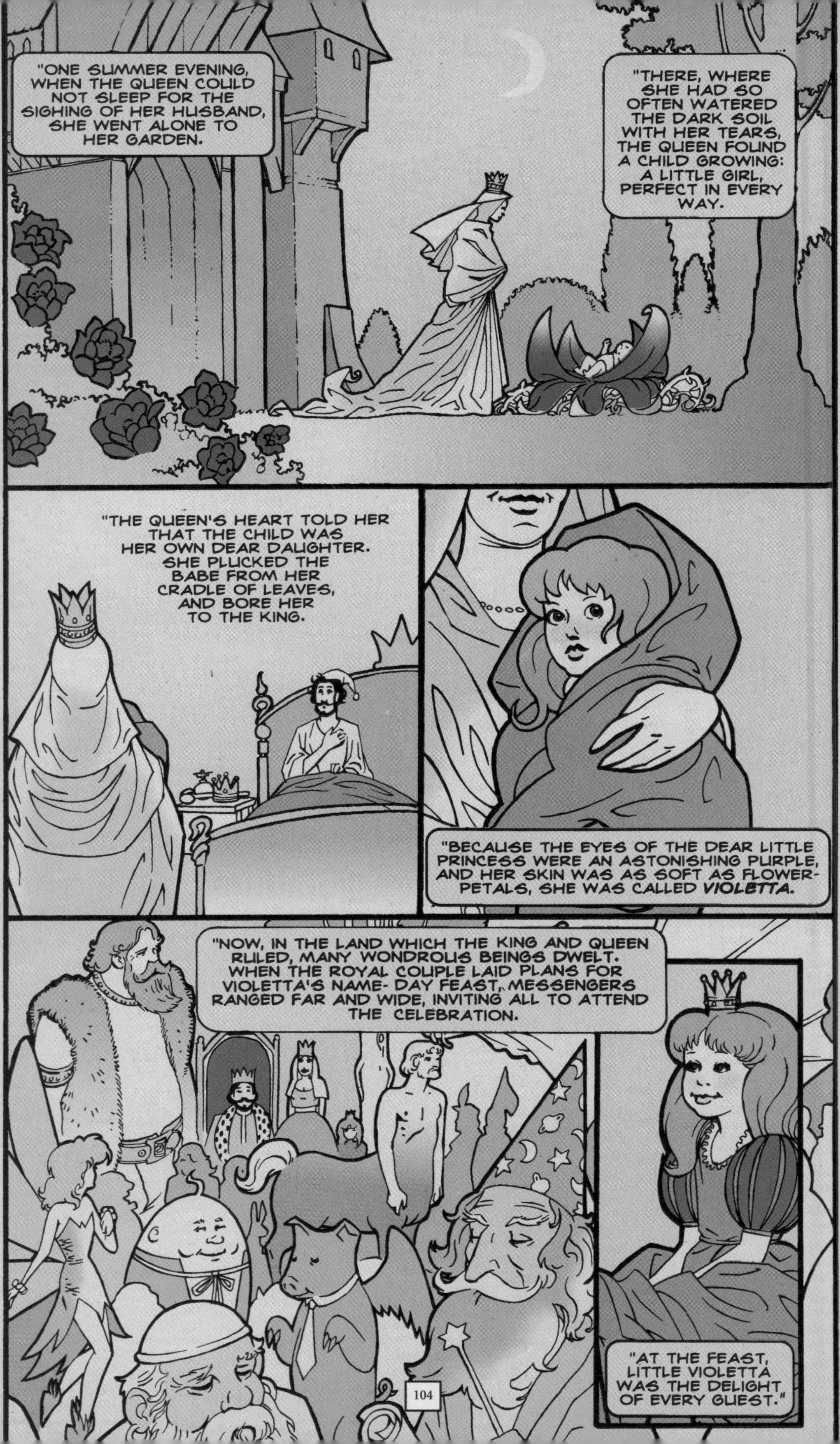
"ONE SUMMER EVENING, WHEN THE QUEEN COULD NOT SLEEP FOR THE SIGHING OF HER HUSBAND, SHE WENT ALONE TO HER GARDEN.
"THERE, WHERE SHE HAD SO OFTEN WATERED THE DARK SOIL WITH HER TEARS, THE QUEEN FOUND A CHILD GROWING: A LITTLE GIRL, PERFECT IN EVERY WAY.
"THE QUEEN'S HEART TOLD HER THAT THE CHILD WAS HER OWN DEAR DAUGHTER. SHE PLUCKED THE BABE FROM HER CRADLE OF LEAVES, AND BORE HER TO THE KING.
"BECAUSE THE EYES OF THE DEAR LITTLE PRINCESS WERE AN ASTONISHING PURPLE, AND HER SKIN WAS AS SOFT AS FLOWER-PETALS, SHE WAS CALLED *VIOLETTA.*
"NOW, IN THE LAND WHICH THE KING AND QUEEN RULED, MANY WONDROUS BEINGS DWELT. WHEN THE ROYAL COUPLE LAID PLANS FOR VIOLETTA'S NAME- DAY FEAST, MESSENGERS RANGED FAR AND WIDE, INVITING ALL TO ATTEND THE CELEBRATION.
"AT THE FEAST, LITTLE VIOLETTA WAS THE DELIGHT OF EVERY GUEST."

"'WHAT A DEAR LITTLE THING SHE IS!" MURMURED THE HOOVED MAN, WHEN VIOLETTA SAT QUIETLY IN HIS LAP, UNDAUNTED BY HIS BURNING EYES.

"HE GAVE HER A RUBY AS A NAMING-GIFT, AND TOLD HER MOTHER: 'LET THE PRINCESS CARRY THIS STONE IN HER MOUTH WHEN SHE GROWS OLDER, AND MANY A PRINCE WILL WISH TO WED HER.'

"'WHAT A DEAR LITTLE THING SHE IS!" SIGHED THE SCALED MAN, WHEN VIOLETTA DID NOT RECOIL FROM THE TOUCH OF HIS COLD HAND.

"HE GAVE HER AN EMERALD AS A NAMING-GIFT, AND TOLD HER MOTHER: 'LET THE PRINCESS WEAR THIS STONE ON HER BREAST WHEN SHE GROWS OLDER, AND MANY A KING WILL WISH TO WED HER.'

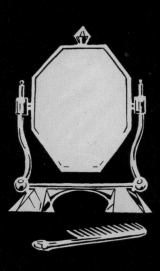

"'WHAT A DEAR LITTLE THING SHE IS!" WHISPERED THE CRYSTAL MAN, WHEN VIOLETTA REACHED UP TO TOUCH HIS FACE, SEEING HER OWN FACE REFLECTED THERE.

"HE GAVE HER A CRYSTAL COMB AND MIRROR AS NAMING-GIFTS, AND TOLD HER MOTHER: 'LET HER SIT BEFORE THE MIRROR AND COMB HER HAIR EACH MORNING, AND WHEN SHE COMES OF AGE, HER BEAUTY WILL BRING EMPERORS AND HEROES TO THEIR KNEES.'"

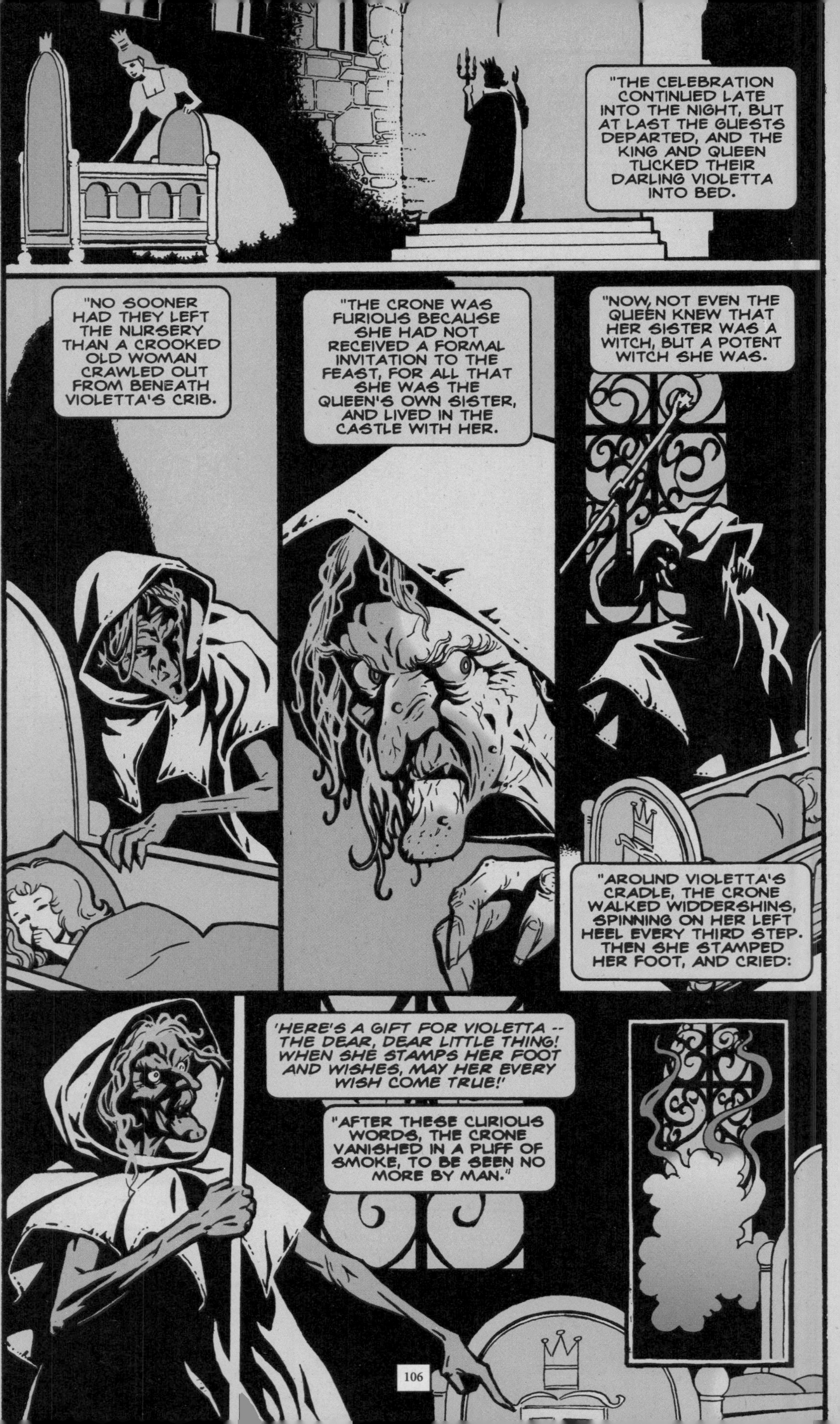
"THE CELEBRATION CONTINUED LATE INTO THE NIGHT, BUT AT LAST THE GUESTS DEPARTED, AND THE KING AND QUEEN TUCKED THEIR DARLING VIOLETTA INTO BED.
"NO SOONER HAD THEY LEFT THE NURSERY THAN A CROOKED OLD WOMAN CRAWLED OUT FROM BENEATH VIOLETTA'S CRIB.
"THE CRONE WAS FURIOUS BECAUSE SHE HAD NOT RECEIVED A FORMAL INVITATION TO THE FEAST, FOR ALL THAT SHE WAS THE QUEEN'S OWN SISTER, AND LIVED IN THE CASTLE WITH HER.
"NOW, NOT EVEN THE QUEEN KNEW THAT HER SISTER WAS A WITCH, BUT A POTENT WITCH SHE WAS.
"AROUND VIOLETTA'S CRADLE, THE CRONE WALKED WIDDERSHINS, SPINNING ON HER LEFT HEEL EVERY THIRD STEP. THEN SHE STAMPED HER FOOT, AND CRIED:
'HERE'S A GIFT FOR VIOLETTA -- THE DEAR, DEAR LITTLE THING! WHEN SHE STAMPS HER FOOT AND WISHES, MAY HER EVERY WISH COME TRUE!'
"AFTER THESE CURIOUS WORDS, THE CRONE VANISHED IN A PUFF OF SMOKE, TO BE SEEN NO MORE BY MAN."

"YEARS PASSED, AND VIOLETTA GREW TO BE A WOMAN.

"EVERY MORNING, SHE SAT FOR HOURS BEFORE THE MIRROR, COMBING HER HAIR. OFTEN SHE SMILED AT THE LOVELY SELF SHE SAW THERE.

"THEN SHE WOULD TAKE THE RUBY INTO HER MOUTH, AND PLACE THE EMERALD ON HER BREAST, AND LEAVE HER ROOM TO WALK THE CASTLE.

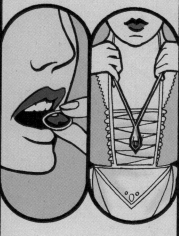

"THE RUBY WAS HEAVY ON HER TONGUE, BUT IT WAS A COMFORTING WEIGHT. WHEN UNKIND THOUGHTS CAME TO HER MIND, THE STONE GREW HEAVIER, PREVENTING HER FROM SPEAKING WORDS SHE WOULD REGRET.

"THE EMERALD CHILLED HER HEART, BUT SHE DID NOT MIND THE COLD. WHEN ONE OF HER SUITORS LOOKED AT HER OR TOUCHED HER IN A MANNER SHE FOUND DISTURBING, THE COLD CALMED HER.

"IT MADE HER FEEL AS THOUGH SHE WERE QUITE ANOTHER PERSON: A PRINCESS IN TRUTH, IMPERVIOUS TO ANGER, SHAME, AND UNSETTLING CURIOSITY.

"IS IT TO BE WONDERED AT THAT A MAIDEN BLESSED WITH SUCH BEAUTY, CHARM, AND DIGNITY SHOULD BE THE OBJECT OF A THOUSAND TENDER HOPES?

"AS VIOLETTA'S BENEFACTORS HAD FORETOLD ON HER NAMING DAY, COUNTLESS KINGS AND PRINCES PETITIONED FOR HER HAND.

"EMPERORS AND HEROES KNELT AT HER FEET, PLEADING, HOPING THAT THE DEAR LITTLE THING WOULD CONSENT TO BE THEIR OWN."

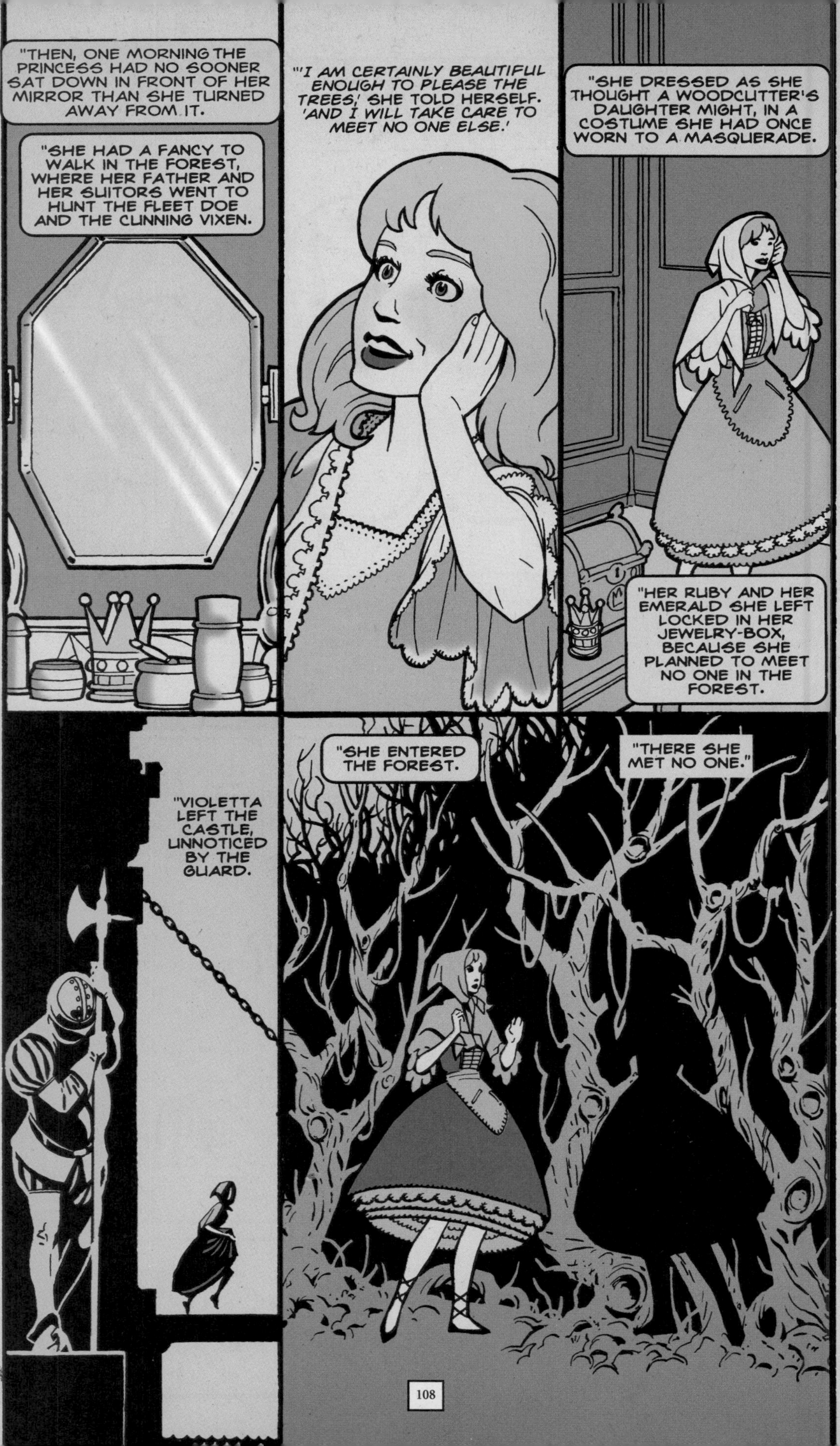
"THEN, ONE MORNING THE PRINCESS HAD NO SOONER SAT DOWN IN FRONT OF HER MIRROR THAN SHE TURNED AWAY FROM IT.
"SHE HAD A FANCY TO WALK IN THE FOREST, WHERE HER FATHER AND HER SUITORS WENT TO HUNT THE FLEET DOE AND THE CUNNING VIXEN.
"'I AM CERTAINLY BEAUTIFUL ENOUGH TO PLEASE THE TREES,' SHE TOLD HERSELF. 'AND I WILL TAKE CARE TO MEET NO ONE ELSE.'
"SHE DRESSED AS SHE THOUGHT A WOODCUTTER'S DAUGHTER MIGHT, IN A COSTUME SHE HAD ONCE WORN TO A MASQUERADE.
"HER RUBY AND HER EMERALD SHE LEFT LOCKED IN HER JEWELRY-BOX, BECAUSE SHE PLANNED TO MEET NO ONE IN THE FOREST.
"VIOLETTA LEFT THE CASTLE, UNNOTICED BY THE GUARD.
"SHE ENTERED THE FOREST.
"THERE SHE MET NO ONE."

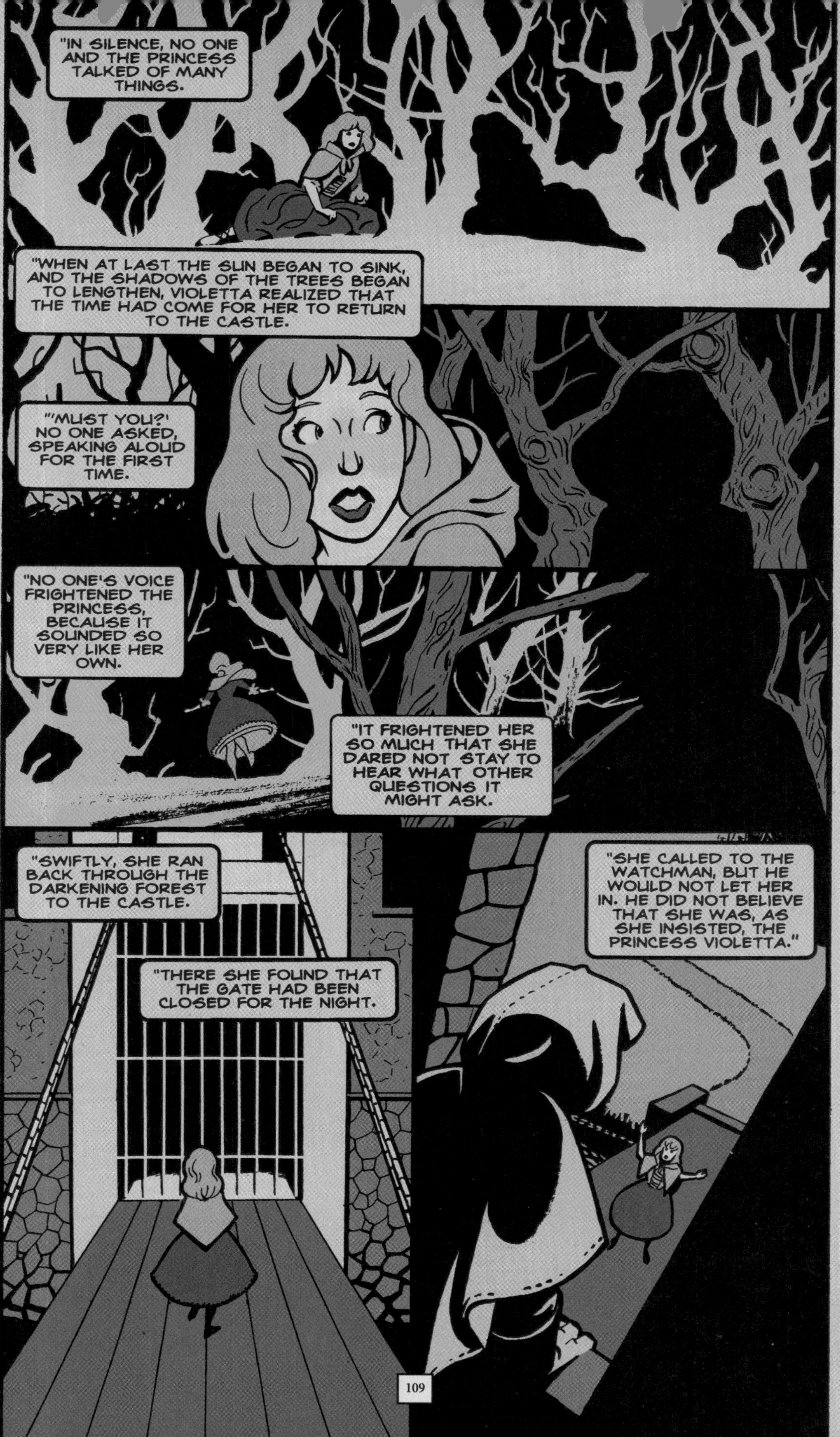
"IN SILENCE, NO ONE AND THE PRINCESS TALKED OF MANY THINGS.
"WHEN AT LAST THE SUN BEGAN TO SINK, AND THE SHADOWS OF THE TREES BEGAN TO LENGTHEN, VIOLETTA REALIZED THAT THE TIME HAD COME FOR HER TO RETURN TO THE CASTLE.
"'MUST YOU?' NO ONE ASKED, SPEAKING ALOUD FOR THE FIRST TIME.
"NO ONE'S VOICE FRIGHTENED THE PRINCESS, BECAUSE IT SOUNDED SO VERY LIKE HER OWN.
"IT FRIGHTENED HER SO MUCH THAT SHE DARED NOT STAY TO HEAR WHAT OTHER QUESTIONS IT MIGHT ASK.
"SWIFTLY, SHE RAN BACK THROUGH THE DARKENING FOREST TO THE CASTLE.
"THERE SHE FOUND THAT THE GATE HAD BEEN CLOSED FOR THE NIGHT.
"SHE CALLED TO THE WATCHMAN, BUT HE WOULD NOT LET HER IN. HE DID NOT BELIEVE THAT SHE WAS, AS SHE INSISTED, THE PRINCESS VIOLETTA."

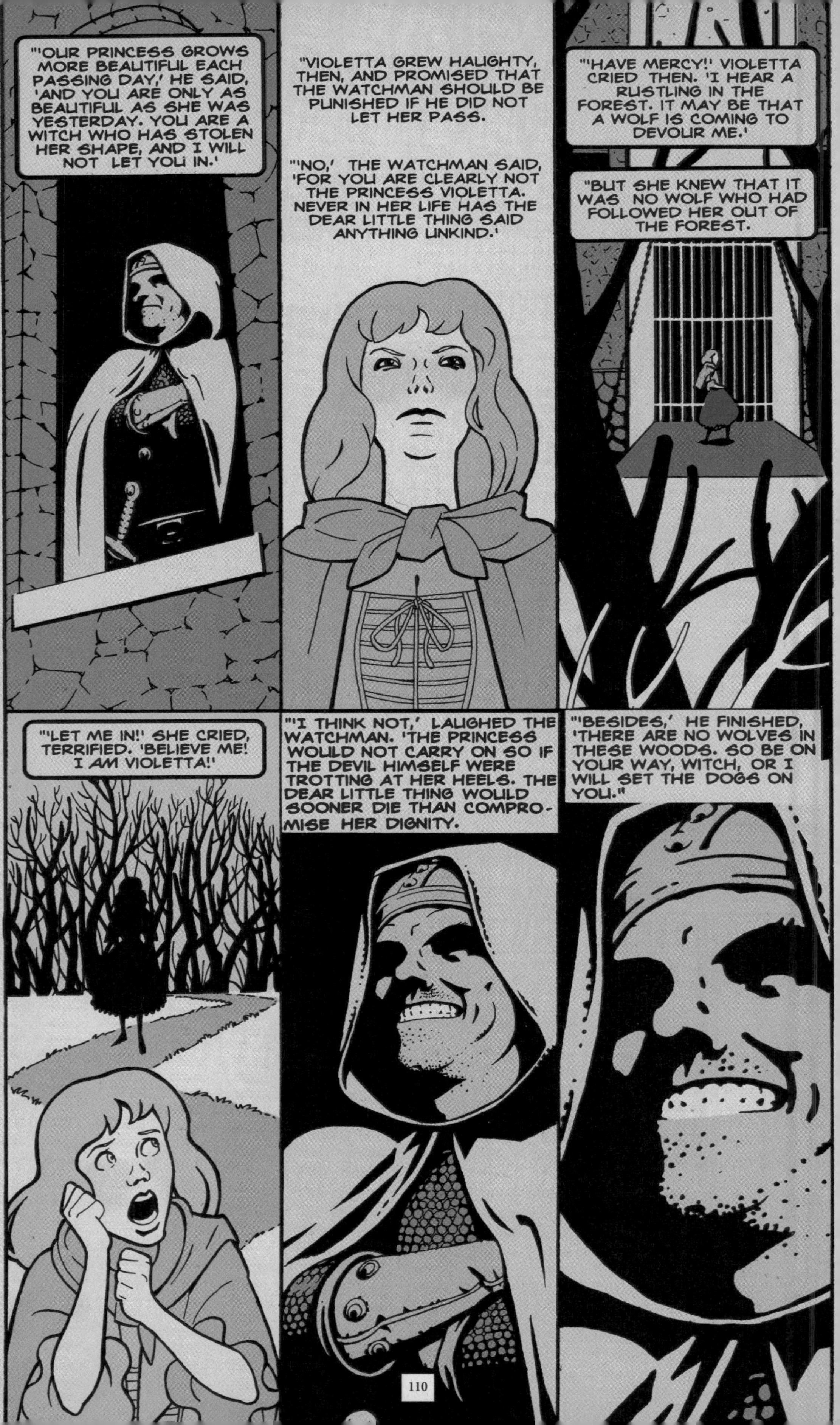
"'OUR PRINCESS GROWS MORE BEAUTIFUL EACH PASSING DAY,' HE SAID, 'AND YOU ARE ONLY AS BEAUTIFUL AS SHE WAS YESTERDAY. YOU ARE A WITCH WHO HAS STOLEN HER SHAPE, AND I WILL NOT LET YOU IN.'
"VIOLETTA GREW HAUGHTY, THEN, AND PROMISED THAT THE WATCHMAN SHOULD BE PUNISHED IF HE DID NOT LET HER PASS.
"'NO,' THE WATCHMAN SAID, 'FOR YOU ARE CLEARLY NOT THE PRINCESS VIOLETTA. NEVER IN HER LIFE HAS THE DEAR LITTLE THING SAID ANYTHING UNKIND.'
"'HAVE MERCY!' VIOLETTA CRIED THEN. 'I HEAR A RUSTLING IN THE FOREST. IT MAY BE THAT A WOLF IS COMING TO DEVOUR ME.'
"BUT SHE KNEW THAT IT WAS NO WOLF WHO HAD FOLLOWED HER OUT OF THE FOREST.
"'LET ME IN!' SHE CRIED, TERRIFIED. 'BELIEVE ME! I *AM* VIOLETTA!'
"'I THINK NOT,' LAUGHED THE WATCHMAN. 'THE PRINCESS WOULD NOT CARRY ON SO IF THE DEVIL HIMSELF WERE TROTTING AT HER HEELS. THE DEAR LITTLE THING WOULD SOONER DIE THAN COMPROMISE HER DIGNITY.
"'BESIDES,' HE FINISHED, 'THERE ARE NO WOLVES IN THESE WOODS. SO BE ON YOUR WAY, WITCH, OR I WILL SET THE DOGS ON YOU."

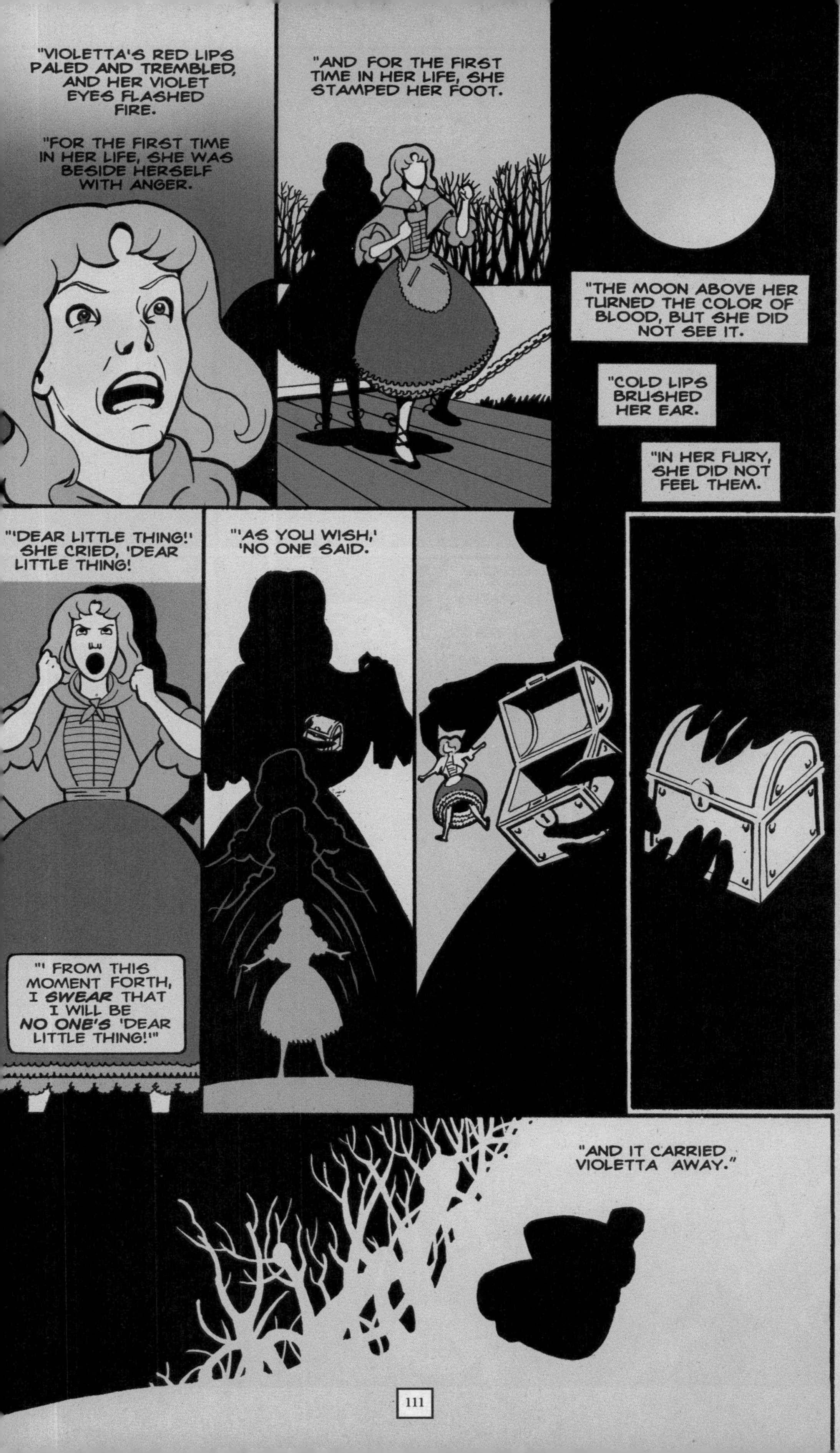
"VIOLETTA'S RED LIPS PALED AND TREMBLED, AND HER VIOLET EYES FLASHED FIRE.
"FOR THE FIRST TIME IN HER LIFE, SHE WAS BESIDE HERSELF WITH ANGER.
"AND FOR THE FIRST TIME IN HER LIFE, SHE STAMPED HER FOOT.
"THE MOON ABOVE HER TURNED THE COLOR OF BLOOD, BUT SHE DID NOT SEE IT.
"COLD LIPS BRUSHED HER EAR.
"IN HER FURY, SHE DID NOT FEEL THEM.
"'DEAR LITTLE THING!' SHE CRIED, 'DEAR LITTLE THING!
"' FROM THIS MOMENT FORTH, I *SWEAR* THAT I WILL BE *NO ONE'S* 'DEAR LITTLE THING!'"
"'AS YOU WISH,' 'NO ONE SAID.
"AND IT CARRIED VIOLETTA AWAY."

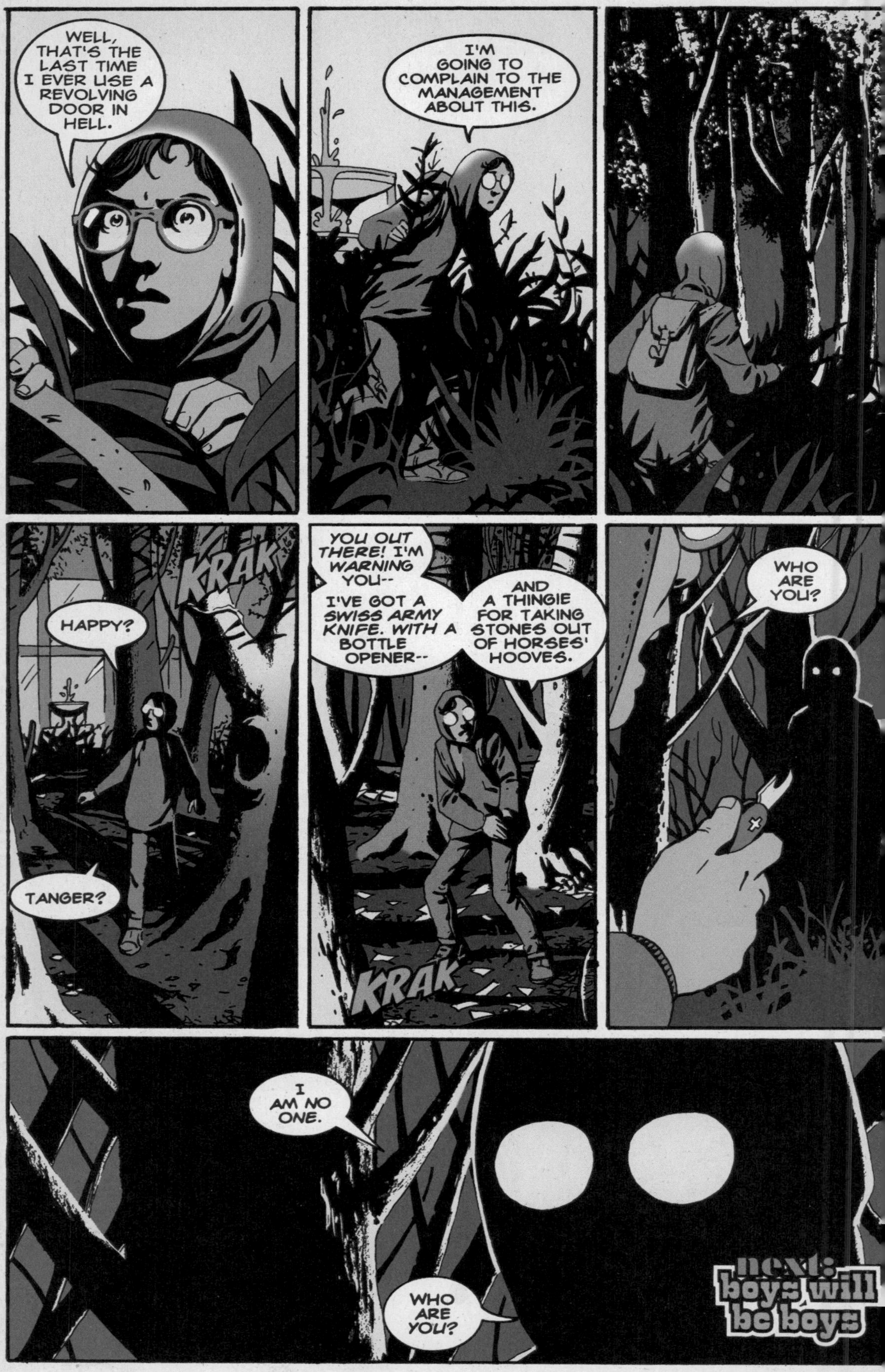
WELL, THAT'S THE LAST TIME I EVER USE A REVOLVING DOOR IN HELL.
I'M GOING TO COMPLAIN TO THE MANAGEMENT ABOUT THIS.
KRAK
HAPPY?
TANGER?
YOU OUT THERE! I'M WARNING YOU--
I'VE GOT A SWISS ARMY KNIFE. WITH A BOTTLE OPENER--
AND A THINGIE FOR TAKING STONES OUT OF HORSES' HOOVES.
KRAK
WHO ARE YOU?
I AM NO ONE.
WHO ARE YOU?
next: boys will be boys

Boys
Will
Be
Boys

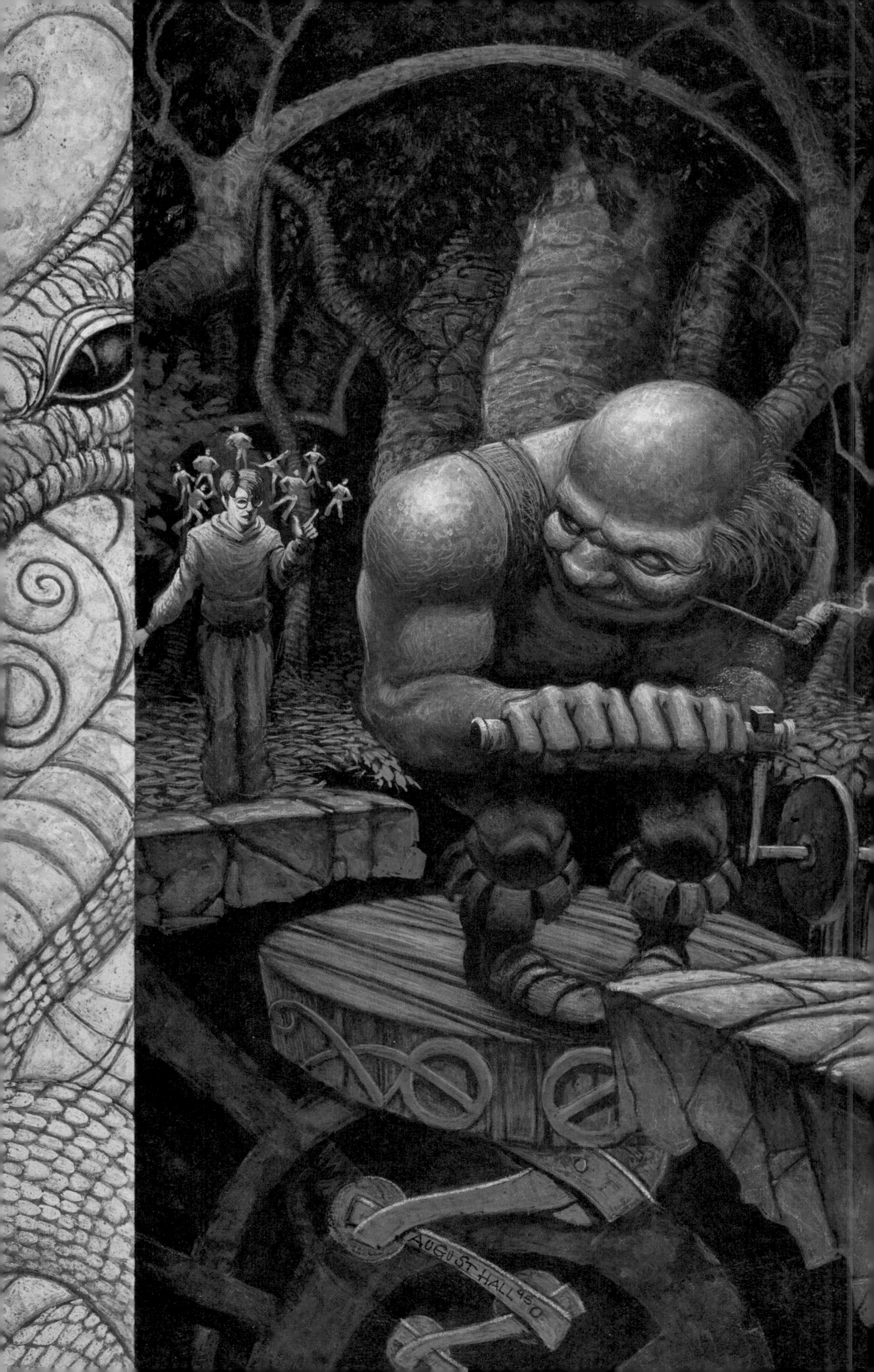
AUGUST HALL 90

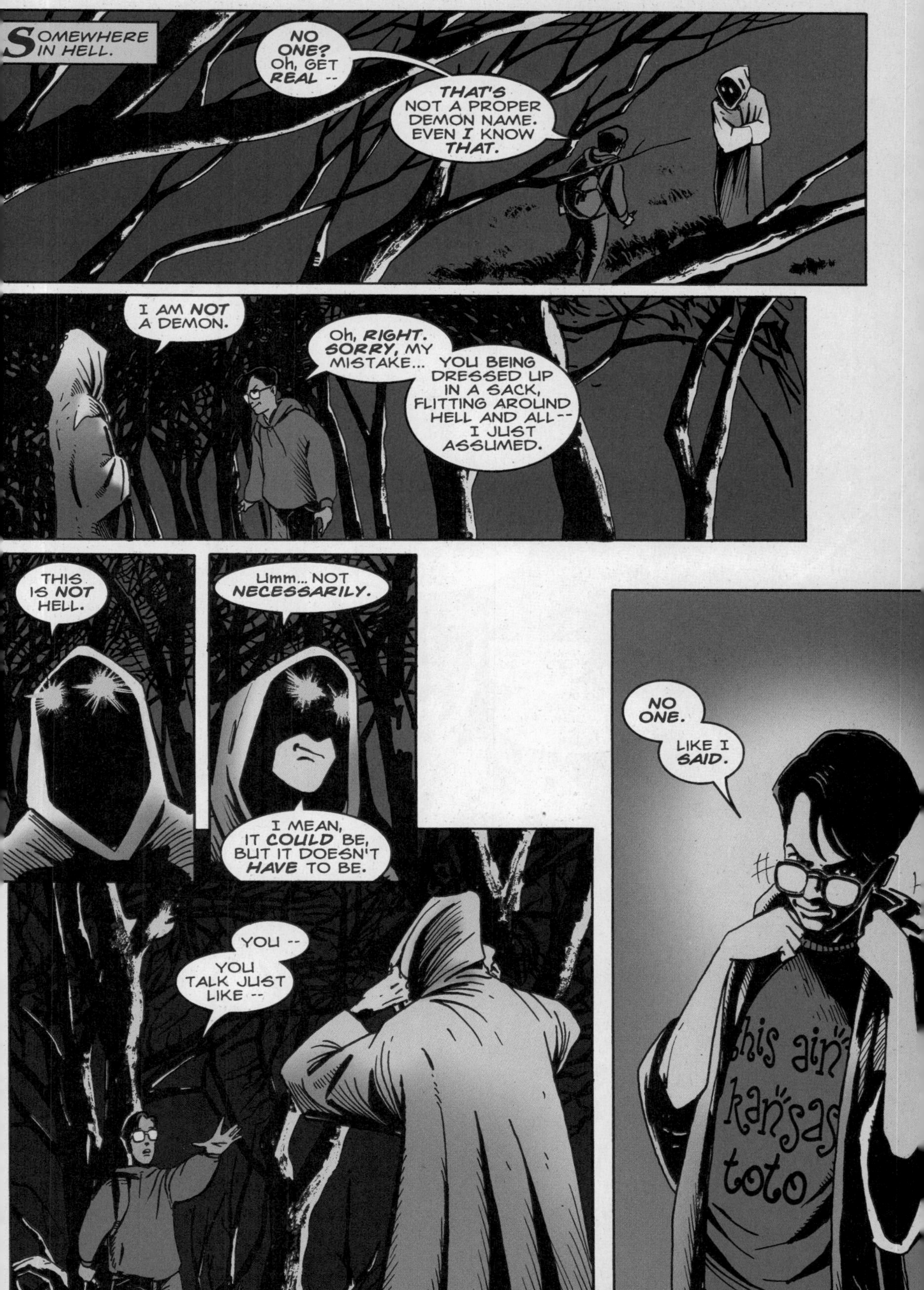
SOMEWHERE IN HELL.
NO ONE? Oh, GET REAL --
THAT'S NOT A PROPER DEMON NAME. EVEN I KNOW THAT.
I AM NOT A DEMON.
Oh, RIGHT. SORRY, MY MISTAKE...
YOU BEING DRESSED UP IN A SACK, FLITTING AROUND HELL AND ALL -- I JUST ASSUMED.
THIS IS NOT HELL.
Umm... NOT NECESSARILY.
I MEAN, IT COULD BE, BUT IT DOESN'T HAVE TO BE.
YOU --
YOU TALK JUST LIKE --
NO ONE.
LIKE I SAID.

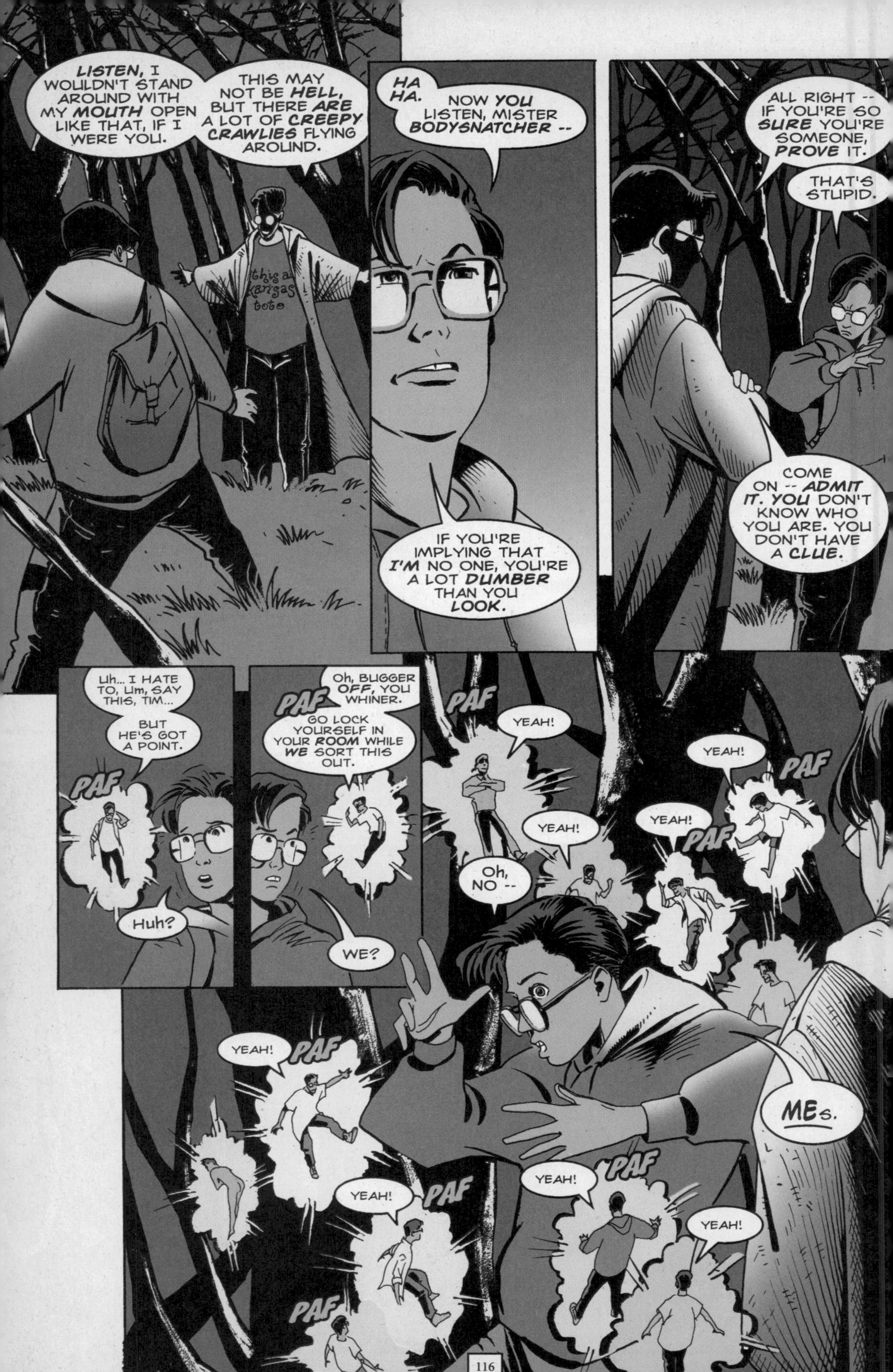
LISTEN, I WOULDN'T STAND AROUND WITH MY MOUTH OPEN LIKE THAT, IF I WERE YOU.
THIS MAY NOT BE HELL, BUT THERE ARE A LOT OF CREEPY CRAWLIES FLYING AROUND.
HA HA.
NOW YOU LISTEN, MISTER BODYSNATCHER --
IF YOU'RE IMPLYING THAT I'M NO ONE, YOU'RE A LOT DUMBER THAN YOU LOOK.
ALL RIGHT -- IF YOU'RE SO SURE YOU'RE SOMEONE, PROVE IT.
THAT'S STUPID.
COME ON -- ADMIT IT. YOU DON'T KNOW WHO YOU ARE. YOU DON'T HAVE A CLUE.
Uh... I HATE TO, Um, SAY THIS, TIM...
BUT HE'S GOT A POINT.
PAF
Huh?
PAF
Oh, BUGGER OFF, YOU WHINER.
GO LOCK YOURSELF IN YOUR ROOM WHILE WE SORT THIS OUT.
WE?
PAF
YEAH!
YEAH!
PAF
YEAH!
YEAH!
PAF
Oh, NO --
YEAH!
PAF
MEs.
YEAH!
PAF
YEAH!
PAF
YEAH!
PAF

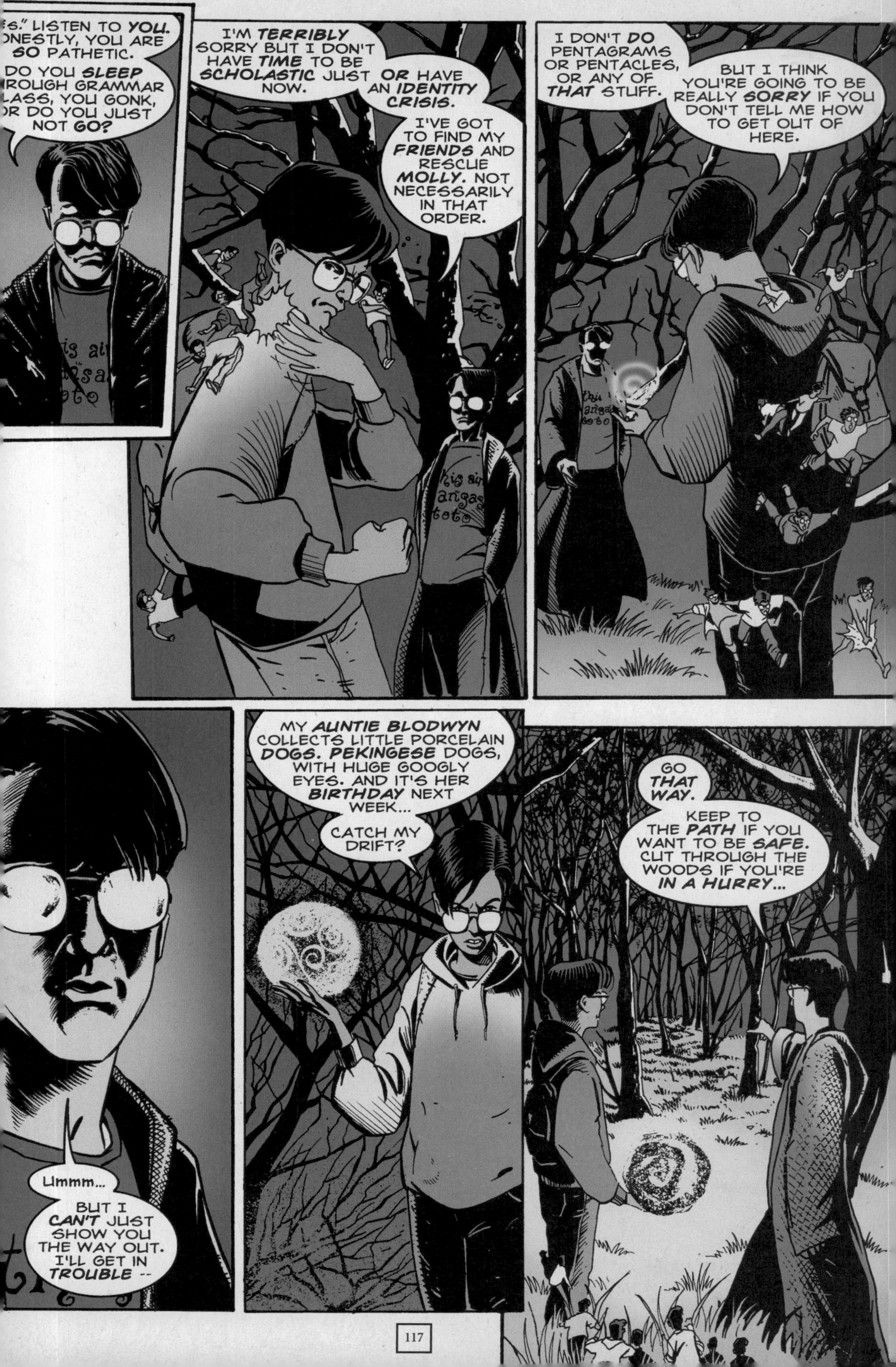

s." LISTEN TO YOU. ONESTLY, YOU ARE SO PATHETIC.
DO YOU SLEEP ROUGH GRAMMAR LASS, YOU GONK, R DO YOU JUST NOT GO?
I'M TERRIBLY SORRY BUT I DON'T HAVE TIME TO BE SCHOLASTIC JUST NOW.
OR HAVE AN IDENTITY CRISIS.
I'VE GOT TO FIND MY FRIENDS AND RESCUE MOLLY. NOT NECESSARILY IN THAT ORDER.
I DON'T DO PENTAGRAMS OR PENTACLES, OR ANY OF THAT STUFF.
BUT I THINK YOU'RE GOING TO BE REALLY SORRY IF YOU DON'T TELL ME HOW TO GET OUT OF HERE.
Ummm...
BUT I CAN'T JUST SHOW YOU THE WAY OUT. I'LL GET IN TROUBLE --
MY AUNTIE BLODWYN COLLECTS LITTLE PORCELAIN DOGS. PEKINGESE DOGS, WITH HUGE GOOGLY EYES. AND IT'S HER BIRTHDAY NEXT WEEK...
CATCH MY DRIFT?
GO THAT WAY.
KEEP TO THE PATH IF YOU WANT TO BE SAFE. CUT THROUGH THE WOODS IF YOU'RE IN A HURRY...

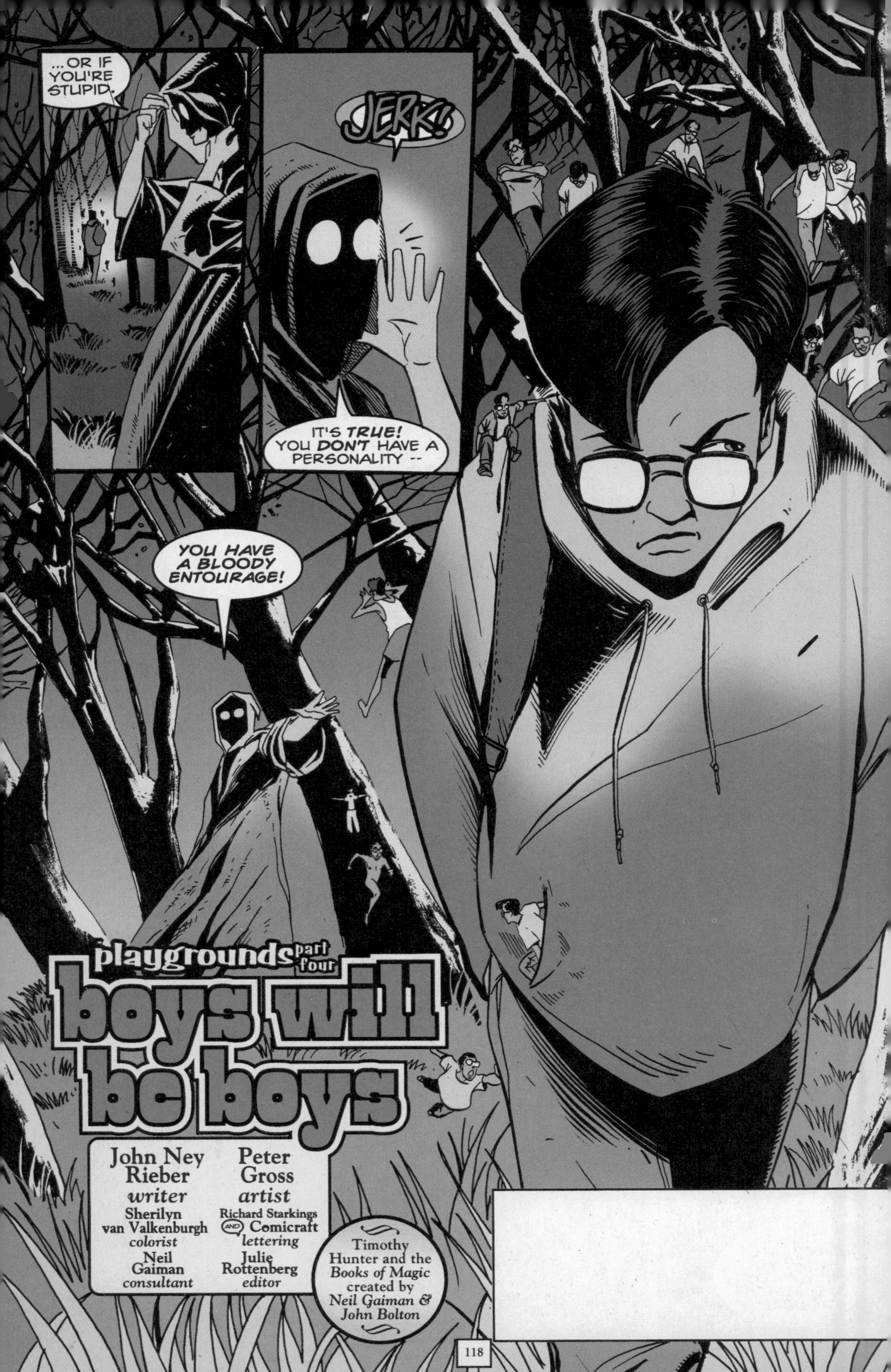

...OR IF YOU'RE STUPID.
JERK!
IT'S TRUE! YOU DON'T HAVE A PERSONALITY --
YOU HAVE A BLOODY ENTOURAGE!
playgrounds part four
boys will be boys
John Ney Rieber writer
Peter Gross artist
Sherilyn van Valkenburgh colorist
Richard Starkings and Comicraft lettering
Neil Gaiman consultant
Julie Rottenberg editor
Timothy Hunter and the Books of Magic created by Neil Gaiman & John Bolton

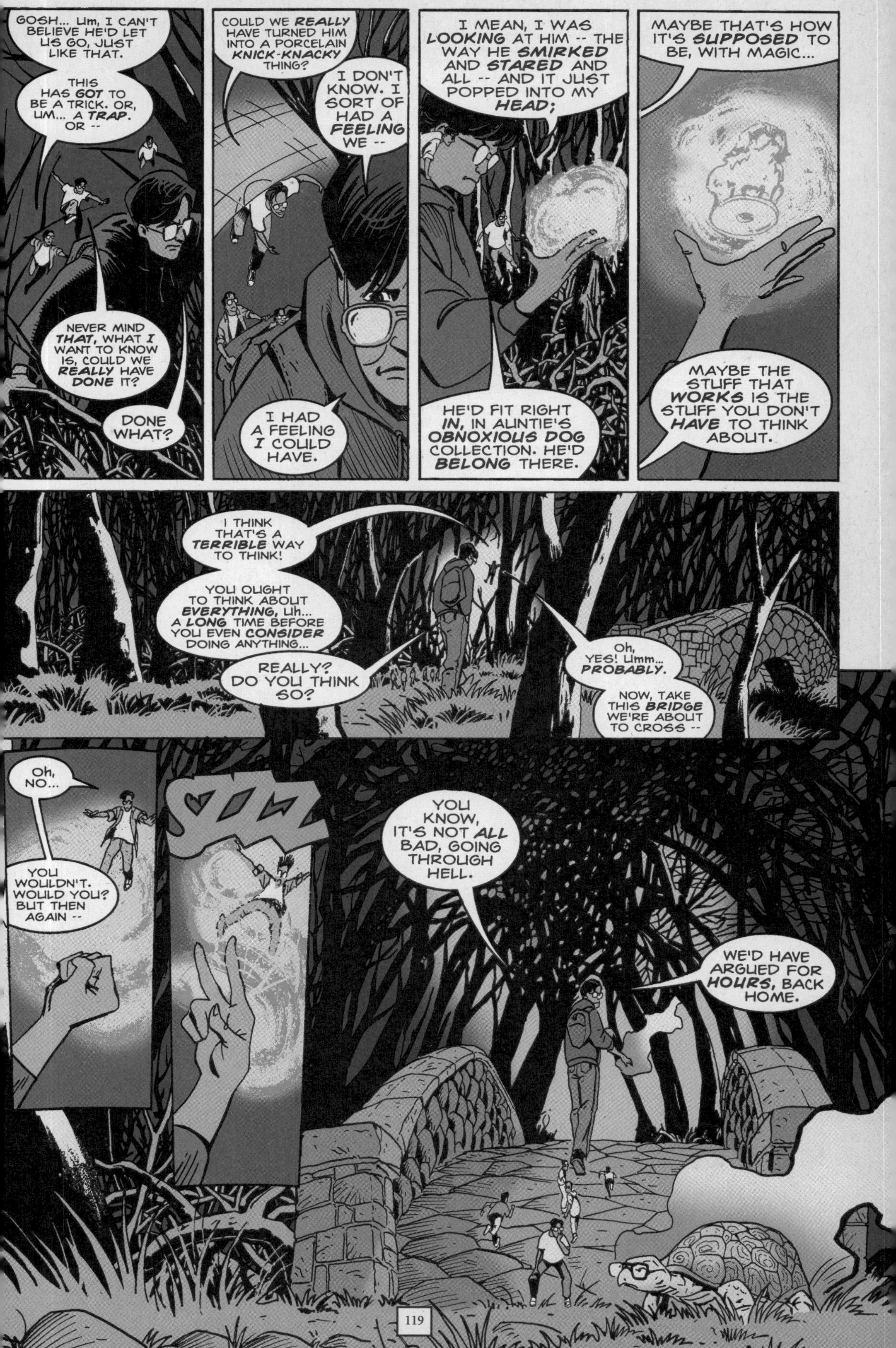
GOSH... UM, I CAN'T BELIEVE HE'D LET US GO, JUST LIKE THAT.
THIS HAS GOT TO BE A TRICK. OR, UM... A TRAP. OR --
NEVER MIND THAT, WHAT I WANT TO KNOW IS, COULD WE REALLY HAVE DONE IT?
DONE WHAT?
COULD WE REALLY HAVE TURNED HIM INTO A PORCELAIN KNICK-KNACKY THING?
I DON'T KNOW. I SORT OF HAD A FEELING WE --
I HAD A FEELING I COULD HAVE.
I MEAN, I WAS LOOKING AT HIM -- THE WAY HE SMIRKED AND STARED AND ALL -- AND IT JUST POPPED INTO MY HEAD;
HE'D FIT RIGHT IN, IN AUNTIE'S OBNOXIOUS DOG COLLECTION. HE'D BELONG THERE.
MAYBE THAT'S HOW IT'S SUPPOSED TO BE, WITH MAGIC...
MAYBE THE STUFF THAT WORKS IS THE STUFF YOU DON'T HAVE TO THINK ABOUT.
I THINK THAT'S A TERRIBLE WAY TO THINK!
YOU OUGHT TO THINK ABOUT EVERYTHING, UH... A LONG TIME BEFORE YOU EVEN CONSIDER DOING ANYTHING...
REALLY? DO YOU THINK SO?
OH, YES! UMM... PROBABLY.
NOW, TAKE THIS BRIDGE WE'RE ABOUT TO CROSS --
OH, NO...
YOU WOULDN'T. WOULD YOU? BUT THEN AGAIN --
SZZ
YOU KNOW, IT'S NOT ALL BAD, GOING THROUGH HELL.
WE'D HAVE ARGUED FOR HOURS, BACK HOME.

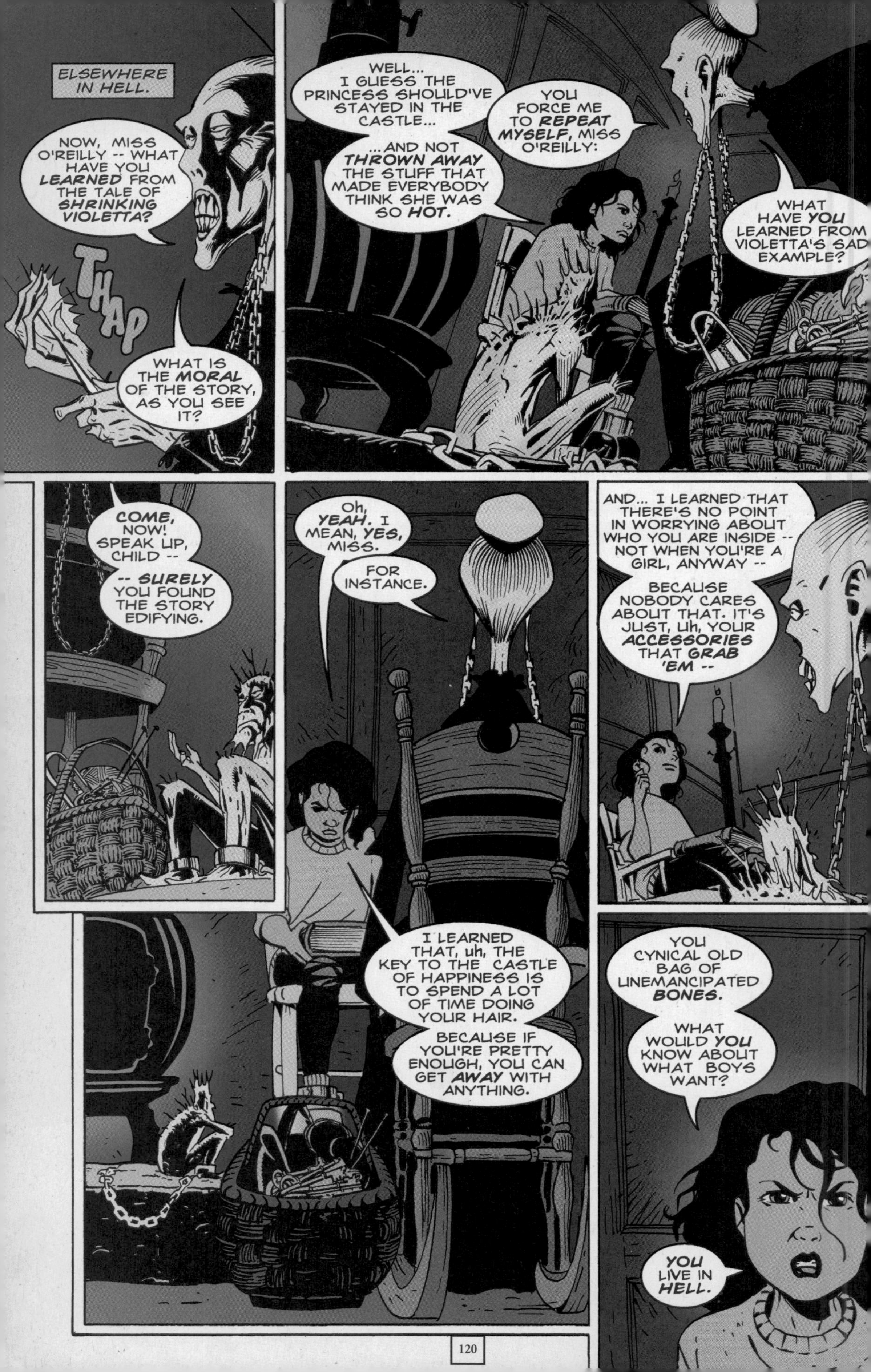
ELSEWHERE IN HELL.
NOW, MISS O'REILLY -- WHAT HAVE YOU LEARNED FROM THE TALE OF SHRINKING VIOLETTA?
THAP
WHAT IS THE MORAL OF THE STORY, AS YOU SEE IT?
WELL... I GUESS THE PRINCESS SHOULD'VE STAYED IN THE CASTLE...
...AND NOT THROWN AWAY THE STUFF THAT MADE EVERYBODY THINK SHE WAS SO HOT.
YOU FORCE ME TO REPEAT MYSELF, MISS O'REILLY:
WHAT HAVE YOU LEARNED FROM VIOLETTA'S SAD EXAMPLE?
COME, NOW! SPEAK UP, CHILD --
-- SURELY YOU FOUND THE STORY EDIFYING.
Oh, YEAH. I MEAN, YES, MISS.
FOR INSTANCE.
I LEARNED THAT, uh, THE KEY TO THE CASTLE OF HAPPINESS IS TO SPEND A LOT OF TIME DOING YOUR HAIR.
BECAUSE IF YOU'RE PRETTY ENOUGH, YOU CAN GET AWAY WITH ANYTHING.
AND... I LEARNED THAT THERE'S NO POINT IN WORRYING ABOUT WHO YOU ARE INSIDE -- NOT WHEN YOU'RE A GIRL, ANYWAY --
BECAUSE NOBODY CARES ABOUT THAT. IT'S JUST, uh, YOUR ACCESSORIES THAT GRAB 'EM --
YOU CYNICAL OLD BAG OF UNEMANCIPATED BONES.
WHAT WOULD YOU KNOW ABOUT WHAT BOYS WANT?
YOU LIVE IN HELL.

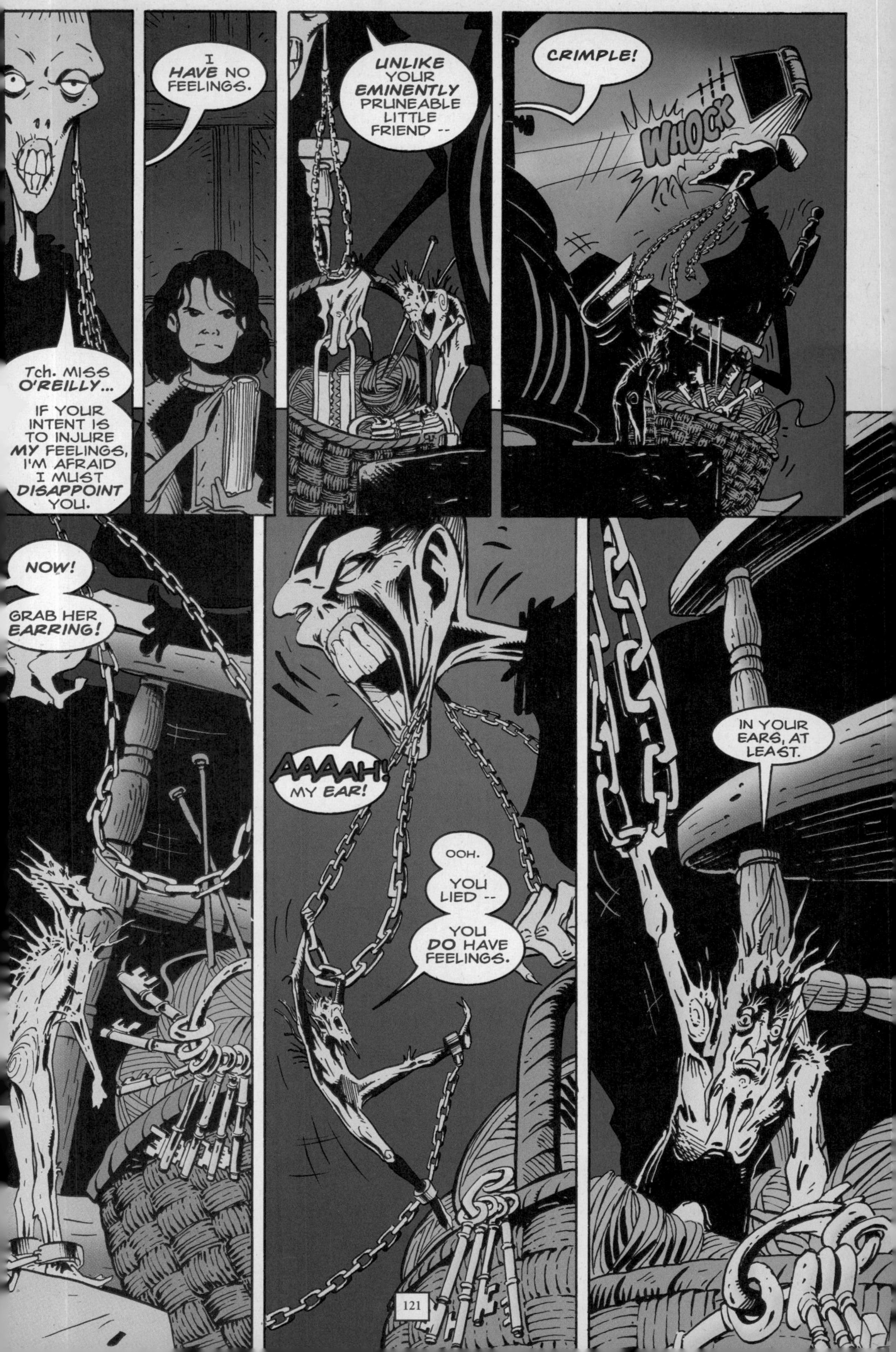
Tch. MISS O'REILLY...
IF YOUR INTENT IS TO INJURE MY FEELINGS, I'M AFRAID I MUST DISAPPOINT YOU.
I HAVE NO FEELINGS.
UNLIKE YOUR EMINENTLY PRUNEABLE LITTLE FRIEND --
CRIMPLE!
WHOCK
NOW!
GRAB HER EARRING!
AAAAH! MY EAR!
OOH.
YOU LIED --
YOU DO HAVE FEELINGS.
IN YOUR EARS, AT LEAST.

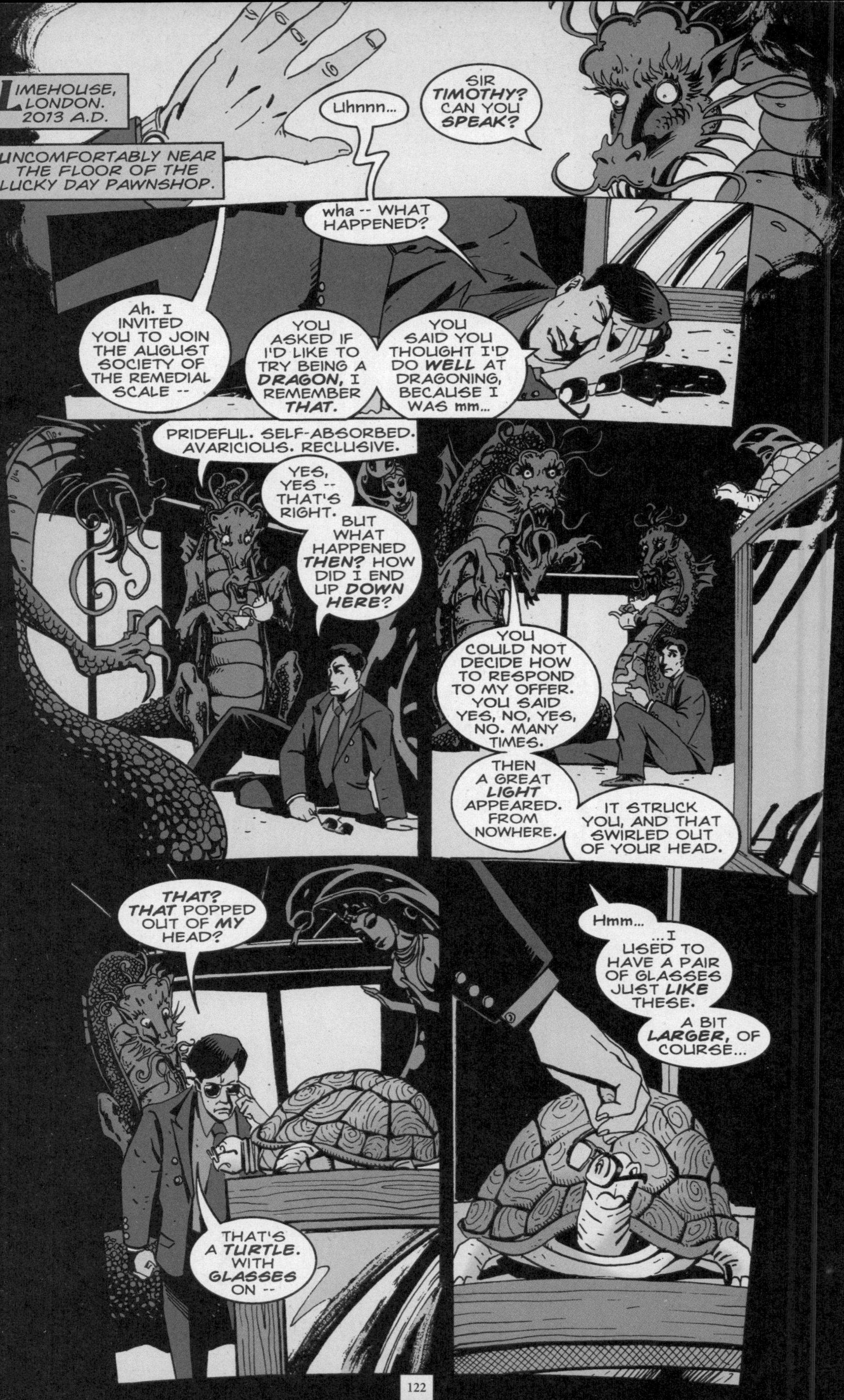

LIMEHOUSE, LONDON. 2013 A.D.
UNCOMFORTABLY NEAR THE FLOOR OF THE LUCKY DAY PAWNSHOP.
Uhnnn...
SIR TIMOTHY? CAN YOU SPEAK?
wha -- WHAT HAPPENED?
Ah. I INVITED YOU TO JOIN THE AUGUST SOCIETY OF THE REMEDIAL SCALE --
YOU ASKED IF I'D LIKE TO TRY BEING A DRAGON, I REMEMBER THAT.
YOU SAID YOU THOUGHT I'D DO WELL AT DRAGONING, BECAUSE I WAS mm...
PRIDEFUL. SELF-ABSORBED. AVARICIOUS. RECLUSIVE.
YES, YES -- THAT'S RIGHT.
BUT WHAT HAPPENED THEN? HOW DID I END UP DOWN HERE?
YOU COULD NOT DECIDE HOW TO RESPOND TO MY OFFER. YOU SAID YES, NO, YES, NO. MANY TIMES.
THEN A GREAT LIGHT APPEARED. FROM NOWHERE.
IT STRUCK YOU, AND THAT SWIRLED OUT OF YOUR HEAD.
THAT? THAT POPPED OUT OF MY HEAD?
THAT'S A TURTLE. WITH GLASSES ON --
Hmm...
...I USED TO HAVE A PAIR OF GLASSES JUST LIKE THESE.
A BIT LARGER, OF COURSE...

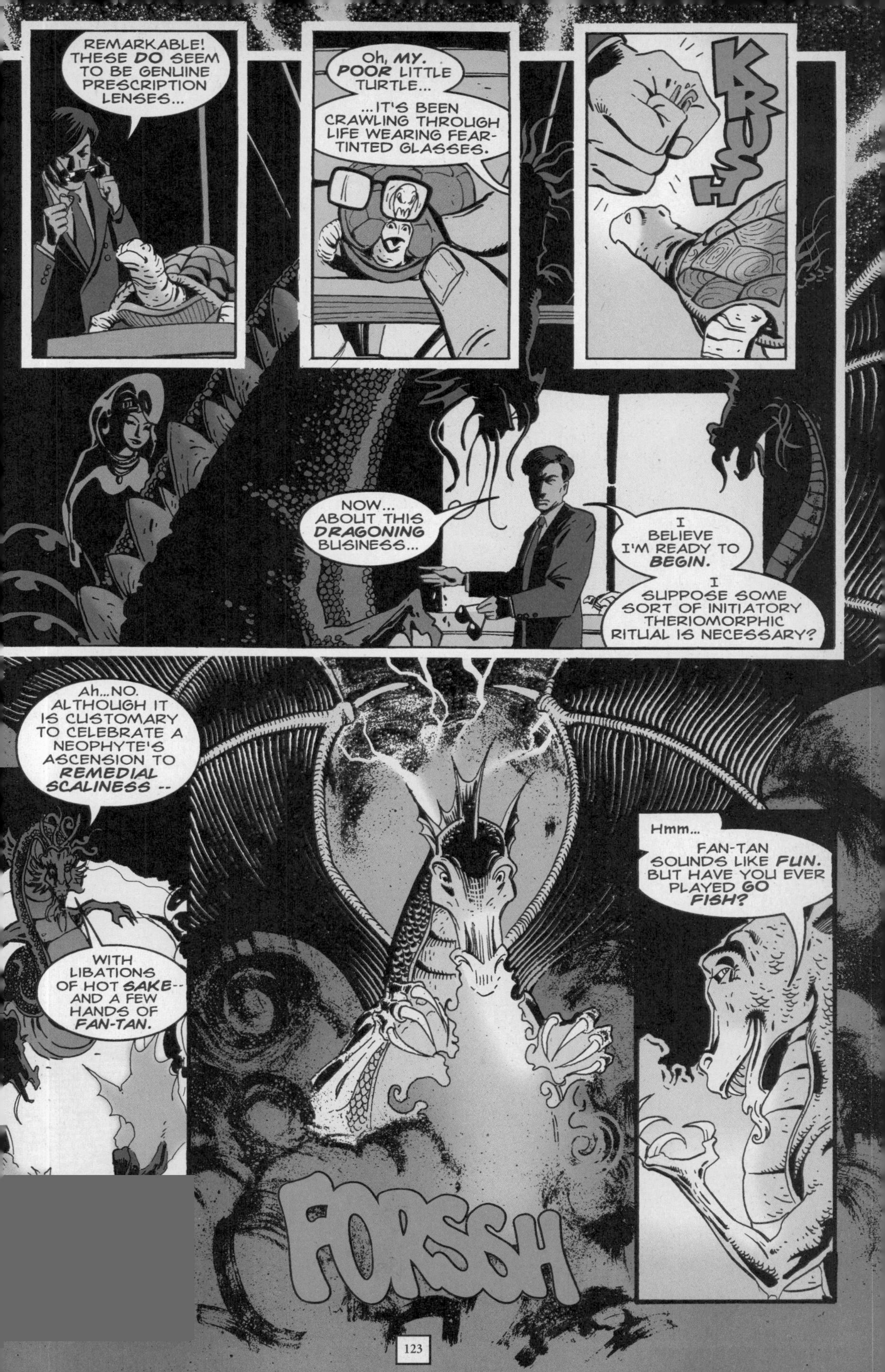
REMARKABLE! THESE DO SEEM TO BE GENUINE PRESCRIPTION LENSES...
Oh, MY. POOR LITTLE TURTLE...
...IT'S BEEN CRAWLING THROUGH LIFE WEARING FEAR-TINTED GLASSES.
KRUSH
NOW... ABOUT THIS DRAGONING BUSINESS...
I BELIEVE I'M READY TO BEGIN.
I SUPPOSE SOME SORT OF INITIATORY THERIOMORPHIC RITUAL IS NECESSARY?
Ah...NO. ALTHOUGH IT IS CUSTOMARY TO CELEBRATE A NEOPHYTE'S ASCENSION TO REMEDIAL SCALINESS --
WITH LIBATIONS OF HOT SAKE-- AND A FEW HANDS OF FAN-TAN.
FORSSH
Hmm...
FAN-TAN SOUNDS LIKE FUN. BUT HAVE YOU EVER PLAYED GO FISH?

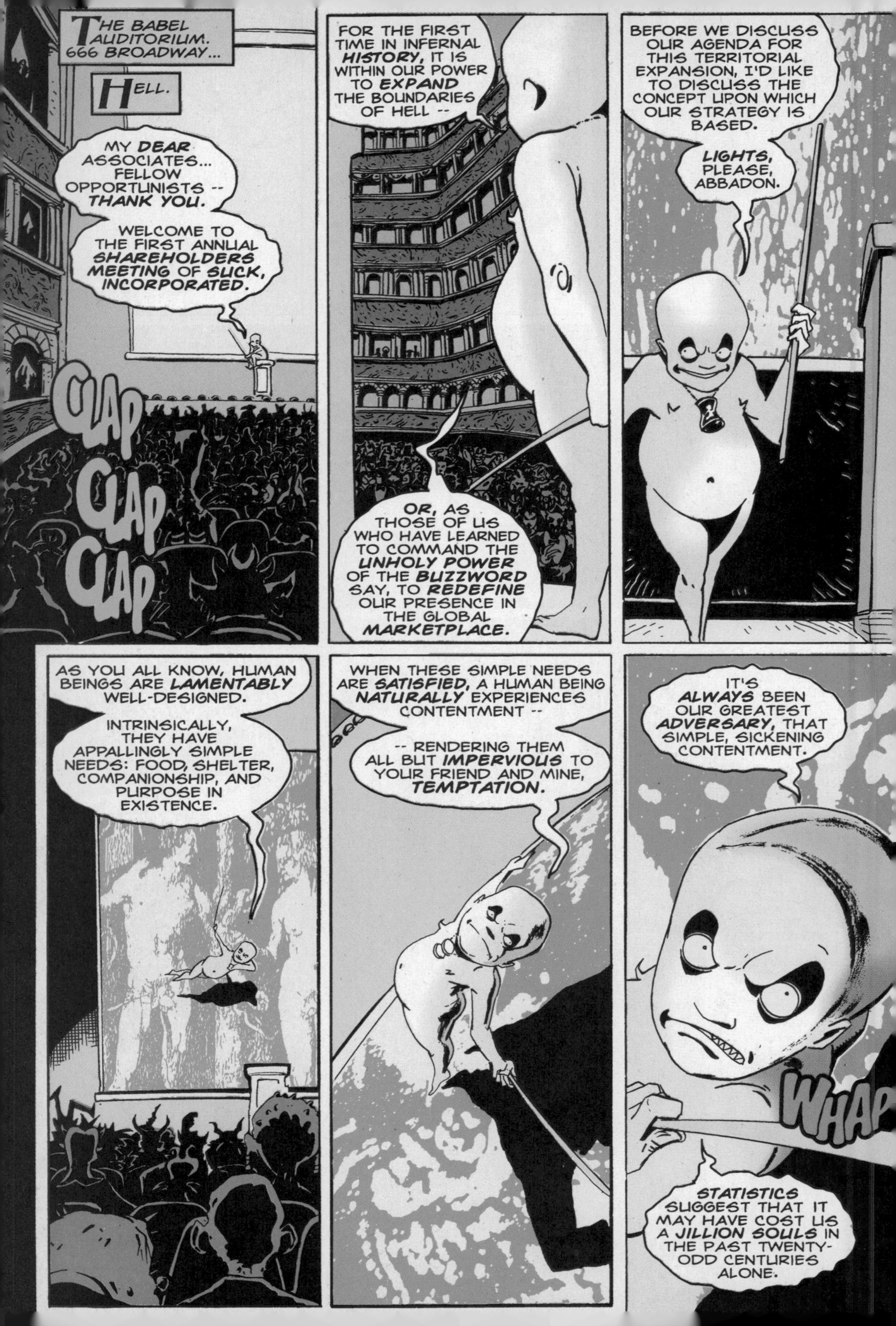
THE BABEL AUDITORIUM. 666 BROADWAY...
HELL.
MY DEAR ASSOCIATES... FELLOW OPPORTUNISTS -- THANK YOU.
WELCOME TO THE FIRST ANNUAL SHAREHOLDERS MEETING OF SUCK, INCORPORATED.
CLAP CLAP CLAP
FOR THE FIRST TIME IN INFERNAL HISTORY, IT IS WITHIN OUR POWER TO EXPAND THE BOUNDARIES OF HELL --
OR, AS THOSE OF US WHO HAVE LEARNED TO COMMAND THE UNHOLY POWER OF THE BUZZWORD SAY, TO REDEFINE OUR PRESENCE IN THE GLOBAL MARKETPLACE.
BEFORE WE DISCUSS OUR AGENDA FOR THIS TERRITORIAL EXPANSION, I'D LIKE TO DISCUSS THE CONCEPT UPON WHICH OUR STRATEGY IS BASED.
LIGHTS, PLEASE, ABBADON.
AS YOU ALL KNOW, HUMAN BEINGS ARE LAMENTABLY WELL-DESIGNED.
INTRINSICALLY, THEY HAVE APPALLINGLY SIMPLE NEEDS: FOOD, SHELTER, COMPANIONSHIP, AND PURPOSE IN EXISTENCE.
WHEN THESE SIMPLE NEEDS ARE SATISFIED, A HUMAN BEING NATURALLY EXPERIENCES CONTENTMENT --
-- RENDERING THEM ALL BUT IMPERVIOUS TO YOUR FRIEND AND MINE, TEMPTATION.
IT'S ALWAYS BEEN OUR GREATEST ADVERSARY, THAT SIMPLE, SICKENING CONTENTMENT.
WHAP
STATISTICS SUGGEST THAT IT MAY HAVE COST US A JILLION SOULS IN THE PAST TWENTY-ODD CENTURIES ALONE.

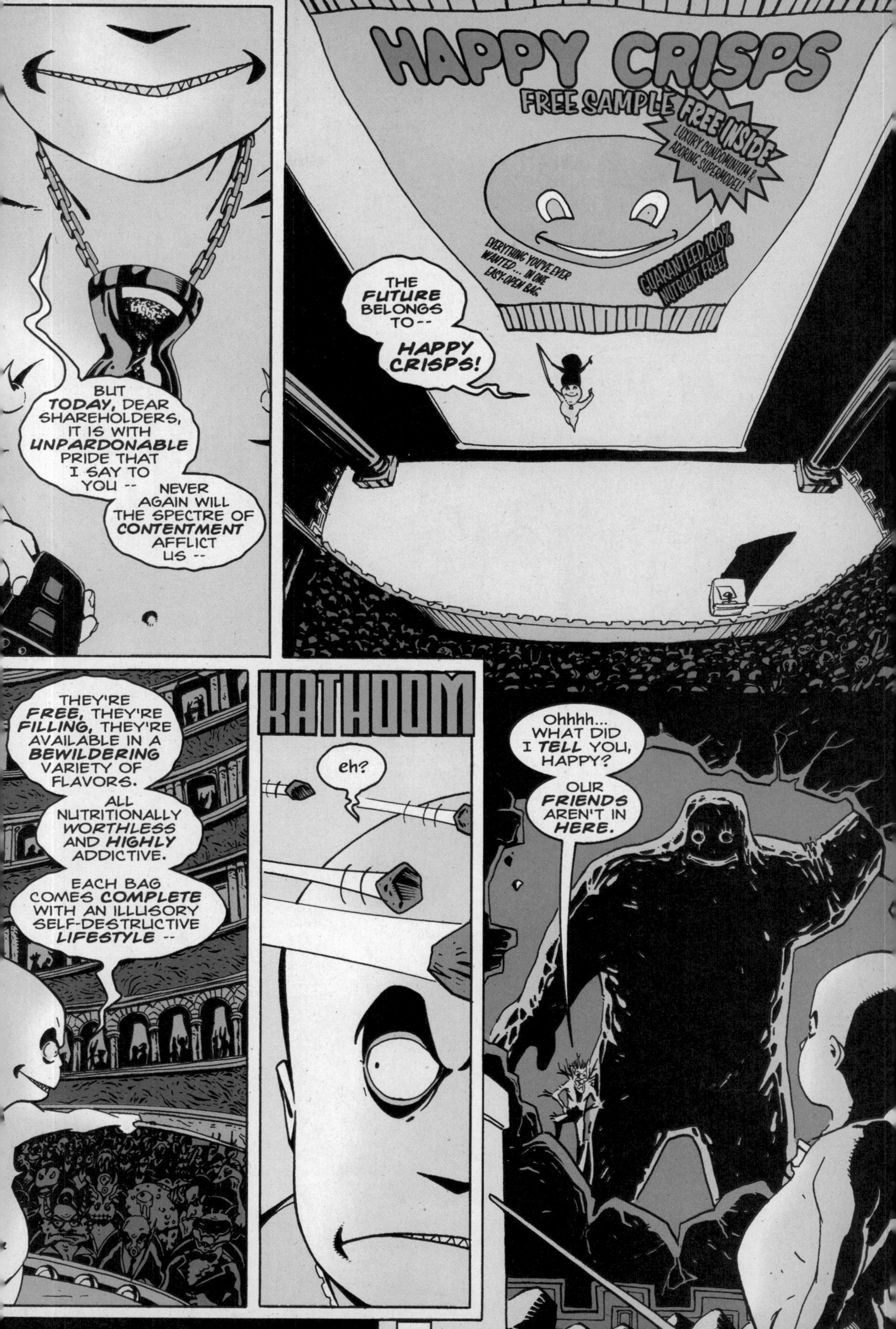

BUT TODAY, DEAR SHAREHOLDERS, IT IS WITH UNPARDONABLE PRIDE THAT I SAY TO YOU --
NEVER AGAIN WILL THE SPECTRE OF CONTENTMENT AFFLICT US --
HAPPY CRISPS
FREE SAMPLE
FREE INSIDE
LUXURY CONDOMINIUM & ADORING SUPERMODEL!
EVERYTHING YOU'VE EVER WANTED... IN ONE EASY-OPEN BAG.
GUARANTEED 100% NUTRIENT FREE!
THE FUTURE BELONGS TO --
HAPPY CRISPS!
THEY'RE FREE, THEY'RE FILLING, THEY'RE AVAILABLE IN A BEWILDERING VARIETY OF FLAVORS.
ALL NUTRITIONALLY WORTHLESS AND HIGHLY ADDICTIVE.
EACH BAG COMES COMPLETE WITH AN ILLUSORY SELF-DESTRUCTIVE LIFESTYLE --
KATHOOM
eh?
Ohhhh... WHAT DID I TELL YOU, HAPPY?
OUR FRIENDS AREN'T IN HERE.

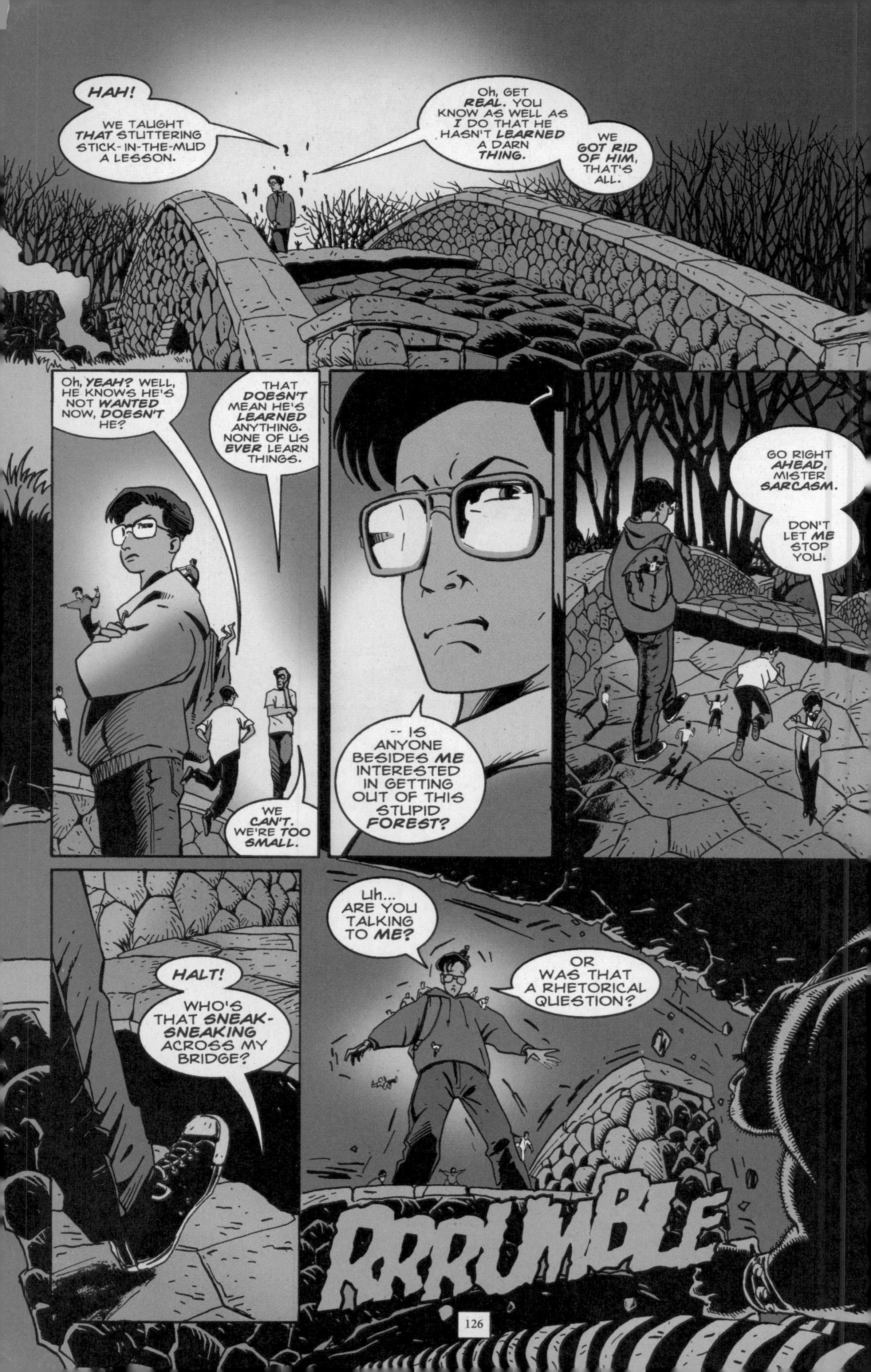
HAH!
WE TAUGHT THAT STUTTERING STICK-IN-THE-MUD A LESSON.
Oh, GET REAL. YOU KNOW AS WELL AS I DO THAT HE HASN'T LEARNED A DARN THING.
WE GOT RID OF HIM, THAT'S ALL.
Oh, YEAH? WELL, HE KNOWS HE'S NOT WANTED NOW, DOESN'T HE?
THAT DOESN'T MEAN HE'S LEARNED ANYTHING. NONE OF US EVER LEARN THINGS.
WE CAN'T. WE'RE TOO SMALL.
-- IS ANYONE BESIDES ME INTERESTED IN GETTING OUT OF THIS STUPID FOREST?
GO RIGHT AHEAD, MISTER SARCASM.
DON'T LET ME STOP YOU.
HALT!
WHO'S THAT SNEAK-SNEAKING ACROSS MY BRIDGE?
Uh... ARE YOU TALKING TO ME?
OR WAS THAT A RHETORICAL QUESTION?
RRRUMBLE

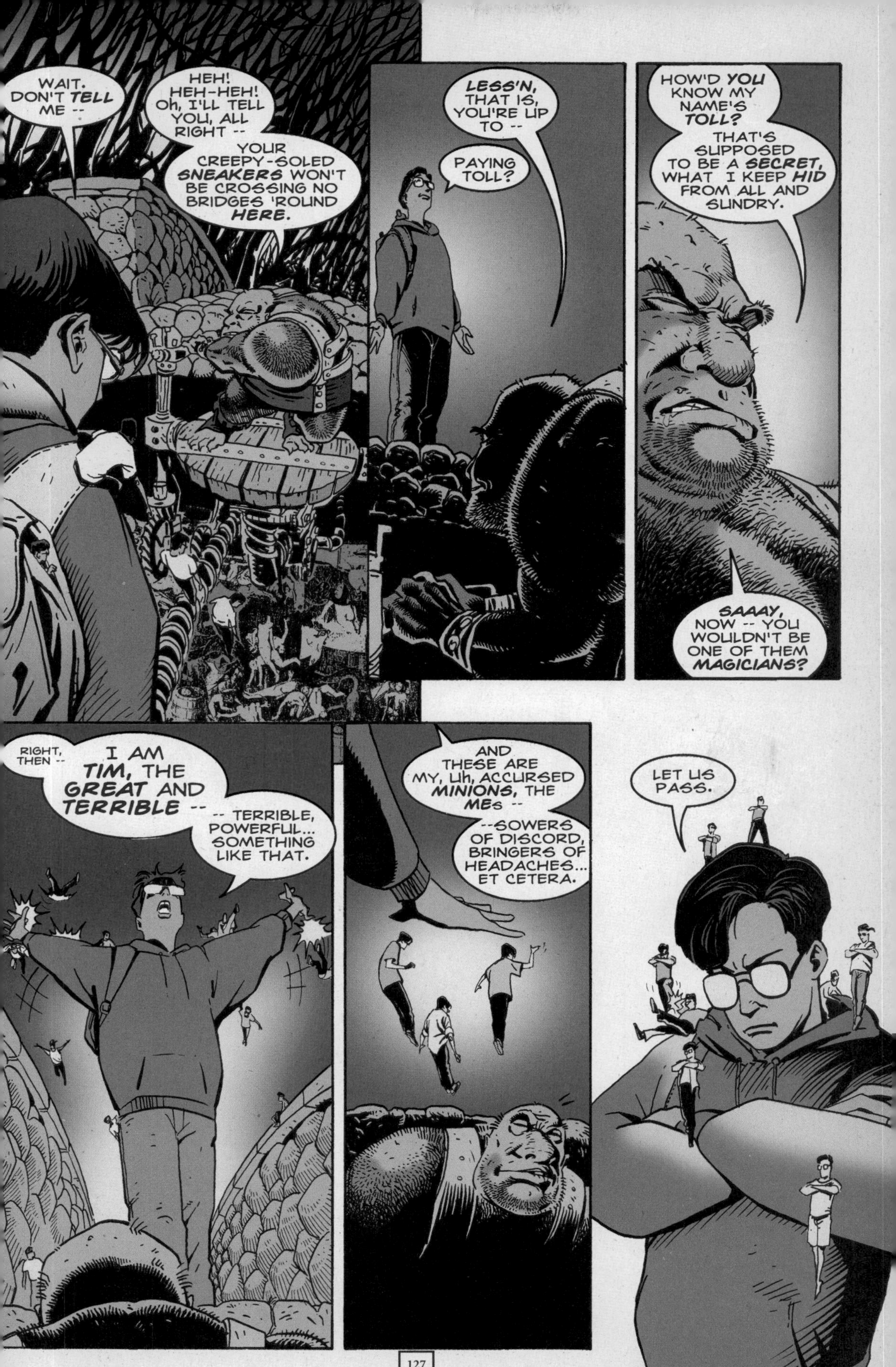
WAIT. DON'T TELL ME --
HEH! HEH-HEH! Oh, I'LL TELL YOU, ALL RIGHT --
YOUR CREEPY-SOLED SNEAKERS WON'T BE CROSSING NO BRIDGES 'ROUND HERE.
LESS'N, THAT IS, YOU'RE UP TO --
PAYING TOLL?
HOW'D YOU KNOW MY NAME'S TOLL?
THAT'S SUPPOSED TO BE A SECRET, WHAT I KEEP HID FROM ALL AND SUNDRY.
SAAAY, NOW -- YOU WOULDN'T BE ONE OF THEM MAGICIANS?
RIGHT, THEN -- I AM TIM, THE GREAT AND TERRIBLE --
-- TERRIBLE, POWERFUL... SOMETHING LIKE THAT.
AND THESE ARE MY, Uh, ACCURSED MINIONS, THE MEs --
--SOWERS OF DISCORD, BRINGERS OF HEADACHES... ET CETERA.
LET US PASS.

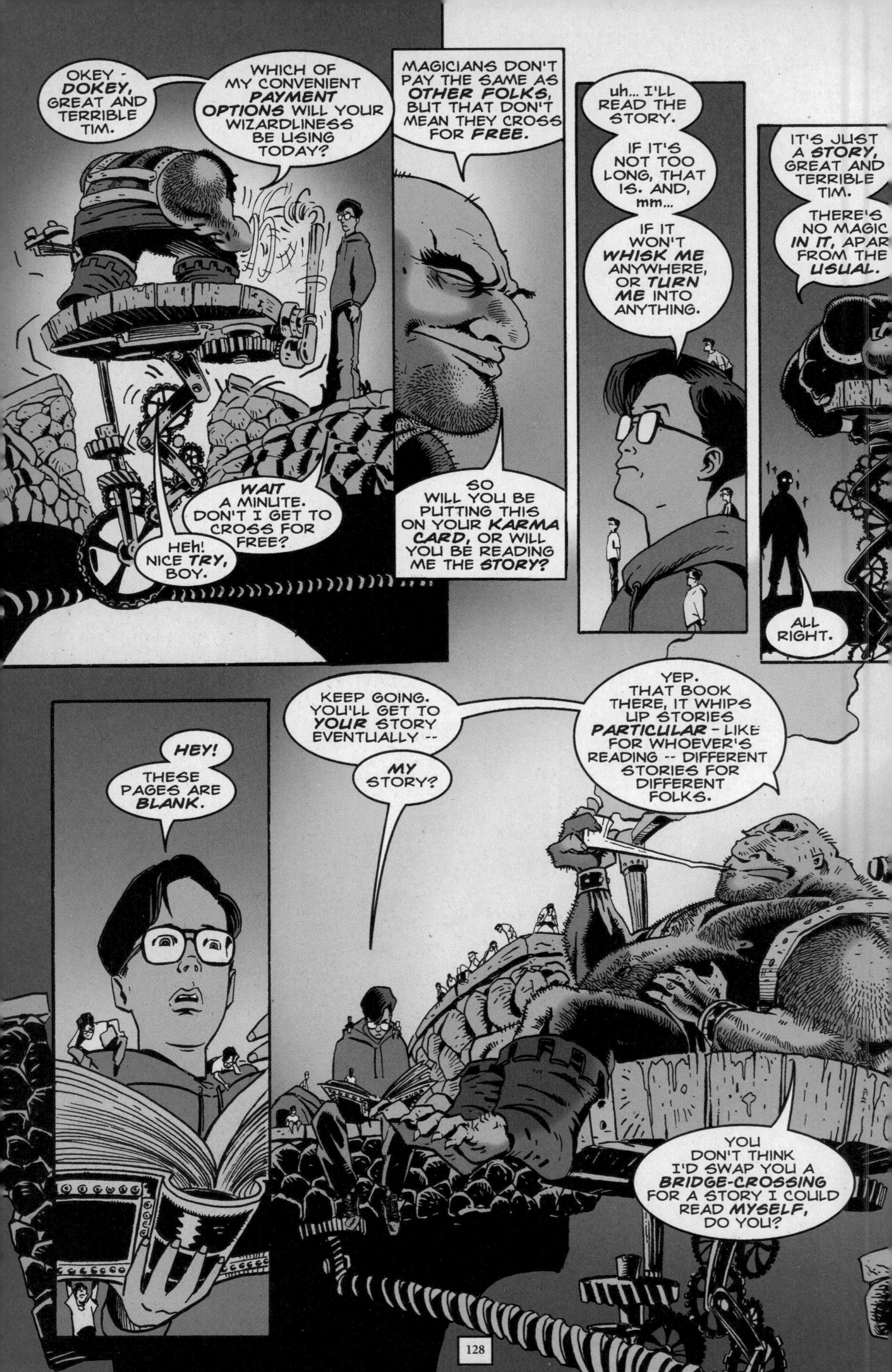
OKEY-DOKEY, GREAT AND TERRIBLE TIM.
WHICH OF MY CONVENIENT PAYMENT OPTIONS WILL YOUR WIZARDLINESS BE USING TODAY?
WAIT A MINUTE. DON'T I GET TO CROSS FOR FREE?
HEH! NICE TRY, BOY.
MAGICIANS DON'T PAY THE SAME AS OTHER FOLKS, BUT THAT DON'T MEAN THEY CROSS FOR FREE.
SO WILL YOU BE PUTTING THIS ON YOUR KARMA CARD, OR WILL YOU BE READING ME THE STORY?
uh... I'LL READ THE STORY.
IF IT'S NOT TOO LONG, THAT IS. AND, mm...
IF IT WON'T WHISK ME ANYWHERE, OR TURN ME INTO ANYTHING.
IT'S JUST A STORY, GREAT AND TERRIBLE TIM.
THERE'S NO MAGIC IN IT, APAR FROM THE USUAL.
ALL RIGHT.
HEY!
THESE PAGES ARE BLANK.
KEEP GOING. YOU'LL GET TO YOUR STORY EVENTUALLY --
MY STORY?
YEP. THAT BOOK THERE, IT WHIPS UP STORIES PARTICULAR - LIKE FOR WHOEVER'S READING -- DIFFERENT STORIES FOR DIFFERENT FOLKS.
YOU DON'T THINK I'D SWAP YOU A BRIDGE-CROSSING FOR A STORY I COULD READ MYSELF, DO YOU?

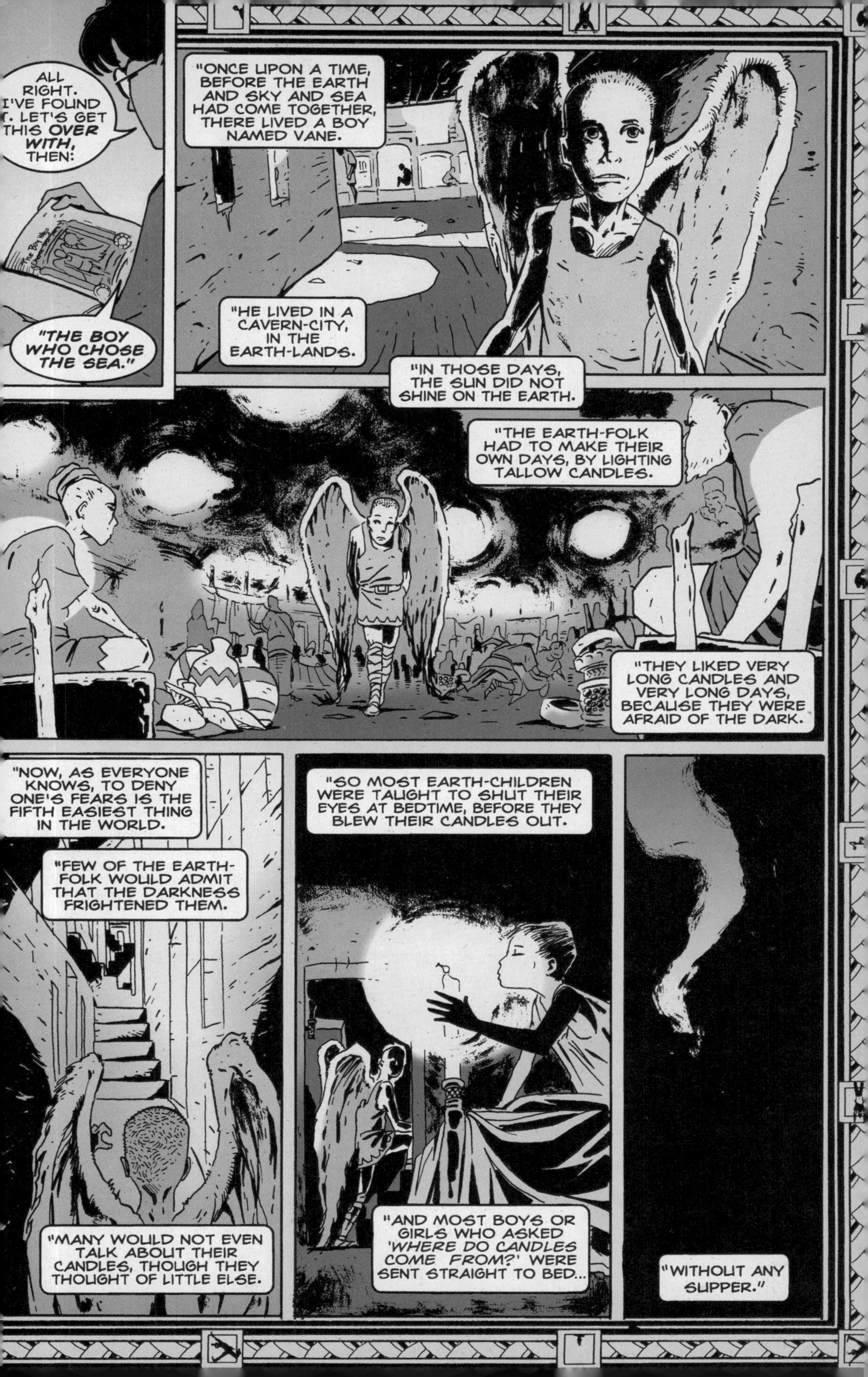
ALL RIGHT. I'VE FOUND IT. LET'S GET THIS OVER WITH, THEN:
"THE BOY WHO CHOSE THE SEA."
"ONCE UPON A TIME, BEFORE THE EARTH AND SKY AND SEA HAD COME TOGETHER, THERE LIVED A BOY NAMED VANE.
"HE LIVED IN A CAVERN-CITY, IN THE EARTH-LANDS.
"IN THOSE DAYS, THE SUN DID NOT SHINE ON THE EARTH.
"THE EARTH-FOLK HAD TO MAKE THEIR OWN DAYS, BY LIGHTING TALLOW CANDLES.
"THEY LIKED VERY LONG CANDLES AND VERY LONG DAYS, BECAUSE THEY WERE AFRAID OF THE DARK.
"NOW, AS EVERYONE KNOWS, TO DENY ONE'S FEARS IS THE FIFTH EASIEST THING IN THE WORLD.
"FEW OF THE EARTH-FOLK WOULD ADMIT THAT THE DARKNESS FRIGHTENED THEM.
"MANY WOULD NOT EVEN TALK ABOUT THEIR CANDLES, THOUGH THEY THOUGHT OF LITTLE ELSE.
"SO MOST EARTH-CHILDREN WERE TAUGHT TO SHUT THEIR EYES AT BEDTIME, BEFORE THEY BLEW THEIR CANDLES OUT.
"AND MOST BOYS OR GIRLS WHO ASKED 'WHERE DO CANDLES COME FROM?' WERE SENT STRAIGHT TO BED...
"WITHOUT ANY SUPPER."

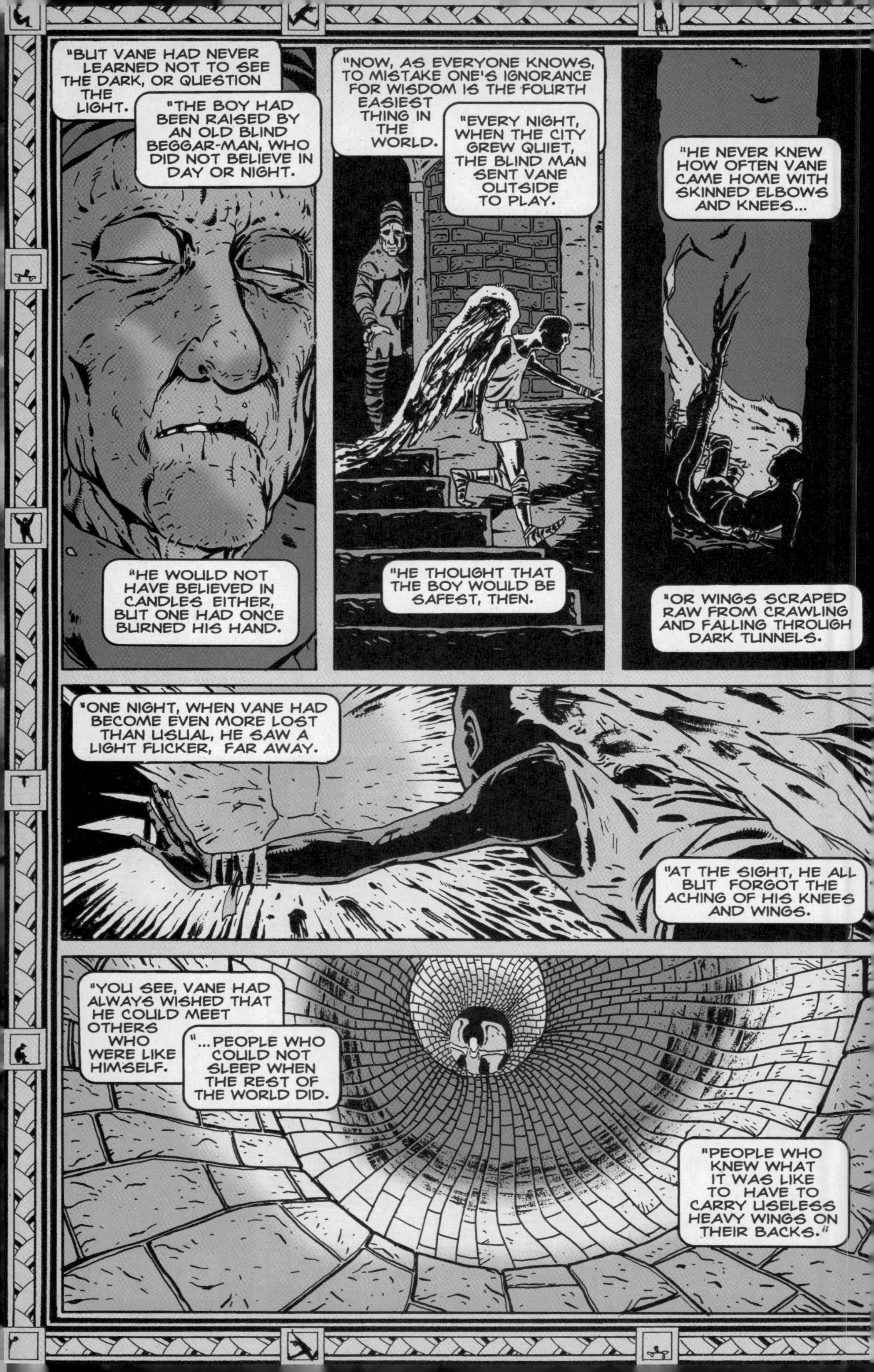
"BUT VANE HAD NEVER LEARNED NOT TO SEE THE DARK, OR QUESTION THE LIGHT.
"THE BOY HAD BEEN RAISED BY AN OLD BLIND BEGGAR-MAN, WHO DID NOT BELIEVE IN DAY OR NIGHT.
"HE WOULD NOT HAVE BELIEVED IN CANDLES EITHER, BUT ONE HAD ONCE BURNED HIS HAND.
"NOW, AS EVERYONE KNOWS, TO MISTAKE ONE'S IGNORANCE FOR WISDOM IS THE FOURTH EASIEST THING IN THE WORLD.
"EVERY NIGHT, WHEN THE CITY GREW QUIET, THE BLIND MAN SENT VANE OUTSIDE TO PLAY.
"HE THOUGHT THAT THE BOY WOULD BE SAFEST, THEN.
"HE NEVER KNEW HOW OFTEN VANE CAME HOME WITH SKINNED ELBOWS AND KNEES...
"OR WINGS SCRAPED RAW FROM CRAWLING AND FALLING THROUGH DARK TUNNELS.
"ONE NIGHT, WHEN VANE HAD BECOME EVEN MORE LOST THAN USUAL, HE SAW A LIGHT FLICKER, FAR AWAY.
"AT THE SIGHT, HE ALL BUT FORGOT THE ACHING OF HIS KNEES AND WINGS.
"YOU SEE, VANE HAD ALWAYS WISHED THAT HE COULD MEET OTHERS WHO WERE LIKE HIMSELF.
"...PEOPLE WHO COULD NOT SLEEP WHEN THE REST OF THE WORLD DID.
"PEOPLE WHO KNEW WHAT IT WAS LIKE TO HAVE TO CARRY USELESS HEAVY WINGS ON THEIR BACKS."

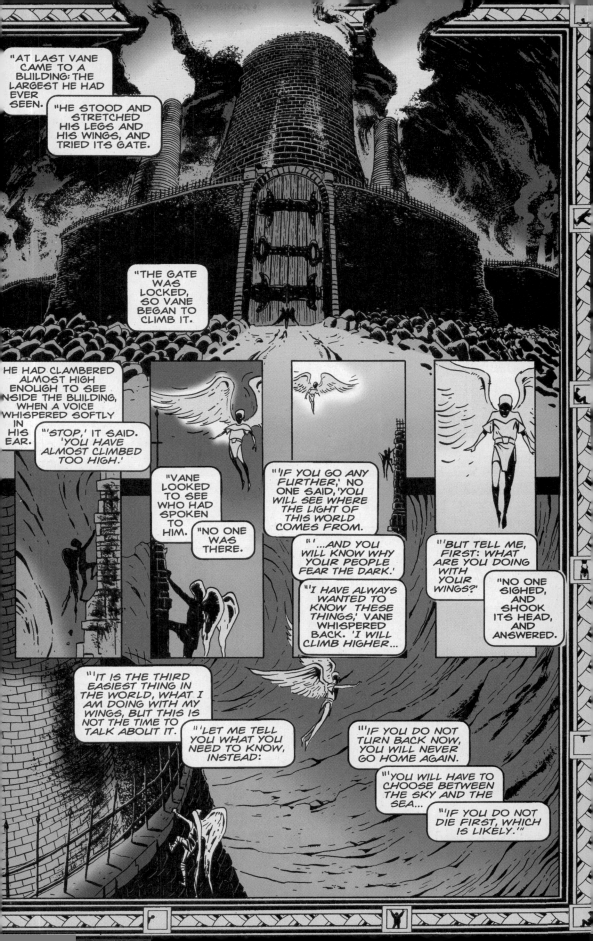

"AT LAST VANE CAME TO A BUILDING: THE LARGEST HE HAD EVER SEEN.

"HE STOOD AND STRETCHED HIS LEGS AND HIS WINGS, AND TRIED ITS GATE.

"THE GATE WAS LOCKED, SO VANE BEGAN TO CLIMB IT.

HE HAD CLAMBERED ALMOST HIGH ENOUGH TO SEE INSIDE THE BUILDING, WHEN A VOICE WHISPERED SOFTLY IN HIS EAR.

"'STOP,' IT SAID. 'YOU HAVE ALMOST CLIMBED TOO HIGH.'

"VANE LOOKED TO SEE WHO HAD SPOKEN TO HIM.

"NO ONE WAS THERE.

"'IF YOU GO ANY FURTHER,' NO ONE SAID, 'YOU WILL SEE WHERE THE LIGHT OF THIS WORLD COMES FROM.

"'...AND YOU WILL KNOW WHY YOUR PEOPLE FEAR THE DARK.'

"'I HAVE ALWAYS WANTED TO KNOW THESE THINGS,' VANE WHISPERED BACK. 'I WILL CLIMB HIGHER...

"'BUT TELL ME, FIRST: WHAT ARE YOU DOING WITH YOUR WINGS?'

"NO ONE SIGHED, AND SHOOK ITS HEAD, AND ANSWERED.

"'IT IS THE THIRD EASIEST THING IN THE WORLD, WHAT I AM DOING WITH MY WINGS, BUT THIS IS NOT THE TIME TO TALK ABOUT IT.

"'LET ME TELL YOU WHAT YOU NEED TO KNOW, INSTEAD:

"'IF YOU DO NOT TURN BACK NOW, YOU WILL NEVER GO HOME AGAIN.

"'YOU WILL HAVE TO CHOOSE BETWEEN THE SKY AND THE SEA...

"'IF YOU DO NOT DIE FIRST, WHICH IS LIKELY.'"

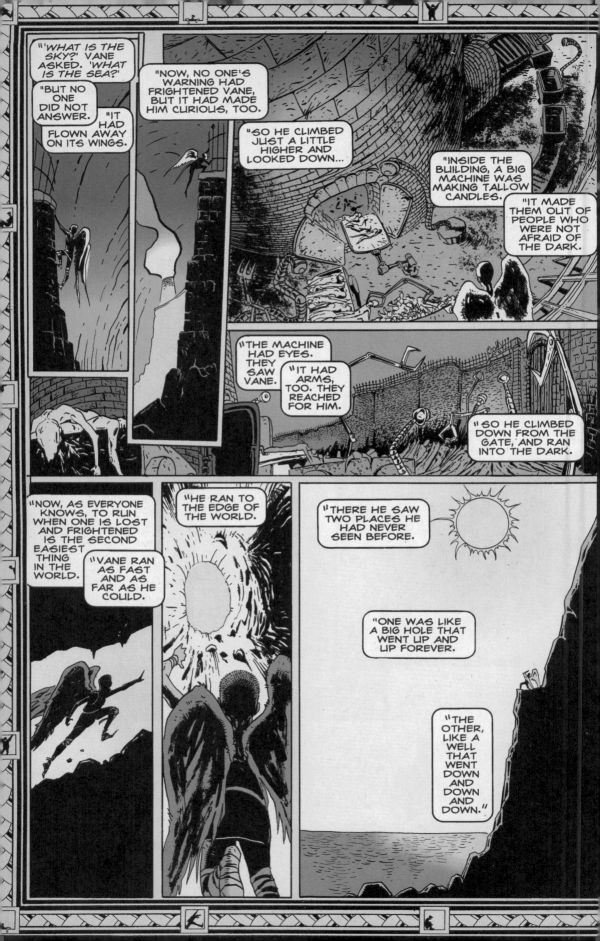

"'WHAT IS THE SKY?' VANE ASKED. 'WHAT IS THE SEA?'

"BUT NO ONE DID NOT ANSWER.

"IT HAD FLOWN AWAY ON ITS WINGS.

"NOW, NO ONE'S WARNING HAD FRIGHTENED VANE, BUT IT HAD MADE HIM CURIOUS, TOO.

"SO HE CLIMBED JUST A LITTLE HIGHER AND LOOKED DOWN...

"INSIDE THE BUILDING, A BIG MACHINE WAS MAKING TALLOW CANDLES.

"IT MADE THEM OUT OF PEOPLE WHO WERE NOT AFRAID OF THE DARK.

"THE MACHINE HAD EYES. THEY SAW VANE.

"IT HAD ARMS, TOO. THEY REACHED FOR HIM.

"SO HE CLIMBED DOWN FROM THE GATE, AND RAN INTO THE DARK.

"NOW, AS EVERYONE KNOWS, TO RUN WHEN ONE IS LOST AND FRIGHTENED IS THE SECOND EASIEST THING IN THE WORLD.

"VANE RAN AS FAST AND AS FAR AS HE COULD.

"HE RAN TO THE EDGE OF THE WORLD.

"THERE HE SAW TWO PLACES HE HAD NEVER SEEN BEFORE.

"ONE WAS LIKE A BIG HOLE THAT WENT UP AND UP FOREVER.

"THE OTHER, LIKE A WELL THAT WENT DOWN AND DOWN AND DOWN."

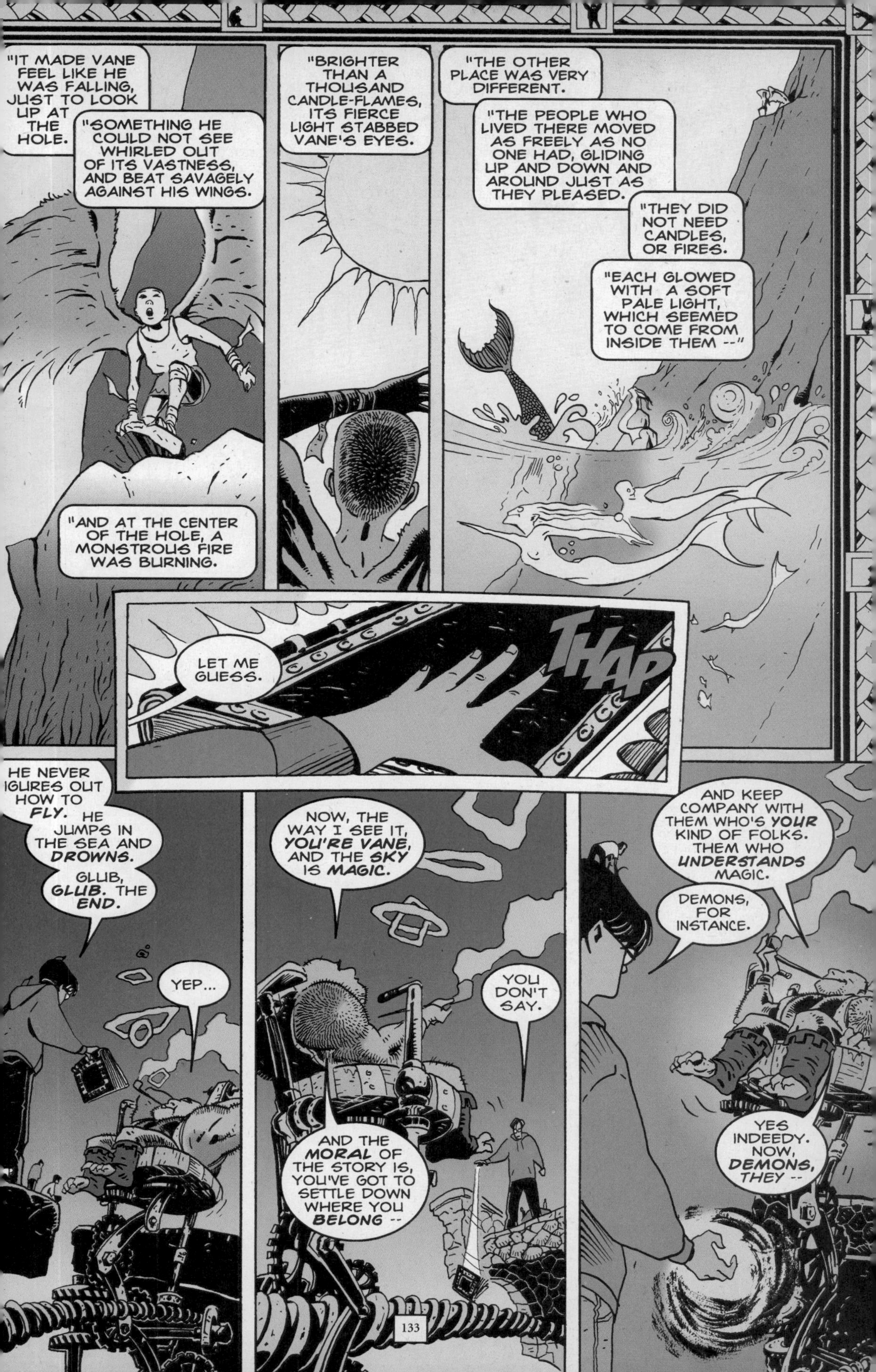
"IT MADE VANE FEEL LIKE HE WAS FALLING, JUST TO LOOK UP AT THE HOLE.
"SOMETHING HE COULD NOT SEE WHIRLED OUT OF ITS VASTNESS, AND BEAT SAVAGELY AGAINST HIS WINGS.
"AND AT THE CENTER OF THE HOLE, A MONSTROUS FIRE WAS BURNING.
"BRIGHTER THAN A THOUSAND CANDLE-FLAMES, ITS FIERCE LIGHT STABBED VANE'S EYES.
"THE OTHER PLACE WAS VERY DIFFERENT.
"THE PEOPLE WHO LIVED THERE MOVED AS FREELY AS NO ONE HAD, GLIDING UP AND DOWN AND AROUND JUST AS THEY PLEASED.
"THEY DID NOT NEED CANDLES, OR FIRES.
"EACH GLOWED WITH A SOFT PALE LIGHT, WHICH SEEMED TO COME FROM INSIDE THEM --"
LET ME GUESS.
THAP
HE NEVER IGURES OUT HOW TO FLY. HE JUMPS IN THE SEA AND DROWNS.
GLUB, GLUB. THE END.
YEP...
NOW, THE WAY I SEE IT, YOU'RE VANE, AND THE SKY IS MAGIC.
AND THE MORAL OF THE STORY IS, YOU'VE GOT TO SETTLE DOWN WHERE YOU BELONG --
YOU DON'T SAY.
AND KEEP COMPANY WITH THEM WHO'S YOUR KIND OF FOLKS. THEM WHO UNDERSTANDS MAGIC.
DEMONS, FOR INSTANCE.
YES INDEEDY. NOW, DEMONS, THEY --

SHUT UP.

YOU KNOW, ALL MY *LIFE* PEOPLE LIKE YOU HAVE BEEN CRAMMING FAIRYTALES DOWN MY THROAT.

"DO *THIS* AND YOU'LL BE HAPPY." "DO *THAT* AND YOU'LL HAVE FRIENDS."

"BE A *GOOD* LITTLE SCAREDY - CAT FROG, AND *SOMEDAY* YOU'LL TURN INTO A BLOODY *PRINCE*."

WELL, I DON'T *WANT* TO LIVE YOUR ROTTEN OLD FAIRYTALES.

RRRUMBLE KRRRAK SKRRNIP

I WANT TO LIVE MINE.

COOL. A *NEW* BRIDGE.

UH... DOES IT HAVE TROLLS?

THAT *WASN'T* A TROLL, YOU IDIOT. THAT WAS A DEMON.

UMM... IT *LOOKS* LIKE A *SUPER* BRIDGE -- BUT WHERE DOES IT GO?

TO *MOLLY*, SILLY.

WHERE *ELSE?*

DARN IT --

THERE GOES *MY* PROMOTION.

134

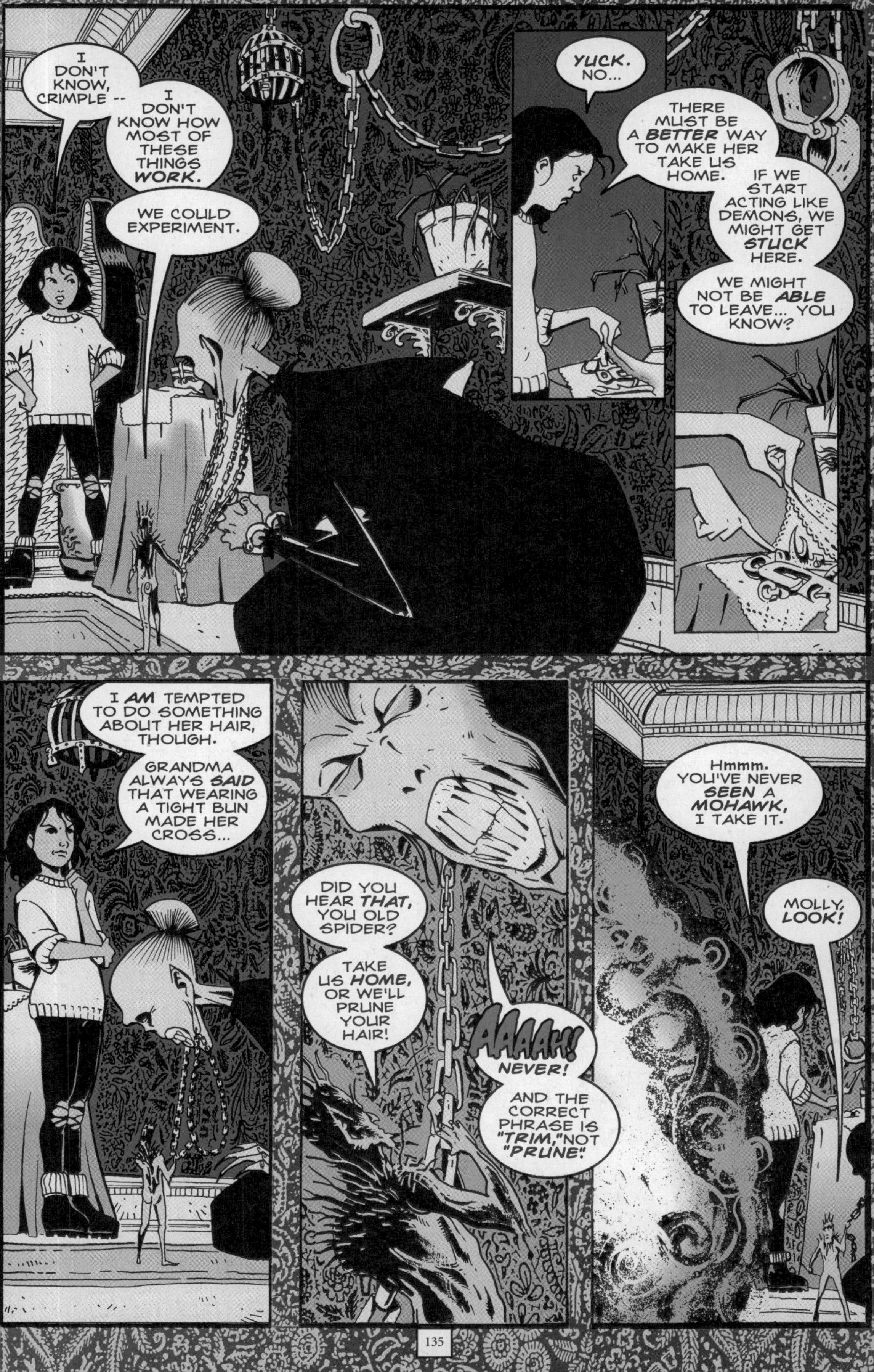
I DON'T KNOW, CRIMPLE --
I DON'T KNOW HOW MOST OF THESE THINGS WORK.
WE COULD EXPERIMENT.
YUCK. NO...
THERE MUST BE A BETTER WAY TO MAKE HER TAKE US HOME.
IF WE START ACTING LIKE DEMONS, WE MIGHT GET STUCK HERE.
WE MIGHT NOT BE ABLE TO LEAVE... YOU KNOW?
I AM TEMPTED TO DO SOMETHING ABOUT HER HAIR, THOUGH.
GRANDMA ALWAYS SAID THAT WEARING A TIGHT BUN MADE HER CROSS...
DID YOU HEAR THAT, YOU OLD SPIDER?
TAKE US HOME, OR WE'LL PRUNE YOUR HAIR!
AAAAH!
NEVER!
AND THE CORRECT PHRASE IS "TRIM," NOT "PRUNE"!
Hmmm. YOU'VE NEVER SEEN A MOHAWK, I TAKE IT.
MOLLY, LOOK!

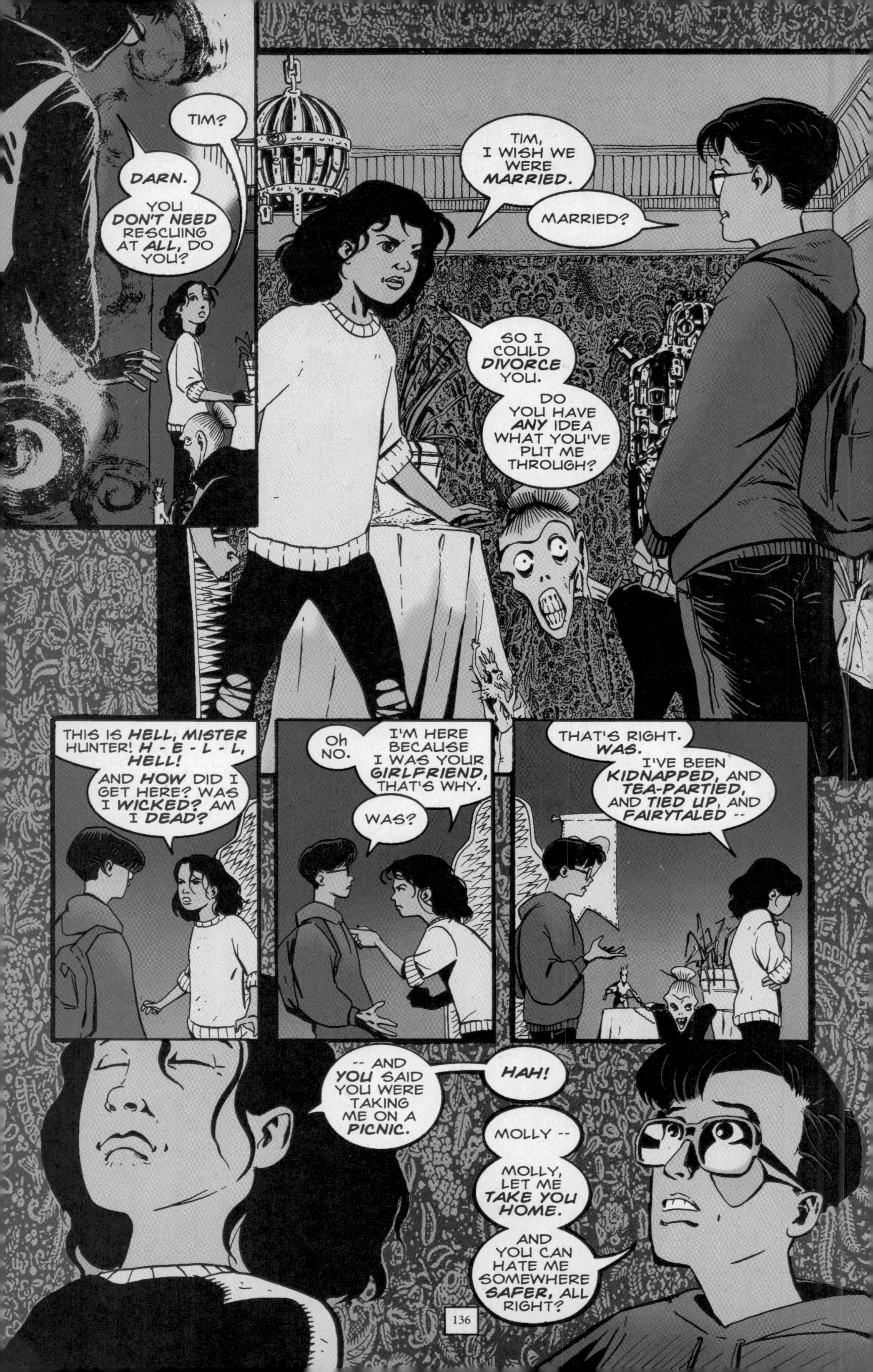
TIM?
DARN.
YOU DON'T NEED RESCUING AT ALL, DO YOU?
TIM, I WISH WE WERE MARRIED.
MARRIED?
SO I COULD DIVORCE YOU.
DO YOU HAVE ANY IDEA WHAT YOU'VE PUT ME THROUGH?
THIS IS HELL, MISTER HUNTER! H - E - L - L, HELL!
AND HOW DID I GET HERE? WAS I WICKED? AM I DEAD?
Oh NO.
I'M HERE BECAUSE I WAS YOUR GIRLFRIEND, THAT'S WHY.
WAS?
THAT'S RIGHT. WAS.
I'VE BEEN KIDNAPPED, AND TEA-PARTIED, AND TIED UP, AND FAIRYTALED --
-- AND YOU SAID YOU WERE TAKING ME ON A PICNIC.
HAH!
MOLLY --
MOLLY, LET ME TAKE YOU HOME.
AND YOU CAN HATE ME SOMEWHERE SAFER, ALL RIGHT?

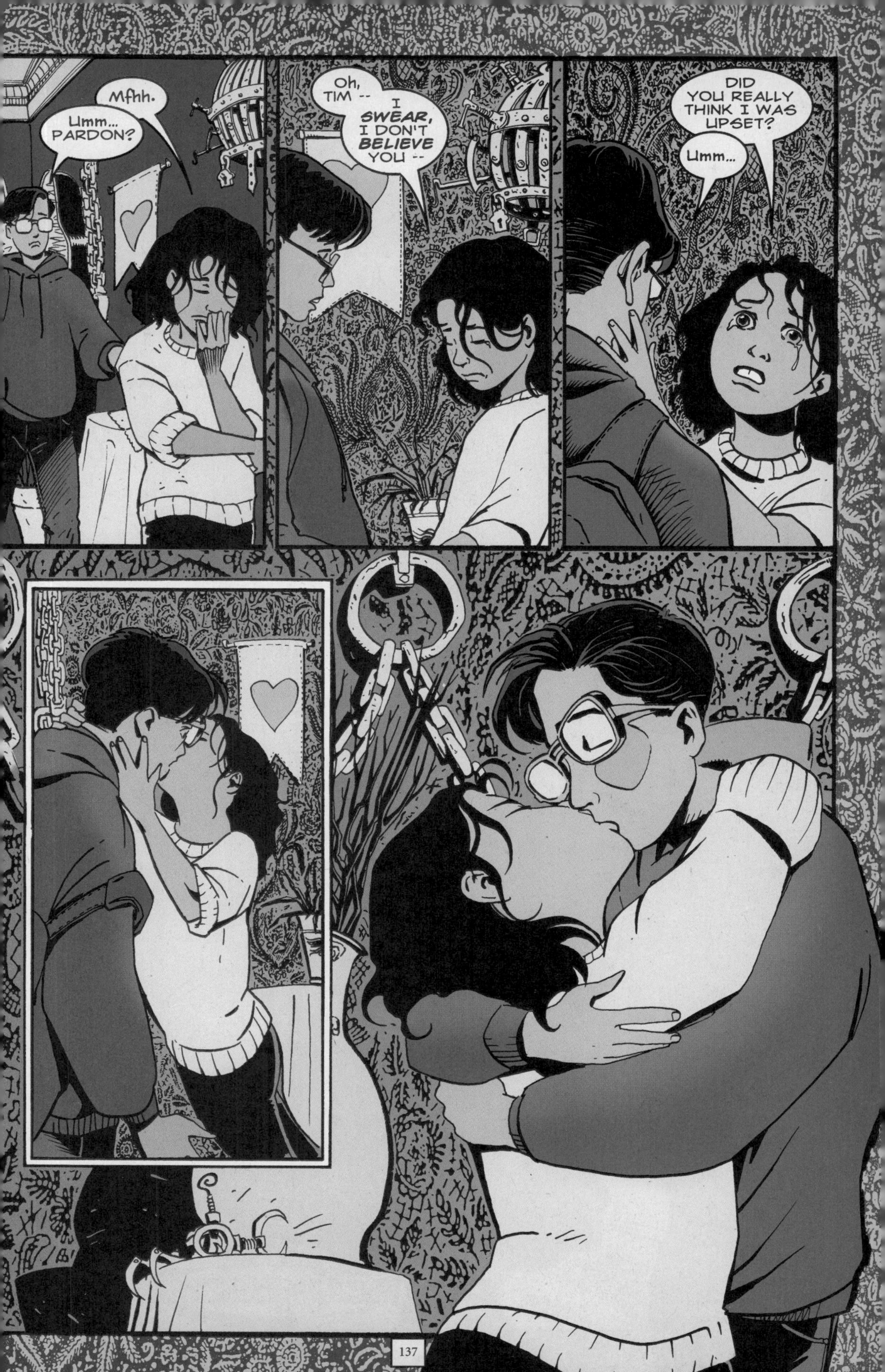
Mfhh.
Umm... PARDON?
Oh, TIM --
I SWEAR, I DON'T BELIEVE YOU --
DID YOU REALLY THINK I WAS UPSET?
Umm...

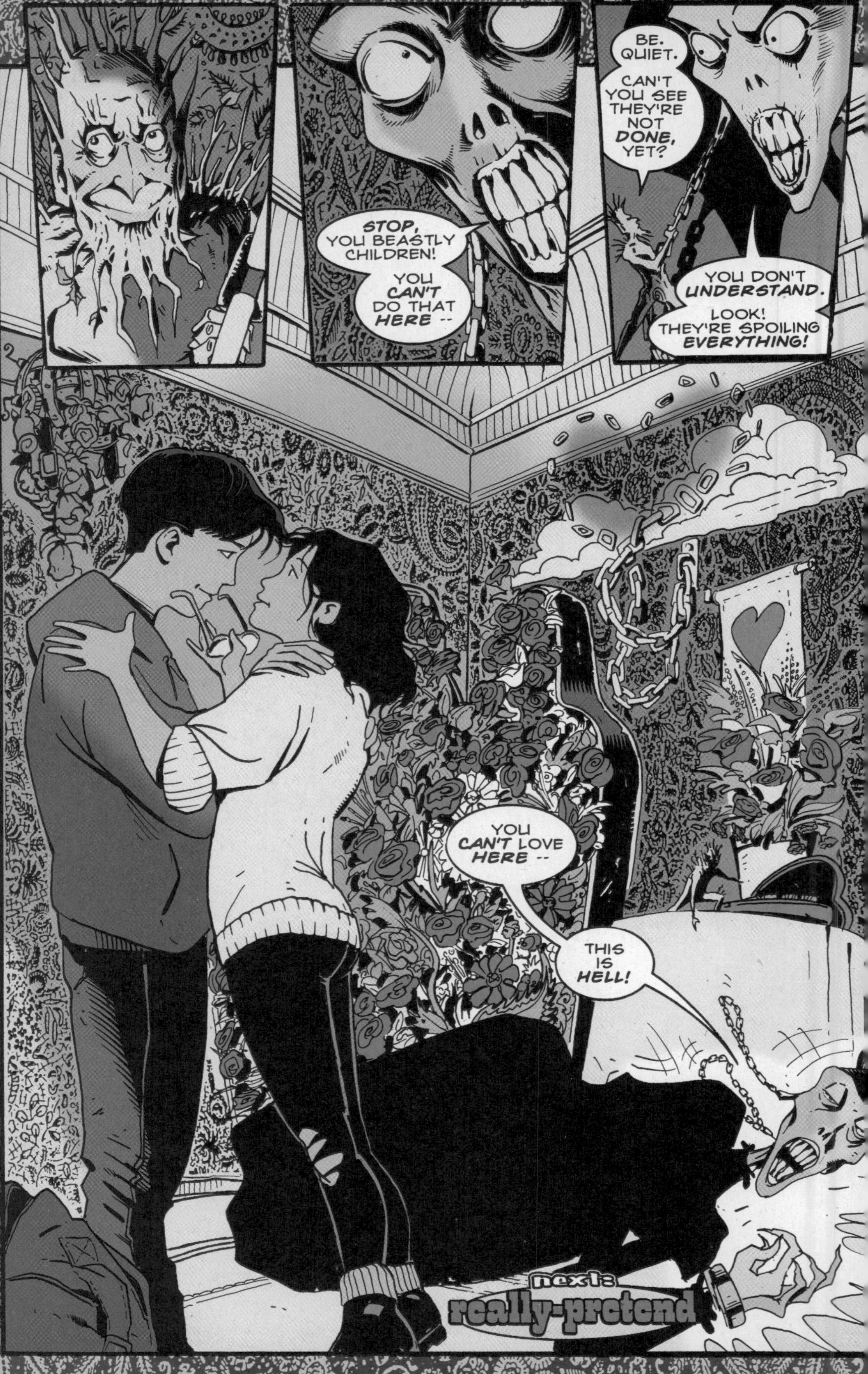
STOP, YOU BEASTLY CHILDREN!
YOU CAN'T DO THAT HERE --
BE. QUIET.
CAN'T YOU SEE THEY'RE NOT DONE, YET?
YOU DON'T UNDERSTAND.
LOOK! THEY'RE SPOILING EVERYTHING!
YOU CAN'T LOVE HERE --
THIS IS HELL!
next:
really-pretend

Really-Pretend

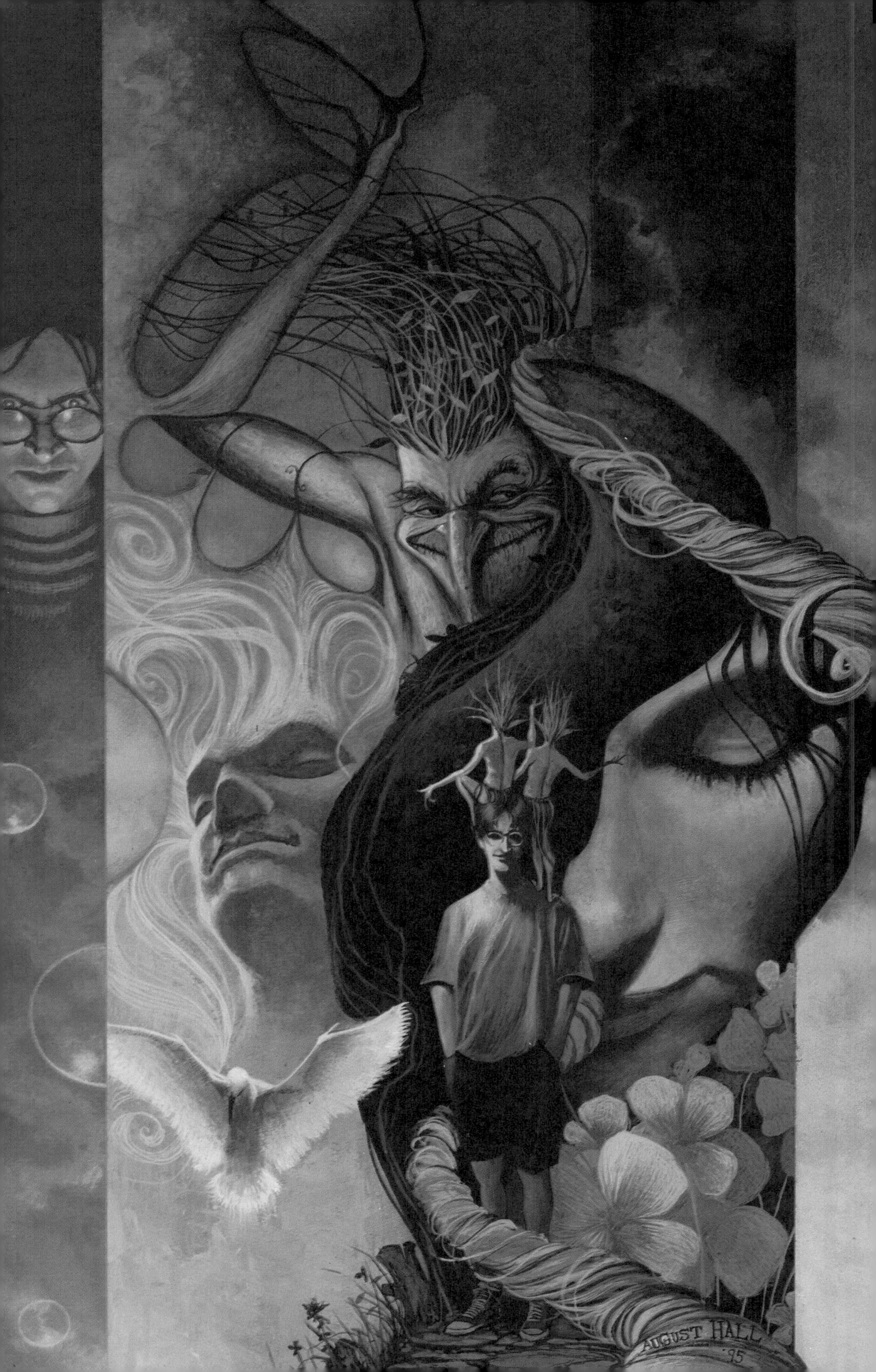
AUGUST HALL
'95

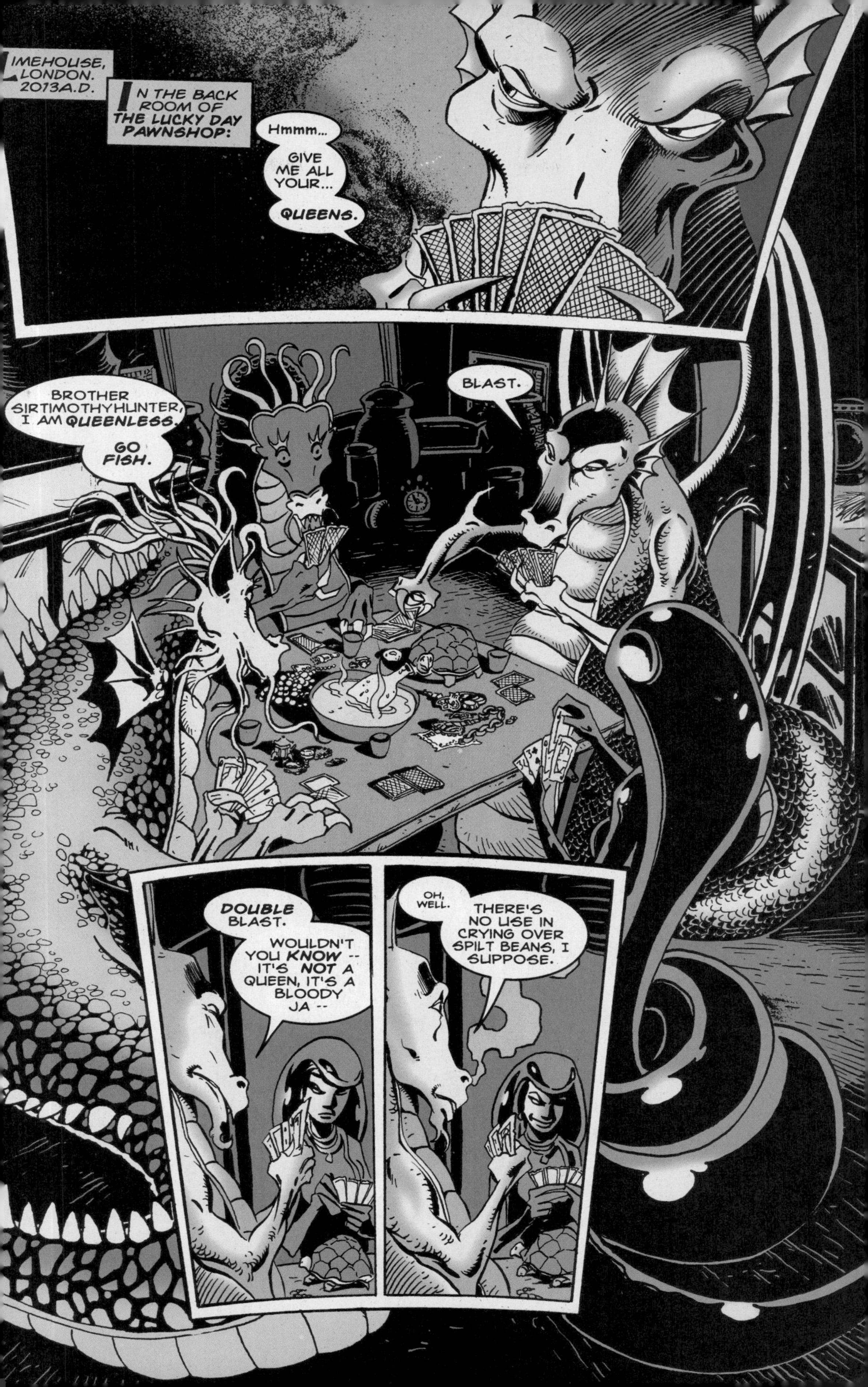
LIMEHOUSE, LONDON. 2013 A.D.
IN THE BACK ROOM OF THE LUCKY DAY PAWNSHOP:
Hmmm... GIVE ME ALL YOUR... QUEENS.
BROTHER SIRTIMOTHYHUNTER, I AM QUEENLESS. GO FISH.
BLAST.
DOUBLE BLAST.
WOULDN'T YOU KNOW -- IT'S NOT A QUEEN, IT'S A BLOODY JA --
OH, WELL.
THERE'S NO USE IN CRYING OVER SPILT BEANS, I SUPPOSE.

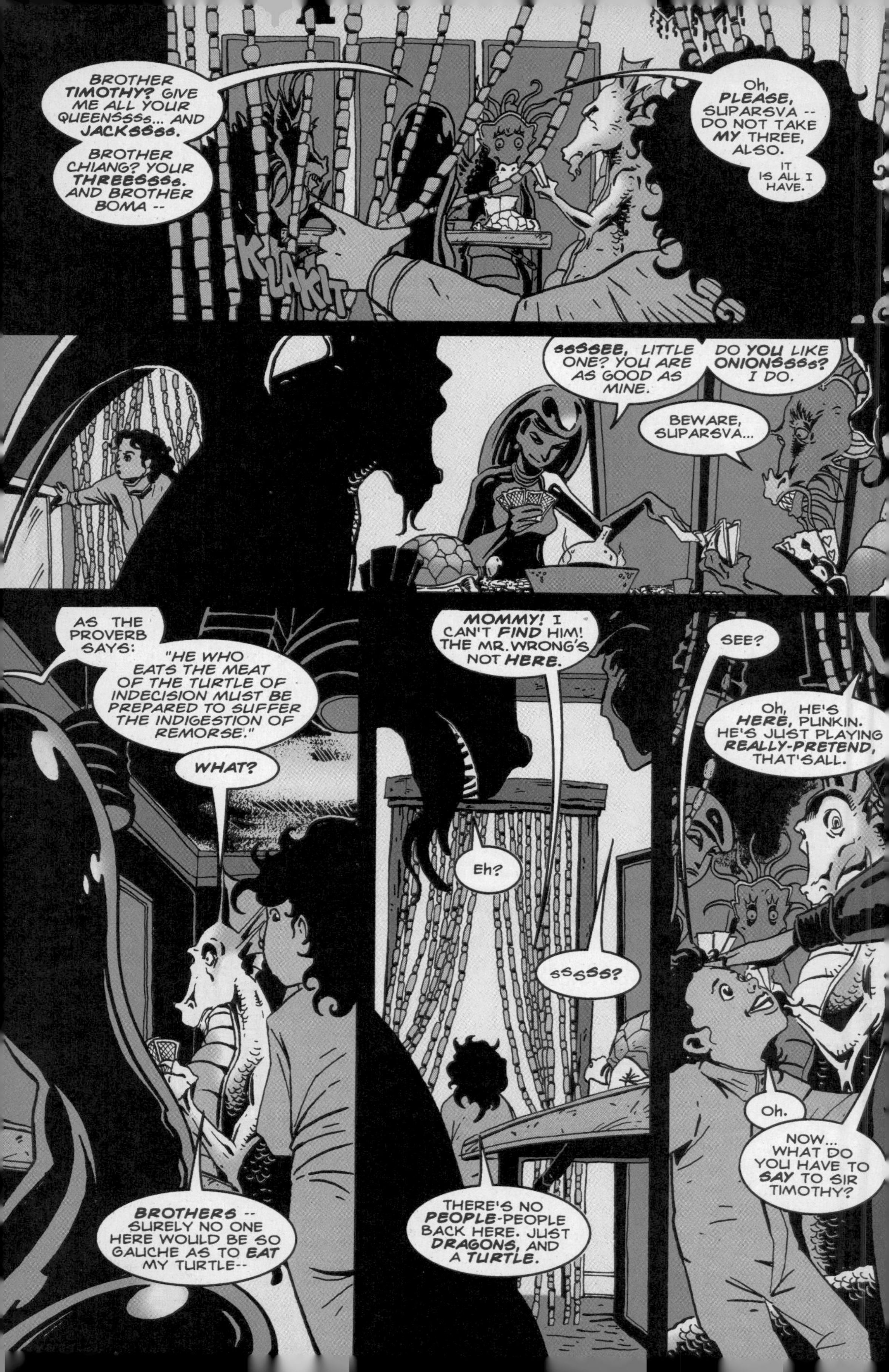
BROTHER TIMOTHY? GIVE ME ALL YOUR QUEENSSSs... AND JACKSSSs.
BROTHER CHIANG? YOUR THREESSSs. AND BROTHER BOMA --
Oh, PLEASE, SUPARSVA -- DO NOT TAKE MY THREE, ALSO.
IT IS ALL I HAVE.
KLAKIT
SSSSEE, LITTLE ONE? YOU ARE AS GOOD AS MINE.
DO YOU LIKE ONIONSSSs? I DO.
BEWARE, SUPARSVA...
AS THE PROVERB SAYS: "HE WHO EATS THE MEAT OF THE TURTLE OF INDECISION MUST BE PREPARED TO SUFFER THE INDIGESTION OF REMORSE."
WHAT?
BROTHERS -- SURELY NO ONE HERE WOULD BE SO GAUCHE AS TO EAT MY TURTLE--
MOMMY! I CAN'T FIND HIM! THE MR. WRONG'S NOT HERE.
Eh?
SSSSS?
THERE'S NO PEOPLE-PEOPLE BACK HERE. JUST DRAGONS, AND A TURTLE.
SEE?
Oh, HE'S HERE, PUNKIN. HE'S JUST PLAYING REALLY-PRETEND, THAT'SALL.
Oh.
NOW... WHAT DO YOU HAVE TO SAY TO SIR TIMOTHY?

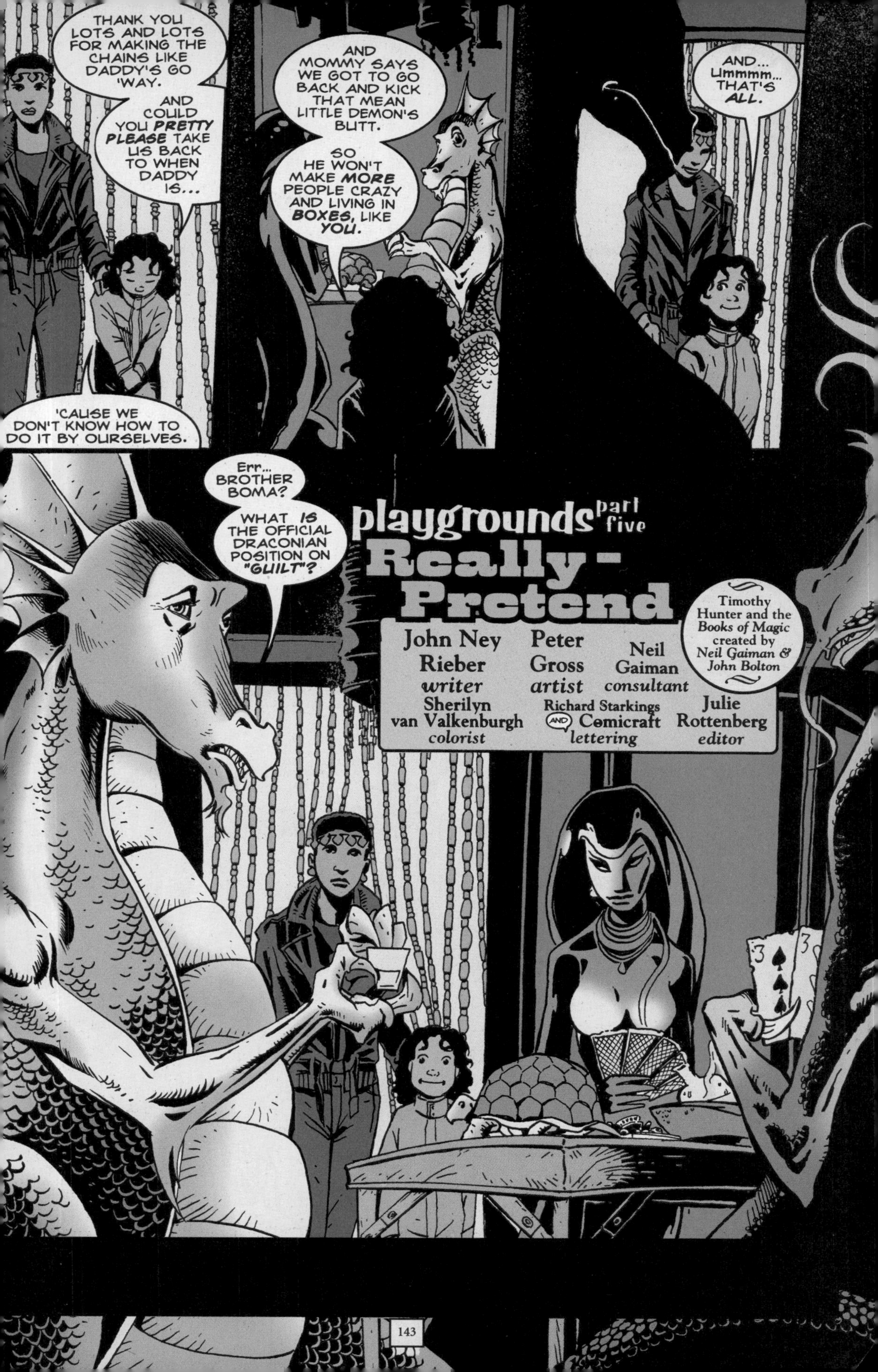
THANK YOU LOTS AND LOTS FOR MAKING THE CHAINS LIKE DADDY'S GO 'WAY.
AND COULD YOU PRETTY PLEASE TAKE US BACK TO WHEN DADDY IS...
'CAUSE WE DON'T KNOW HOW TO DO IT BY OURSELVES.
AND MOMMY SAYS WE GOT TO GO BACK AND KICK THAT MEAN LITTLE DEMON'S BUTT.
SO HE WON'T MAKE MORE PEOPLE CRAZY AND LIVING IN BOXES, LIKE YOU.
AND... Ummmm... THAT'S ALL.
Err... BROTHER BOMA?
WHAT IS THE OFFICIAL DRACONIAN POSITION ON "GUILT"?
playgrounds part five
Really-Pretend
John Ney Rieber writer
Peter Gross artist
Neil Gaiman consultant
Timothy Hunter and the Books of Magic created by Neil Gaiman & John Bolton
Sherilyn van Valkenburgh colorist
Richard Starkings AND Comicraft lettering
Julie Rottenberg editor

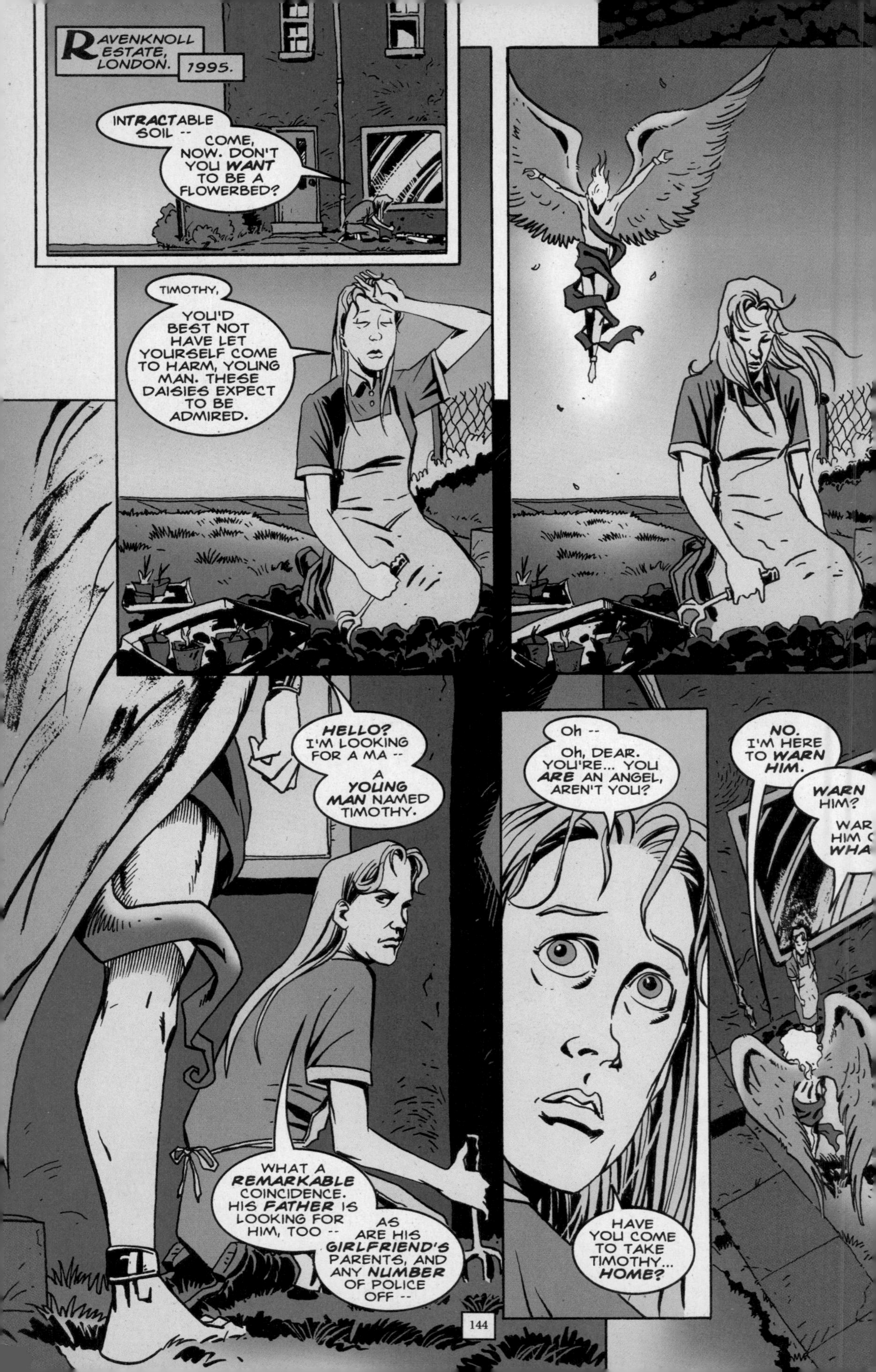
RAVENKNOLL ESTATE, LONDON.
1995.
INTRACTABLE SOIL --
COME, NOW. DON'T YOU WANT TO BE A FLOWERBED?
TIMOTHY,
YOU'D BEST NOT HAVE LET YOURSELF COME TO HARM, YOUNG MAN. THESE DAISIES EXPECT TO BE ADMIRED.
HELLO? I'M LOOKING FOR A MA --
A YOUNG MAN NAMED TIMOTHY.
WHAT A REMARKABLE COINCIDENCE. HIS FATHER IS LOOKING FOR HIM, TOO --
AS ARE HIS GIRLFRIEND'S PARENTS, AND ANY NUMBER OF POLICE OFF --
Oh --
Oh, DEAR. YOU'RE... YOU ARE AN ANGEL, AREN'T YOU?
HAVE YOU COME TO TAKE TIMOTHY... HOME?
NO. I'M HERE TO WARN HIM.
WARN HIM?
WAR HIM WHA

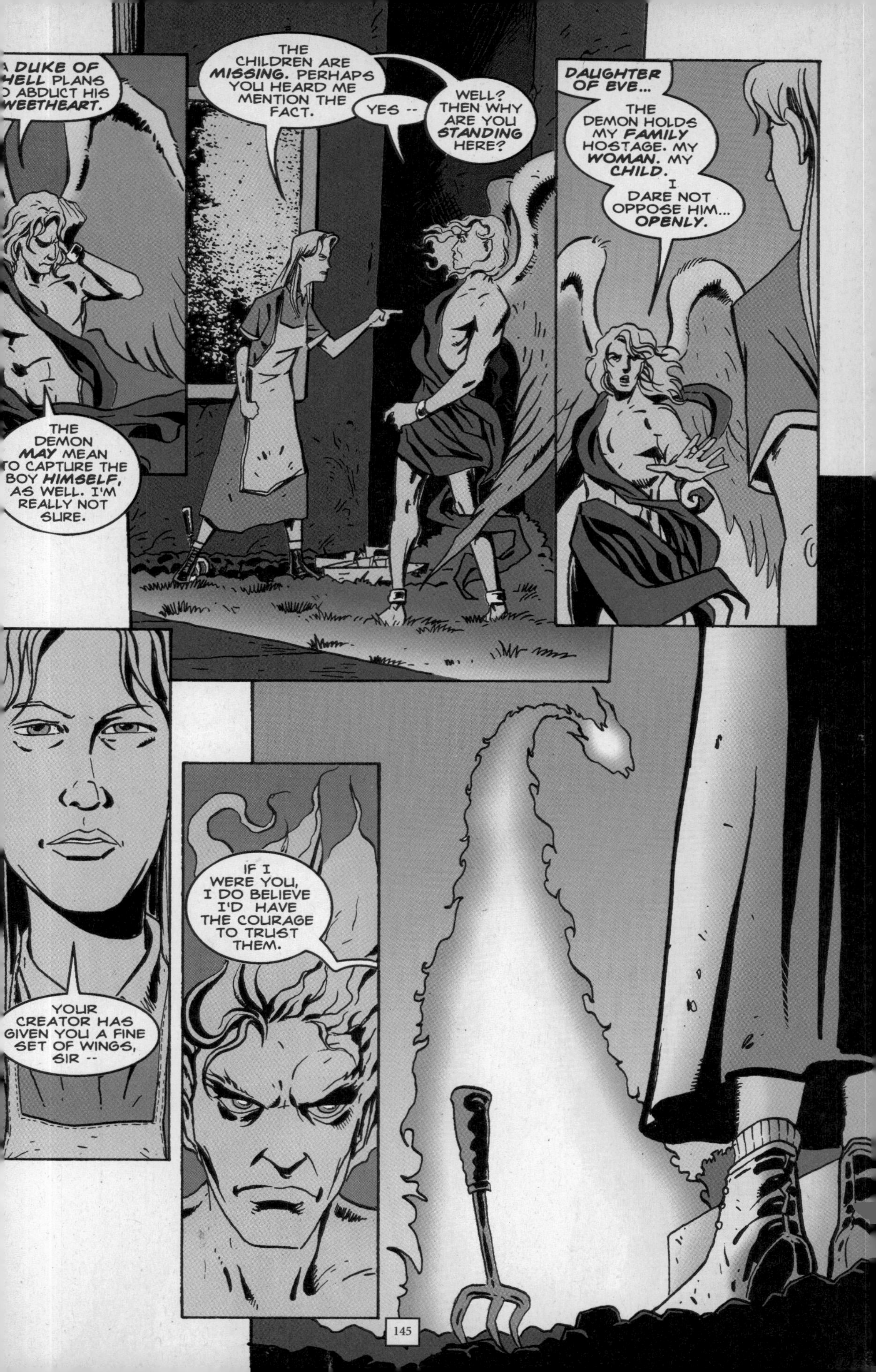
A DUKE OF HELL PLANS TO ABDUCT HIS SWEETHEART.
THE DEMON MAY MEAN TO CAPTURE THE BOY HIMSELF, AS WELL. I'M REALLY NOT SURE.
THE CHILDREN ARE MISSING. PERHAPS YOU HEARD ME MENTION THE FACT.
YES --
WELL? THEN WHY ARE YOU STANDING HERE?
DAUGHTER OF EVE...
THE DEMON HOLDS MY FAMILY HOSTAGE. MY WOMAN. MY CHILD.
I DARE NOT OPPOSE HIM... OPENLY.
YOUR CREATOR HAS GIVEN YOU A FINE SET OF WINGS, SIR --
IF I WERE YOU, I DO BELIEVE I'D HAVE THE COURAGE TO TRUST THEM.

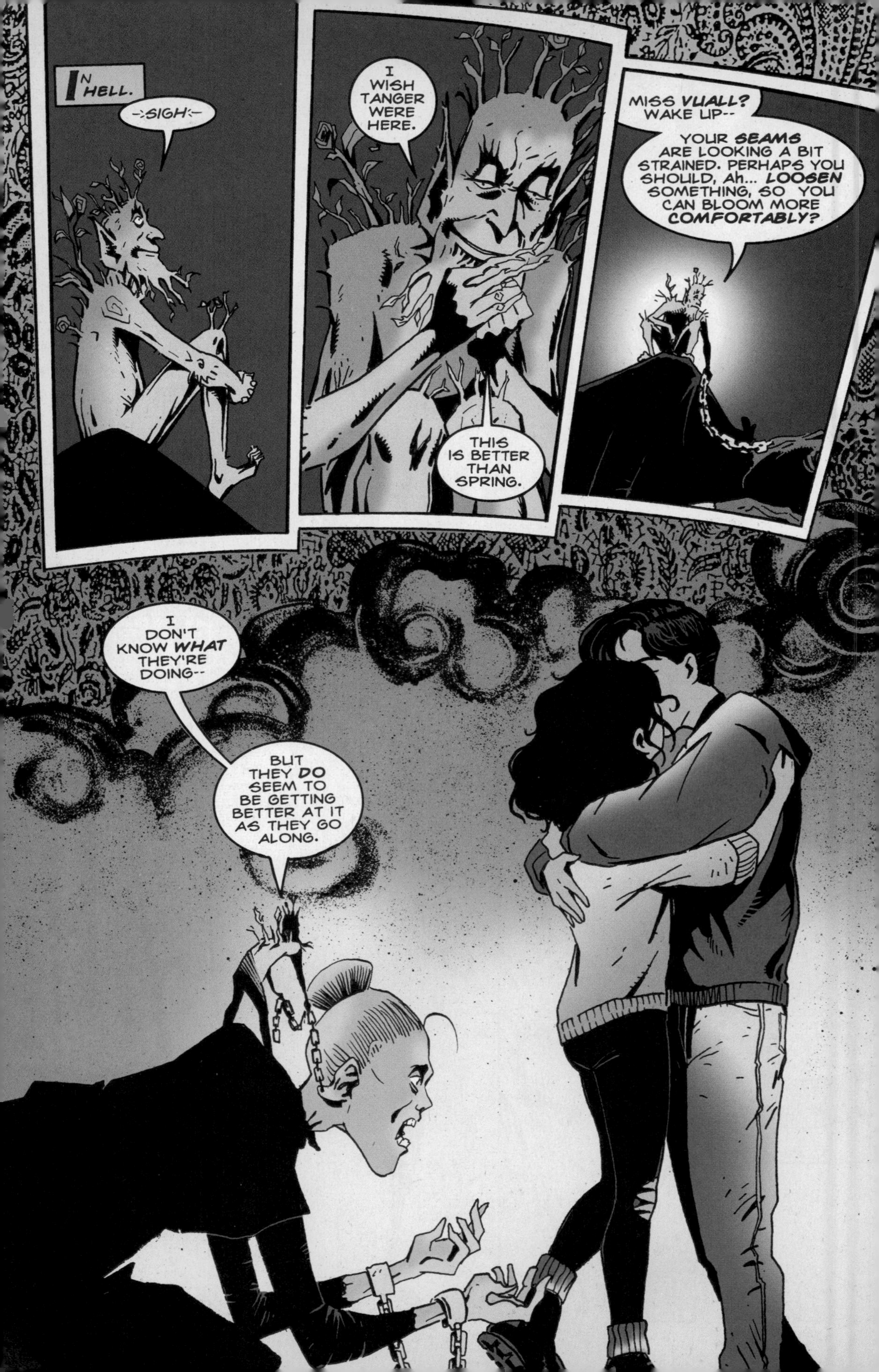
IN HELL.
-SIGH-
I WISH TANGER WERE HERE.
THIS IS BETTER THAN SPRING.
MISS VUALL? WAKE UP--
YOUR SEAMS ARE LOOKING A BIT STRAINED. PERHAPS YOU SHOULD, Ah... LOOSEN SOMETHING, SO YOU CAN BLOOM MORE COMFORTABLY?
I DON'T KNOW WHAT THEY'RE DOING--
BUT THEY DO SEEM TO BE GETTING BETTER AT IT AS THEY GO ALONG.

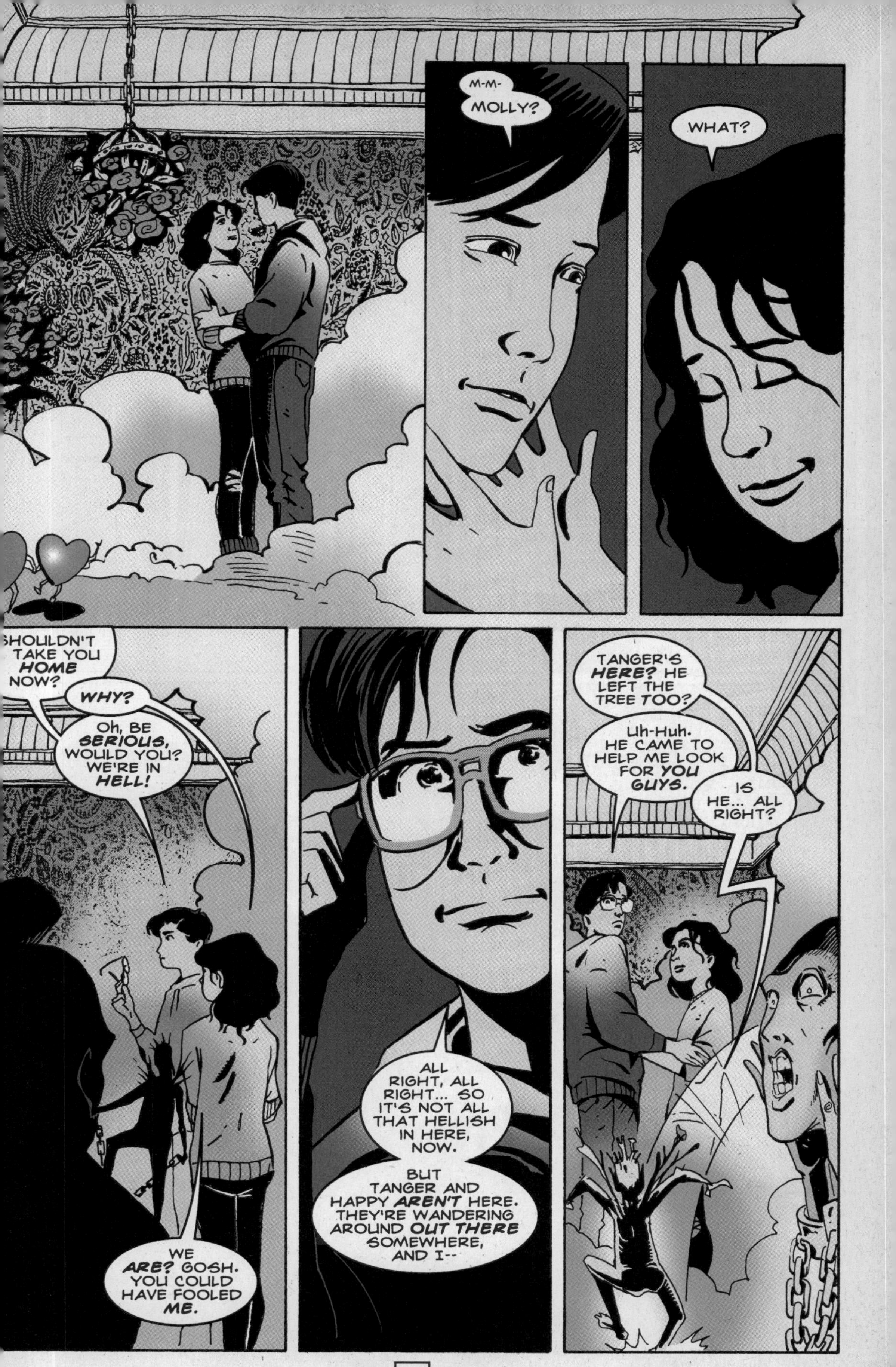
M-M-
MOLLY?
WHAT?
SHOULDN'T TAKE YOU HOME NOW?
WHY?
Oh, BE SERIOUS, WOULD YOU? WE'RE IN HELL!
WE ARE? GOSH. YOU COULD HAVE FOOLED ME.
ALL RIGHT, ALL RIGHT... SO IT'S NOT ALL THAT HELLISH IN HERE, NOW.
BUT TANGER AND HAPPY AREN'T HERE. THEY'RE WANDERING AROUND OUT THERE SOMEWHERE, AND I--
TANGER'S HERE? HE LEFT THE TREE TOO?
Uh-Huh. HE CAME TO HELP ME LOOK FOR YOU GUYS.
IS HE... ALL RIGHT?

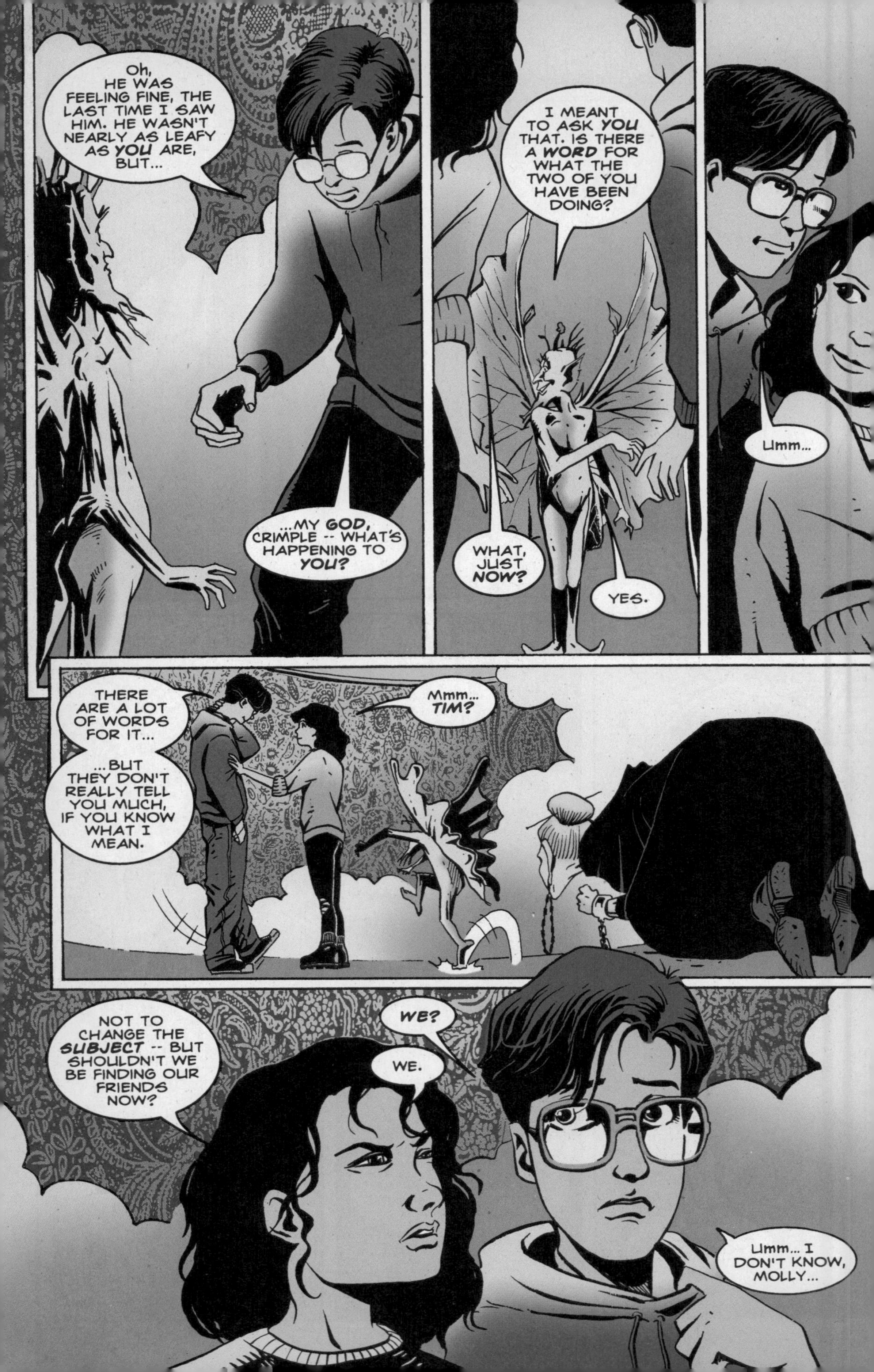

Oh, HE WAS FEELING FINE, THE LAST TIME I SAW HIM. HE WASN'T NEARLY AS LEAFY AS YOU ARE, BUT...
...MY GOD, CRIMPLE -- WHAT'S HAPPENING TO YOU?
I MEANT TO ASK YOU THAT. IS THERE A WORD FOR WHAT THE TWO OF YOU HAVE BEEN DOING?
WHAT, JUST NOW?
YES.
Umm...
THERE ARE A LOT OF WORDS FOR IT...
...BUT THEY DON'T REALLY TELL YOU MUCH, IF YOU KNOW WHAT I MEAN.
Mmm... TIM?
NOT TO CHANGE THE SUBJECT -- BUT SHOULDN'T WE BE FINDING OUR FRIENDS NOW?
WE?
WE.
Umm... I DON'T KNOW, MOLLY...

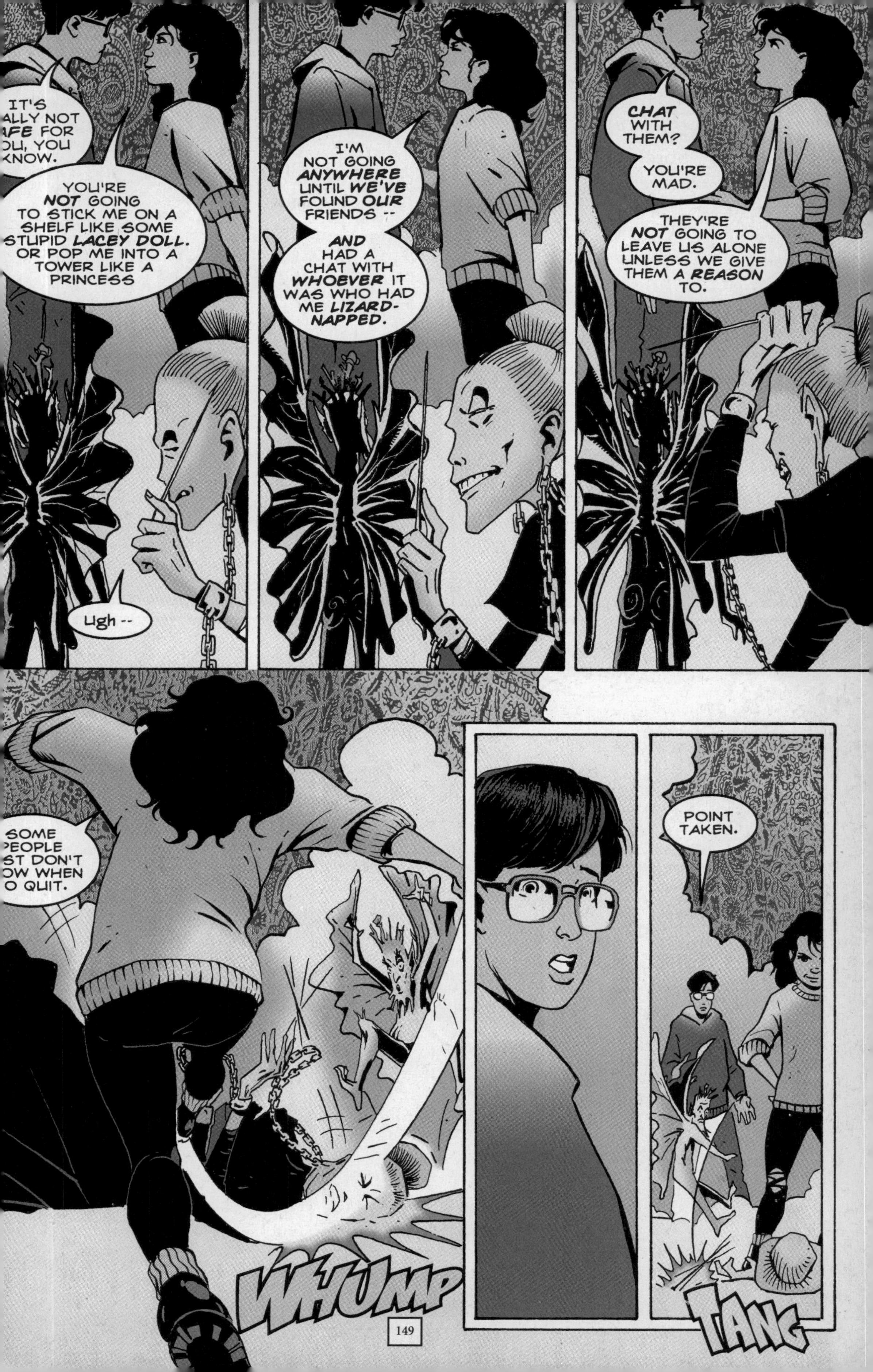
IT'S ALLY NOT AFE FOR OU, YOU KNOW.
YOU'RE NOT GOING TO STICK ME ON A SHELF LIKE SOME STUPID LACEY DOLL. OR POP ME INTO A TOWER LIKE A PRINCESS
Ugh --
I'M NOT GOING ANYWHERE UNTIL WE'VE FOUND OUR FRIENDS --
AND HAD A CHAT WITH WHOEVER IT WAS WHO HAD ME LIZARD-NAPPED.
CHAT WITH THEM?
YOU'RE MAD.
THEY'RE NOT GOING TO LEAVE US ALONE UNLESS WE GIVE THEM A REASON TO.
SOME PEOPLE ST DON'T OW WHEN O QUIT.
WHUMP
POINT TAKEN.
TANG

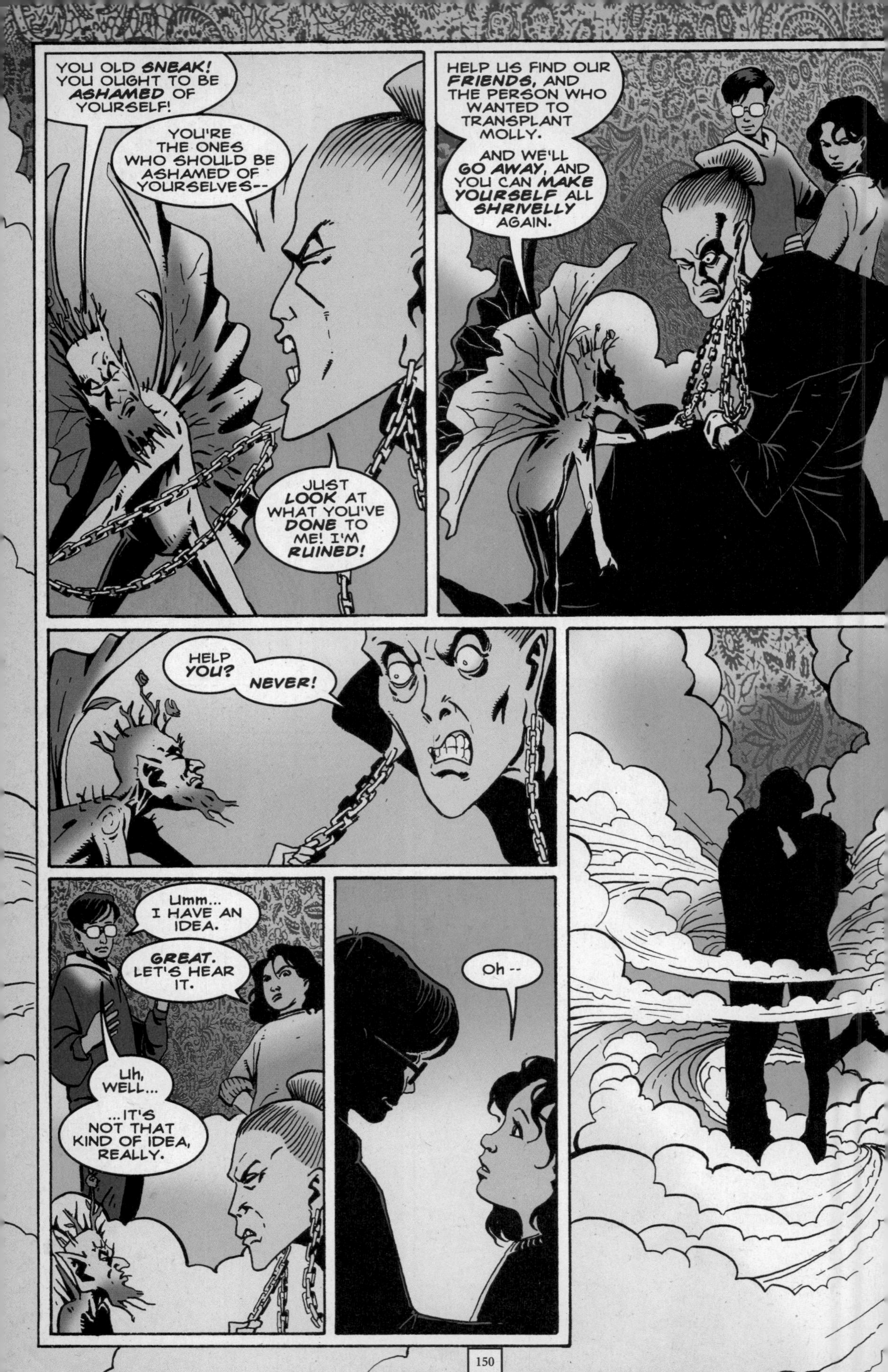
YOU OLD SNEAK! YOU OUGHT TO BE ASHAMED OF YOURSELF!
YOU'RE THE ONES WHO SHOULD BE ASHAMED OF YOURSELVES--
JUST LOOK AT WHAT YOU'VE DONE TO ME! I'M RUINED!
HELP US FIND OUR FRIENDS, AND THE PERSON WHO WANTED TO TRANSPLANT MOLLY.
AND WE'LL GO AWAY, AND YOU CAN MAKE YOURSELF ALL SHRIVELLY AGAIN.
HELP YOU? NEVER!
Umm... I HAVE AN IDEA.
GREAT. LET'S HEAR IT.
Uh, WELL...
...IT'S NOT THAT KIND OF IDEA, REALLY.
Oh --

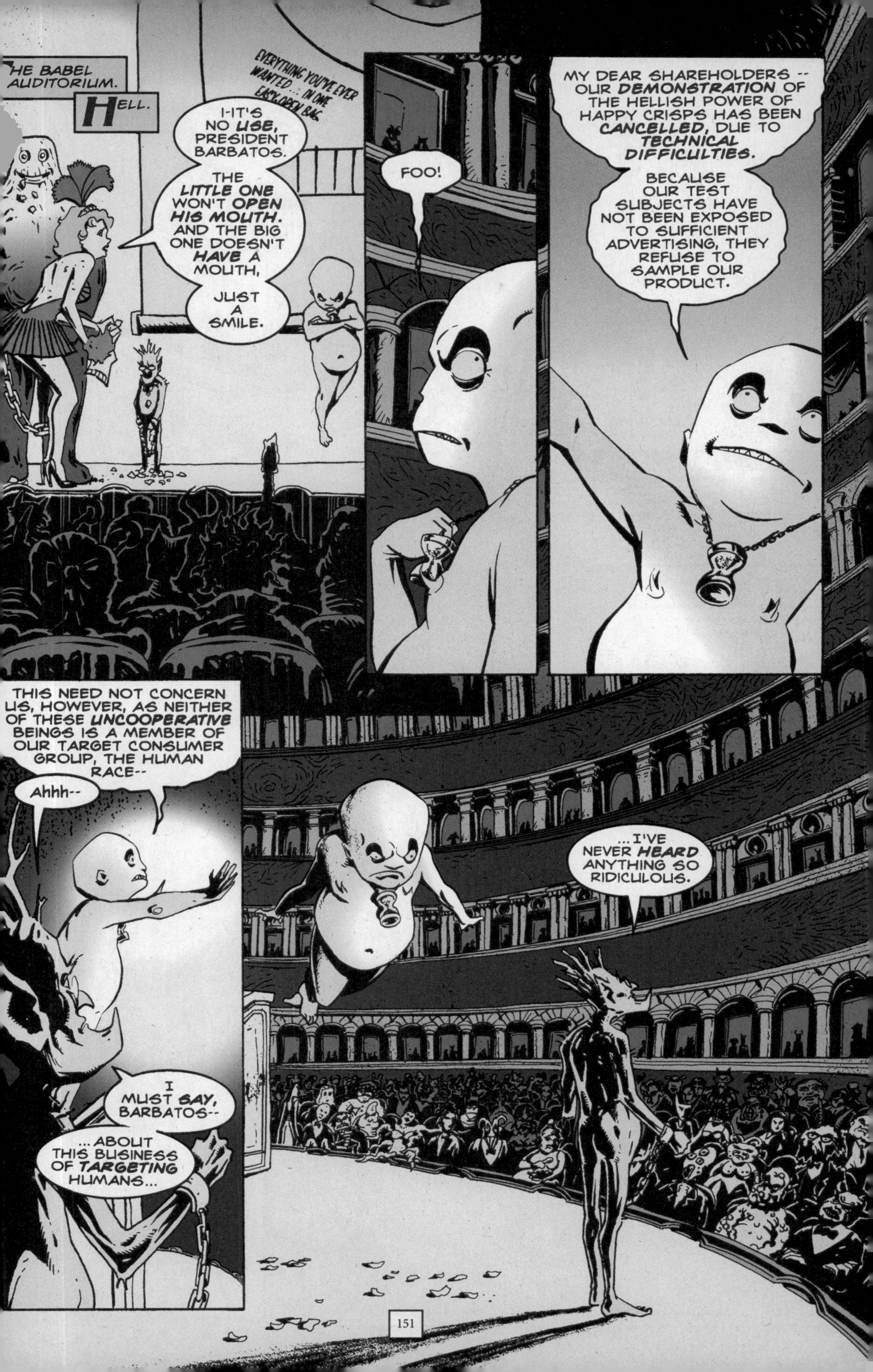
HE BABEL AUDITORIUM.
HELL.
EVERYTHING YOU'VE EVER WANTED... IN ONE EASY-OPEN BAG.
I-IT'S NO USE, PRESIDENT BARBATOS.
THE LITTLE ONE WON'T OPEN HIS MOUTH. AND THE BIG ONE DOESN'T HAVE A MOUTH,
JUST A SMILE.
FOO!
MY DEAR SHAREHOLDERS -- OUR DEMONSTRATION OF THE HELLISH POWER OF HAPPY CRISPS HAS BEEN CANCELLED, DUE TO TECHNICAL DIFFICULTIES.
BECAUSE OUR TEST SUBJECTS HAVE NOT BEEN EXPOSED TO SUFFICIENT ADVERTISING, THEY REFUSE TO SAMPLE OUR PRODUCT.
THIS NEED NOT CONCERN US, HOWEVER, AS NEITHER OF THESE UNCOOPERATIVE BEINGS IS A MEMBER OF OUR TARGET CONSUMER GROUP, THE HUMAN RACE--
Ahhh--
I MUST SAY, BARBATOS--
...ABOUT THIS BUSINESS OF TARGETING HUMANS...
...I'VE NEVER HEARD ANYTHING SO RIDICULOUS.

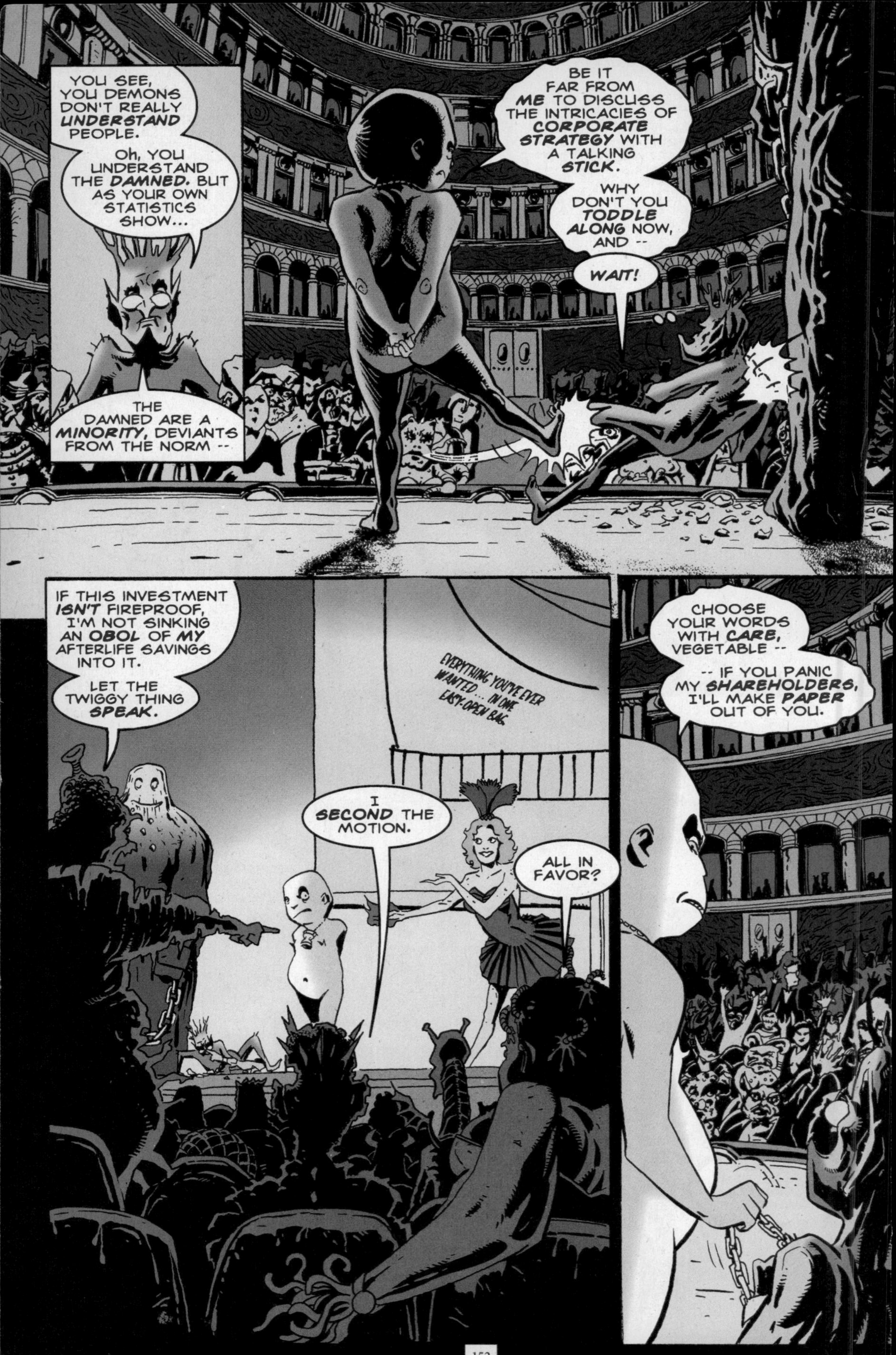
YOU SEE, YOU DEMONS DON'T REALLY UNDERSTAND PEOPLE.
Oh, YOU UNDERSTAND THE DAMNED. BUT AS YOUR OWN STATISTICS SHOW...
THE DAMNED ARE A MINORITY, DEVIANTS FROM THE NORM --
BE IT FAR FROM ME TO DISCUSS THE INTRICACIES OF CORPORATE STRATEGY WITH A TALKING STICK.
WHY DON'T YOU TODDLE ALONG NOW, AND --
WAIT!
IF THIS INVESTMENT ISN'T FIREPROOF, I'M NOT SINKING AN OBOL OF MY AFTERLIFE SAVINGS INTO IT.
LET THE TWIGGY THING SPEAK.
EVERYTHING YOU'VE EVER WANTED... IN ONE EASY-OPEN BAG.
I SECOND THE MOTION.
ALL IN FAVOR?
CHOOSE YOUR WORDS WITH CARE, VEGETABLE --
-- IF YOU PANIC MY SHAREHOLDERS, I'LL MAKE PAPER OUT OF YOU.

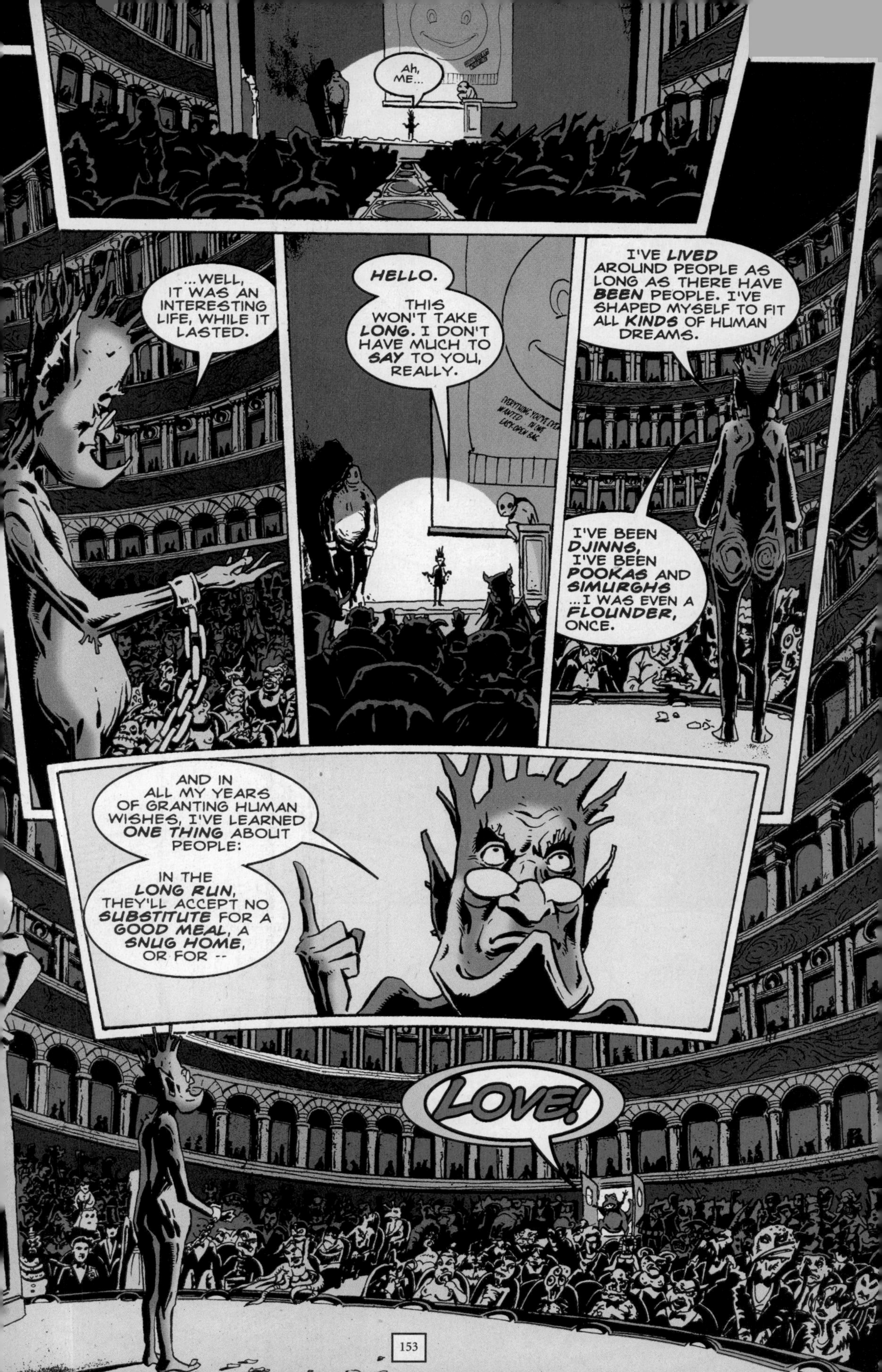
Ah, ME...
...WELL, IT WAS AN INTERESTING LIFE, WHILE IT LASTED.
HELLO.
THIS WON'T TAKE LONG. I DON'T HAVE MUCH TO SAY TO YOU, REALLY.
I'VE LIVED AROUND PEOPLE AS LONG AS THERE HAVE BEEN PEOPLE. I'VE SHAPED MYSELF TO FIT ALL KINDS OF HUMAN DREAMS.
I'VE BEEN DJINNS, I'VE BEEN POOKAS AND SIMURGHS ...I WAS EVEN A FLOUNDER, ONCE.
AND IN ALL MY YEARS OF GRANTING HUMAN WISHES, I'VE LEARNED ONE THING ABOUT PEOPLE:
IN THE LONG RUN, THEY'LL ACCEPT NO SUBSTITUTE FOR A GOOD MEAL, A SNUG HOME, OR FOR --
LOVE!

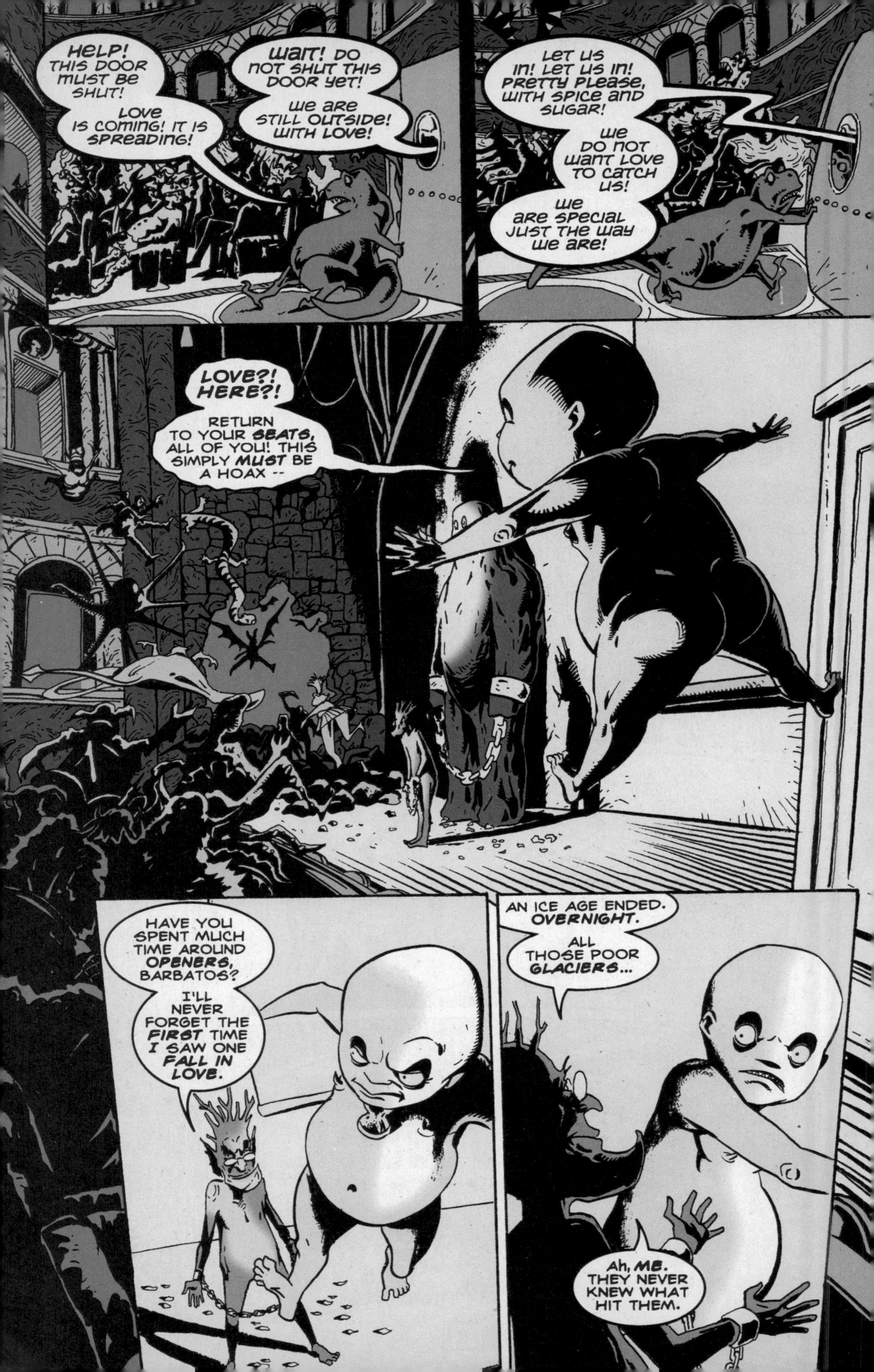
HELP! THIS DOOR MUST BE SHUT!
LOVE IS COMING! IT IS SPREADING!
WAIT! DO NOT SHUT THIS DOOR YET!
WE ARE STILL OUTSIDE! WITH LOVE!
LET US IN! LET US IN! PRETTY PLEASE, WITH SPICE AND SUGAR!
WE DO NOT WANT LOVE TO CATCH US!
WE ARE SPECIAL JUST THE WAY WE ARE!
LOVE?! HERE?!
RETURN TO YOUR SEATS, ALL OF YOU! THIS SIMPLY MUST BE A HOAX --
HAVE YOU SPENT MUCH TIME AROUND OPENERS, BARBATOS?
I'LL NEVER FORGET THE FIRST TIME I SAW ONE FALL IN LOVE.
AN ICE AGE ENDED. OVERNIGHT.
ALL THOSE POOR GLACIERS...
Ah, ME. THEY NEVER KNEW WHAT HIT THEM.

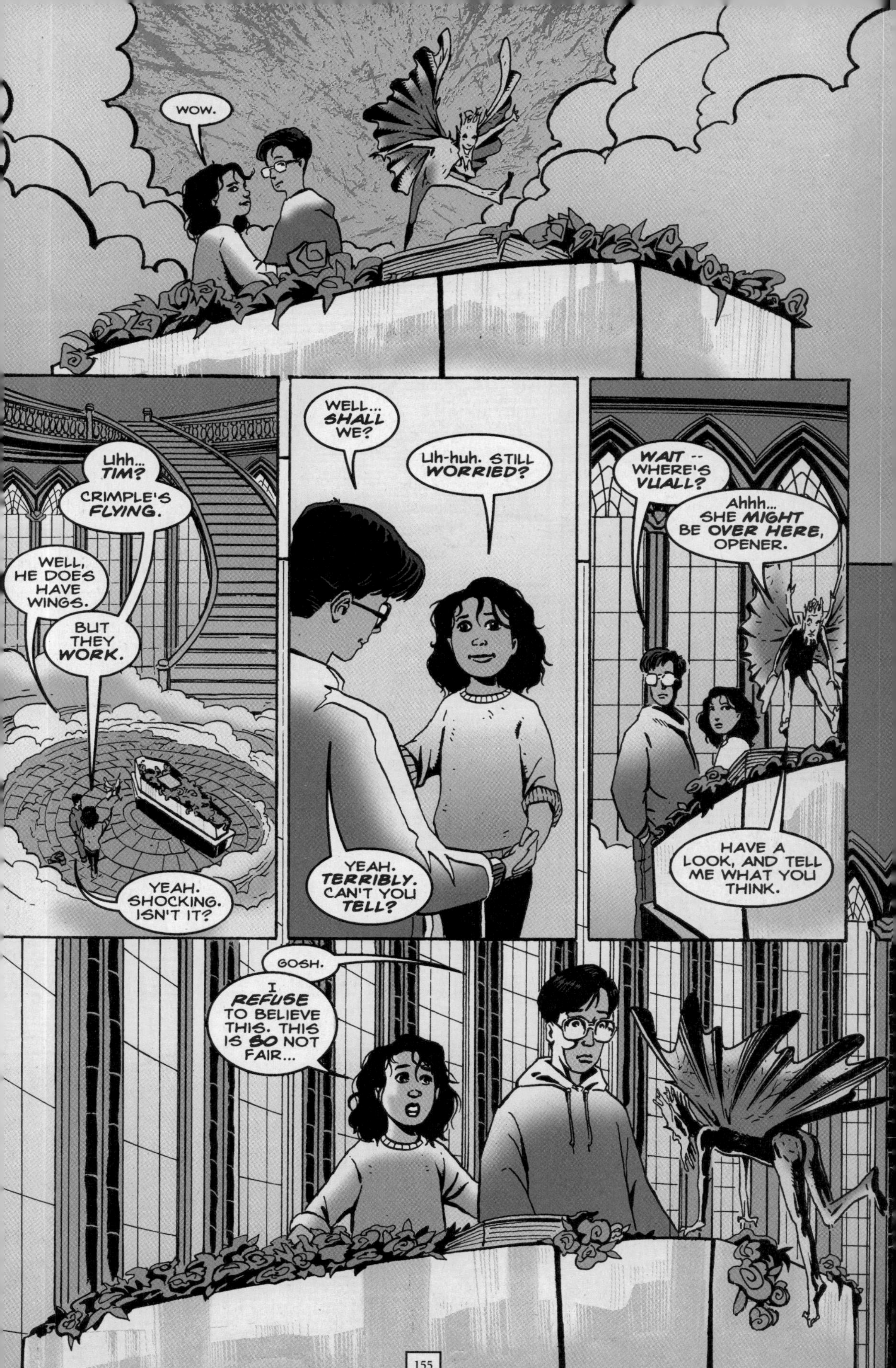
WOW.
UHH... TIM?
CRIMPLE'S FLYING.
WELL, HE DOES HAVE WINGS.
BUT THEY WORK.
YEAH. SHOCKING. ISN'T IT?
WELL... SHALL WE?
UH-HUH. STILL WORRIED?
YEAH. TERRIBLY. CAN'T YOU TELL?
WAIT -- WHERE'S VUALL?
AHHH... SHE MIGHT BE OVER HERE, OPENER.
HAVE A LOOK, AND TELL ME WHAT YOU THINK.
GOSH.
I REFUSE TO BELIEVE THIS. THIS IS SO NOT FAIR...

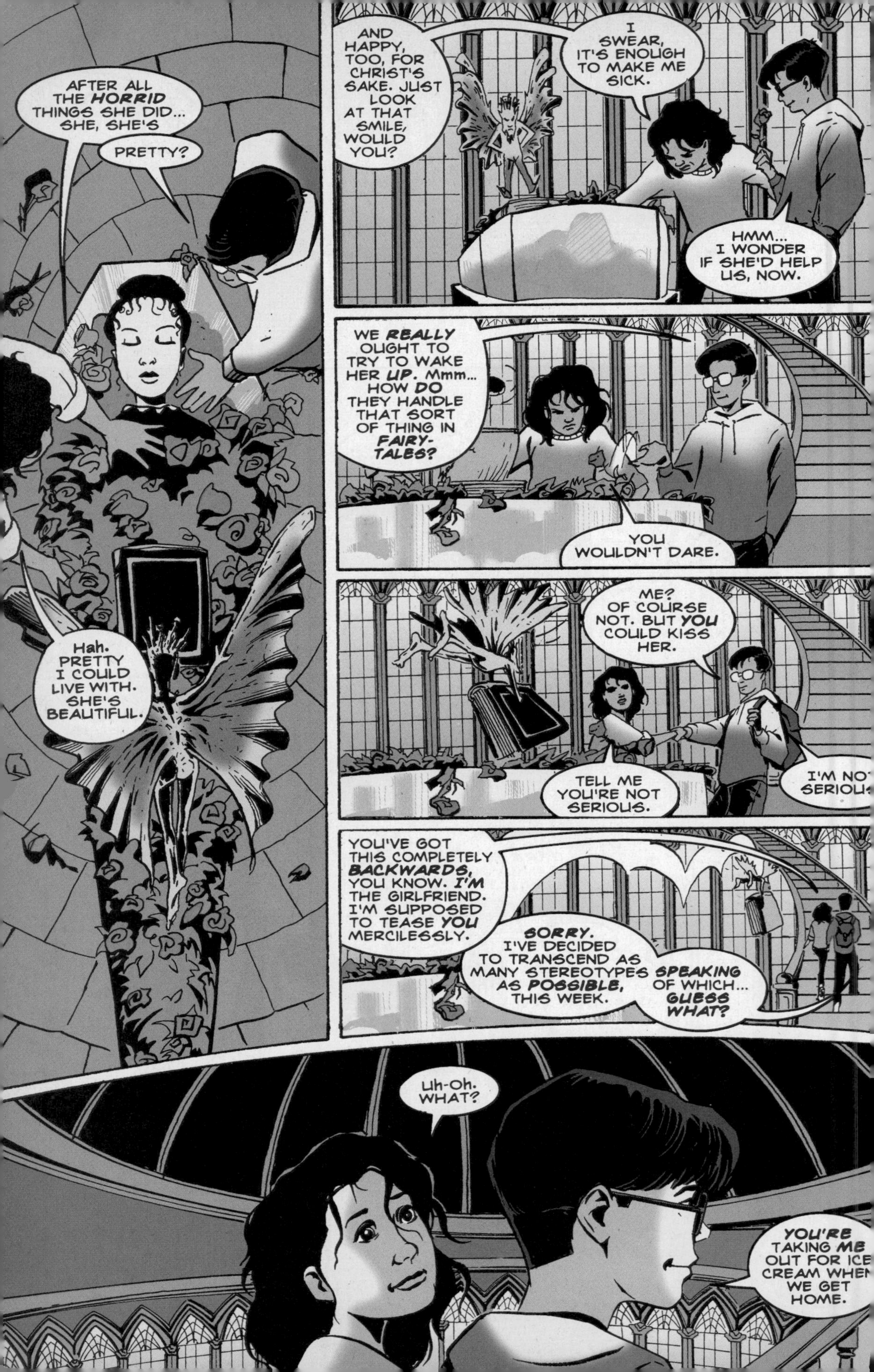
AFTER ALL THE HORRID THINGS SHE DID... SHE, SHE'S
PRETTY?
Hah. PRETTY I COULD LIVE WITH. SHE'S BEAUTIFUL.
AND HAPPY, TOO, FOR CHRIST'S SAKE. JUST LOOK AT THAT SMILE, WOULD YOU?
I SWEAR, IT'S ENOUGH TO MAKE ME SICK.
HMM... I WONDER IF SHE'D HELP US, NOW.
WE REALLY OUGHT TO TRY TO WAKE HER UP. Mmm... HOW DO THEY HANDLE THAT SORT OF THING IN FAIRY-TALES?
YOU WOULDN'T DARE.
ME? OF COURSE NOT. BUT YOU COULD KISS HER.
TELL ME YOU'RE NOT SERIOUS.
I'M NOT SERIOUS.
YOU'VE GOT THIS COMPLETELY BACKWARDS, YOU KNOW. I'M THE GIRLFRIEND. I'M SUPPOSED TO TEASE YOU MERCILESSLY.
SORRY. I'VE DECIDED TO TRANSCEND AS MANY STEREOTYPES AS POSSIBLE, THIS WEEK.
SPEAKING OF WHICH... GUESS WHAT?
Uh-Oh. WHAT?
YOU'RE TAKING ME OUT FOR ICE CREAM WHEN WE GET HOME.

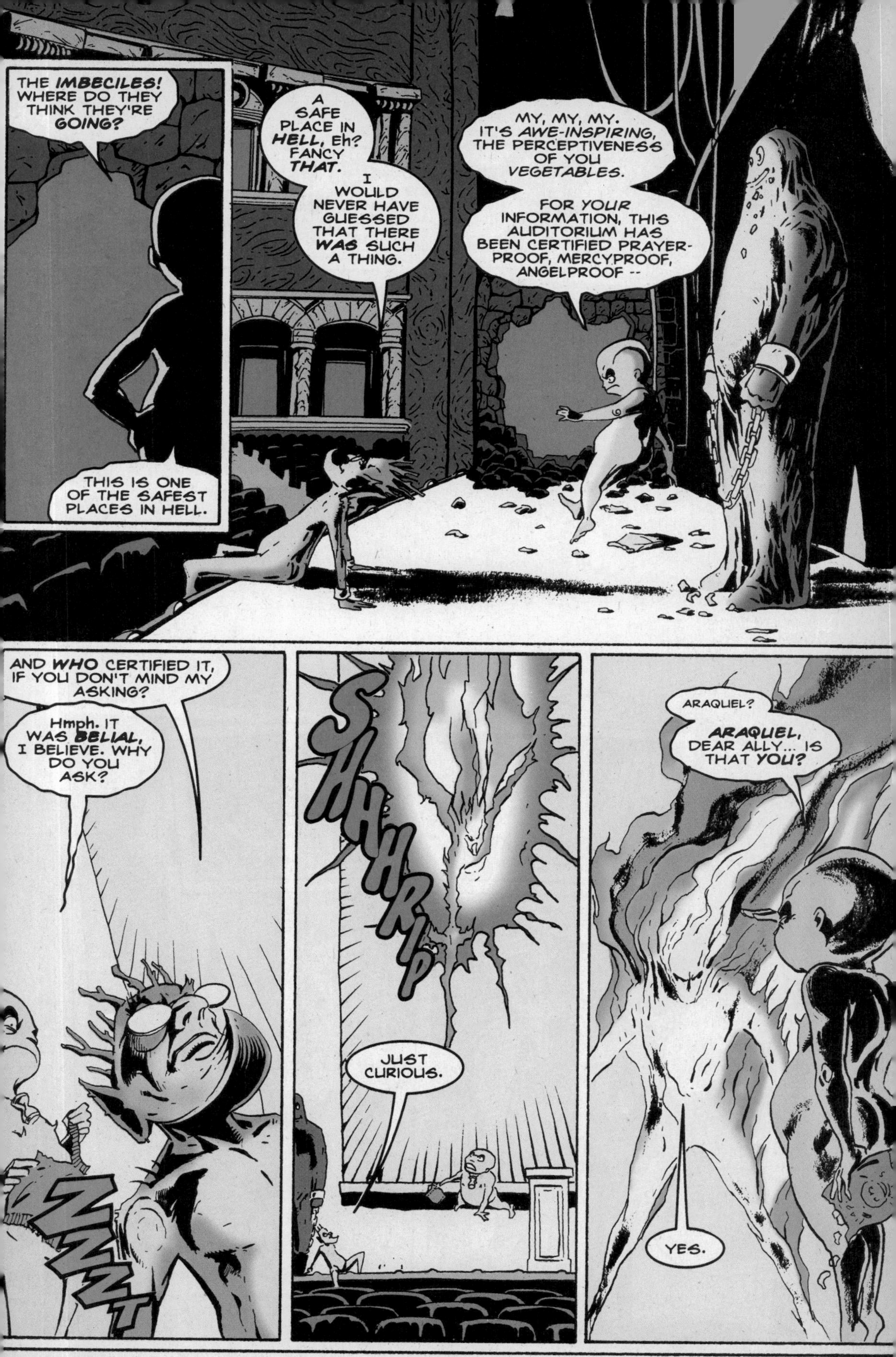

THE *IMBECILES!* WHERE DO THEY THINK THEY'RE *GOING?*
THIS IS ONE OF THE SAFEST PLACES IN HELL.
A SAFE PLACE IN *HELL*, Eh? FANCY *THAT*.
I WOULD NEVER HAVE GUESSED THAT THERE *WAS* SUCH A THING.
MY, MY, MY. IT'S *AWE-INSPIRING*, THE PERCEPTIVENESS OF YOU *VEGETABLES*.
FOR *YOUR* INFORMATION, THIS AUDITORIUM HAS BEEN CERTIFIED PRAYER-PROOF, MERCYPROOF, ANGELPROOF --
AND *WHO* CERTIFIED IT, IF YOU DON'T MIND MY ASKING?
Hmph. IT WAS *BELIAL*, I BELIEVE. WHY DO YOU ASK?
MMMZZT
SHHHRRIP
JUST CURIOUS.
ARAQUEL?
ARAQUEL, DEAR ALLY... IS THAT *YOU?*
YES.

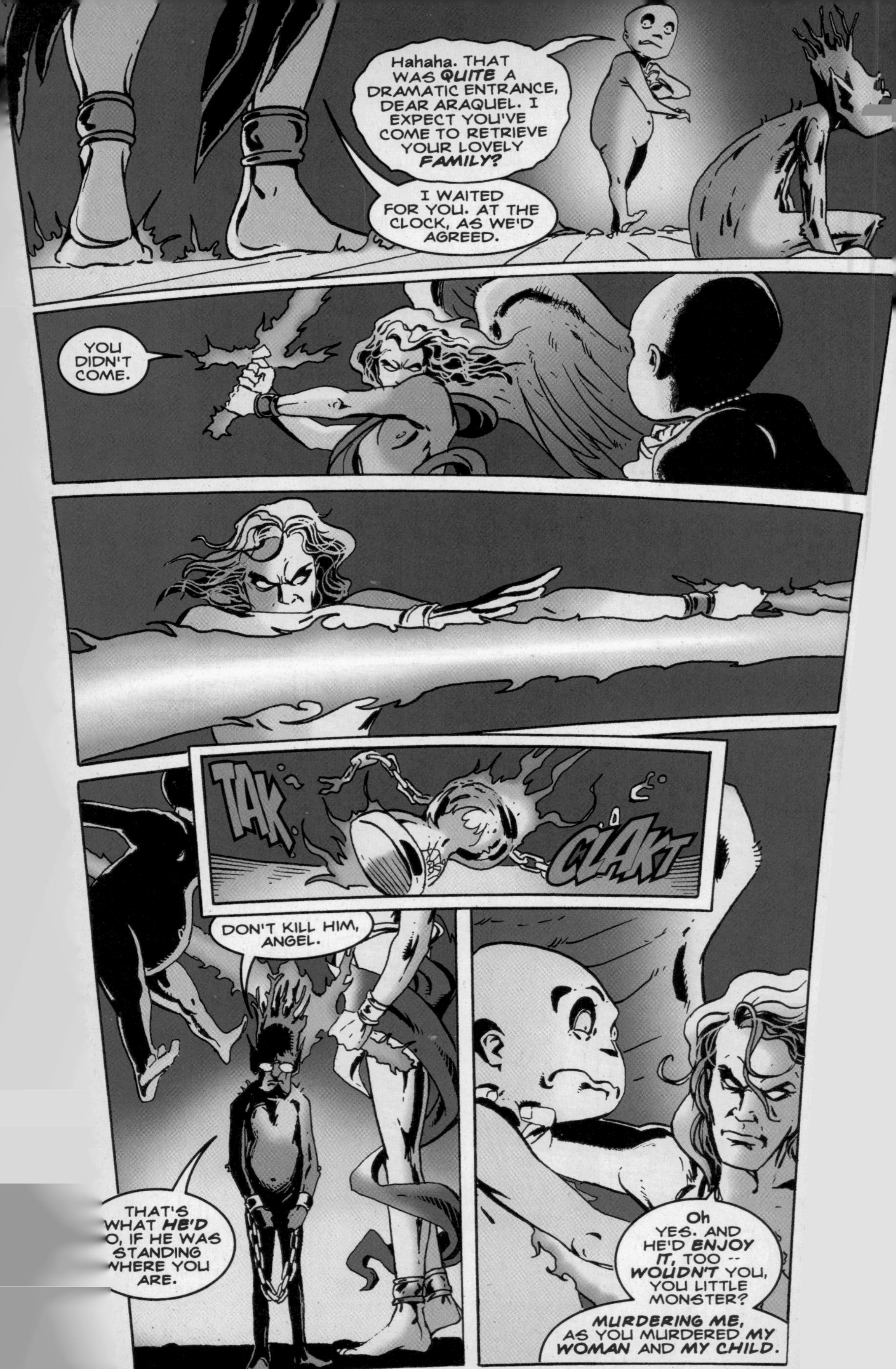
Hahaha. THAT WAS QUITE A DRAMATIC ENTRANCE, DEAR ARAQUEL. I EXPECT YOU'VE COME TO RETRIEVE YOUR LOVELY FAMILY?
I WAITED FOR YOU. AT THE CLOCK, AS WE'D AGREED.
YOU DIDN'T COME.
TAK
CLAKT
DON'T KILL HIM, ANGEL.
THAT'S WHAT HE'D O, IF HE WAS STANDING WHERE YOU ARE.
Oh YES. AND HE'D ENJOY IT, TOO -- WOUDN'T YOU, YOU LITTLE MONSTER?
MURDERING ME, AS YOU MURDERED MY WOMAN AND MY CHILD.

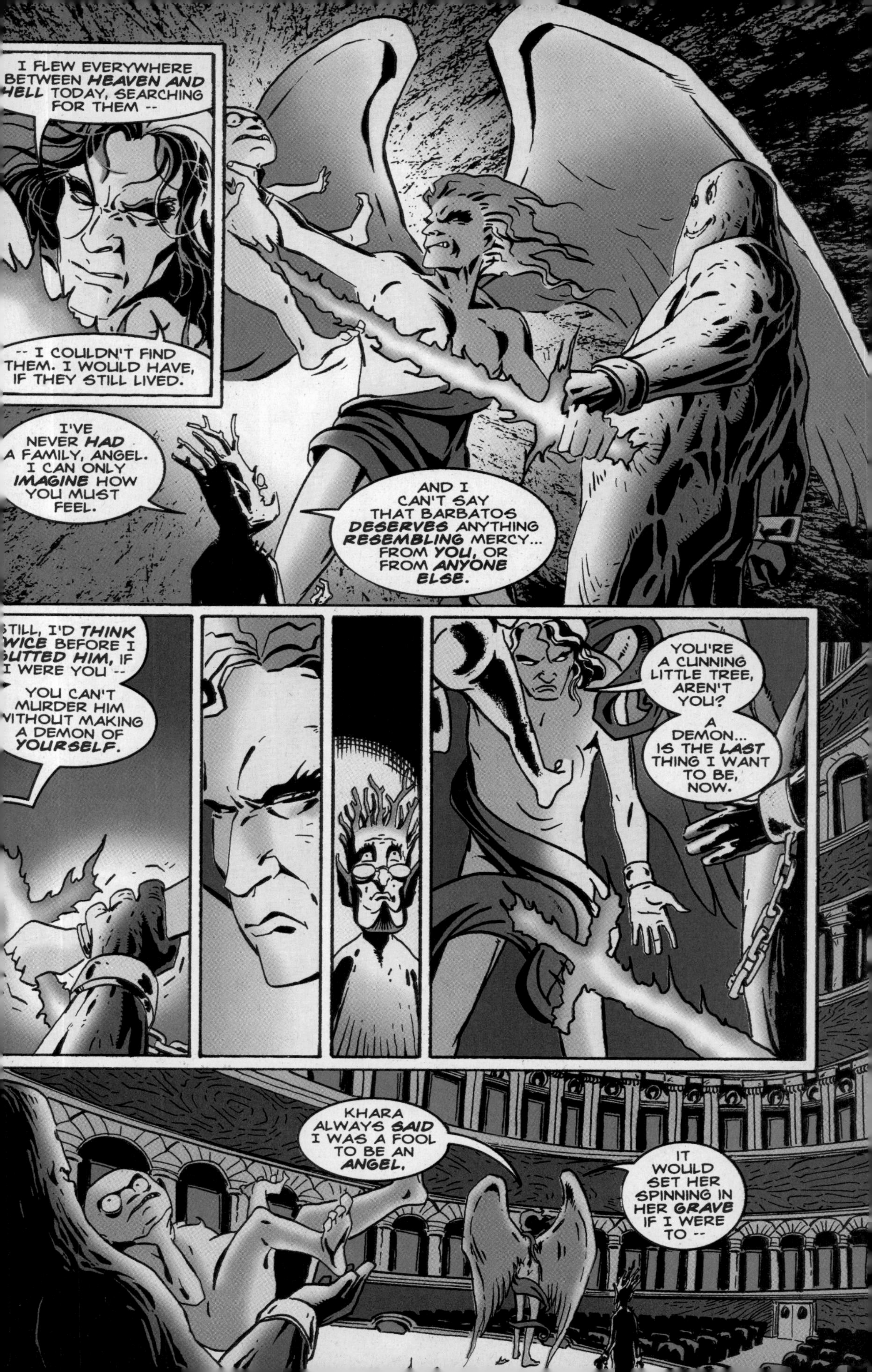
I FLEW EVERYWHERE BETWEEN HEAVEN AND HELL TODAY, SEARCHING FOR THEM --
-- I COULDN'T FIND THEM. I WOULD HAVE, IF THEY STILL LIVED.
I'VE NEVER HAD A FAMILY, ANGEL. I CAN ONLY IMAGINE HOW YOU MUST FEEL.
AND I CAN'T SAY THAT BARBATOS DESERVES ANYTHING RESEMBLING MERCY... FROM YOU, OR FROM ANYONE ELSE.
STILL, I'D THINK WICE BEFORE I GUTTED HIM, IF I WERE YOU --
YOU CAN'T MURDER HIM WITHOUT MAKING A DEMON OF YOURSELF.
YOU'RE A CUNNING LITTLE TREE, AREN'T YOU?
A DEMON... IS THE LAST THING I WANT TO BE, NOW.
KHARA ALWAYS SAID I WAS A FOOL TO BE AN ANGEL.
IT WOULD SET HER SPINNING IN HER GRAVE IF I WERE TO --

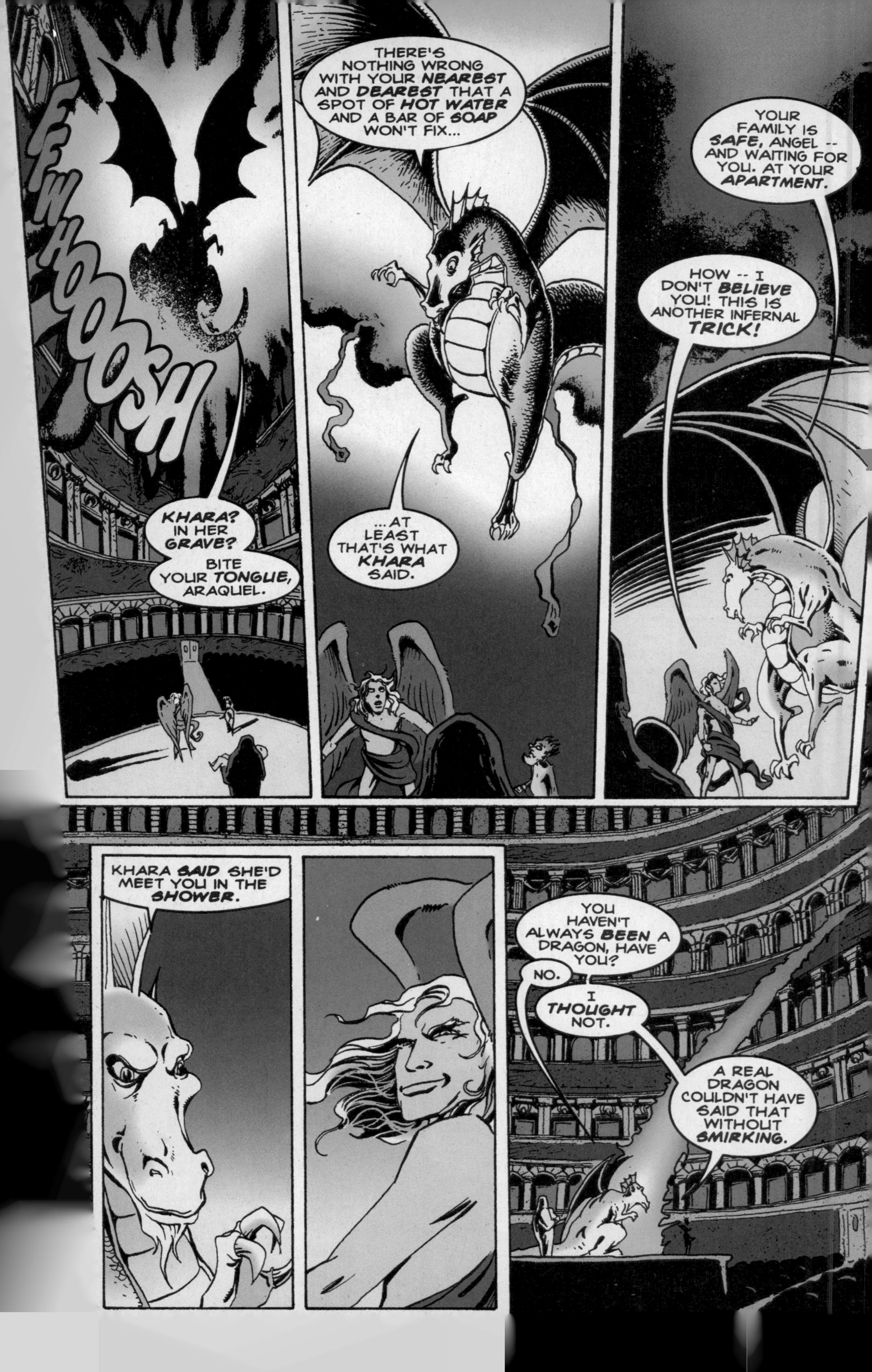
FFWHOOOSH
KHARA? IN HER GRAVE?
BITE YOUR TONGUE, ARAQUEL.
THERE'S NOTHING WRONG WITH YOUR NEAREST AND DEAREST THAT A SPOT OF HOT WATER AND A BAR OF SOAP WON'T FIX...
...AT LEAST THAT'S WHAT KHARA SAID.
YOUR FAMILY IS SAFE, ANGEL -- AND WAITING FOR YOU. AT YOUR APARTMENT.
HOW -- I DON'T BELIEVE YOU! THIS IS ANOTHER INFERNAL TRICK!
KHARA SAID SHE'D MEET YOU IN THE SHOWER.
YOU HAVEN'T ALWAYS BEEN A DRAGON, HAVE YOU?
NO.
I THOUGHT NOT.
A REAL DRAGON COULDN'T HAVE SAID THAT WITHOUT SMIRKING.

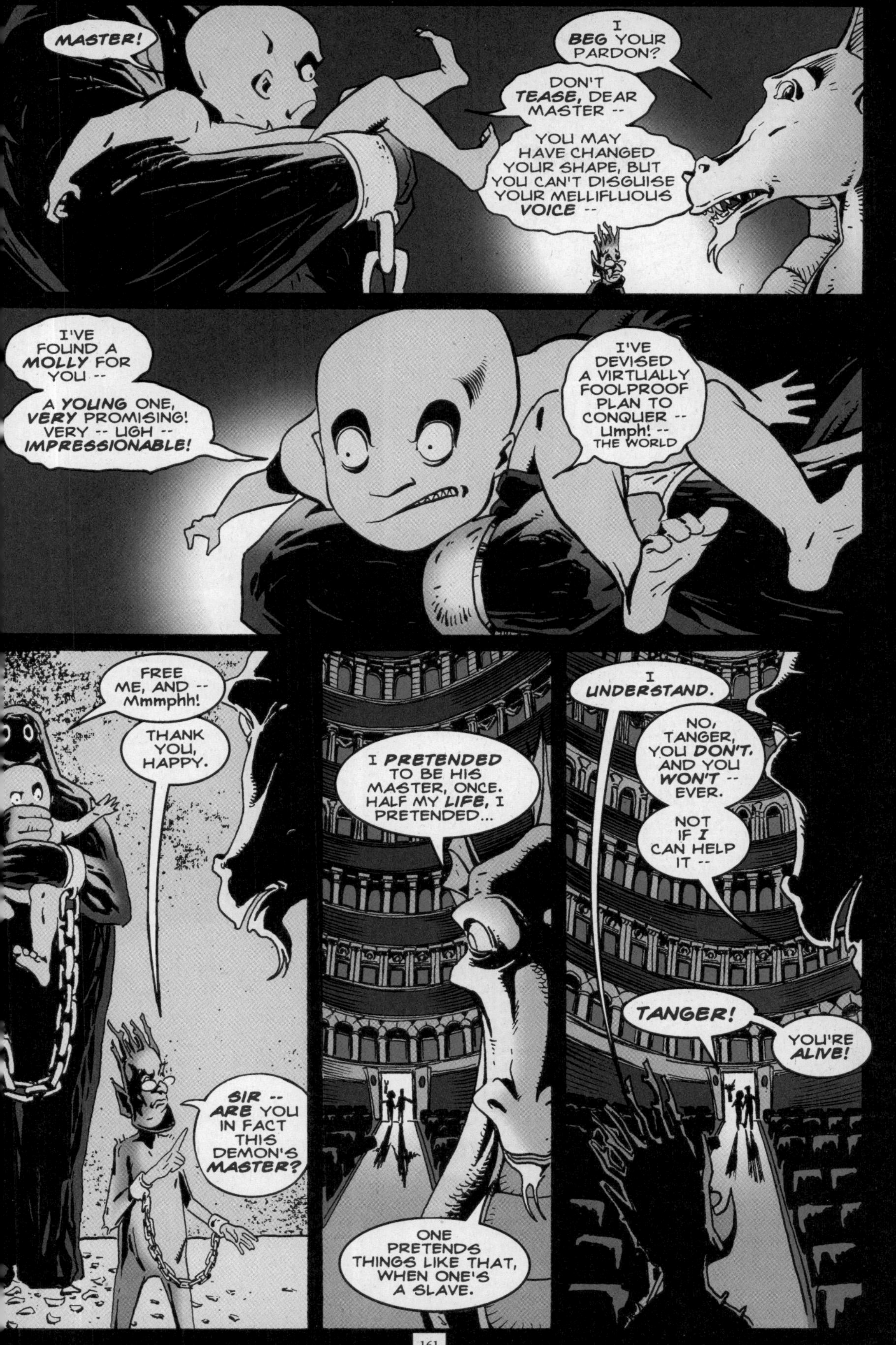
MASTER!
I BEG YOUR PARDON?
DON'T TEASE, DEAR MASTER --
YOU MAY HAVE CHANGED YOUR SHAPE, BUT YOU CAN'T DISGUISE YOUR MELLIFLUOUS VOICE --
I'VE FOUND A MOLLY FOR YOU --
A YOUNG ONE, VERY PROMISING! VERY -- UGH -- IMPRESSIONABLE!
I'VE DEVISED A VIRTUALLY FOOLPROOF PLAN TO CONQUER -- Umph! -- THE WORLD
FREE ME, AND -- Mmmphh!
THANK YOU, HAPPY.
SIR -- ARE YOU IN FACT THIS DEMON'S MASTER?
I PRETENDED TO BE HIS MASTER, ONCE. HALF MY LIFE, I PRETENDED...
ONE PRETENDS THINGS LIKE THAT, WHEN ONE'S A SLAVE.
I UNDERSTAND.
NO, TANGER, YOU DON'T. AND YOU WON'T -- EVER.
NOT IF I CAN HELP IT --
TANGER!
YOU'RE ALIVE!

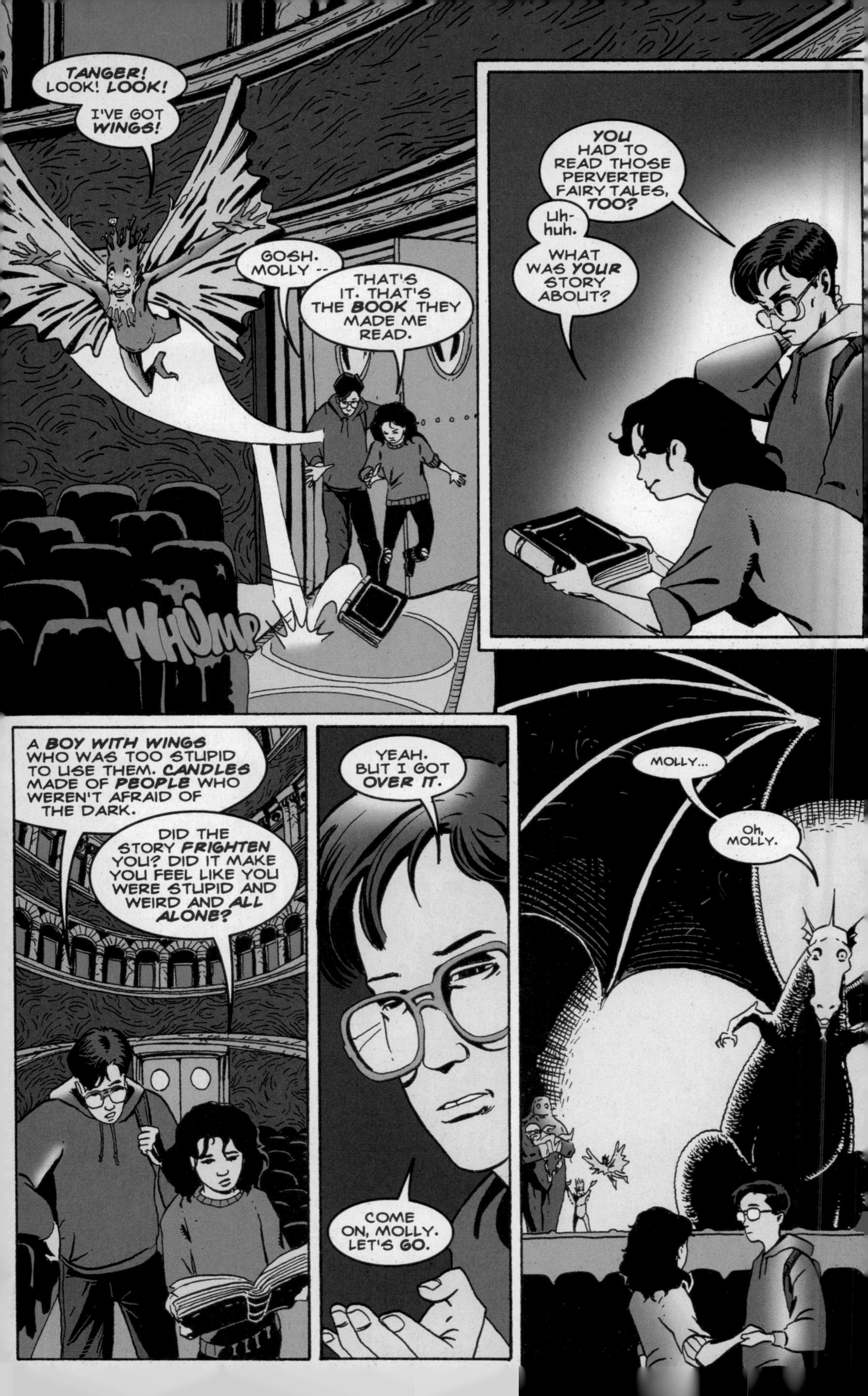
TANGER! LOOK! LOOK!
I'VE GOT WINGS!
GOSH. MOLLY --
THAT'S IT. THAT'S THE BOOK THEY MADE ME READ.
WHUMP
YOU HAD TO READ THOSE PERVERTED FAIRY TALES, TOO?
Uh-huh.
WHAT WAS YOUR STORY ABOUT?
A BOY WITH WINGS WHO WAS TOO STUPID TO USE THEM. CANDLES MADE OF PEOPLE WHO WEREN'T AFRAID OF THE DARK.
DID THE STORY FRIGHTEN YOU? DID IT MAKE YOU FEEL LIKE YOU WERE STUPID AND WEIRD AND ALL ALONE?
YEAH. BUT I GOT OVER IT.
COME ON, MOLLY. LET'S GO.
MOLLY...
Oh, MOLLY.

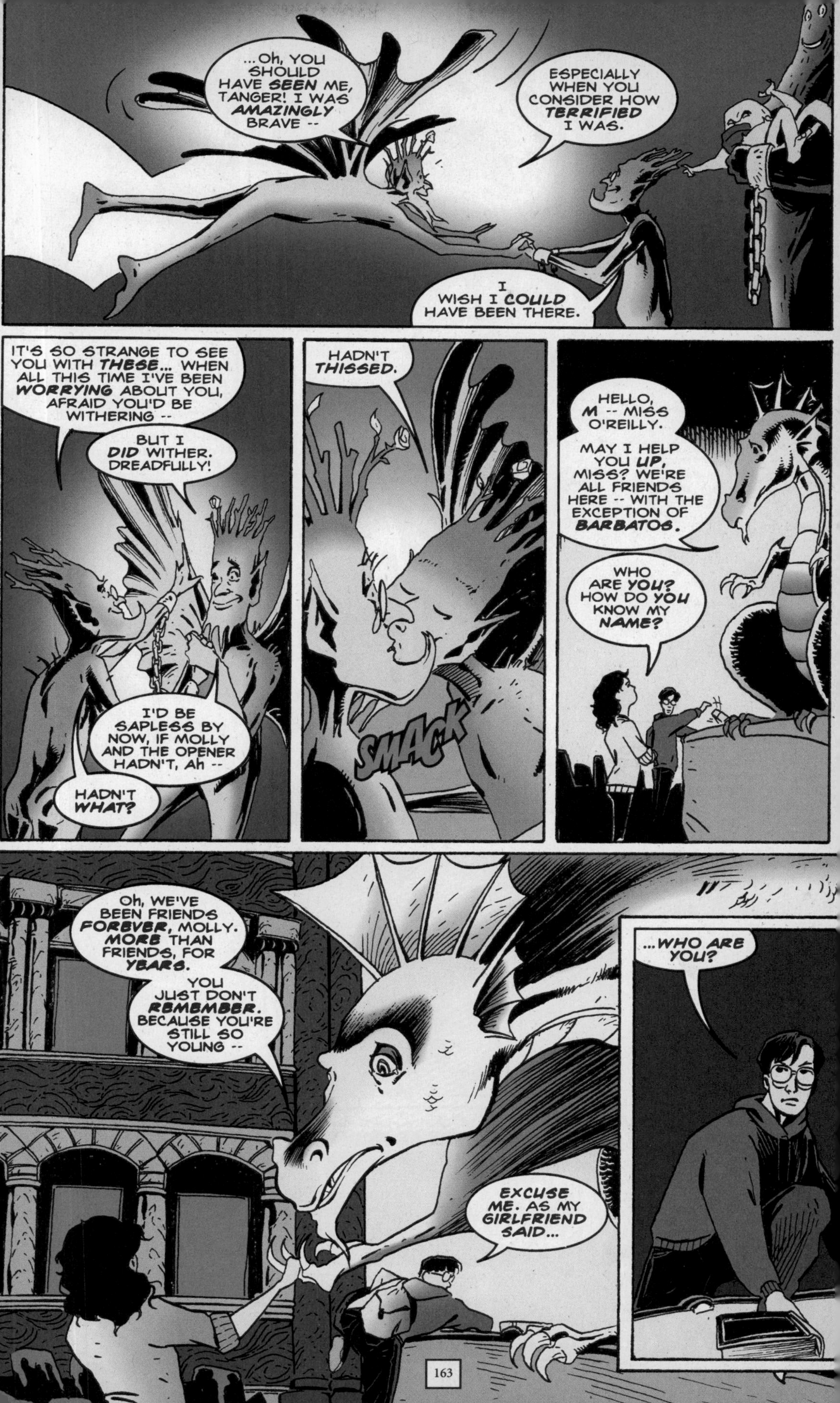
...Oh, YOU SHOULD HAVE SEEN ME, TANGER! I WAS AMAZINGLY BRAVE --
ESPECIALLY WHEN YOU CONSIDER HOW TERRIFIED I WAS.
I WISH I COULD HAVE BEEN THERE.
IT'S SO STRANGE TO SEE YOU WITH THESE... WHEN ALL THIS TIME I'VE BEEN WORRYING ABOUT YOU, AFRAID YOU'D BE WITHERING --
BUT I DID WITHER. DREADFULLY!
I'D BE SAPLESS BY NOW, IF MOLLY AND THE OPENER HADN'T, Ah --
HADN'T WHAT?
HADN'T THISSED.
SMACK
HELLO, M -- MISS O'REILLY.
MAY I HELP YOU UP, MISS? WE'RE ALL FRIENDS HERE -- WITH THE EXCEPTION OF BARBATOS.
WHO ARE YOU? HOW DO YOU KNOW MY NAME?
Oh, WE'VE BEEN FRIENDS FOREVER, MOLLY. MORE THAN FRIENDS, FOR YEARS.
YOU JUST DON'T REMEMBER. BECAUSE YOU'RE STILL SO YOUNG --
EXCUSE ME. AS MY GIRLFRIEND SAID...
...WHO ARE YOU?

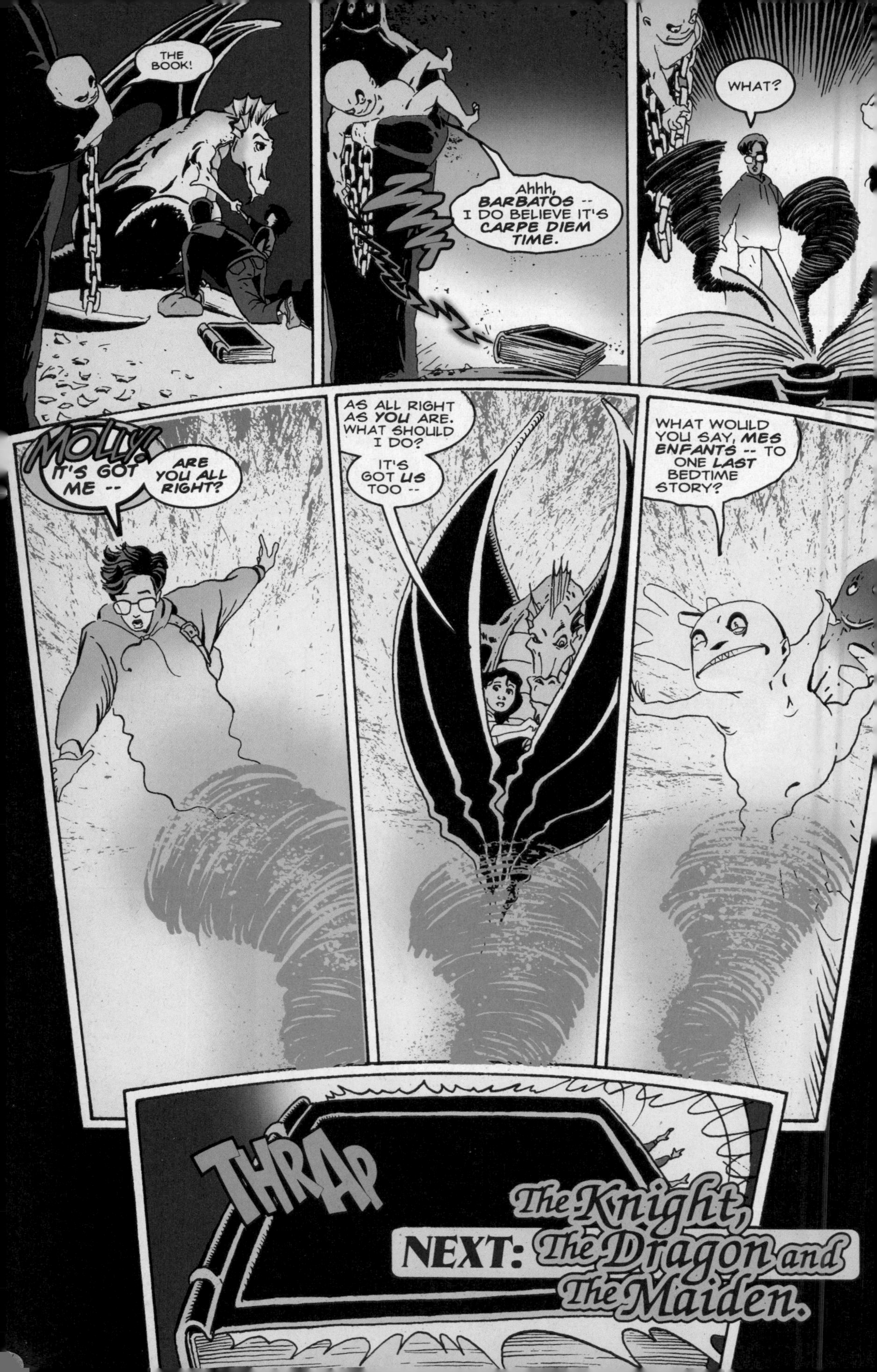
THE BOOK!
Ahhh, BARBATOS -- I DO BELIEVE IT'S CARPE DIEM TIME.
WHAT?
MOLLY! IT'S GOT ME --
ARE YOU ALL RIGHT?
AS ALL RIGHT AS YOU ARE. WHAT SHOULD I DO?
IT'S GOT US TOO --
WHAT WOULD YOU SAY, MES ENFANTS -- TO ONE LAST BEDTIME STORY?
THRAP
NEXT: The Knight, The Dragon and The Maiden.

The Knight,
The Dragon,
& The Maiden

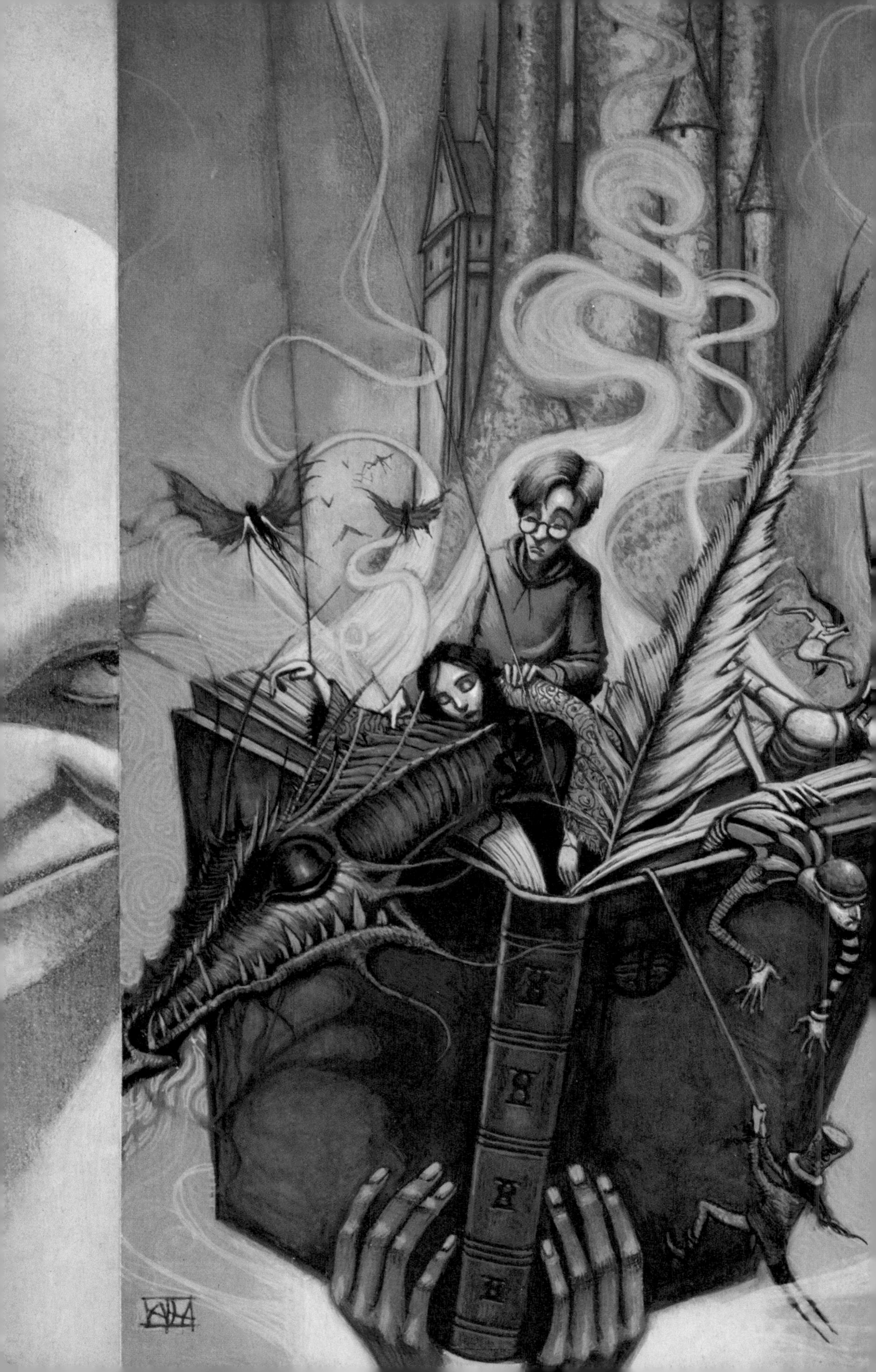

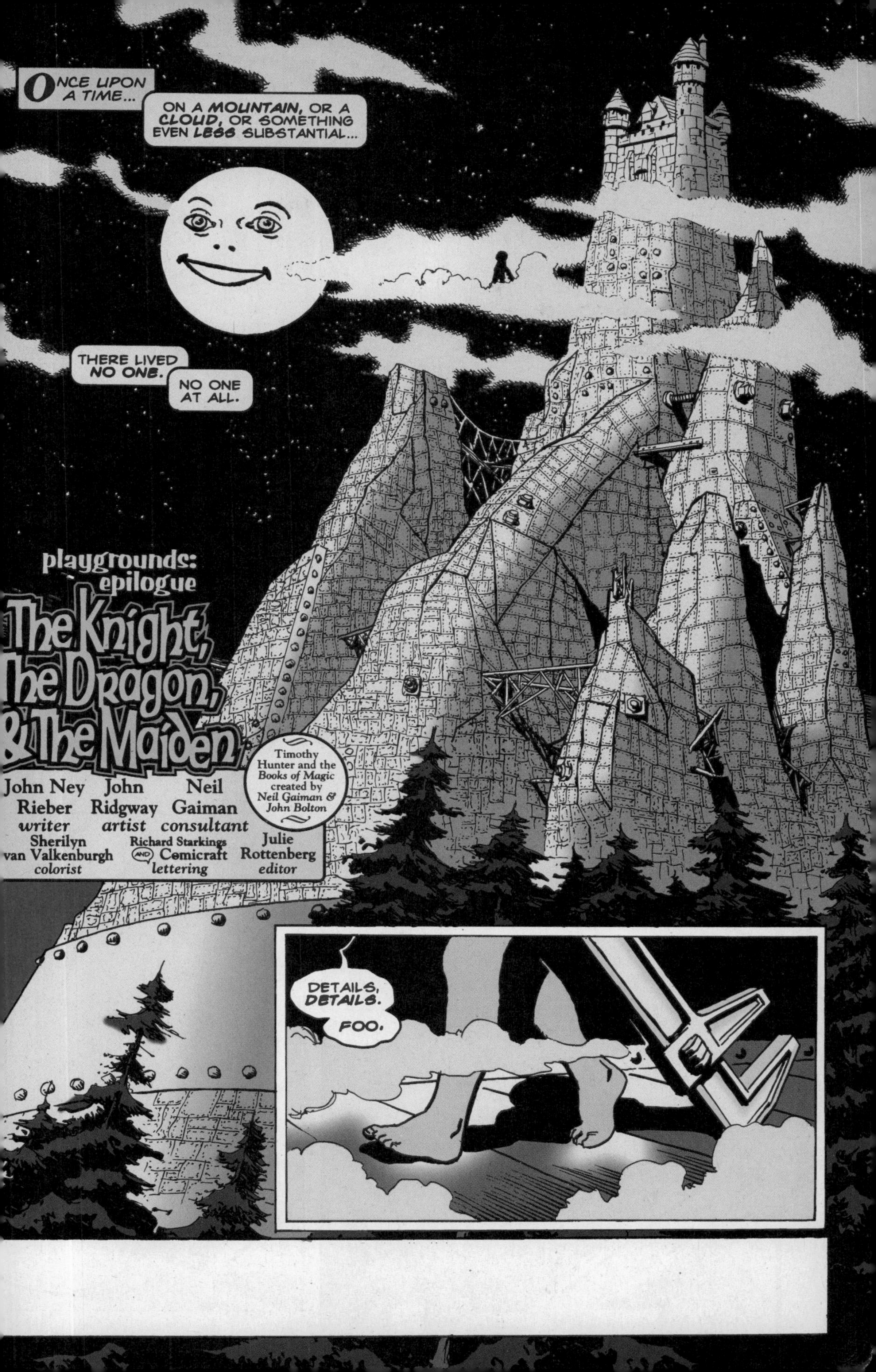
ONCE UPON A TIME...
ON A MOUNTAIN, OR A CLOUD, OR SOMETHING EVEN LESS SUBSTANTIAL...
THERE LIVED NO ONE.
NO ONE AT ALL.
playgrounds: epilogue
The Knight, The Dragon, & The Maiden
John Ney Rieber writer
John Ridgway artist
Neil Gaiman consultant
Sherilyn van Valkenburgh colorist
Richard Starkings and Comicraft lettering
Julie Rottenberg editor
Timothy Hunter and the Books of Magic created by Neil Gaiman & John Bolton
DETAILS, DETAILS.
FOO.

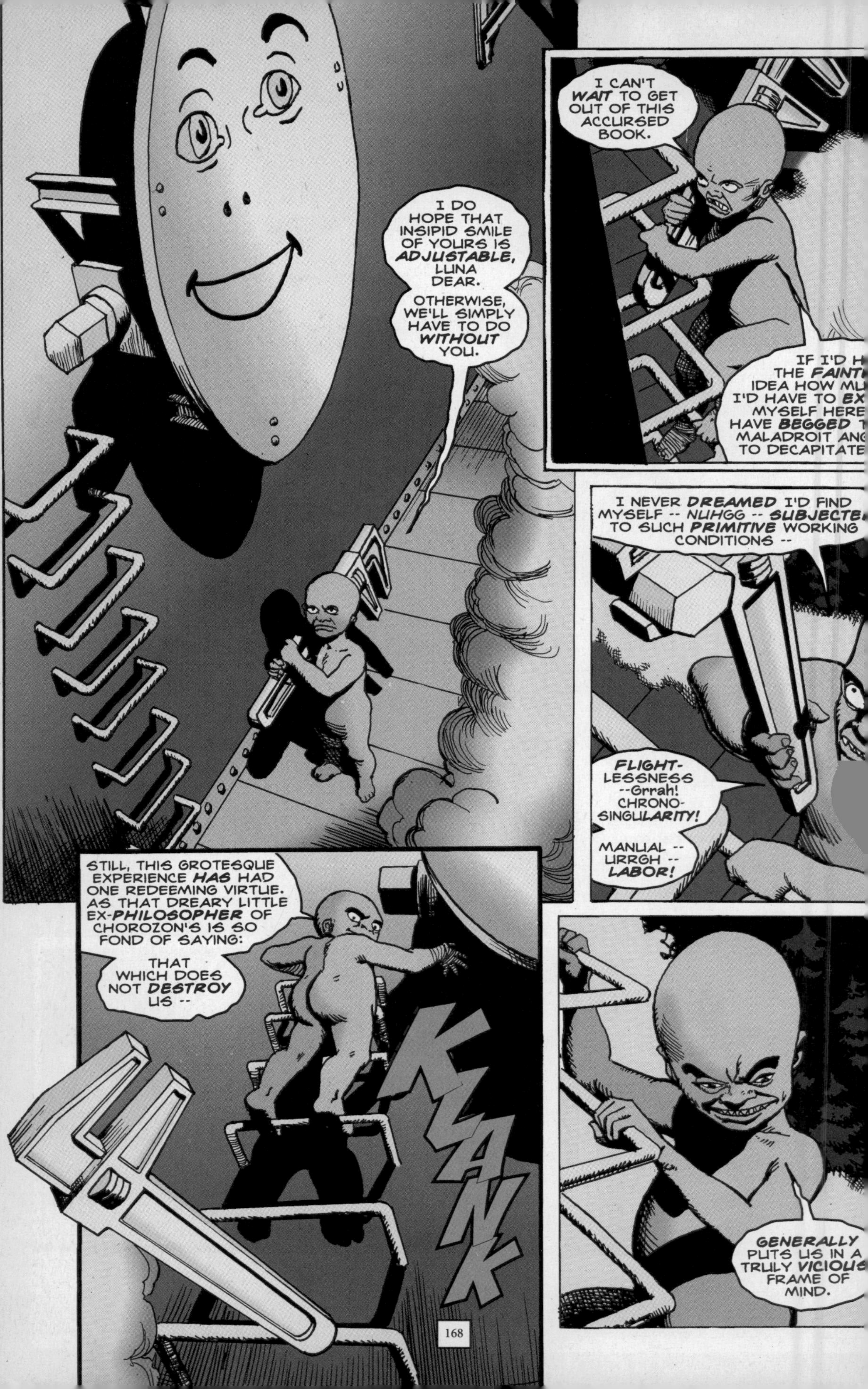

I DO HOPE THAT INSIPID SMILE OF YOURS IS ADJUSTABLE, LUNA DEAR.
OTHERWISE, WE'LL SIMPLY HAVE TO DO WITHOUT YOU.
I CAN'T WAIT TO GET OUT OF THIS ACCURSED BOOK.
IF I'D H
THE FAINT
IDEA HOW MU
I'D HAVE TO EX
MYSELF HERE
HAVE BEGGED T
MALADROIT ANG
TO DECAPITATE
I NEVER DREAMED I'D FIND MYSELF -- NUHGG -- SUBJECTE TO SUCH PRIMITIVE WORKING CONDITIONS --
FLIGHT-LESSNESS --Grrah! CHRONO-SINGULARITY!
MANUAL -- URRGH -- LABOR!
STILL, THIS GROTESQUE EXPERIENCE HAS HAD ONE REDEEMING VIRTUE. AS THAT DREARY LITTLE EX-PHILOSOPHER OF CHOROZON'S IS SO FOND OF SAYING:
THAT WHICH DOES NOT DESTROY US --
KLANK
GENERALLY PUTS US IN A TRULY VICIOUS FRAME OF MIND.

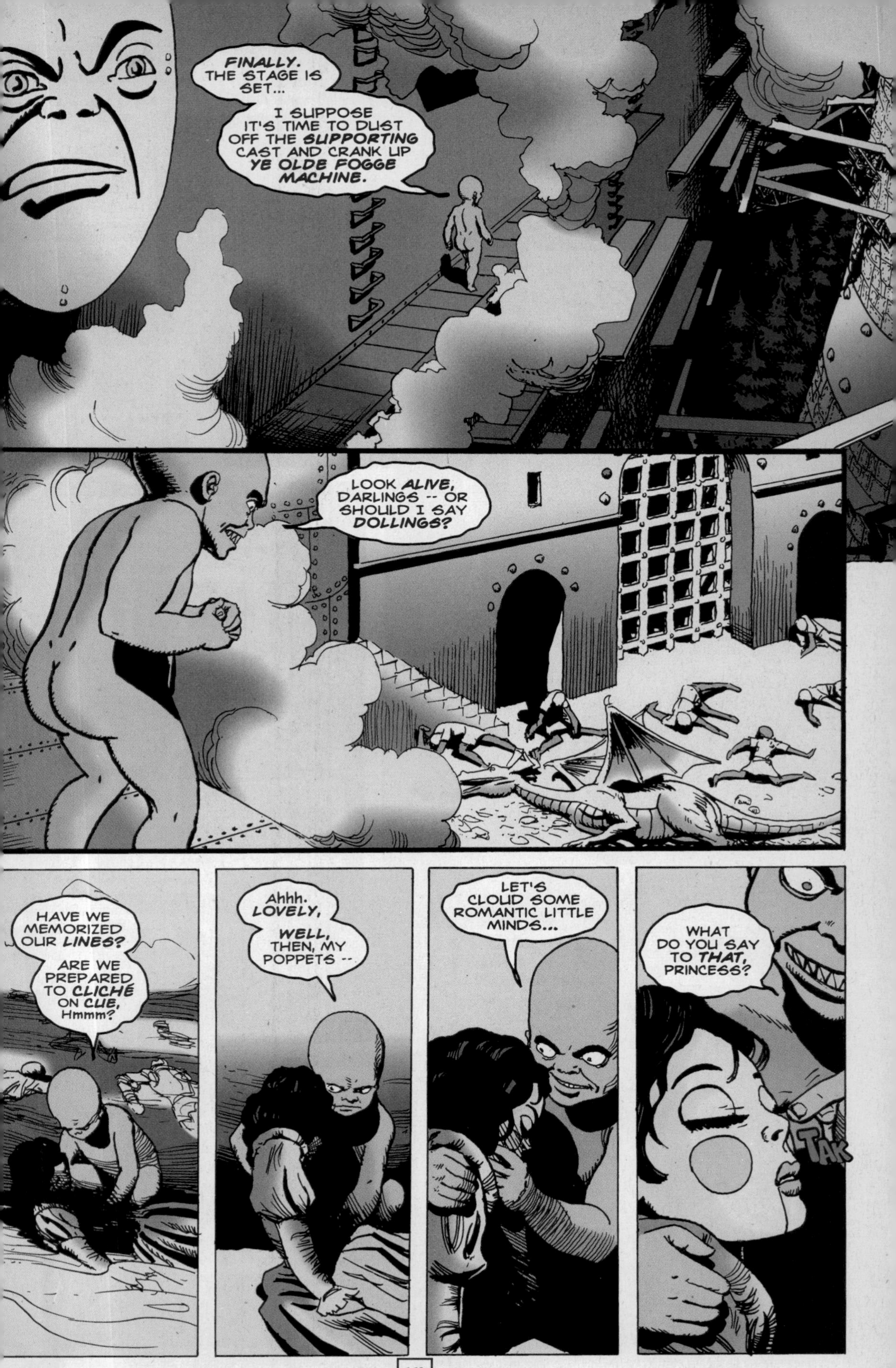
FINALLY. THE STAGE IS SET...
I SUPPOSE IT'S TIME TO DUST OFF THE SUPPORTING CAST AND CRANK UP YE OLDE FOGGE MACHINE.
LOOK ALIVE, DARLINGS -- OR SHOULD I SAY DOLLINGS?
HAVE WE MEMORIZED OUR LINES?
ARE WE PREPARED TO CLICHÉ ON CUE, Hmmm?
Ahhh. LOVELY.
WELL, THEN, MY POPPETS --
LET'S CLOUD SOME ROMANTIC LITTLE MINDS...
WHAT DO YOU SAY TO THAT, PRINCESS?
TAK

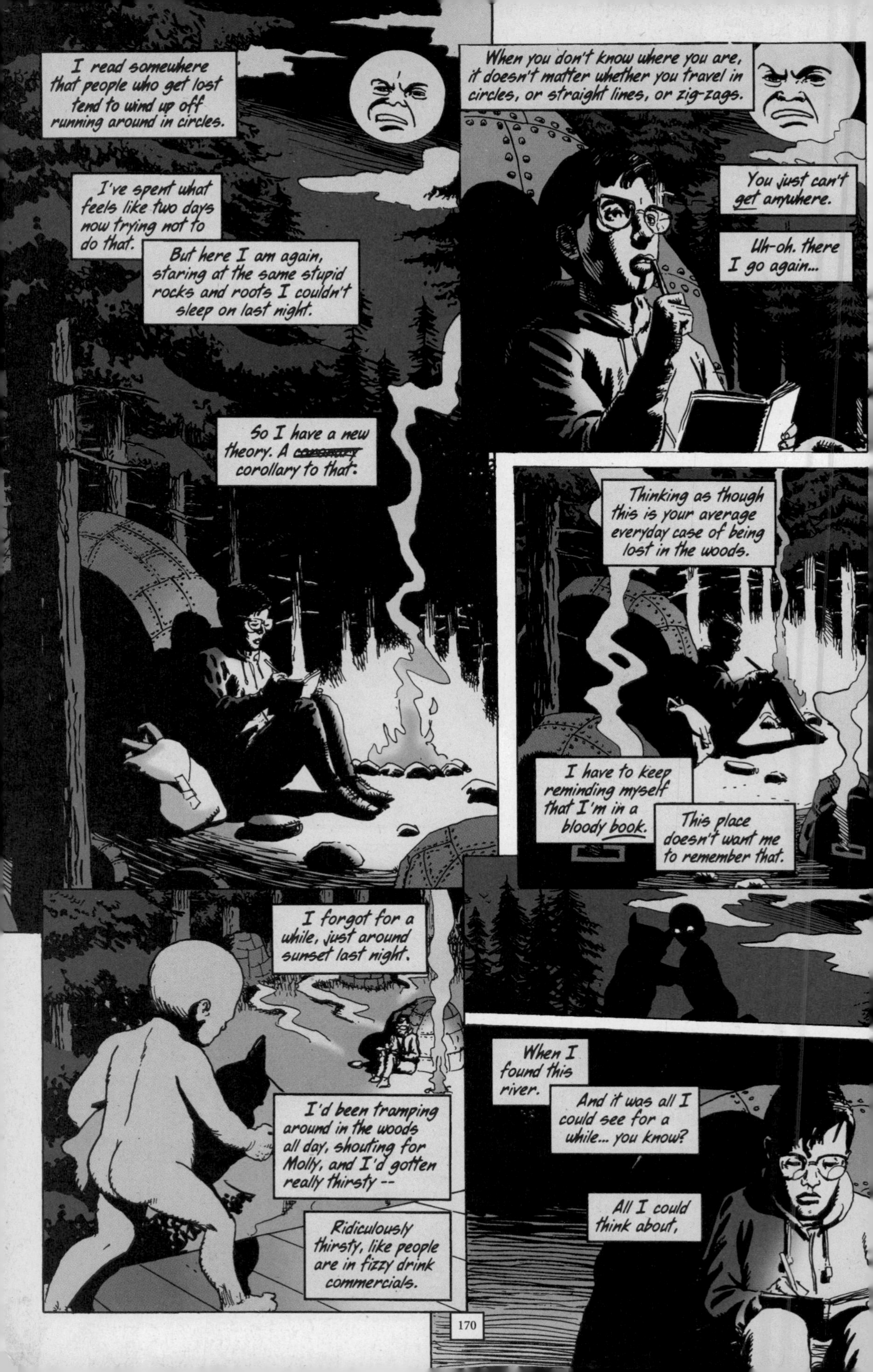
I read somewhere that people who get lost tend to wind up off running around in circles.
I've spent what feels like two days now trying not to do that.
But here I am again, staring at the same stupid rocks and roots I couldn't sleep on last night.
So I have a new theory. A corollary to that.
When you don't know where you are, it doesn't matter whether you travel in circles, or straight lines, or zig-zags.
You just can't get anywhere.
Uh-oh. there I go again...
Thinking as though this is your average everyday case of being lost in the woods.
I have to keep reminding myself that I'm in a bloody book.
This place doesn't want me to remember that.
I forgot for a while, just around sunset last night.
I'd been tramping around in the woods all day, shouting for Molly, and I'd gotten really thirsty --
Ridiculously thirsty, like people are in fizzy drink commercials.
When I found this river.
And it was all I could see for a while... you know?
All I could think about,

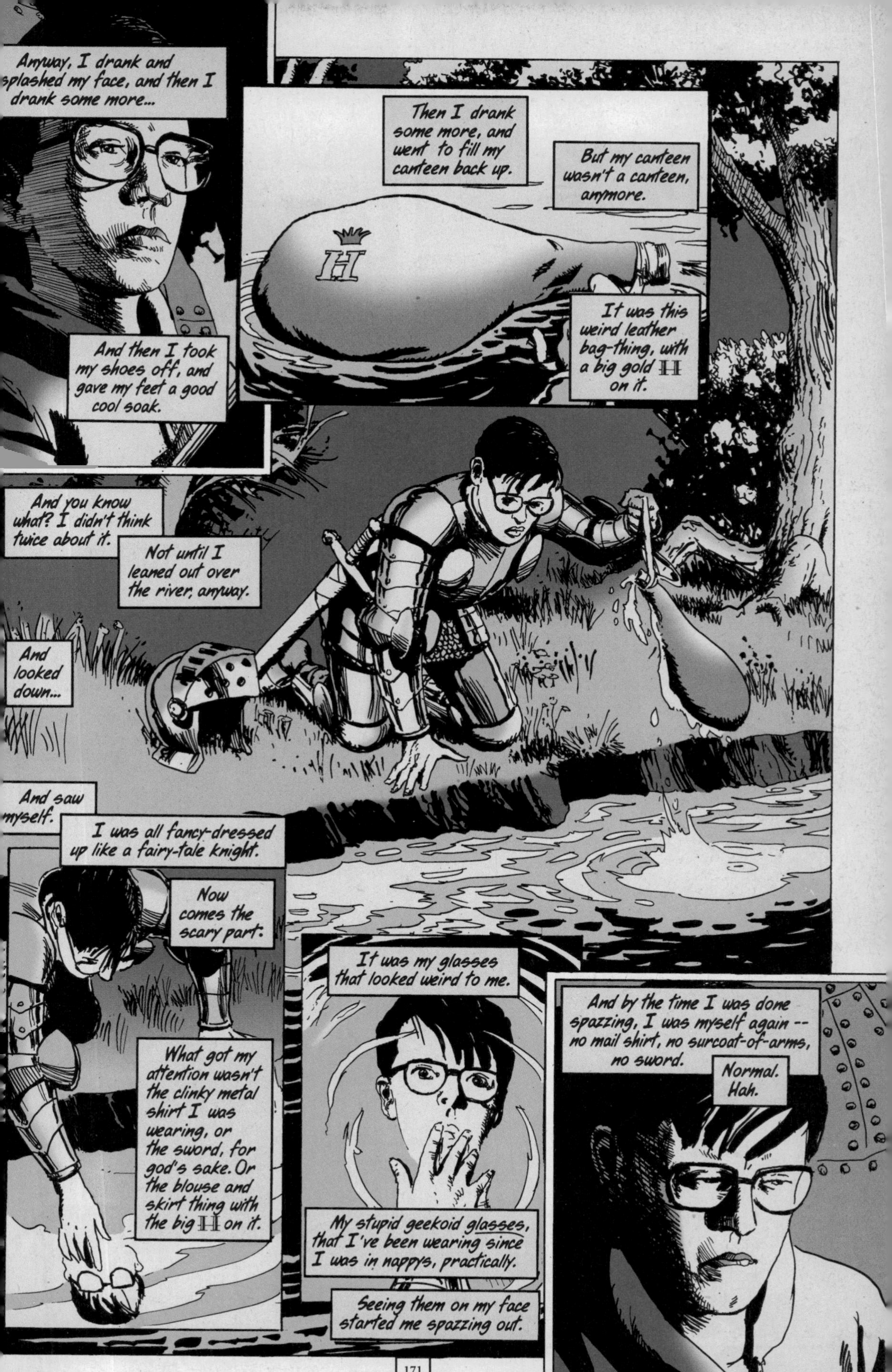
Anyway, I drank and splashed my face, and then I drank some more...
And then I took my shoes off, and gave my feet a good cool soak.
Then I drank some more, and went to fill my canteen back up.
But my canteen wasn't a canteen, anymore.
It was this weird leather bag-thing, with a big gold H on it.
And you know what? I didn't think twice about it.
Not until I leaned out over the river, anyway.
And looked down...
And saw myself.
I was all fancy-dressed up like a fairy-tale knight.
Now comes the scary part:
What got my attention wasn't the clinky metal shirt I was wearing, or the sword, for god's sake. Or the blouse and skirt thing with the big H on it.
It was my glasses that looked weird to me.
My stupid geekoid glasses, that I've been wearing since I was in nappys, practically.
Seeing them on my face started me spazzing out.
And by the time I was done spazzing, I was myself again -- no mail shirt, no surcoat-of-arms, no sword.
Normal. Hah.

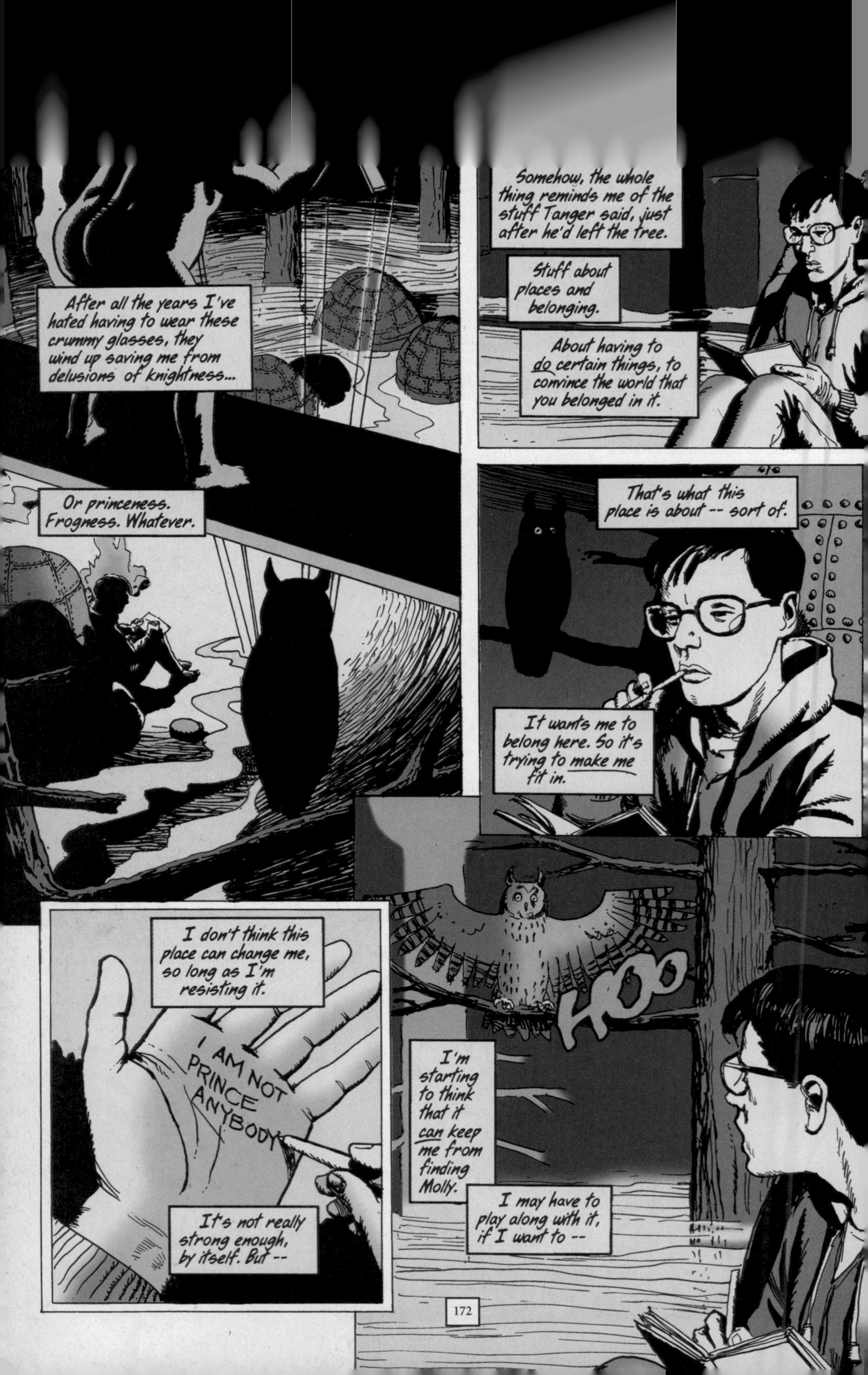
After all the years I've hated having to wear these crummy glasses, they wind up saving me from delusions of knightness...
Somehow, the whole thing reminds me of the stuff Tanger said, just after he'd left the tree.
Stuff about places and belonging.
About having to do certain things, to convince the world that you belonged in it.
Or princeness. Frogness. Whatever.
That's what this place is about -- sort of.
It wants me to belong here. So it's trying to make me fit in.
I don't think this place can change me, so long as I'm resisting it.
I AM NOT PRINCE ANYBODY
It's not really strong enough, by itself. But --
HOO
I'm starting to think that it can keep me from finding Molly.
I may have to play along with it, if I want to --

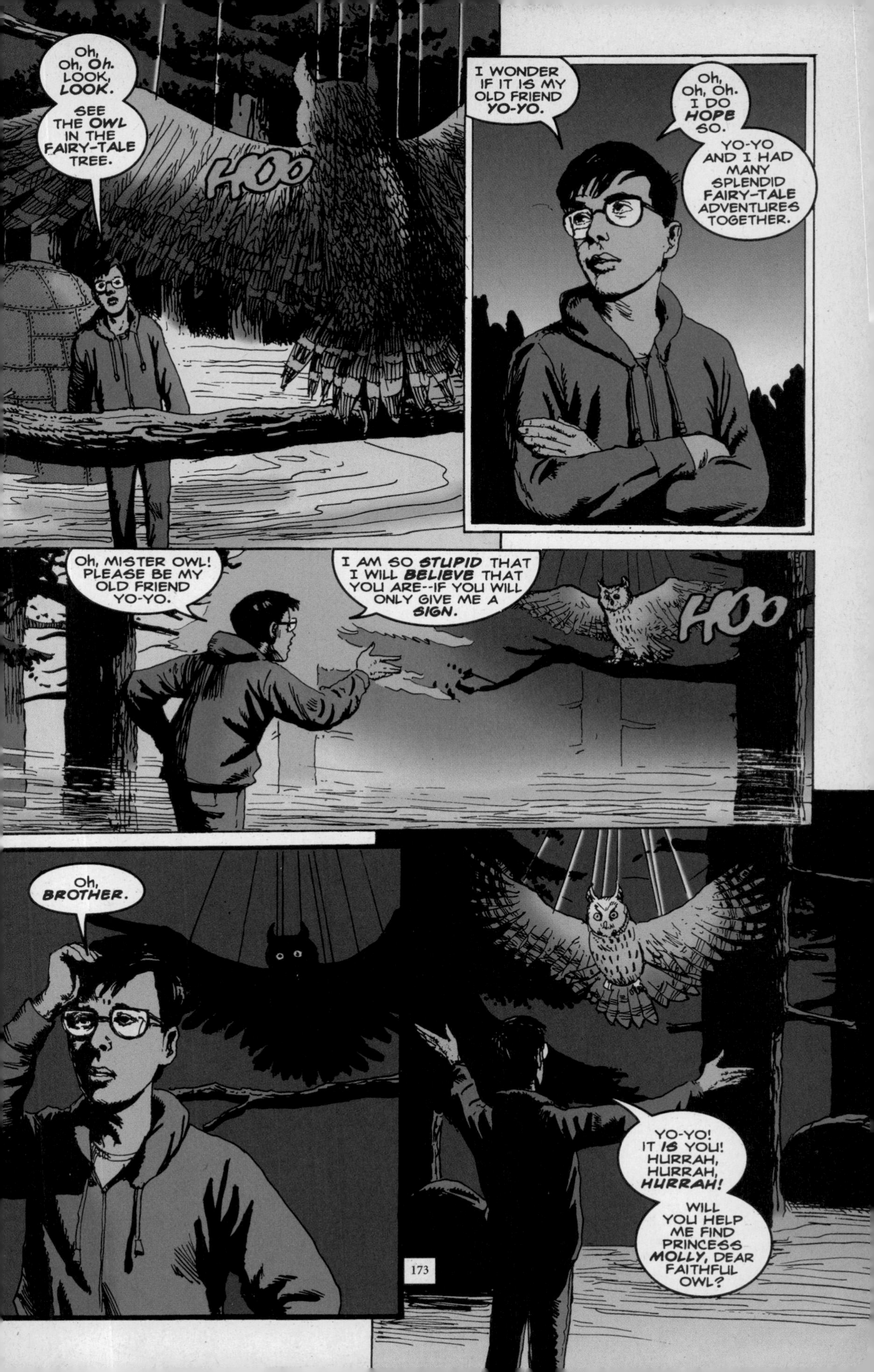

Oh, Oh, Oh. LOOK, LOOK.
SEE THE OWL IN THE FAIRY-TALE TREE.
HOO
I WONDER IF IT IS MY OLD FRIEND YO-YO.
Oh, Oh, Oh. I DO HOPE SO.
YO-YO AND I HAD MANY SPLENDID FAIRY-TALE ADVENTURES TOGETHER.
Oh, MISTER OWL! PLEASE BE MY OLD FRIEND YO-YO.
I AM SO STUPID THAT I WILL BELIEVE THAT YOU ARE--IF YOU WILL ONLY GIVE ME A SIGN.
HOO
Oh, BROTHER.
YO-YO! IT IS YOU! HURRAH, HURRAH, HURRAH!
WILL YOU HELP ME FIND PRINCESS MOLLY, DEAR FAITHFUL OWL?

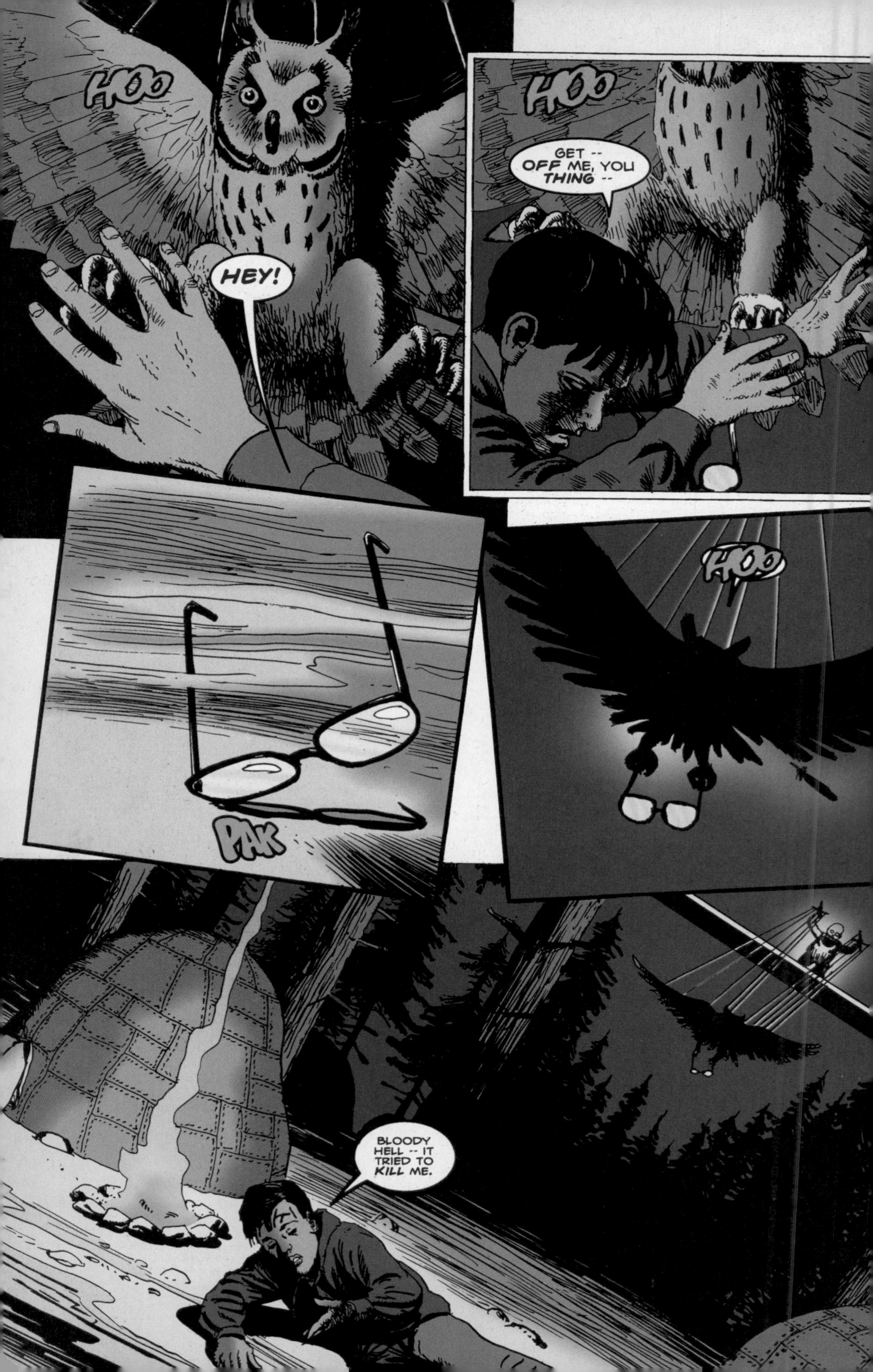
HOO
HEY!
HOO
GET -- OFF ME, YOU THING --
PAK
HOO
BLOODY HELL -- IT TRIED TO KILL ME.

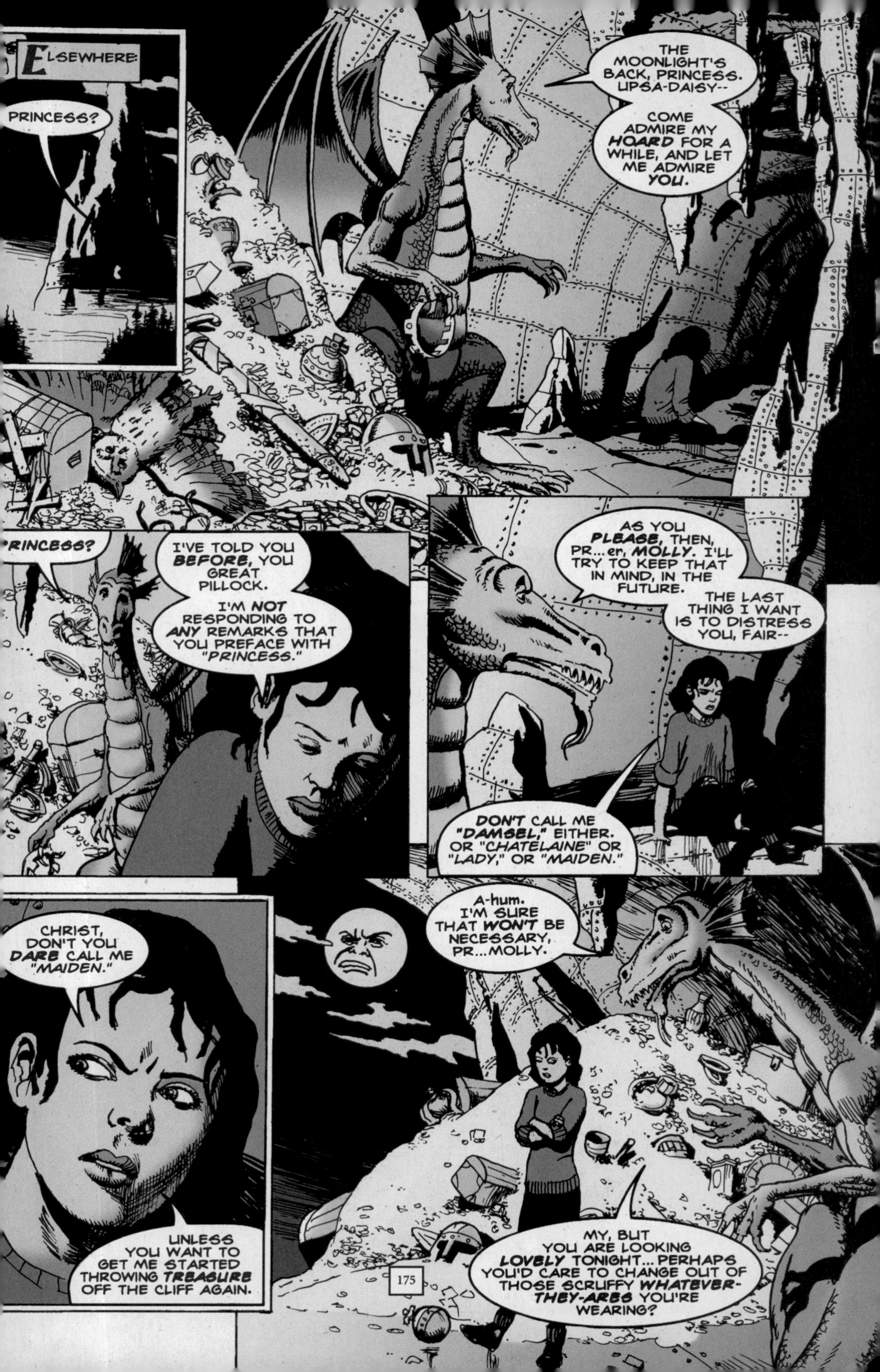

ELSEWHERE:
PRINCESS?
THE MOONLIGHT'S BACK, PRINCESS. UPSA-DAISY--
COME ADMIRE MY HOARD FOR A WHILE, AND LET ME ADMIRE YOU.
PRINCESS?
I'VE TOLD YOU BEFORE, YOU GREAT PILLOCK.
I'M NOT RESPONDING TO ANY REMARKS THAT YOU PREFACE WITH "PRINCESS."
AS YOU PLEASE, THEN, PR... er, MOLLY. I'LL TRY TO KEEP THAT IN MIND, IN THE FUTURE.
THE LAST THING I WANT IS TO DISTRESS YOU, FAIR--
DON'T CALL ME "DAMSEL," EITHER. OR "CHATELAINE" OR "LADY," OR "MAIDEN."
CHRIST, DON'T YOU DARE CALL ME "MAIDEN."
UNLESS YOU WANT TO GET ME STARTED THROWING TREASURE OFF THE CLIFF AGAIN.
A-hum. I'M SURE THAT WON'T BE NECESSARY, PR...MOLLY.
MY, BUT YOU ARE LOOKING LOVELY TONIGHT... PERHAPS YOU'D CARE TO CHANGE OUT OF THOSE SCRUFFY WHATEVER-THEY-ARES YOU'RE WEARING?

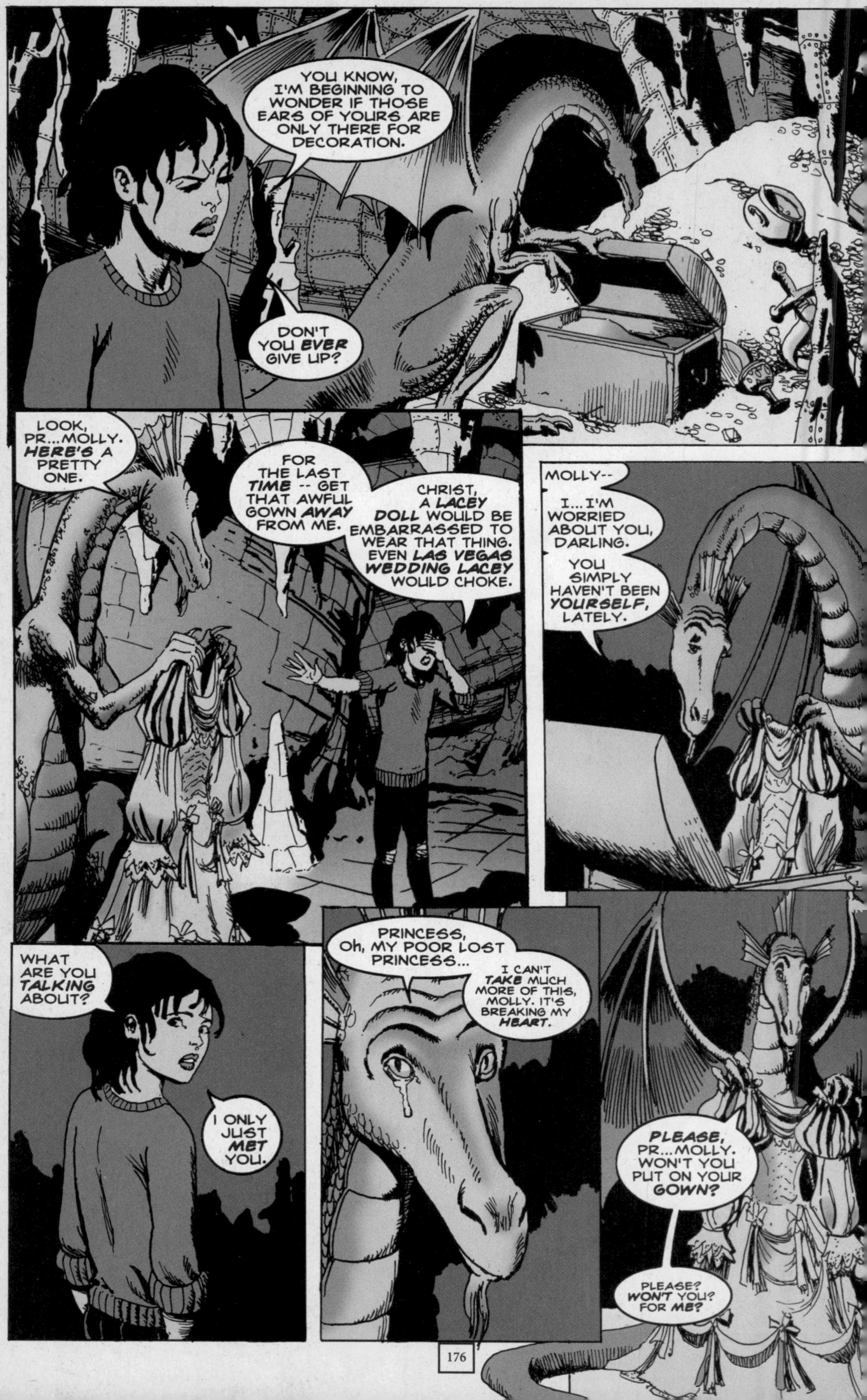
YOU KNOW, I'M BEGINNING TO WONDER IF THOSE EARS OF YOURS ARE ONLY THERE FOR DECORATION.
DON'T YOU **EVER** GIVE UP?
LOOK, PR...MOLLY. **HERE'S** A PRETTY ONE.
FOR THE LAST **TIME** -- GET THAT AWFUL GOWN **AWAY** FROM ME.
CHRIST, A **LACEY DOLL** WOULD BE EMBARRASSED TO WEAR THAT THING. EVEN **LAS VEGAS WEDDING LACEY** WOULD CHOKE.
MOLLY--
I...I'M WORRIED ABOUT YOU, DARLING.
YOU SIMPLY HAVEN'T BEEN **YOURSELF,** LATELY.
WHAT ARE YOU **TALKING** ABOUT?
I ONLY JUST **MET** YOU.
PRINCESS, Oh, MY POOR LOST PRINCESS...
I CAN'T **TAKE** MUCH MORE OF THIS, MOLLY. IT'S BREAKING MY **HEART**.
PLEASE, PR...MOLLY. WON'T YOU PUT ON YOUR **GOWN?**
PLEASE? **WON'T** YOU? FOR **ME?**

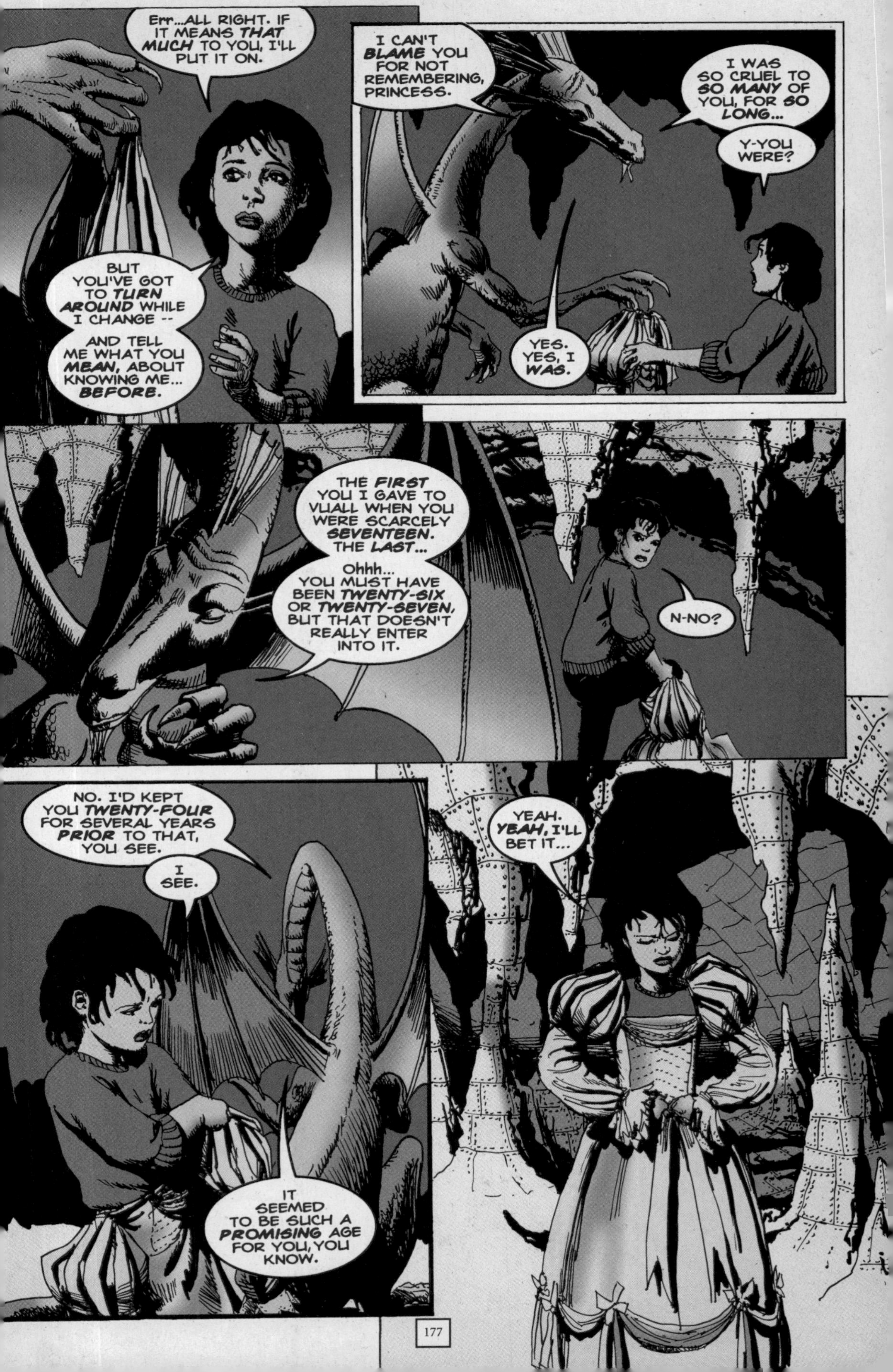
Err...ALL RIGHT. IF IT MEANS THAT MUCH TO YOU, I'LL PUT IT ON.
BUT YOU'VE GOT TO TURN AROUND WHILE I CHANGE --
AND TELL ME WHAT YOU MEAN, ABOUT KNOWING ME... BEFORE.
I CAN'T BLAME YOU FOR NOT REMEMBERING, PRINCESS.
I WAS SO CRUEL TO SO MANY OF YOU, FOR SO LONG...
Y-YOU WERE?
YES. YES, I WAS.
THE FIRST YOU I GAVE TO VUALL WHEN YOU WERE SCARCELY SEVENTEEN. THE LAST...
Ohhh... YOU MUST HAVE BEEN TWENTY-SIX OR TWENTY-SEVEN, BUT THAT DOESN'T REALLY ENTER INTO IT.
N-NO?
NO. I'D KEPT YOU TWENTY-FOUR FOR SEVERAL YEARS PRIOR TO THAT, YOU SEE.
I SEE.
IT SEEMED TO BE SUCH A PROMISING AGE FOR YOU, YOU KNOW.
YEAH. YEAH, I'LL BET IT...

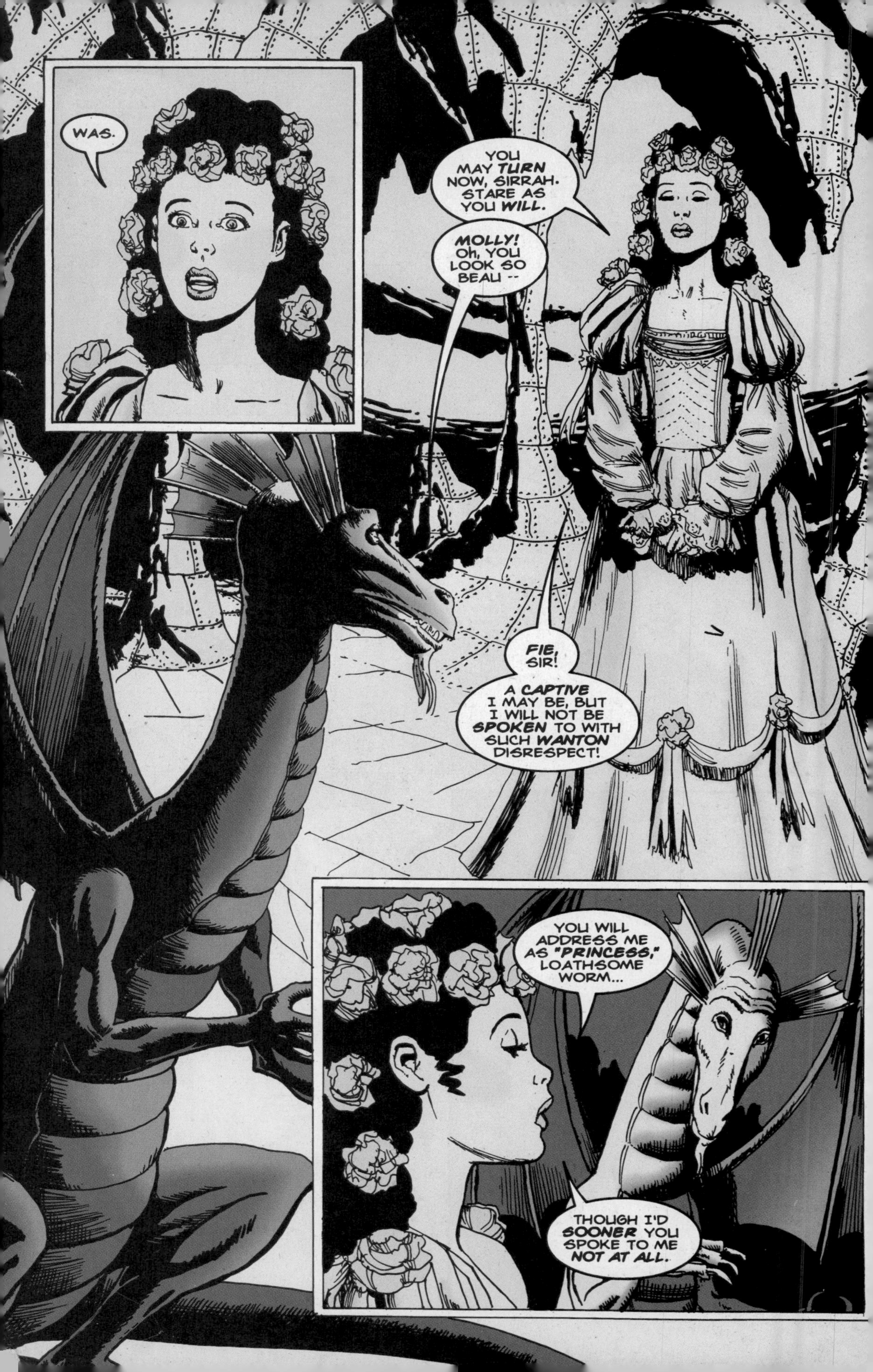

WAS.
YOU MAY TURN NOW, SIRRAH. STARE AS YOU WILL.
MOLLY! Oh, YOU LOOK SO BEAU --
FIE, SIR!
A CAPTIVE I MAY BE, BUT I WILL NOT BE SPOKEN TO WITH SUCH WANTON DISRESPECT!
YOU WILL ADDRESS ME AS "PRINCESS," LOATHSOME WORM...
THOUGH I'D SOONER YOU SPOKE TO ME NOT AT ALL.

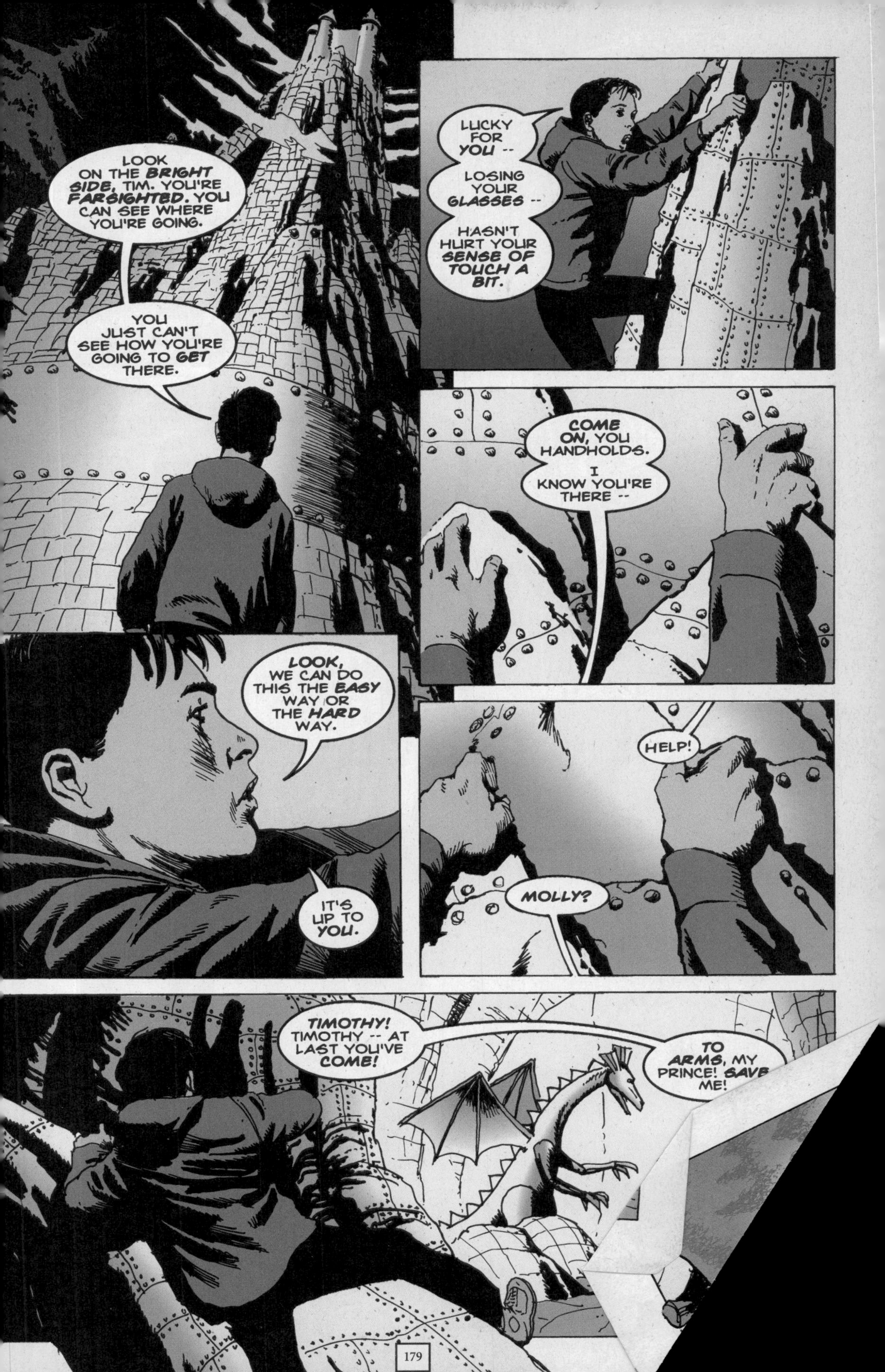
LOOK ON THE BRIGHT SIDE, TIM. YOU'RE FARSIGHTED. YOU CAN SEE WHERE YOU'RE GOING.
YOU JUST CAN'T SEE HOW YOU'RE GOING TO GET THERE.
LUCKY FOR YOU --
LOSING YOUR GLASSES --
HASN'T HURT YOUR SENSE OF TOUCH A BIT.
COME ON, YOU HANDHOLDS.
I KNOW YOU'RE THERE --
LOOK, WE CAN DO THIS THE EASY WAY OR THE HARD WAY.
IT'S UP TO YOU.
HELP!
MOLLY?
TIMOTHY! TIMOTHY -- AT LAST YOU'VE COME!
TO ARMS, MY PRINCE! SAVE ME!

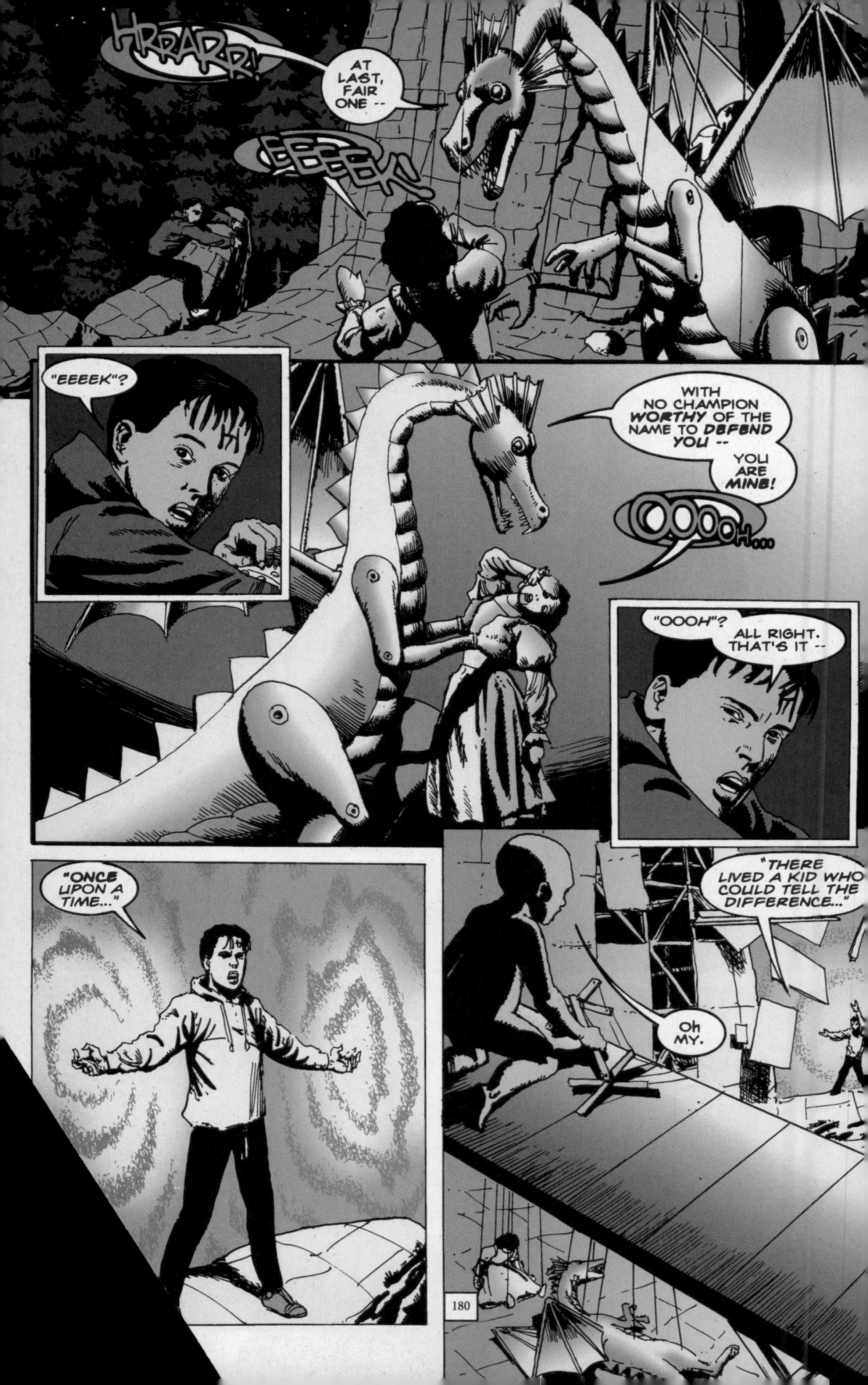
HRRARR!
AT LAST, FAIR ONE --
EEEEK!
"EEEEK"?
WITH NO CHAMPION WORTHY OF THE NAME TO DEFEND YOU --
YOU ARE MINE!
OOOOH...
"OOOH"? ALL RIGHT. THAT'S IT --
"ONCE UPON A TIME..."
"THERE LIVED A KID WHO COULD TELL THE DIFFERENCE..."
Oh MY.

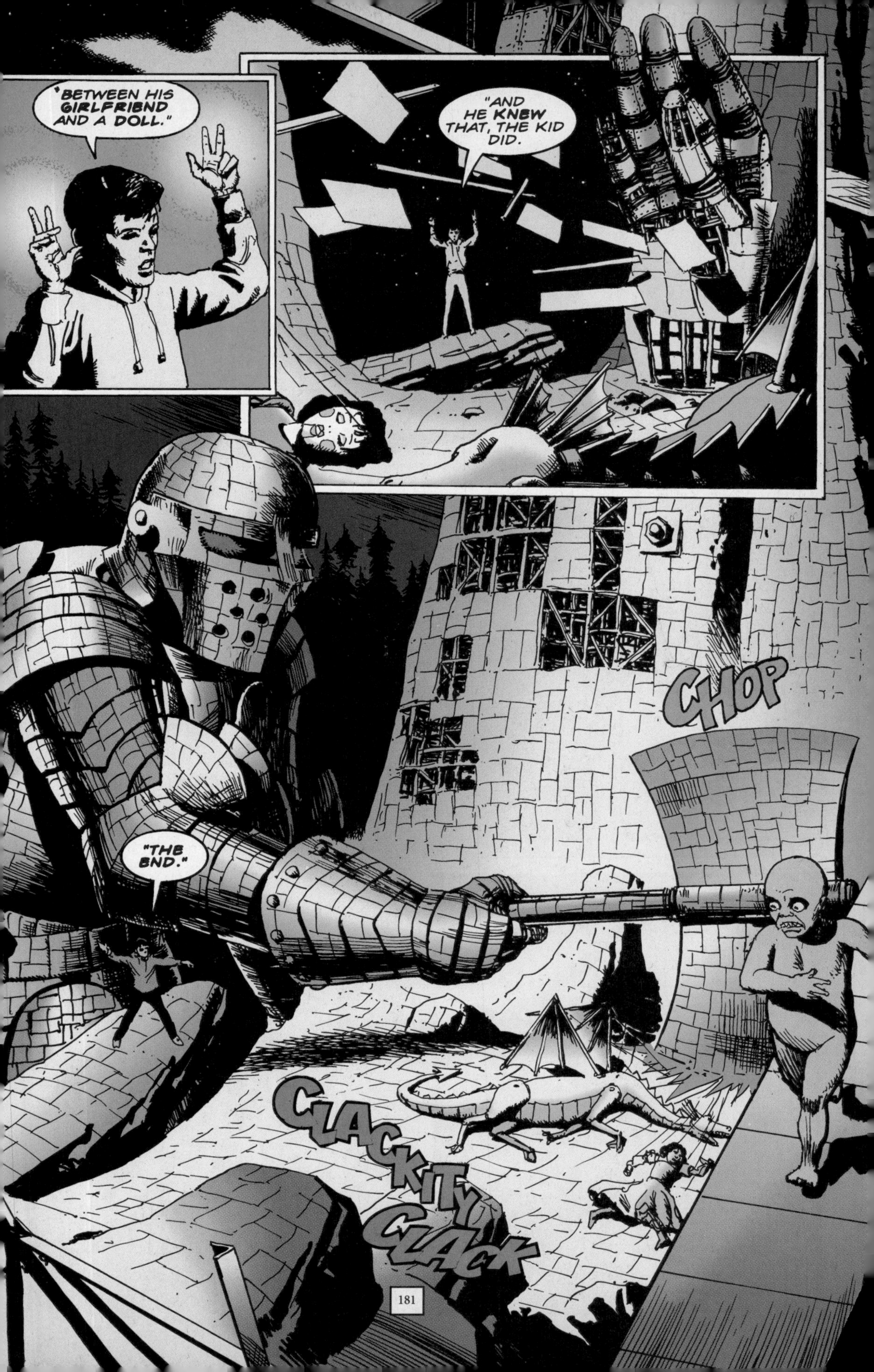
"BETWEEN HIS GIRLFRIEND AND A DOLL."
"AND HE KNEW THAT, THE KID DID.
CHOP
"THE END."
CLACKITY CLACK

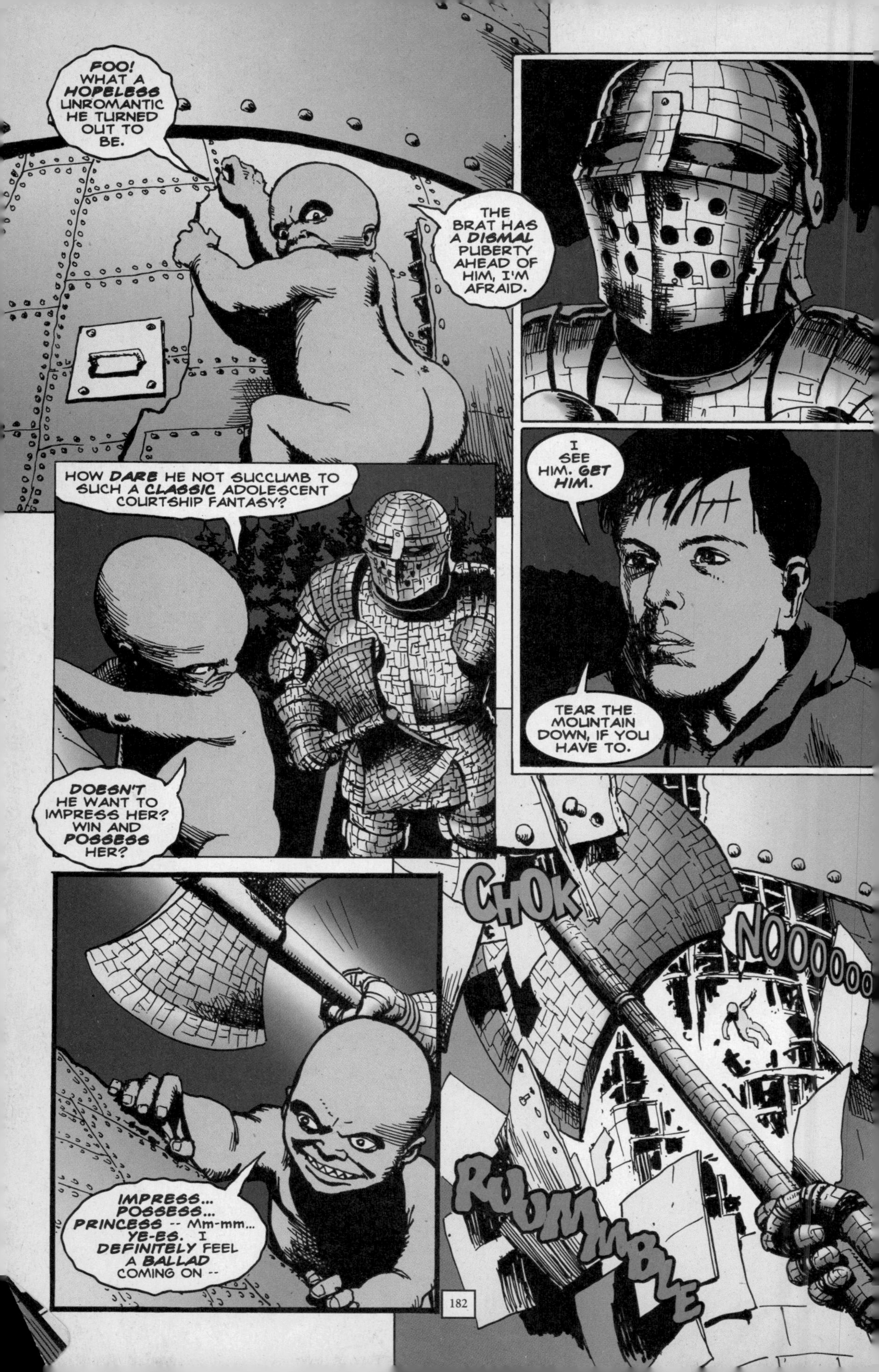
FOO! WHAT A HOPELESS UNROMANTIC HE TURNED OUT TO BE.
THE BRAT HAS A DISMAL PUBERTY AHEAD OF HIM, I'M AFRAID.
HOW DARE HE NOT SUCCUMB TO SUCH A CLASSIC ADOLESCENT COURTSHIP FANTASY?
DOESN'T HE WANT TO IMPRESS HER? WIN AND POSSESS HER?
I SEE HIM. GET HIM.
TEAR THE MOUNTAIN DOWN, IF YOU HAVE TO.
IMPRESS... POSSESS... PRINCESS -- Mm-mm... YE-ES. I DEFINITELY FEEL A BALLAD COMING ON --
CHOK
NOOOOOO
RUUMMBLE

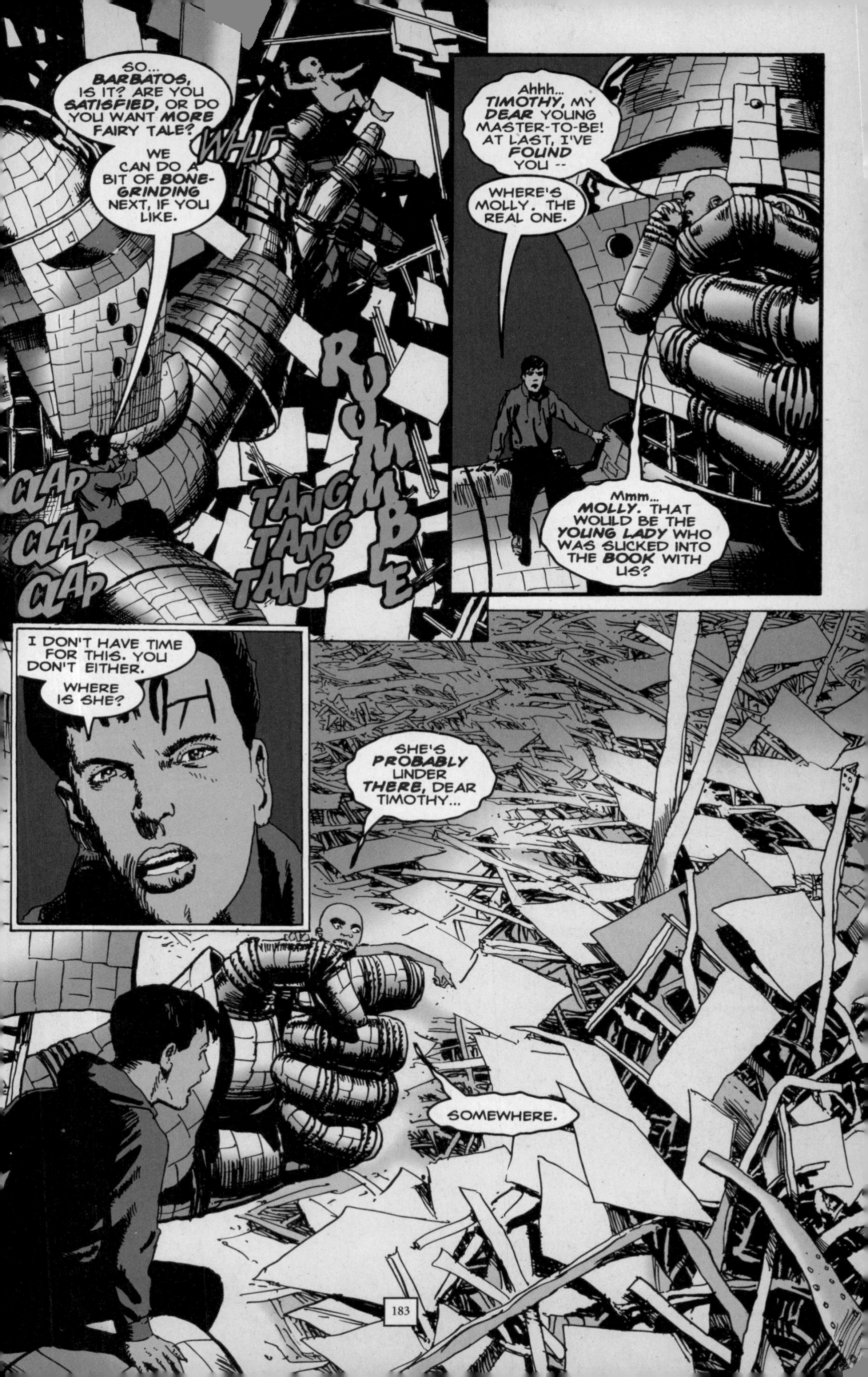
SO... BARBATOS, IS IT? ARE YOU SATISFIED, OR DO YOU WANT MORE FAIRY TALE?
WE CAN DO A BIT OF BONE-GRINDING NEXT, IF YOU LIKE.
WHUF
CLAP CLAP CLAP
TANG TANG TANG
RUMMMBLE
Ahhh... TIMOTHY, MY DEAR YOUNG MASTER-TO-BE! AT LAST, I'VE FOUND YOU --
WHERE'S MOLLY. THE REAL ONE.
Mmm... MOLLY. THAT WOULD BE THE YOUNG LADY WHO WAS SUCKED INTO THE BOOK WITH US?
I DON'T HAVE TIME FOR THIS. YOU DON'T EITHER.
WHERE IS SHE?
SHE'S PROBABLY UNDER THERE, DEAR TIMOTHY...
SOMEWHERE.

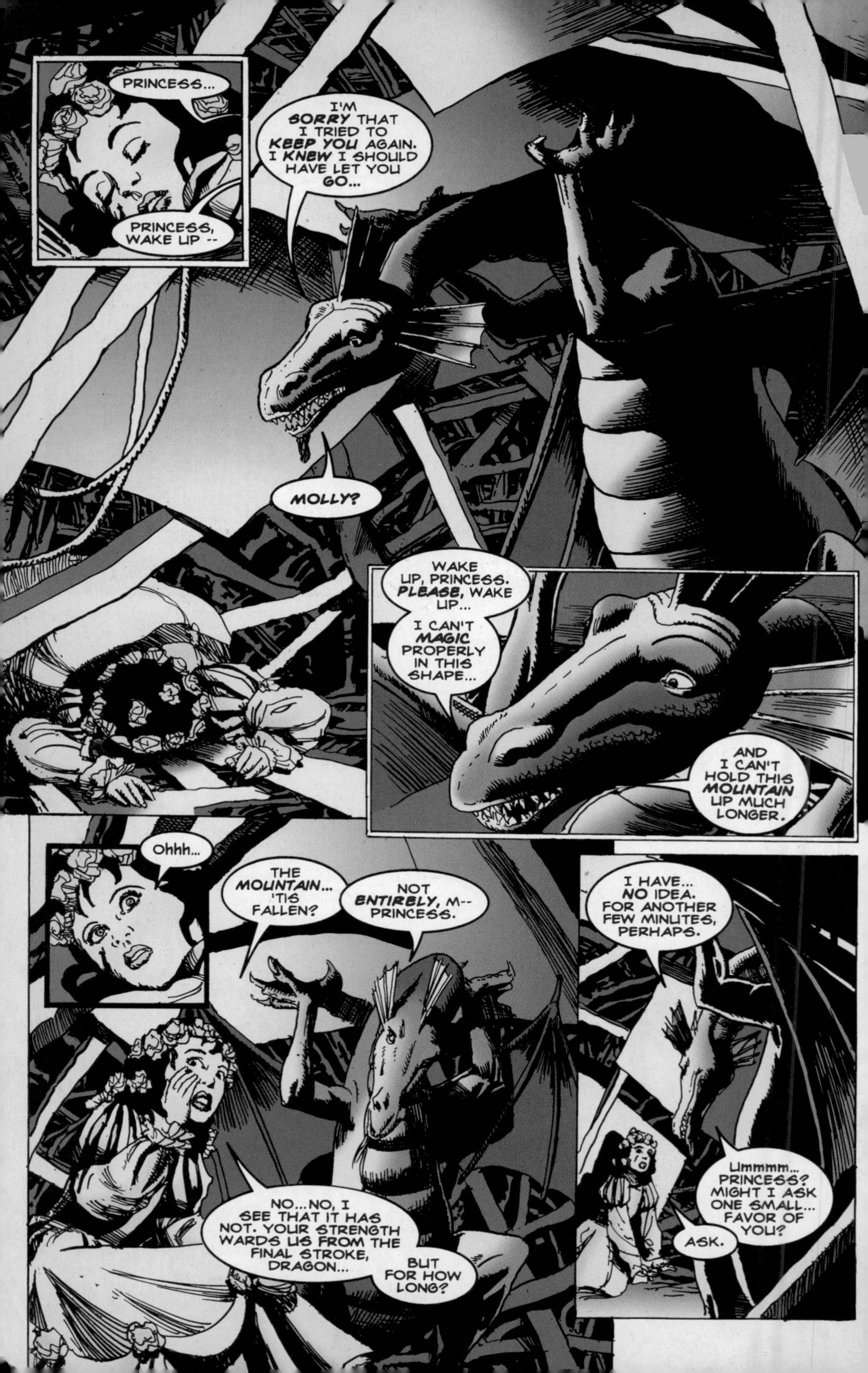
PRINCESS...
PRINCESS, WAKE UP --
I'M SORRY THAT I TRIED TO KEEP YOU AGAIN. I KNEW I SHOULD HAVE LET YOU GO...
MOLLY?
WAKE UP, PRINCESS. PLEASE, WAKE UP...
I CAN'T MAGIC PROPERLY IN THIS SHAPE...
AND I CAN'T HOLD THIS MOUNTAIN UP MUCH LONGER.
Ohhh...
THE MOUNTAIN... 'TIS FALLEN?
NOT ENTIRELY, M-- PRINCESS.
NO...NO, I SEE THAT IT HAS NOT. YOUR STRENGTH WARDS US FROM THE FINAL STROKE, DRAGON...
BUT FOR HOW LONG?
I HAVE... NO IDEA. FOR ANOTHER FEW MINUTES, PERHAPS.
Ummmm... PRINCESS? MIGHT I ASK ONE SMALL... FAVOR OF YOU?
ASK.

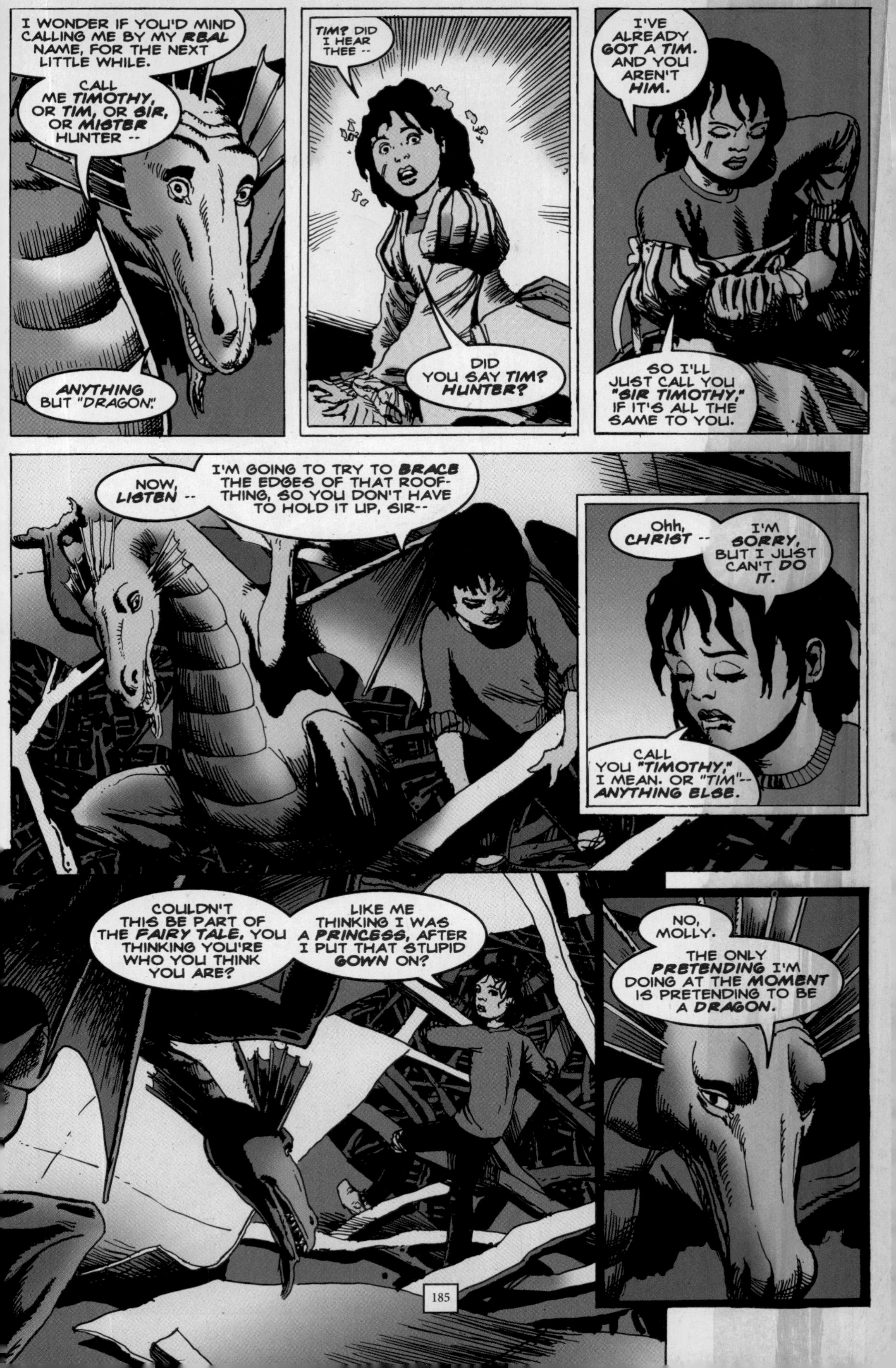
I WONDER IF YOU'D MIND CALLING ME BY MY REAL NAME, FOR THE NEXT LITTLE WHILE.
CALL ME TIMOTHY, OR TIM, OR SIR, OR MISTER HUNTER --
ANYTHING BUT "DRAGON."
TIM? DID I HEAR THEE --
DID YOU SAY TIM? HUNTER?
I'VE ALREADY GOT A TIM. AND YOU AREN'T HIM.
SO I'LL JUST CALL YOU "SIR TIMOTHY," IF IT'S ALL THE SAME TO YOU.
NOW, LISTEN --
I'M GOING TO TRY TO BRACE THE EDGES OF THAT ROOF-THING, SO YOU DON'T HAVE TO HOLD IT UP, SIR--
Ohh, CHRIST --
I'M SORRY, BUT I JUST CAN'T DO IT.
CALL YOU "TIMOTHY," I MEAN. OR "TIM"-- ANYTHING ELSE.
COULDN'T THIS BE PART OF THE FAIRY TALE, YOU THINKING YOU'RE WHO YOU THINK YOU ARE?
LIKE ME THINKING I WAS A PRINCESS, AFTER I PUT THAT STUPID GOWN ON?
NO, MOLLY.
THE ONLY PRETENDING I'M DOING AT THE MOMENT IS PRETENDING TO BE A DRAGON.

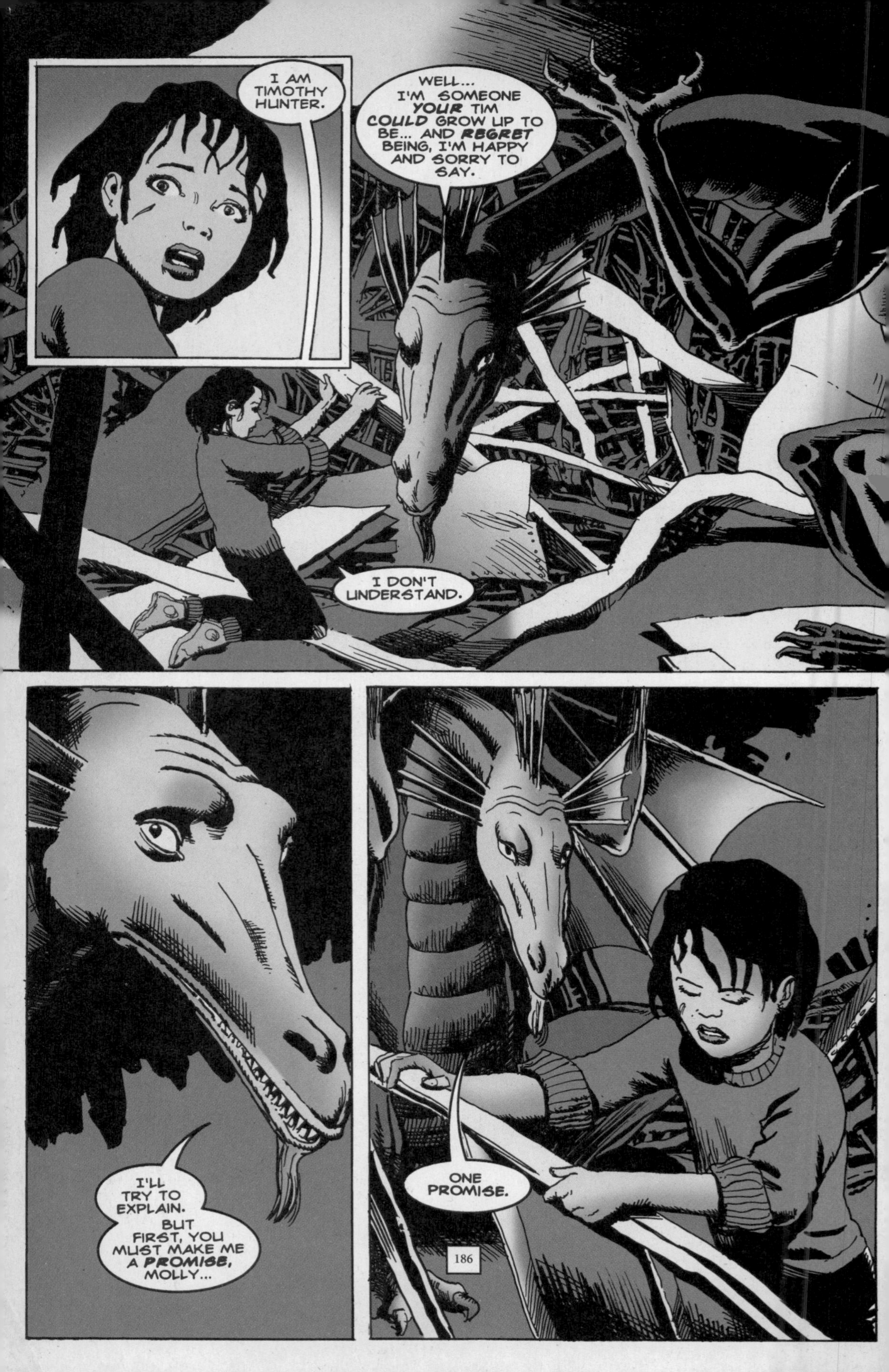
I AM TIMOTHY HUNTER.
WELL... I'M SOMEONE YOUR TIM COULD GROW UP TO BE... AND REGRET BEING, I'M HAPPY AND SORRY TO SAY.
I DON'T UNDERSTAND.
I'LL TRY TO EXPLAIN.
BUT FIRST, YOU MUST MAKE ME A PROMISE, MOLLY...
ONE PROMISE.

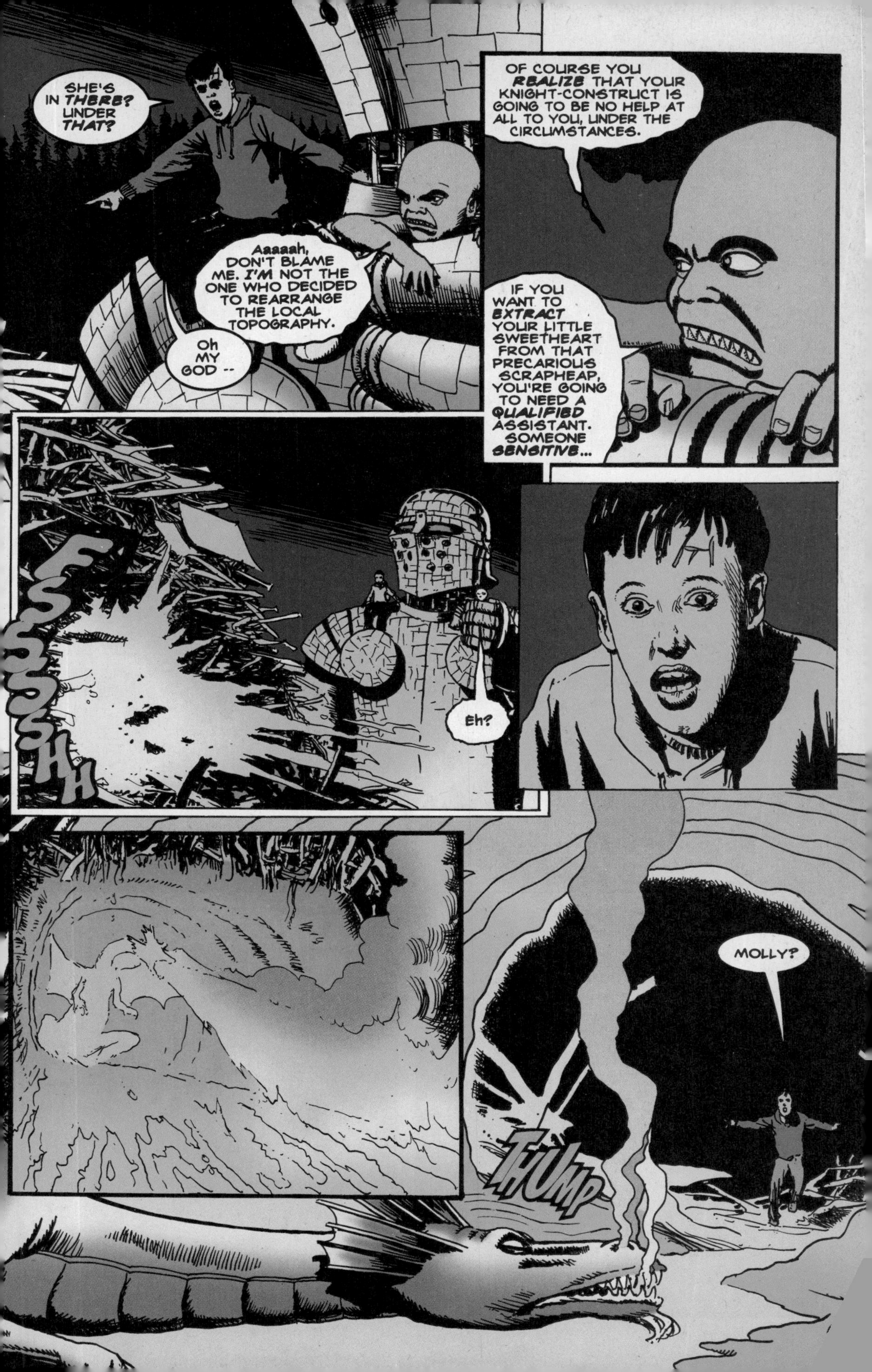
SHE'S IN THERE? UNDER THAT?
Aaaaah, DON'T BLAME ME. I'M NOT THE ONE WHO DECIDED TO REARRANGE THE LOCAL TOPOGRAPHY.
Oh MY GOD --
OF COURSE YOU REALIZE THAT YOUR KNIGHT-CONSTRUCT IS GOING TO BE NO HELP AT ALL TO YOU, UNDER THE CIRCUMSTANCES.
IF YOU WANT TO EXTRACT YOUR LITTLE SWEETHEART FROM THAT PRECARIOUS SCRAPHEAP, YOU'RE GOING TO NEED A QUALIFIED ASSISTANT. SOMEONE SENSITIVE...
FSSSSHH
Eh?
MOLLY?
THUMP

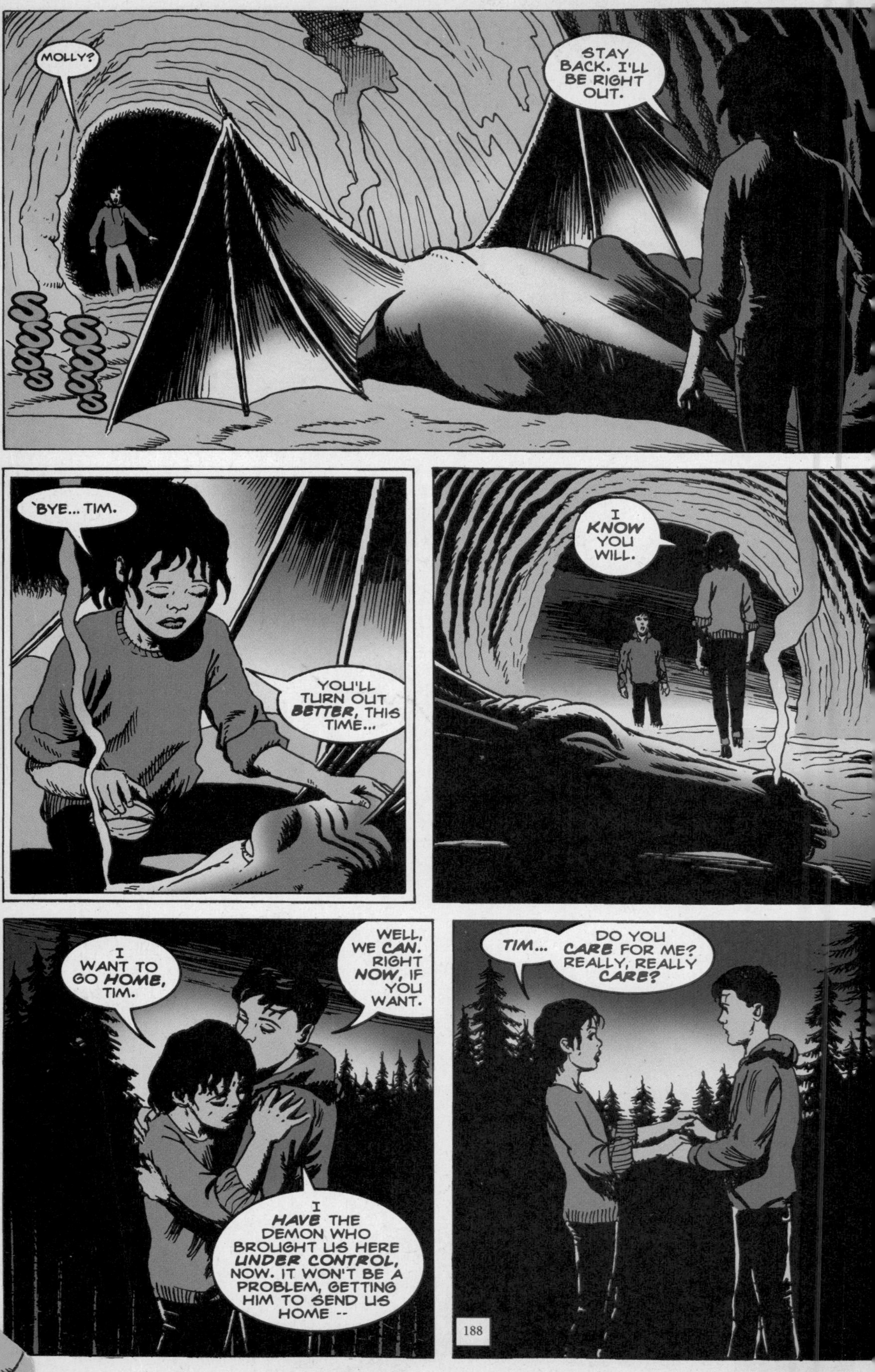
MOLLY?
STAY BACK. I'LL BE RIGHT OUT.
SSSS
SSSS
`BYE... TIM.
YOU'LL TURN OUT BETTER, THIS TIME...
I KNOW YOU WILL.
I WANT TO GO HOME, TIM.
WELL, WE CAN. RIGHT NOW, IF YOU WANT.
I HAVE THE DEMON WHO BROUGHT US HERE UNDER CONTROL, NOW. IT WON'T BE A PROBLEM, GETTING HIM TO SEND US HOME --
TIM...
DO YOU CARE FOR ME? REALLY, REALLY CARE?

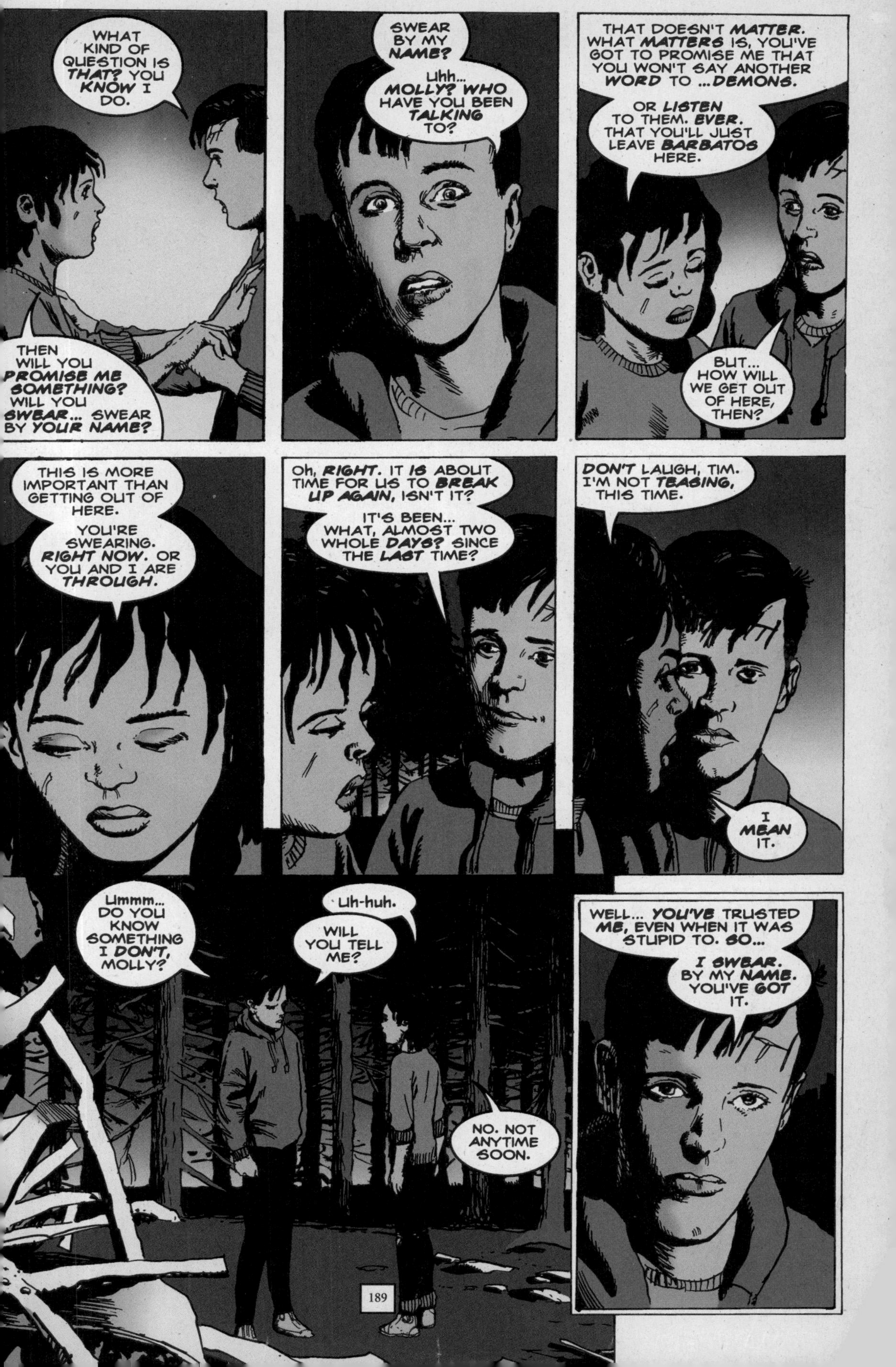
WHAT KIND OF QUESTION IS THAT? YOU KNOW I DO.
THEN WILL YOU PROMISE ME SOMETHING? WILL YOU SWEAR... SWEAR BY YOUR NAME?
SWEAR BY MY NAME?
Uhh... MOLLY? WHO HAVE YOU BEEN TALKING TO?
THAT DOESN'T MATTER. WHAT MATTERS IS, YOU'VE GOT TO PROMISE ME THAT YOU WON'T SAY ANOTHER WORD TO ...DEMONS.
OR LISTEN TO THEM. EVER. THAT YOU'LL JUST LEAVE BARBATOS HERE.
BUT... HOW WILL WE GET OUT OF HERE, THEN?
THIS IS MORE IMPORTANT THAN GETTING OUT OF HERE.
YOU'RE SWEARING. RIGHT NOW. OR YOU AND I ARE THROUGH.
Oh, RIGHT. IT IS ABOUT TIME FOR US TO BREAK UP AGAIN, ISN'T IT?
IT'S BEEN... WHAT, ALMOST TWO WHOLE DAYS? SINCE THE LAST TIME?
DON'T LAUGH, TIM. I'M NOT TEASING, THIS TIME.
I MEAN IT.
Ummm... DO YOU KNOW SOMETHING I DON'T, MOLLY?
Uh-huh.
WILL YOU TELL ME?
NO. NOT ANYTIME SOON.
WELL... YOU'VE TRUSTED ME, EVEN WHEN IT WAS STUPID TO. SO...
I SWEAR. BY MY NAME. YOU'VE GOT IT.

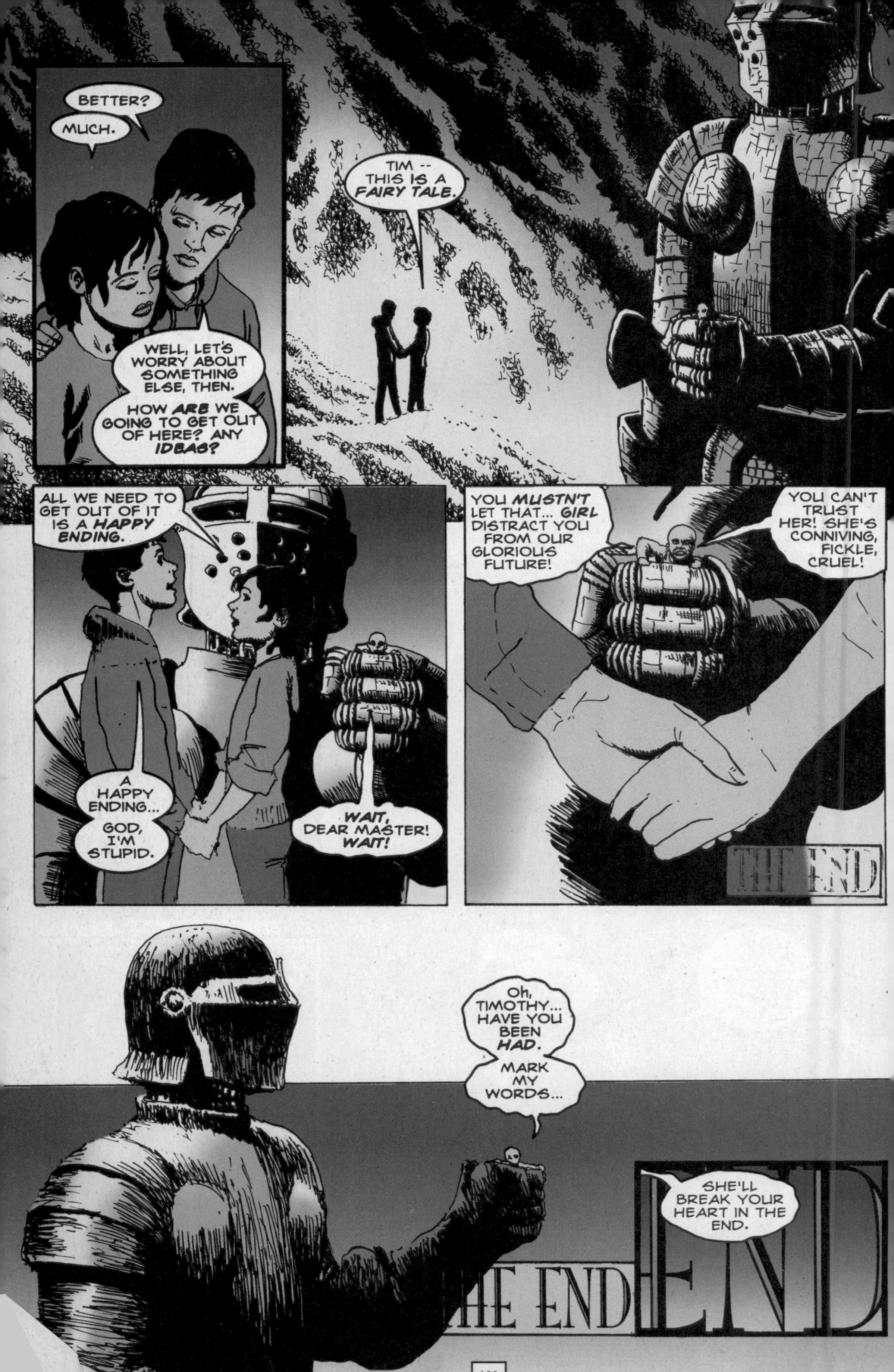
BETTER?
MUCH.
WELL, LET'S WORRY ABOUT SOMETHING ELSE, THEN.
HOW ARE WE GOING TO GET OUT OF HERE? ANY IDEAS?
TIM -- THIS IS A FAIRY TALE.
ALL WE NEED TO GET OUT OF IT IS A HAPPY ENDING.
A HAPPY ENDING...
GOD, I'M STUPID.
WAIT, DEAR MASTER! WAIT!
YOU MUSTN'T LET THAT... GIRL DISTRACT YOU FROM OUR GLORIOUS FUTURE!
YOU CAN'T TRUST HER! SHE'S CONNIVING, FICKLE, CRUEL!
THE END
Oh, TIMOTHY... HAVE YOU BEEN HAD.
MARK MY WORDS...
SHE'LL BREAK YOUR HEART IN THE END.
HE END END